A HIGHLAND TRILOGY

First published in 2002
Reprinted in 2004 by

Scottish Cultural Press

Unit 6, Newbattle Abbey Business Park
Newbattle Road, DALKEITH EH22 3LJ Scotland
Tel: +44 (0)131 660 6366 • Fax: +44 (0)131 660 4666
Email: info@scottishbooks.com

website: www.scottishbooks.com

The publisher acknowledges subsidy from

THE SCOTTISH **ARTS** COUNCIL

towards the publication of this volume

BRITISH LIBRARY CATALOGUING IN PUBLICATION DATA
A catalogue record for this book is available from the British Library

ISBN: 1 84017 046 8

Printed and bound by Bell & Bain Ltd, Glasgow

A

HIGHLAND TRILOGY

Dan

The Summer is Ended

West of the World

Kenneth Steven

SCOTTISH CULTURAL PRESS

Kenneth Steven is a widely published novelist, poet and children's author. On behalf of the Scottish Arts Council he undertakes readings, lectures and writing workshops all across the country, both at school and community level.

He began writing early, finding the people and landscape of Scotland the primary inspiration for both poetry and prose. His mother's family are from the north-west Highlands, and it is their stories and experience which form the background to much of his work.

His acclaimed first novel, **Dan**, was published by Scottish Cultural Press in 1994, followed by his first major poetry collection, **The Missing Days** in 1995. **The Summer is Ended** appeared in 1997, but **West of the World** has never before been published.

Dan

For Donald Stewart
of Croftgarrow

and to remember Lexie Walker –
the last Gaelic speaker of Glen Lyon

one

It was thawing. He could tell that even before he got up that morning, before he had made his way to the window to let the light in. There was a thrush singing, the notes thick and rich as blood. He could hear Kate out in the yard behind the house, her feet going through slush. And then the drops from the window; chimes of bright water.

He would not get up yet. He lay still, looking around him at the familiar room. On the chest of drawers, beyond the thin layer of dust, he could see the faded photograph of his mother and father – the tall, dark man, unsmiling, his black coat tightly buttoned; his mother, still young, her head tilted slightly, her hands folded, curved as though they might have been holding a young bird. That was before his older brother had been born, he mused – Andrew, the boy who had gone to France to be killed. And then the picture of Andrew himself, in uniform. The boy's moustache, the lean, intelligent face with its high cheekbones, the woman's hands. He had been killed in 1918, one week before war's end.

He could see the clock, still keeping its steady time. It brought back vivid memories of his grandfather, Alan, who had been in this glen and on this farm before them all. He could see his face so clearly, with a silver beard, as he took him out as a little boy to see the horses. That clock had been on the mantelpiece then, above the open fire; it was shaped like a sphinx and had mahogany shoulders.

The sun burst into the room, between the faded curtains which did not meet. He wanted to be up, to see the fields and hills now that the fresh green of spring was being reborn; the unexpected fall of snow had not lasted long. Still he did not get up. The room was a protection, a place that was his own, that did not change like the road which had been the bringer-in of a new world with strange ways. In this room Dan had been born, and here his mother had died. It was also the room that he and Catriona had shared for so many years. All of them were together, it now seemed to him, their ghosts in the separate compartments of his mind, like the clean drawers of the chest itself. They were now both comfort and nightmare; they were as naked white hands beneath the weakness of his old age, supporting him although they could no longer speak.

He must get up. He heard Rory barking in the yard, and imagined him bouncing around Kate as she came back from the sheep. There was the creaking of the back door and the sound of her steps. He sat up, reached for his mother's old hand mirror and looked at himself; there were red flecks about the edges of his eyes. For a moment Dan was vividly aware of Catriona; it was as though he could feel her hands on the wooden edges of his shoulders, her warm breath on his cheek; but then she was gone, the moment of remembering past. He shuddered and pulled back the heavy old homespun blankets, his hands foolish and stumbling with their blue veins of cold. It took him a long time to get dressed, to draw the thick trousers over the pathetic thinness of his legs; he felt sharp needles in his arms as he drew the sweater over his head.

A faint sound of fluttering drew his attention to the window. He went over to draw back the curtains and saw the butterfly, a tortoiseshell. Its wings were still slow and heavy after winter sleep, and it did not attempt to escape as the old man held out his forefinger and let it settle. The sun, coming down in folds from the side of Beinn Dobhran, spilled on to his hand, lighting the chain of blue lacing on the edges of its wings. Suddenly a memory came back of the last summer before his brother had left for France. Dan had been five then, just old enough for his brother to take him and show him things of wonder in the fields and woods around the farm – deep exciting caves, trees where squirrels were often to be seen, big pools in the river where salmon came, butterflies in the fields' edges. He still recalled how he had tried to catch a butterfly, and how his frustration grew as it repeatedly flew further away at his approach; and Andrew had laughed as he had forgotten to look where he was going and had fallen into a shallow ditch, howling with pain and rage.

That memory sparked off another. One day he had been sailing a toy boat on the small pond; Andrew came and knelt beside him.

'A present for you, Danny,' he had said, with more than usual gentleness.

'What is it?' Dan had replied, not looking up, so absorbed was he in the progress of his boat.

His brother, for reply, dropped a parcel on the ground beside him. Inside were toy sheep, cows and hens. He could still recall how, although he had said his thanks as he had been taught, his disappointment had shown; he had felt himself to have grown past such childish things. He had immediately turned back to his boat, and hardly looked up as his brother said goodbye and started walking down the track. Only much later did he understand the meaning of the gift – when he found on his father's desk the paper, with its message so simply written that it sounded almost harsh:

'I want you to know, father, that Danny is to take over the farm instead of me. Whatever happens while I am in France, I do not want you to think that I will one day be master of Achnagreine. If I come back, I will find a way to get to university and become a teacher. That is what I want.'

But what did all that mean to him as a young boy? Just as long as he was free to roam the woods, to find birds' nests in the spring and chestnuts and hazel nuts in the autumn, to watch fish in the pools and – if he was lucky enough – occasionally otters at play on the river bank, he was content. Day and night were one, that long summer before school began – the world of the farm was warm with his mother, and beyond the back door stretched eternity.

For a while, though, it seemed as if the skies were black without Andrew; but soon the time of the chestnuts came and he forgot.

The butterfly dipped its wings on the old man's hand and suddenly flew away. Dan opened the window and gently guided the fragile creature to its edge, watching as it rose like a red leaf into the sunlight and was lost to view. He went out of the room and descended the wooden staircase with slow and painful steps. At the foot, he stopped and looked up at the three paintings which his mother had done during her last illness – geese in the field south of Achnagreine, with the long line of elms behind; the view west to Beinn Dobhran in autumn; and the fallow field running down to the ruins of the old Lodge. He could see her still, painting that last canvas in her room, could visualise so clearly the pale oval of her face and the sensitive artist's hands. She would not allow him to look until she had finished. The work had taken her a long time.

Rory had heard him coming down. Dan had tried to be quiet so that Kate would not hear him; but now the collie came padding out of the kitchen and thrust his wet nose into the old man's hand. He looked down into the wise eyes and whispered to him in Gaelic; then they went in together to where Kate was working at the range. There was a smell of fresh baking; she had put wood on the fire and flames leaped up like sleek wolfhounds. Rory lay down on the sheepskin rug, his head on his paws, the blue eyes looking warily at Kate.

'And what are you doing there, dog?' she said sharply. 'You're getting soft too young.'

'Ach, let him lie,' Dan answered her gently as he came over to the warmth of the fire. She didn't turn towards him; she was lifting a heavy pan on to the edge of the sink.

'I'm . . . I'm thinking of going up to Beinn Dobhran today,' he heard himself say; the statement had an air of uncertainty which he immediately regretted.

'What, now?' she answered loudly. He saw that she had tied back her long, straight hair and that it was beginning to grey. 'Rory! Will you go out when you're told!' There was an edge to her voice now. She left the sink and came over to the old man, wiping her hands on her apron. Rory slunk off to the back door and thumped down with a heavy sigh. 'You must be out of your mind, even thinking of going out on a day like this!' she continued. 'One slip on this slush and you'll land somewhere none of us may be able to find you.'

He felt his cheeks beginning to redden. Treating him like a child again! He put out a hand to the mantelpiece to steady himself; he could feel his heart starting to thud. 'I'll not be gone all that long,' he defended himself weakly. 'And there's plenty of light in the day . . . ' his voice trailed away. 'There's one or two things I want to see before . . . '

'Before what?' she demanded.

'Am I a prisoner in my own house?' he exclaimed in sudden anger, stretching himself to his full height from where he had been leaning against the fireplace. He noted that even so she was still almost as tall as himself.

'Surely you can understand perfectly well why I'm concerned,' she now said in a gentler tone, turning back to the range and lifting the heavy kettle which was blowing a thin mist of steam. 'There are still plenty of drifts higher up that haven't melted yet, and who knows what might happen to you? But of course if you've set your mind to go I can't stop you. Anyway, at least have your porridge first.'

He sat down heavily at the table and she brought over his steaming bowl of porridge, which he ate in the time-honoured way, dipping each spoonful into a cup of creamy milk so that the porridge remained hot. He finished it and looked up at her.

'Right then, I'll be off.'

She returned his look, her expression kindly almost, but not quite, smiling. Then he rose and went out without another word.

two

At the very door the cold seemed to strike him. There was a wind coming from the north, and he went back into the porch to find his warm mitts and his shepherd's crook. The door made the same creak as it had done for as long as he could remember; even now he could hear it as he had when his father went out in the early dark to the lambing. It had been a good feeling then, as he lay cosily in the sanctuary of his nest, imagining the cold outside, the studs of frost stars on the blue-black cloth of the sky, and the snow lying in thin ridges like watching wolves. Glad to be inside, yet wishing for the exultation of the fierce outdoors. But soon he would go back to sleep.

He did not take Rory. In fact the collie showed no sign of wanting to go with him, which was unusual, although Dan reckoned he was glad enough to be nearer the fire after a long spell at the sheep with Kate. He heard the river at once; fuller now than it had been for months, a deep booming as it charged through the gorge. That had been his favourite haunt when school was over. He would come in, breathless after running, to find his mother and wolf his tea and scones; then he would be off, running through the yard, over the field, scrambling down to the river. Once he had found a deep black cairngorm pebble in one of the pools, smooth and rounded, and when he held it up to the light it had seemed hollow, its heart as if on fire. And when the river was low again, spring past with water coming down over the falls like little more than spittle over a bearded chin, he would go down to Donnie's Pool, the one he knew best of all, to guddle for trout. Andrew had given him his first lessons in the art that last summer before he left; when he did not come back, Angus from further up the glen, Andrew's great friend, continued to teach him until he knew every inch of the pool's edge, every bank where fish would be lying. Sometimes he would be nearly driven mad by the midges; they would swarm in a misty cloud around his head on a summer's evening; or his hands would be numb with cold, and hunger would gnaw at his stomach. But something would always draw him back again. As he leant out of his window late at night, long after he should have been asleep, a sudden thumping would begin in his heart and sweat would break out on his palms. Then, stealthily, he would open his window inch by inch, terrified lest his father might come upstairs; and soon he was free, out into the cool night and away down to the river.

Only once had he been caught, and the memory still had the power to make his heart beat faster. His father had been waiting for him as he came creeping in; a lamp blazed in his face.

'And what's the meaning of this?'

It was the deadly quietness of the voice that had appalled Dan. Far more deadly than shouting.

'I . . . I got a fish, Dad . . . ' The trout was torn out of hands.

'Don't ever dare to trick us like that again. Andrew never behaved like this! And do you know, boy, what day this is?'

The question had seemed to hang quivering in the air.

'Answer me.'

'The . . . the Sabbath, Dad. I forgot.'

'You forgot! The Sabbath. Breaking God's holy law, the fourth commandment, the day of rest. Have you no shame, after all you have been taught?'

Dan stood there silent, feeling his lip begin to tremble, the tears ready to flow.

'You'll go to your bed now and you'll pray for forgiveness. Remember this – turn back from God too often and the door will close; you will be cast out. You have shamed this house today!'

Dan had held back the tears till he reached the safety of his room. Then huge sobs had torn him as he pressed his face deep into the pillow. 'Please Lord, forgive. Oh please, Lord Jesus, do not cast me out!' It was a long time before peace came to him and he slept that night.

Now the old man turned on the path towards the river and looked far down the glen. More memories, far more vivid than those of last year's events, came flooding back. Somewhere around the folds of the hills stood the church, by the village of Drumbeg. Each Sabbath they had marched there, he chafing against the stiffness of his best clothes, longing to be free to search for nests, to pick flowers, to climb trees. There was always so much to see – the high floating of an eagle, perhaps, as it sailed out wooden and straight from the high Corrie of Ben Dobhran; a heron at its fishing by the river bank – he had to make do with these pleasures. Sometimes it would be raining and he would find the going hard, and there was nothing to do but follow endlessly the stride of his father in front of him; it had seemed like a relentless march that would never end. Then it was a relief to reach the sanctuary of the church, to hear the drumming of the rain on the roof while he nestled close to his mother on the hard bench, growing warm again.

He would always remember one window which was his great comfort. It was of stained glass, and showed Jesus holding a small boy in his arms. Later, he had realised that there had been much controversy before it had been accepted by the elders; it was a gift from the laird, disapproved of by some because the churches of the time were severely plain and unadorned. But in the end the more liberal faction had won. When he learned about this, how glad he was that they had! Underneath the picture were the simple words: 'Suffer the little children to come unto me.'

When the long, long sermon was about to begin, there would always be a peppermint to suck, pressed into his hand by one of the old women, a tide of rustling passing around the pews. And when he trembled to hear the stern old minister warn the congregation of judgement to come, his eyes would turn at once to that one window with its message, and find solace in seeing the gentle face of Christ. Fancying that He was looking down at him, he would imagine himself the small boy held in the arms of the One who was a friend of fishermen – after all he, Danny, was a fisherman too. Somehow he felt that Jesus would be happy to come with him to the river, to see the pools where the salmon lay.

Thinking of the river always sent his mind wandering to his next fishing trip; soon he would go further afield, to explore new pools that he had never yet reached, far up on the shoulder of Beinn Dobhran. He would go tomorrow, after school! The peppermint burned in the corner of his cheek until it was away to nothing. He became restless and shifted endlessly on the hard seat. He looked along at his father; he seemed carved out of stone, his face stern and pale, his eyes fixed resolutely on the old man in the pulpit. Sometimes his mother would slip her opal brooch to him, the one that had been her own mother'. He would then sit with bowed head holding the thin bar of gold with its single oval stone, fascinated by the colours, blue and orange and red, as he turned it in the light.

At last the sermon was over and the last psalm sung. There would be a low murmur of voices as the congregation pressed out through the door, shaking hands solemnly with the minister and gathering in sober groups. He would see other children there, looking as uncomfortable in their stiff clothes as he felt in his. Although the boys were intensely aware of the girls and eyed them covertly, they never spoke to them; except one day, he recalled, when his parents were deep in conversation with the parents of Jean MacBride, and he was told to walk along the road with her until they were ready. He never could stand Jean; she had a pernickety manner, and stood with her nose in the air talking to two of her elderly aunts who looked, he thought, like crows in their black shawls and long black skirts. Jean always wore the same white dress on summer Sundays along with a white hat with pink bows. Suddenly overcome by devilment, he could not resist walking behind her as they rounded the first bend, grabbing a large stone and lashing it down into one of the muddy pools she had just passed so that an arc of black drops splashed her back and bottom. She screamed with rage and tried to kick him, then burst into angry tears and ran back to the grown-ups while he choked with laughter. It was worth the thrashing he received.

Once the memories had been unleashed, it seemed as if they came like a flood. Forgetful of the spring cold, the old man sat down on the bench in the yard and thought about his parents. From an early age he had been conscious of the differences between them, his father's sternness in even sharper contrast because of his mother's extreme gentleness. There was just no hardness in her at all, he mused. And it was especially in the matter of their religious faith that the difference came to a head – his father a good man, honest to a fault, yet always aware of the necessity to keep the rules. Like the old minister – putting fear into your heart, telling you about the judgement to come. There was kindness in his father, though; yet Dan could not recall neighbours coming to him in trouble. With his mother, now, it was different; people made for her door in times of need – never a sick-bed for miles around but she would be there. She too had had a strong faith, but she did not talk about it much. It showed in all she did.

It was on those Sabbaths long ago that he had become aware of these things, he thought. He remembered the seemingly interminable afternoons, when he would have to sit in the parlour, with the choice of either Bunyan's *Pilgrim's Progress* or the Bible. He much preferred the Bible – the Pilgrim's Progress put the fear of death on him. The smell of that front room came back to him now. It was damp and fusty, used only on Sundays and special days like New Year, and he would sit as near the window as he could, to smell instead the flowers his mother would have put there – hyacinths in spring, lilac perhaps in summer – strongly scented flowers as if she too wanted to drown the fustiness. The river would be shouting for him to come; it often seemed like some terrible conspiracy that the skies should be clearer than usual, the world outside more than ever filled with waiting treasure. Never did the hands of the clock move more slowly than on Sabbath afternoons.

But then the whole aspect of the day would change. At five o'clock precisely, his father would leave the house, to begin the long tramp back again for the evening service. It seemed to Dan as if a dark shadow had been removed; his mother would build up the fire, and they would sit beside it in happy and relaxed companionship. When the flames had died down, leaving a glowing red heart, she would bring down the long brass toasting fork from its hook by the mantelpiece and leave him with slices of bread to toast, while she fetched the rest of their supper – milk, oatcakes with cheese or honey, and a banana, a great treat in those days – and spread butter on the hot toast where it melted in golden pools, and it was soft and hot in his mouth.

Often he begged his mother to tell him stories about the old days, when she was a child; he drank in all she said, asking endless questions. Or she would read him a story. Afterwards he would lie in bed cocooned in warmth and utter contentment; and long before his father returned he would be asleep.

What he certainly recognised in his mother was a kind of underlying sadness. Sometimes he would hear her crying upstairs after an exchange with his father; and he would tiptoe upstairs and listen quietly outside their door until he had summoned up enough courage to knock. But she never answered. An hour or so after he would find her down at the kitchen stove once more, singing softly to herself, turning to him with her gentle smile, with only the tell-tale edges of red about her eyes.

Dan now became aware of the cold and moved over towards the last of the barns. The river was louder; he could see a white tail of it higher up, reminding him of the scut of a rabbit as the water bounced down with its load of snow. There was time to go inside for a moment.

He smelled that warm darkness which he loved. The wooden door closed with a soft knock; a little light came from underneath. Two skylights let in their own narrow shafts of silver. The thick air was filled with dust and golden flecks of hay danced in the pillars that struck the damp floor. To his left, in a corner, a lamb bleated. It was in a little pen and he saw its black legs folded under the frail shivering body. Born just this morning, he guessed, and its mother had refused to accept it. Dan knelt down and stretched out his hand; the lamb tried to rise on trembling legs, bleating in expectation of a further bottle, then collapsed back into the corner, a black face turned towards Dan. He tickled the tight curls in the middle of its forehead and got up, feeling the strain in his knees. He looked around. The same bales of hay stacked here, the same air of secrecy, the same sense of sanctuary. How far back these feelings went! This was where he had come with Jess, he remembered, smiling inwardly. She had been so shy of him, so much in awe of his father. Her family had come from the very top of the glen, from Camus Lurgan. That second year at school he had seen her; it was as if something in her face caught him every time he looked at her and paralysed him. He could never find any words to say to her; afterwards he would kick himself for his stupidity, and plan what he would say to her next time. Once, the day before he knew she was to be coming to Achnagreine, he had lain awake half the night, promising himself that this time would be different.

The next morning he had waited, trembling with nervousness, for a sight of her father's cart as the farmer made his way down to Abercree for the market. They had sat among the hay bales because she had not wanted to meet his father. He had brought out a bottle of his mother's best home-made lemonade, a special treat, and a plate of her shortbread; for the first time he felt at home with her, and chattered away about fishing, and about things that had been happening that week at the school. She had been sitting at right angles to him, he remembered, the light coming down from the skylight and striking her face, and suddenly, quite beside himself, he leaned forward and planted a loud kiss in the middle of her cheek. She turned to him bewildered, like a deer startled in a glade, then leapt up and was away in a flash through the barn door, which banged loudly behind her. Dismay overwhelmed him. What had he done wrong? That was what the other boys had told him they had done, and all seemed to have gone well enough for them.

He trailed disconsolately to school the following Monday and kept as far away from her as he could; but his eyes burned into her back and a mixture of longing and shame struggled inside him. She never came to Achnagreine again. Once his mother asked if he would like her to invite Jess for tea one Saturday, but he made excuses about all the work he had to do, and the subject was never brought up again.

How strange, he thought now, that her shadow was still there in the old barn after all these years. She had grown up into a beautiful, rather aloof woman, had married young and left the glen many a long year ago. He never heard what had become of her.

Now the barn was in sore need of repair. He saw the white chinks in the walls where the light came in like steel arrows. So much work to be done! It surged through him, the longing to begin all over again, to have everything in good working order, to have whole days ahead – aye, and months, and years – ready to be filled with satisfying hard work. If he only had the time, and the strength! Time ran like water, now, through his hands. He could not bear to think of it. Leaving this beautiful world that was his. And yet, what did he have here any more? Memories surged back of days that were past, when he would come to this barn tired and broken at the day's end, to hang tools on their hooks before that final walk home into the golden light of the kitchen and the warmth of the fire – and Catriona. Sometimes before leaving the barn he would look up through the skylight at the jagged edges of the stars with their golden and red fires, or the light of the moon as it etched white cornices on Beinn Dobhran's sharp ridges. That sky was the same as it had always been, he thought now. The first man that came there and cut down the trees – began turning the earth to plant his poor seed – he too must have stood there and seen the same fragments of light burn in that sky, and the same haunting shoulders of the mountain lit up with rich mantles of moonbeams. It was as though they were kindred, separated by the long ages of time, yet somehow together, their hands on the same plough. They were born of the same earth, and in their veins was the sound of the same song. What he, Dan, did here would in a sense never be finished; they would come after him and stand in this place, their eyes drawn upward to the same sky. There were times he had almost felt their presence, as though their spirits somehow had been fused into one memory that lingered on, brushing occasionally against the world of his own day, as though re-visiting, remembering. Once, looking down from an upstairs room, he fancied he saw the half-bent back of a man ploughing, making a straight furrow in the field that ran down to the lodge. Only a moment and the figure was gone; drawing his hand over his eyes, he saw only peewits making their ragged half-circles; weeping over the spring field. He said nothing to his mother; there were too many ghosts haunting her grey eyes already.

Three times in his life he had heard the crying of a woman in the small shed where he kept birch logs stacked for winter, three times so widely spaced through his life that he could not easily have told at what time of the year they had occurred. Wait, though – it was surely in those strange days between summer and autumn, days of a kind of waiting, when there was a stillness in the trees and fields, almost an unexplained anxiety. Dusk was coming earlier, yet the light hung blue and strange after the sun's fall and the hills were lit with a glow of ochre, unreal and tainted as if with blood. It was almost as though the glen strained with all its might against the chains that pulled onward into autumn, towards sleep and the certainty of death. Each time, he had been coming up the path towards the house, weary and thinking of nothing, hearing only the sound made by his feet as they trod on the stones. And then, the muffled sound of crying, as if the woman's hands covered her face. Each time he went to the shed and opened the door as quietly as he could; never was there anything to be seen. There was the dark, deep smell of wood, but nothing else.

three

He had gone at once to tell his grandmother about the crying that he had heard – Granny Drummond, wife of Alan, mother of John, his father, in whose hands Achnagreine now lay. Memories surged over him as he thought of her now – one of whose love he had been so sure always, who had time for him and would listen to his tales and share his joys and anxieties, even when he seemed to be in the way of the others who were always so busy. Granny Drummond with her wrinkled, kind face; a face more than a little like a man's with its strong features and sometimes a half-frown which could give the impression of annoyance – until she smiled, and you were at once put at your ease. And when she spoke you caught the soft music of the islands in her voice.

Looking back, Dan had often wondered why it was that no one, not even his mother, had told him any of the things that he so much wanted to know about his grandparents. Why they so seldom came to Achnagreine, for example; they would come to the big family dinner at New Year, but hardly any other time. And they never seemed to want to stay long even then. It was only very gradually, as the years went past, that he came to know these things by himself – simply by listening and asking questions, and then putting two and two together. About their attitude to his mother, for instance. They did not altogether approve of her, of that he was sure. Much later he understood why; it had to do with her painting pictures. Nobody in the glen ever thought of doing such a thing – least of all a woman. Artists occasionally came to the glen and could be seen sitting with their easels painting Beinn Dobhran, perhaps, or a view of the river. But for working folk, painting was a frivolous thing, a waste of precious time; there was always so much else to be done. Only Dan knew how his mother worked to save the time for her art, how early she rose in the morning, how she set aside a single afternoon for it, and never another minute. It wasn't exactly a disgrace that she painted pictures – more of an embarrassment; not as if she, the wife of an elder, had worn trousers, or been seen smoking! These things were unheard of.

Then there was the question of the farm. It gradually dawned on the boy that his grandparents came visiting so seldom partly because they just could not bear to see the place that had been their own home for so long, their precious land, in the hands of another, even of their own son. He was aware that they had moved some years back to the cottage at Balree because his grandfather was almost crippled with rheumatism. If he had not been, they would still have been at Achnagreine, the place they loved.

But in their cottage Danny was welcomed like a king. It was little but Gaelic he heard beneath the low roof of their cosy living room. Never simply another language to him; more a bigger world, a living link with the old, old days; a tongue that expressed exactly the feel of things, that captured the looming of a storm, or the ecstasy of a sunny morning. The words came to his own tongue as smoothly as English. And then there were the songs and stories his grandfather told him. He would have been up at Balree every day if his parents had let him; after all it was only two miles up the glen.

What had really taken a very long time to fathom, though, was the strange, vexed question of his grandmother's second sight. Again his mind went back over the years and he smiled inwardly as he remembered the first time it was mentioned to him; he had been a very small boy, not long in school, when a class-mate had said to him: 'My mother says your granny has the second sight.' It had not bothered him at all – of course, his granny had just got her first pair of spectacles! That must be what they meant. Gradually, as the years went past, he learned the truth bit by bit. How little adults give credit to children, or at least to sensitive children, for their awareness, he mused. He had learned to listen, while pretending to be totally absorbed in his own pursuits, when women visiting his mother would adopt a certain tone, an air of secrecy, a sort of conspiratorial whispering. And he heard more than once of how at times his granny, walking with a friend, had moved to the side of the road to allow a funeral to go past; the friend had of course seen nothing. But his granny would have 'seen' the chief mourners and knew who was about to die. There was another time, too, when her sister was seriously ill following an operation – they had always been close to each other although Mairi had been in Canada for many a long year. It seemed that his granny had known the exact hour she had been taken ill; she had noted it, and this had been confirmed later in a letter.

These pieces of information, stealthily acquired, bothered him greatly; he would lie in bed at night turning them over in his mind. Was his granny queer in some way? And then he would go up to Balree, and there she would be in the warmth of the kitchen with the range glowing red, and the delicious smell of the oatcakes she was baking would start his mouth watering; and she would turn round with her special smile of welcome, her face flushed with the heat of the fire. And he thought how stupid he had been to worry; there was nothing queer about her at all. She was the kindest and the wisest person he knew. And anyway she was his granny and he loved her.

One day when he was perhaps about twelve, he finally dared to ask his mother about her.

'What is second sight, Mother?' He enquired so suddenly that she was startled, and laid down the pan she was lifting with a loud clatter.

'It's . . . it's a kind of gift some people have,' she faltered.

A gift? He pondered this; to him a gift meant the present his parents gave him at New Year. How could this strange power be called a gift? He tried again.

'Is it a sort of . . . a sort of superstition?'

This time his mother showed no uncertainty at all. 'Certainly not,' she said with conviction. 'Get that out of your head this minute, Danny. Remember this – your granny is a devout Christian, a godly woman who cares nothing for superstition. And she didn't ask to have this gift.'

Then, perhaps to end the conversation, she told him the story of how his grandmother had come to this glen from the island of Skye.

She had arrived, in her teens, to go into service at the Lodge. It was then that she had seen the young and handsome Alan Drummond, up on the hill at Achnagreine in all weathers, coming down with his beautiful horses to the dykes that ran very nearly to the Lodge. For long enough he did not appear to see her, despite many efforts, discreet though they were, on her part. But he saw her in the end – she made sure of that.

Mrs Bolton, the laird's wife, was a tyrant towards her servants and would not have contemplated allowing any courtship while Eliza was in her service. But she had not reckoned with this girl; she was not to be deterred that easily. Every Saturday evening Mrs Bolton, dressed in her fine tweeds, set out in her carriage to visit her only close friend in the district, an elderly lady who had lived most of her life in London but who had come, nobody knew why, to live in a small lodge near Drumbeg with two servants to look after her. It gave Eliza her only chance. Hoisting her long skirts to climb the dyke at the rear of the Lodge, she would speed through the damp grass towards the lights of Achnagreine whenever the carriage was out of sight. Quiet as a moth, she would return before the lady of the house, slipping stealthily up the back stairs, afraid lest the servants too would hear her and their suspicions be aroused.

But one night the end came. Mistress Bolton set off down the glen at her usual time, only to find that the road was flooded at one point. On her early return, she had called at once for Eliza. The housekeeper could not find her and her room was empty. Furious, the old lady had summoned her to the breakfast table next morning and demanded an explanation and an apology. Neither was forthcoming. Eliza had no intention of humiliating herself before this selfish woman who had virtually imprisoned her servants within the Lodge walls. Mrs Bolton, surprised and angered by this stubborn pride, told her to leave that very day. What was Eliza to do? Alan had been slow to take the hint; it was time, she decided, to make things clear. He spotted her from the stables as she dragged her cumbersome trunk down the steps; he had come running over, tearing his cap from his head, and had seen her standing in the sunlight smiling at him.

'Eliza, you can't be going!' he cried.

'No,' she had calmly replied, 'I'm coming,' nodding in the direction of the house. And so it had been. He had taken her home to his parents, who had arranged lodgings for her with the gamekeeper's wife for a few days until their marriage could be arranged.

'I'm coming!' These were the famous words she often quoted to tease her husband, as Dan crouched on the rug in front of a roaring fire. Alan would merely grunt as he sat chewing on his old pipe, but the two would exchange a laughing glance which was full of understanding. They were a couple completely at ease with each other.

What Dan loved most of all when he was up at Balree was Granny's Old Box. It was a small battered tin trunk, filled with pieces of the past, which she would drag out from under the bed. There was a box full of gemstones, faceted stones that flashed red and blue and gold when he held them up to the light. There were marbles made of clay that Alan himself had found at Achnagreine, and soldiers made of tin which could join battle on the kitchen floor – they were Redcoats, hunting Jacobites in the hills, and they always lost. There were his granny's wedding gloves, silvery grey with a fine sheen on them and mother-of-pearl buttons. And there were drawings, childish drawings quite unlike his mother's expert ones, tattered at the edges now, but still vivid with the wide sea and the distant Cuillins, in Elgol on the Isle of Skye where her childhood has been spent. Danny had never seen the sea, yet felt himself at one with that world and dreamed of going out in a fishing boat like the one in the picture, with the gulls wheeling around it.

Looking back over the long years, Dan could see how he had gradually grown very close to his grandmother, and how his mother's love and hers had meant security to him; more, it had compensated for his growing alienation from his father. His grandfather, although a kindly and cheerful figure, seemed somehow to have been always in the background; he sat by the fire smoking his pipe, coming to life only when he taught the boy the old songs and told tales of bygone years. But he never had half the vitality of his granny. He grew to realise that she had loved his dead brother Andrew, loved him very much, and as he began to grow up, she spoke more to Dan about him.

Andrew and his father, she said, were as wary of each other as two strange collies; she did not understand why Johnny, her son, had set up barriers between them; indeed she did not always understand her son at all. Dan came to be aware that a certain incident seemed to hold the key. Once, his granny told him, when Andrew was about twelve he had been coming back from Beinn Dobhran after a day's fishing on the hill lochs; he was in a hurry, for dusk was coming on and his supper would be ready.

Suddenly, in the pine wood, he heard a terrible screaming; it could almost have been a child, with its high-pitched urgency, but Andrew knew what it was. He followed the sound, his heart pounding, struggling through the deep heather until he reached the trap, one of his father's, to find the rabbit there with its forepaw caught and bleeding. Working with trembling hands, he freed the terrified creature. He could never bear to see an animal's suffering, his grandmother explained; it pained him almost more than that of a fellow human being. It was so till the end, she added, when he wrote passionately from France of the horse he had seen drowning in the mud. But that night among the trees, he had told her, he felt that for once he had done something worthwhile; it was this enmity between farmers and the creatures of the wild that caused him deep distress, that in fact had made him in some ways actually hate the life at Achnagreine, so that he already knew his future could not lie there. He went on towards his home with a feeling that something had been, in a sense, restored; he was at peace with himself. But when he entered the farm kitchen, his father rose up black from the fireside; he was hauled upstairs and belted without mercy. His grief, his granny said, was far less for his own pain than for the depth of the misunderstanding between his father and himself. As she told Danny the story, he looked at her and saw tears in her eyes.

'Many a time I have prayed to be able to forgive my son,' she added quietly, 'but I have never truly forgiven him.'

One thing she never did tell him, he recalled, was that she herself had known the exact moment when Andrew had been killed in France. But his mother had told him.

Now, as an old man, Dan marvelled that the thought of what came next should still have the power to cast such a deep shadow over him. And yet, how could anyone possibly forget a thing so terrible? It was his grandfather who had told him, one day when he was up at Balree, that his granny was deeply upset because of 'a thing she had seen'. She was in bed upstairs that day; Dan had been up to take her a cup of tea, for she was recovering from a bout of sickness. He had never known her to be so quiet before; she looked at him without a smile, all the sparkle completely gone out of her. He did not know what to say himself, so sat silently with his arm around her shoulders while she drank the tea. Then she simply said: 'You're a good lad, Danny,' and lay down with a long sigh; and he tiptoed away, a dark cloud on his spirit.

'Aye, she's in a bad way,' was all his grandfather said, which worried him even more. He was about to leave when his grandfather asked him to tell his father to come up that evening – another thing so extremely unusual as to cause him concern again. When he arrived home and passed on the message his father only grunted.

He was a long time in sleeping that night. The weather was hot and sultry and he tossed and turned, finally falling into an uneasy sleep. Some hours later, he awoke to the sound of voices from the next room. He knew at once that his father and mother were having an argument. Very quietly he got up and, trembling lest he should be discovered, crouched by their door and listened. At first he could make out nothing; then his father's voice was raised in anger:

'For the last time I'm telling you, Rena, I will not go and make a fool of myself telling them a foolish old woman's fancies.'

There was a pause, and he heard his mother reply, but could not hear what she said. Again his father's voice, with an edge to it:

'I'm telling you, woman, I will not do it! They'll say it's just superstition, and they'll be right.'

Afterwards he was sure he heard his mother crying, but did not dare to intrude. He went miserably back to bed, and eventually slept.

It was August and the school holidays; he got up later than usual and found that his father was out attending to the animals. His mother looked drained, as if she had not slept a wink. He burst out at once:

'I know my granny has seen something terrible – tell me what it is.'

His mother hesitated for a moment, then answered quietly. 'She says she has seen the Lodge burned to the ground and some of the family lost. She . . . she begged your father to warn them, but he refuses to do it.'

Dan was speechless, horrified; it was even worse than he had imagined. Just then his father came in. His mother brought the porridge to the table; his father said grace and they ate, then he pushed back his chair and went out, with no word spoken. Dan watched him and saw that he was deeply upset. He now saw him go with Corrie into the high field, where he set about mending a fence. Still Dan kept watching him; he hung about the kitchen with no will to do anything, until his mother sent him out to cut kindling for the fire; stifling hot though the day was, cooking still had to be done on the kitchen range.

When he returned with the wood, he could not help asking his mother what she felt about his grandmother's fears.

'I don't honestly know, Danny,' she replied with a sigh. 'All we can do is pray that she's wrong . . . this time.'

But he knew that she, like himself, would be thinking of the many times she had not been wrong. He looked at his mother with love – her long delicate hands, far too delicate, he thought, for some of the rough work she had to do; soft hair tied back so that it left her white forehead bare. The sun fell in a dusty pillar from the window, flickering and golden. His gaze then turned back to the far, bent form of his father, the hammer swinging in a wide arc as he drove a new post into the hard earth.

Dan hated these August days when the sun turned the sky copper and there was not a breath of wind, the hills shrouded in a pale haze of heat. Only hives of midges danced over the yard, weaving their grey patterns and then shifting without warning into new circles. He felt within himself a mixture of fear and excitement; he did not want to feel excited, and felt guilty about it, but he was, and that was the truth. Yet a battle went on in his spirit. Why did his father not warn the Boltons? How could he go on working up there in the field, with this terrible thing hanging over them all? In a way he understood, though. They probably would laugh, and call the whole thing superstition. They would not know what Highland folk had known for centuries. His father would be ashamed; and anyway, his strong religious beliefs obviously made him deeply uneasy over this strange gift his mother had. But she shared these beliefs, Dan thought; as his mother had once told him, she had not asked for this gift. It was all too much for him.

He thought again about the Bolton family. Granny Drummond had told him plenty of stories, from her days in service in the Lodge, about old Rachel Bolton and her selfish and cruel ways. But since then a generation had gone by. Rachel had died a sad, wandered old woman and, since she had no children, her nephew, a business man in London, had fallen heir to the estate. He had come north for the shooting once or twice, but had little inclination for the dreary autumns in the glen, nor indeed for the house and gardens which were slowly falling into disrepair. He would have sold up without a second thought had it not been for his wife. Cornelia Bolton had become almost obsessively loyal to the family since she had married Roger. She was aghast that he should even think of selling the estate; she saw it as a symbol of their past which they could not lightly cast off, an inheritance Rachel Bolton had intended them to preserve. Besides, it would be good for their young son Charles to spend his summers in the glen, rather than in London. And she and Roger could hold parties there, become acquainted with the country gentry and invite friends north for the shooting and fishing. Eventually her husband reluctantly agreed, not without some misgivings that it would be throwing good money after bad.

So the Lodge came to life again, with its summer staff and the family from London. Roger, after spending the first two seasons pottering rather aimlessly in the garden and working on business reports, began to take an interest in the place, and found enjoyment in taking his son to fish the hill lochs. On one occasion Johnny Drummond had been approached and asked politely whether his son Andrew would be willing to teach young Charles the finer points of fly-fishing; curtly he replied that he was too busy. It was customary for the Boltons to hold open house on their last evening before returning south, as a gesture of friendship to the glen folk; no invitation came that year to the Drummonds of Achnagreine. Johnny merely snorted; he would be happy, he said, never to set foot in the Lodge again in his life, after all he had heard from his mother of her unhappy days there. But they all knew the enmity went far deeper than that. Once, before Johnny was born, Rachel Bolton had threatened to turn his father off Achnagreine, asserting that she could do so whenever she chose; the fear of this had remained with his father until he left the farm for Balree – and he had passed it on to his son. Johnny, who loved Achnagreine above all else, inherited as it were a loaded gun of pride and defensiveness which was forever pointed towards the Lodge.

So it was that, on a thundery day in August with the threat of something terrible hanging over them all, Danny, aware at least to some extent of the struggle which must be going on in his father's mind, could not settle to any of his usual tasks, and told his mother he was going up the river to Donnie's Pool to have a swim. He found the pool too shallow now for swimming, but he sunned himself on a rock and watched a pair of buzzards circling high above, as though caught in their own blue whirlpool. Still he felt listless and heavy, ill at ease. The sky was beginning to cloud over, seeming to be laced on every side with yellow-orange flames that melted and swelled; the heat was oppressive; not a breath moved the branches of the low birches around the river.

Suddenly he thought of his grandmother. She had been ill, and he had not even been back to see her; he knew that it was concern for her that was partly possessing him. He would go at once to Balree! In a few leaps he was back on the Achnagreine side of the burn; if he followed the same way back, it would be gentler going with the sheep track most of the way; but there was always the chance that his mother would want him and he would be kept at home. If he traversed the slopes above the house, he could come down to the road from above the Lodge and save himself a good deal of extra walking. But it would be tiring crossing the steep slope with its heather and bracken. All the same, he would go that way, he decided. He soon caught a glimpse of his father, a tiny figure in the yard, working as always in his long sleeves despite the heat.

Halfway over, he flung himself in the heather, hot and panting. For a moment he was tempted to go down the hill and home; there was still a long way between him and Balree, and a good deal of it uphill. But he was worried about his grandmother, so he got up and went on. Down in the Lodge garden, he could see a little circle of deck-chairs; garish and out of place they seemed to him with the moors about them. There will be visitors up from London, he said to himself. Perhaps Charles has come on holiday. And then, despite the brassy heat of the day, a chill darkness seemed to come about him like a cloak. I am imagining things, he told himself; I have become obsessed by this whole business. Surely my granny must have been wrong; after all, time has passed. So he willed himself not to look at the Lodge again, and continued across until he came to the steep brae with its birch wood; and the road came in sight, curling on its way to Balree. It was good to come into the shade of the trees, and he found a small burn that still had a trickle of water in it, and he drank, and rubbed some water thankfully on his face.

Going into the cottage, he felt the still cool of the kitchen. No fire burned in the grate. Apprehension filled him as he went up to his granny's room. It was the old man's face he saw first, looking up pale and haggard from the chair where he sat beside his wife. Danny knelt by the bed. His granny looked fevered, ill; more, she had an unnatural quietness, a complete absence of her normal vitality which had so worried him before. Not knowing what to do, he went downstairs to fetch them both a cup of milk; then, feeling there was nothing more he could do, he left for home. He would send his mother up to look after them, he thought uneasily. He began to run as fast as he could, hardly knowing why; suddenly he felt he simply must make his father understand that this terrible thing was making his granny suffer too much. It was far more serious than a mere feverish illness. He began to rehearse what he would say to his father; for once, he decided, he really would stand up to him, challenge him.

And then, in the stillness of the coming dusk, he saw a tiny fork of lightning stab the earth. Scared now, he ran faster than ever; he went so fast that he could feel the breeze on his face. But then, almost home, he rounded the corner and stood stock still in sheer unbelief. In the midst of the trees, above the road and through the thick banks of rhododendrons, he saw the red anger of flames. There was a smell in the air, thick and heavy, like that of an October bonfire – a smell he would never be able to forget. The Lodge was burning.

The elderly couple, Cornelia and Roger Bolton, did not retreat in time from their burning wing. He had been out in the garden when Danny had passed above on his way to Balree; she had been giving the cook last-minute instructions for dinner for the first guests for the grouse shooting. She had then gone upstairs for a rest; Roger had had a drink with Charles, who had then gone to meet the guests, and had later gone upstairs himself. When the fire started, only they and the cook, with one kitchen maid, had been in the Lodge. Those downstairs had escaped easily enough; but the staircase was a mass of flames and nobody could get near.

Johnny Drummond was bringing a pail of water in from the spring when a spark caught the edge of his eye. He stood in complete horror and disbelief as they all saw the great house they knew so well rise in a tangled rose of fire, the huge flames like many adders writhing their way up into the sky. Then he ran without a word. Rena, his wife, hugged

Dan to her, leaning his head against her; he wished she would stop, as two girls from the Lodge were standing near. When at last he saw his father returning, he felt he was ready at last to hurl at him all the words he had been storing up inside him for days. But when he looked at his father's face, every one of them was washed away; he looked drained, beaten. His head was bowed as if in despair; he held his big veined hands out in a gesture of hopelessness. Dan said not a word. Instead a dam seemed to burst inside him and he turned into the shelter of his mother's side and wept, as the thunder crashed far away and huge drops of boiling rain hissed against the burning ruins of the Lodge.

four

The old man left the barn and started down the track on his way to the river. He shivered as the sharp wind caught him, the damp, cold air a man here loved and hated. There was a figure coming up towards him; he screwed up his eyes so as to see better, but it was only when he had come close that he saw it was young Roddy, Kate's son.

'How are you, Mr Drummond?' the boy said politely, his voice still a piping treble. His straw hair was tousled with the wind; Dan ruffled it kindly and stopped. He had been walking faster than usual and his breathing was not good. He smiled but did not speak. He had noticed the lilt the boy now had in his voice; although Kate was English and they had not been in the glen all that long, he was already picking up the accent. How would he ever survive at school, wondered the old man, looking with sympathy at the pale city face and the arms thin as a sparrow's; the farmers' lads could tear him apart if they chose. He seemed a lonely fellow too, Roddy; he almost gave the impression of preferring animals to folk, and had no desire to learn to fish, or even to explore the magical woods Dan had so loved as a boy.

'On you go up to the house,' Dan said to him now, 'I'm sure your mother will have the kettle on.'

'I'll not go in,' answered the boy doubtfully; and then, brightening, 'Has Charlie had her kittens yet?'

It was Kate who had given the cat its name; Dan would never have bothered. The original name, Charlotte, had rung oddly in their ears and had been pared down to the Jacobite 'Charlie'. Dan was not sure about the kittens. Kate had said nothing to him and he realised he hadn't seen the cat for days. But he guessed that all was not well between Roddy and his mother. She seemed at times to find him a nuisance, and preferred not to have him round her feet when she was at Achnagreine helping Dan. That meant the boy was often alone in the cottage down at Shian. Kate had come to the glen with no husband, and Roddy had never spoken of a father; Dan had never liked to enquire. He wished he could have spent time with the lonely youngster, perhaps taken him to places this spring where there would be wren's nests, or to the stones under the old bridge where the otters had always had their road and where their fishbones were to be found. But he could be sure of nothing. He no longer knew how he would feel from one day to the next; he was weak now after the long, hard winter; some days he had hardly gone out at all, indeed at times he had done no more than cross the yard from the house from one week's beginning to its end. Now the wind caught him again, making him shiver; he had been going to say he might take him to Donnie's Pool, but the words never came. He turned away; it was too late now.

He came down towards the ford. The thaw had set in; the bushes hung black and dead. He felt they were like himself; the landscape and he had in a sense become one. As far as his eyes could see on every side, this was his world; this was himself. Here were his ghosts. The hands of his grandmother in the twigs of the alder; his father in the never-ending fall and toil of the burn; his mother Beinn Dobhran itself, watching and guarding, blessing with the unchanging strength of her love. He was becoming fanciful, he knew; but these thoughts comforted him. What indeed had he ever known besides? His brother's death, two wars, the loss of Catriona. Now he was here alone, but the land at least remained. The land, his own land! How could anyone fully understand what it meant to him? He remembered his father, how he would say it was idolatry to love the land too much; it was the Creator, not what had been created, that one must be sure to worship. He should have heeded his own words, Dan thought wryly: had he not also loved the land too much?

Now Dan bent down painfully towards the burn and, hardly knowing what he did, plunged his hands into its freezing water, burying them in the deep silt. The burn, he thought to himself, did not change; it did not alter for a moment its endless rushing, but went on and on until its end.

Just so, nothing he himself did would alter even one iota the course of time; nobody would see his footprints any more than they would see the marks of his hands where they had been in the wild surge of the stream. Was that then what he was afraid of? That he would pass without notice? That the people would go by in their cars and never know he had been here at all? That the field would cover him with its own blanket of grass, and nobody even remember?

He went over the burn, turned and looked back at the house, with its jagged pencil of brown smoke etched against the low grey skies. And immediately there returned to his mind a vivid memory of another day, a day he would always remember. Even now, as clear as could be, he saw the figure of his father on the other side of the burn, could hear him calling – he had had to go nearer in order to hear, with the noise of the autumn spate loud in his ears:

'The rowan tree! The old tree behind the barn – it's going to have to come down! Its roots are cracking the barn floor. Don't be long coming back, I need your help!'

He would have been about thirteen at the time, Dan thought; he was on his way to the woods, the place where he always went – for solace, or sometimes just to be alone and think his own thoughts. It seemed to him that he found there something new every time he went. And, give his father his due, he never tried to stop him, provided all the jobs around the house and steading were done. Now, in answer to his father's shout for assistance, he did not shout back but merely nodded; it was little enough his father ever talked to him, except about work that needed doing about the place.

Looking back now over the long years, Dan still wondered what had been eating at his father; why was it that he had grown away from his mother and himself, seeming to withdraw into some far place deep inside himself, to be always searching, never at ease? Even on the Sabbath, which used to be his delight – when he made sure Rena had put flowers in the parlour, and kept a good fire going in that fusty room – even on that day he would go often to the window, his eyes searching out the fields like those of a merlin, restless, withdrawn. Dan would watch him, see the light striking the deep ditches that were coming into his forehead, and the dark hair becoming streaked with grey. Was that it, the boy used to wonder, was his father afraid of growing old? And then there was the land – the love of it, but at the same time the desire somehow to tame it. The young Dan had struggled to understand, dimly aware of some kind of battle his father was fighting within. His mother never complained, never talked of any of it, but the strain showed in her face; and she and Dan drew closer together for comfort. Dan would watch her as she sat quietly sewing, and wonder at her patience and calm.

On the day the rowan was cut down, he remembered, he had gone up to the edge of the wood and sat on the barrow, that strange hillock which long, long ago had been raised for a burial mound – a place of rest, he thought, for the very first men to come to this land, the ones who hunted animals and cut down trees. Again and again he would go there, seeming to feel in it some kind of peace; he would feel part of the earth, and not detached and alone.

He left the barrow and went into the wood. He loved to listen to the wind among these autumn boughs; the beech leaves were curled and dry now and made a hissing sound. He went silently, as he had learned to do long since, hoping for the sight of a squirrel, perhaps, or the white rump of a roe deer. Sometimes he would choose a certain place where the course of the burn became a bottle-neck and, finding a supply of moss and silt, would work feverishly for a while constructing a dam. From time to time he would bring one or two chosen friends there, but he liked best to be alone; it was his place which held so much of what he most loved.

He thought of the wood as a haven, and of the barrow as its guard. Sometimes when the gamekeeper from the Lodge appeared from the western edge of the wood, he would drop down and lie flat and absolutely still until he had passed. How he resented that intrusion into his private, precious world! This was his place; nobody must spoil it or take it away from him.

He remembered that his father had asked him to return early – but realised that he did not want to go back, did not want to help his father cut down the old rowan. He loved that tree; he felt it was like being asked to assist in a murder. The previous spring a blackbird had built its nest in the branches; Dan clearly recalled how the three of them had laughed as they watched from the kitchen window the young fledglings, huddled up on one of the branches on a cold morning, looking for all the world like bad-tempered children who could not face getting up. He thought too of the many times he had used the berries as ammunition when he was younger; he even grudged the birds their share! And his mother, with her pots of clear rowan and apple jelly – she would surely miss the tree as well.

With these thoughts going round in his head he wended his way reluctantly down towards the house. A fox was barking somewhere up on the shoulder of Beinn Dobhran. Dusk was coming earlier, he noted; there was a distinct feel of approaching winter in the air. Then he had reached the barn. His father was standing with a saw in his hand, and clean white chips of the rowan trunk were strewn around his feet. A pile of logs was stacked nearby, and there seemed to be bright red berries everywhere. His father went on sawing while Dan silently and with a heavy heart joined in the work. Then, without looking up, his father said:

'You're late.'

'Sorry,' he replied. 'I was just up in the wood. Is mother in?'

'No, she went up to Balree. Plenty of work to do here before supper.' That was all; and the sawing went on.

She went up to Balree, his father had said. That must mean his granny was poorly again, thought Dan, and a now familiar feeling of guilt came over him. He hardly ever went to see her now. Ever since the burning of the Lodge and the death of the Boltons, his grandmother had changed. Oh, he knew they said she had never fully recovered from the strange sickness which had laid her low at that time. But it went far deeper than that. Sometimes Dan had the feeling that she actually blamed herself in some way for the tragedy – not simply that nobody had warned them, but that it was her fault. She had lost her bright spirit, the vitality that had so drawn him as a young boy to her. He could almost feel afraid of her at times because of her far-away look. And she had taken to spending more and more time in bed. Her Bible was always by the bedside; sometimes she would be reading it, but she would always lay it down when he came in, and ask him about himself; but somehow he could not share his thoughts with her as he used to do. Was it just that he was growing up, he wondered; the Old Box with its treasures no longer held the same appeal for him. But no, it was much more than that. He had in a sense lost his grandmother; she was no longer what she had been to him.

His father seldom went to Balree nowadays. Dan was fully aware that the tragedy at the Lodge, and the fore-warning, had greatly frightened him as well as making him feel a deep sense of personal guilt. Perhaps, he thought, his father was actually afraid of his grandmother, or of the strange gift that she had. Dan himself had grown to hate it. Why could she not have been a normal person like other people's grandmothers? At one time he had persuaded himself that she was! His grandfather, too, was failing; he no longer sang the old Gaelic songs, nor told tales from the past. It was, Dan felt, as if he had depended on his wife for his own vitality, and now that it was gone he too was empty. He was almost bent double now with rheumatism.

So his thoughts ran as together, in silence, they toiled at the cross-cut, and the pile of logs grew. Suddenly Dan looked up at the sound of running footsteps. In the fading light he saw his mother, her skirts lifted, running towards them. His father straightened and turned.

'Granny Drummond . . . she's dead!'

five

That night Dan cried as he had never cried before. He cried for what he remembered – the times he had run to Balree, longing to be with her and hear the Gaelic songs, seeing her busy and happy as she baked her oatcakes, telling her everything that had happened to him, and to have her go here and there with him, chattering and laughing. And then he cried for the times when he had gone up there and found another woman, her eyes without any light in them; he cried too for the times when he had not gone, had neglected her because she had changed; and guilt bled in him as he thought of his failure in love.

That autumn night he cried, hearing the wind hurling itself about the walls and roof. There would be chestnuts down at the manse, he thought, and cried again because never again would he take unopened burrs up to the cottage, to the old woman with the young heart who had loved the joy of splitting them and finding the polished treasures inside. He cried until his chest ached. He stood by the window, his curtains not yet drawn, looking up in the blue-black dark at the vague shoulder of Beinn Dobhran. Why had God taken her away from him? He knew that he was crying too so that his father would hear him; his mother had stayed up at Balree to be with the old man. He had not said a word as they ate their supper, nor afterwards as they had sat by the fire hearing the wind rising outside. He did not care; surely he could not care! His father loved only the land. He showed more kindness to his sheep, his dogs. Let him hear him crying now and know at least that he, Dan, had loved her! But there came a time when he could cry no more. He stood there still at the window, shivering with cold, too tired now to do anything but stare out at the empty whiteness of the yard as the moon broke clear through the sea of cloud and seemed to breathe over the land.

When he saw the shadow that had fallen across the floor he turned sharply, scared, and recognised the tall figure of his father. He heard his own whisper:

'I'll go to bed . . . I . . . wasn't doing anything.' At once he felt his face crumpling and the tears beginning. He staggered, as he felt the big hand on his shoulder.

'Stay there if you want, son. I never came to tell you off, but I . . . heard you . . . just wanted to see how you were.' He spoke quietly.

Dan listened, his head hung. Was this, could this be the same man? Gentle as a lamb with him, his voice as soft as his mother's might have been. But this was his father!

'Come on, back to bed, Danny, you'll catch your death by the window. Here, I'll tuck you in; lie down, that's it now. Man, your hands are cold.'

He struck a match and lit the tiny paraffin lamp by the bed, and then knelt there beside him. Dan looked at the jutting head with its swept-back greying hair, the face that looked as if it had been chipped out of granite.

'Here I am, talking to you at last,' his father went on in the same quiet voice. 'Well, Danny, maybe it had to take a thing like this. Oh, I know fine what you must be thinking; I know you're probably hating me for the sake of your granny, and I don't blame you. I'm just no good at all at showing things . . . never was, I'm afraid.' There was a moment's silence. Then: 'You know, my father was a very hard man; you never saw him like that – he was old, and he had mellowed, before you ever knew him. But he was hard on me all right, even harder than I've been on you. I don't know if I ever really loved him. But your granny! Don't ever think I didn't love *her*. When I was wee, and she could spare the time, we would do all the things you and she did together – we found nests, we gathered hazel nuts, we had picnics and boiled a kettle down by the burn. They were good times . . . but then, that was before she started . . . seeing things. After that I sort of grew away from her. The last few years . . . I couldn't bear it, Dan. I saw her getting old; I saw a kind of darkness in her; I was almost afraid of her. Afraid that her strange gift was not . . . was not of God. I found it hard to reconcile with her faith . . . and my own. Just don't ever think, though, that I didn't love her – my heart nearly broke with love!'

There was a silence, and then:

'At first I tried to tell myself she was just imagining things, it was all coincidence. But that was before . . . before the fire. After that, I found it hard to go near Balree. She had become so strange, so . . . so sort of far away.' He was quiet again for a few moments. Dan said nothing. Then his father said in a muffled voice: 'The sense of guilt – it's a terrible thing. Do you see, Dan, can you understand?'

Dan was struggling with his own thoughts. He had not dreamed ever to see this. To see white stars in his father's eyes, to hear him pleading like this; it was like some strange dream. He simply did not know how to respond.

He whispered: 'I know, Father. I deserted her as well.'

Johnny looked up at that, and went on: 'I wanted to remember her the way she used to be. Out in the field, I would remember a thousand things . . . there's just so much to be sorry for . . . all I said; all I did . . . Andrew especially. Nothing of it can be changed – nothing. It's too late.'

In the dim light, his face seemed to Dan like a twisted mask. He was not sure that he fully understood. But that he had come, that he was here by his side and had said he loved his granny, that was enough! Dan pulled the blankets round him and nestled his head on the pillow, and nodded gently. His father straightened slowly and stood by the bedside, as if unwilling to leave.

'Pray for me, Dan,' he said. 'Maybe you think I'm a strong man. I'm not. I need your prayers.' Again Dan nodded, finding no words.

Then he said, 'Father, can I come to the funeral?'

'Aye, lad, You can come.' Johnny turned and left the room.

That day of rain – he would never forget. The cottage at Balree, with the people crowded into the tiny parlour – the church was never used for funerals in those days – the smell of damp clothes; his grandfather, a man who had been tall, stooped and broken now, holding the book of psalms close to his eyes; his father, gone back as though to stone, his face without expression. His mother, beautiful under all the weight of her black, slipping her cold hand into his for comfort. And the coffin standing there; was his grandmother really inside it? Would he really never see her again, never have the chance to tell her he was sorry for neglecting her? He had not even said goodbye, he thought. He had no tears left now, and felt no desire to cry; he just felt something precious had gone from his life.

The old minister was there, standing inside the front door so that the many crowded outside in the rain could hear, speaking of Mrs Drummond's strong faith and Christian love; and as they sang, in Gaelic, the 23rd psalm the tide broke over him again and the tears came to choke him. Strangely, it was of the rowan tree that he thought at that moment – the tree which had borne such beautiful fruit and now was gone. And his granny, too, had gone forever. The singing, with its poignant cadences, died away; there was a final prayer, and then the coffin was lifted by strong men, and the procession began to move away. Dan could not help at that moment feeling proud that he was one of the men; women and children never went to the graveside, but today he was to go. They had tramped in silence to the ancient burial-ground, and had stood quietly by the open grave; then his father, his face deathly pale against the black suit, stepped over and bent to whisper:

'The minister says you are to hold one of the cords.'

But Dan had turned away, shaking his head, unable to speak. His father had not insisted. He had stood a few feet away then, hearing the dull thud of the clods of earth drumming down on the shiny wood of the box. It seemed to go on and on, until he wanted to scream for them to stop. He felt desperate to shut out the noise and run away from them all, out of the graveyard and up to Balree. And then it came to him that there would be nothing left there – no kettle on the boil, no Gaelic songs, no smell of oatcakes baking. It had not struck him until that moment; he had not imagined the gaping hole that would be left. In the distance he heard the river pounding, following its course through the glen, down to Abercree and, in the end, to the sea. His father was suddenly by his side, was holding his shoulders as if to stay his crying. Then it was over. The men moved away in fragmented groups. Most of the glen people had been there to bid farewell to Eliza Drummond, who had come as a girl from the islands, but had become one of them.

Johnny Drummond had walked with his father, Alan, out through the iron gate. The minister had shaken hands with them silently and left. Dan had followed, seeing how slowly his grandfather walked, his head bent, his eyes on the deep gravel of the path. At first nobody spoke; then:

'You'll come to stay with us now, Father,' Johnny said quietly; it was a statement rather than a question, and no answer was either required or received. Indeed, the old man had not spoken a word all day that Dan had heard; he had looked closely at his grandfather, and although he seemed to have aged already and his face was haggard and pale, yet there seemed almost to be an air of serenity about him. Did he perhaps feel it would not be long till he and she were reunited, the boy wondered. Now his father told him to go on ahead to Achnagreine so that his mother could have a meal ready; he left them in their painfully slow walk, and ran as quickly as he could. His mother held him in a warm embrace when he arrived, but they said little.

At last the two men came in. Rena had a blazing fire going in the range; the room was bright and welcoming. They sat down at the table and the old man, as the senior, said grace before the meal.

Later, Dan and his grandfather sat at the fire while Johnny made ready to go back up to Balree for those things which would be needed for the time being. Dan felt awkward with his grandfather, so unused was he to seeing him sitting there, and he searched his mind for something to say. Then his father came in bearing an armful of logs.

'They're not really ready for burning yet,' he said to his wife, 'but seeing the fire's so hot, they'll keep it going for a good while.' Then he went out.

Old Alan sat looking at the fire for a moment then, for the first time apart from asking the blessing, he spoke.

'Rowan logs?' he said to Rena. 'He didn't . . . didn't cut down the old rowan?'

Dan's mother nodded gently.

'The rowan.' He was almost whimpering now. 'It's been there as long as I can remember . . . what possessed him? She would never have let him, never!' Gently then, Rena led him up to his room.

six

Dan stood still on the far side of the burn. Roddy, Kate's boy, had disappeared. The old man was alone there, his eyes half-mesmerised by the silver flow of the water as it gushed down dark among the pools like a great serpent. Through a small break in the clouds the sun spread out in sudden gold over the land; but down the glen towards Abercree a great grey wall had fallen. The lambing snow! That would be it; the snow his father had so feared, and his grandfather before him. How often Dan had known it; he recalled how the newborn scraps had lain crumpled and shivering beside the ewes, hardly able to bleat for weakness and cold. The snow, he thought, was a more dangerous enemy than any eagle or fox, and no bullet in the world could defeat it. For all the changes he had seen – the new machinery, the sprays and fertilisers – the enemies had not gone. He did not truly think of the animals as enemies; after all, this was their land too – the fox and the badger, the otter and the roe deer, that sometimes raided his crops.

But once he had lost three lambs in the space of one weekend; the carcasses had been left half-eaten in the top field, below the first scree slopes of the Beinn. It had been a hard winter that year; deer, pathetic in their straggling groups, had come low down in their desperate search for food. That time he knew the killings had been the work of a fox, and a hungry one at that. And on the Sabbath he had waited, watching the crystals of snow drop against the light of the lamp. At dawn the snow had stopped, the skies breaking with blue as delicate as a hedge sparrow's egg. He took his gun, and began the steady walk up towards the woods.

He found the tracks quickly enough, here and there around the boulders strewn over the open hillsides, several sets, still quite fresh. Then, quite far away, he spotted them, a flutter of sandy red on the snows. Using whatever cover he could find, he cautiously moved higher; before very long he was near enough to shoot, and he raised the gun to his shoulder. At that moment he made a careless movement with his foot and a stone rolled noisily away. At once the mother fox turned towards him, her three cubs moving restlessly behind her. She did not move an inch, but looked steadily at him. His hand trembled; slowly he lowered the gun. Even as he did so, he could almost hear his father – and his grandfather – 'Call yourself a man of the land? Are you out of your mind?' But what right had he? The cubs would have starved! He had killed foxes before when he had to; he would no doubt kill them again. But not this time.

His mind returned to that time after the death of Eliza, his grandmother, when her husband Alan came to stay again at Achnagreine. At first, Dan recalled, he had been silent, almost as if in a kind of daze, hardly able to take in the enormity of what had happened to him. At times, though, he would be overcome with grief. Crippled as he was, he could do little apart from sitting at the fire; Dan remembered how his mother, with her customary kindness, invariably saw to it that a cheerful blaze was kept going in the kitchen range at all hours. Never again did old Alan refer to the rowan tree.

Dan could not help but notice with what respect Johnny treated his father. In the matter of family worship, for example; as the senior, he was the one to read aloud from the Bible; he it was who also asked a blessing on their meals together.

It seemed now to Dan, looking back, that after a while – he could not be sure just how long – old Alan settled down with the three of them with a surprising serenity; indeed, he remembered it as a happy time in many ways. Thinking of it now, what came back to him was the life of the glen in all its fullness – the ordinary days, filled with hard work; the Sabbath days, when everything was different, even the dishes his mother would bring out, and the best tablecloth and few pieces of silver; visits from neighbours, when there would be much talk and laughter around the fire. You never invited folk in those days, thought Dan – they called at any hour, and the kettle was never far off the boil. And there were the special occasions, of which New Year was the chief (Christmas was an ordinary working day then); but sometimes, for no particular reason, the parlour fire would be on, and in would come a few of his parents' musical friends – Alasdair the roadman with his fiddle; young Iain from the next farm with the old 'squeeze-box' his uncle had sent him, and on which he performed with amazing skill; Peter the post with his 'trump', as they called the Jew's harp. What great nights they were, thought Dan wistfully; when he was very young he would be sent to bed far too early for his liking, and he would creep out of bed and stand outside his bedroom door to hear the music, caring nothing for his icy feet. Sometimes his mother would sing in her lovely, slightly husky voice; it was always a Gaelic song, and it was always a sad one because, she said, they were the most beautiful; and always Dan would have a lump in his throat, and would feel ashamed, because tears were for girls. There was never any drink on these occasions, Dan remembered, not like nowadays; only at New Year would the whisky bottle – otherwise kept for medicinal purposes – be brought out, with glasses on a tray; for the women there would be home-made ginger wine, always served along with his mother's shortbread, dainty pieces cut in crescent and diamond shapes for the occasion.

How well he remembered the humour; there was always plenty of it in the glen, even when times were hard – maybe especially at those times. And nobody, he thought, had seemed to mind the same old jokes being told over and over, not like today, when radio and television had made folk much more demanding. Old Calum from up at Camus Lurgan, now, he was a great one for poaching stories; he had a fund of them which nobody ever tired of hearing. He was a natural storyteller; he would punctuate his tales with remarks like: 'Boys, you'll never guess what happened then!' so that you hung on his words even although you knew fine what the outcome had been.

Some of the glen humour was connected with the nicknames – common, and indeed necessary, in an area where many had the same surnames. He recalled especially Peter the miller, known as 'East-West' because of his habit of mentioning the direction – it was always 'east to Drumbeg' or 'west to the barn'. Whether he was aware of his nickname or not, nobody knew – until one evening by the fire, when the tea was being passed round; Alasdair the roadman handed him the plate of scones, saying slyly, without even a glimmer of a smile, 'Put west your hand and take east a scone.' There was a moment of silence, and then Peter had thrown back his head and roared with laughter; delightedly they had all joined in. Some of the names were more obscure, their origins long since forgotten – like Kate the Hind, and Maggie Heather; some merely incorporated a feature of the person concerned, like 'ruadh' for red-haired; while sometimes an entire family of children had their father's Christian name tacked on to their own.

Humour reached a kind of climax at Hallowe'en, though, Dan reflected. In those days, it had far more to do with practical jokes and sheer fun and games than nowadays, with all the talk of witches and spells. As a child he had dressed up in a weird collection of old clothes, topped off perhaps with a bonnet of his father's, and with his face blackened; and he was allowed to go 'guising' to a few of the houses within easy reach, to recite a poem or sing a song, and then be recognised, or not, by the occupants. But it was the 'big boys' who played the pranks. One Hallowe'en, he remembered, a gang of them had taken away all the gates in the neighbourhood – they had found their own gate next day at the bottom of a pile, neatly stacked beside the road. And then there was the time the chimney smoked so badly that his father had to get a ladder and climb up to find out the reason – which was a huge turnip somebody had placed on top. But for the children, there was not only the fun of 'dooking' for apples, but the almost unknown thrill of being given some pennies; they got nuts and apples too, but the houses at which pennies were given were noted for following years.

April Fool's Day, the first of April, was another time for practical jokes. Dan could remember some of these vividly; some of the older generation, he thought, were merciless towards the youngsters in those days – sending them all the way to the shop in Drumbeg to buy a tin of elbow grease or tartan paint. Or giving them a letter for some friend, with a note inside saying 'Don't laugh, don't smile, send the fool another mile.' Dan had himself once been the victim; it was a long time before somebody finally took pity on him.

Then Dan started to think about New Year again; it was the real highlight. One year he was given a sledge which his father had made for him, secretly, in one of the sheds. No gift in all his life, he felt sure, had ever given him more pleasure. He pictured the scene so clearly now, all these years later; he was beside himself with excitement, bouncing round the room like a dog that knows it is about to go out for a walk.

Then his father chuckled gently as he lit his pipe, and said mock-angrily, 'On you go then. Away and try it out before you drive us all daft.'

Never was there a sledge like that one. And making it had been good for his father, he reflected. It had brought them closer.

But that had always been the trouble – his father simply couldn't allow folk to come too near. Even on those musical evenings long ago, Dan recalled, his grandfather would often seem more part of things than his father. Johnny Drummond, although as a host he was welcoming enough, had a kind of silence about him, a withdrawn look. Yet over the years, how often Dan had comforted himself by remembering that night, the night of his grandmother's death, when for once his father had come close. How much it had meant to him, especially at those times when all his father had said to him amounted to no more than a dozen words in an entire day! Then he would hug to himself the words Johnny had spoken to him that night: 'Here I am, talking to you at last.'

Even if he never talks to me again in that way, he would say to himself, I will never, never forget.

But he remembered also how his father had often said that his own father, Alan, had been hard on him; to Dan, seeing the gentle old man who now lived with them, this was difficult to believe. And strangely enough, it was not until much later, when his grandfather began to lose his memory, to have periods of forgetfulness when he seemed to imagine himself back in the old days and master of Achnagreine again, that he began to understand that what his father had said was indeed true.

At times Alan would lash out suddenly at Dan's father, saying things like: 'I've always told you you're slow and clumsy! You'll never handle ewes for me again!'

Or at other times it was old Mrs Bolton he was addressing; the old fear of losing the precious land was on his mind. He would burst out with angry shouts of: 'Never, Rachel Bolton! I'll never let this land go! There's nothing you can do to take it from me and I'll fight, I tell you! This is my land, do you hear? You bought yours; but this belongs to my people, aye, as far back as you can go!'

A shadow of stark fear would cloud his face then – how that woman must have frightened him, thought Dan – and often he would begin to weep pitifully. And once or twice he had called out, 'Eliza! Come here! Come and tell her!' He would look around as if in a daze; then, seeming to come to himself, would crouch over the fire, and break into uncontrollable grief. Rena would exchange a look with her husband, he would nod gently; then they would take an arm each and help him slowly up the stairs to bed.

That was the beginning of the bad times, Dan remembered sadly; the period of calm was beginning to pass; gradually the lucid intervals became shorter, the outbursts more frequent. As always, Dan had been anxious about his mother; yet sometimes, noting how his grandfather could humiliate his father, he found an unfamiliar sense of sympathy for him; one time, marvelling at his forbearance with the old man, he could not help saying:

'How can you put up with it, Father?'

Quietly, his father had replied, 'The fifth commandment, Dan; remember? Honour thy father and thy mother.'

And as time went on, it was again his mother Dan worried about; sometimes she looked haggard and weary, and he noticed that she never sang at her work around the kitchen any more. It was she, after all, who had the old man on her hands all day long; he and his father could escape for hours at a time. Nowadays, he supposed, a social worker would have been involved and a suitable place found where he would have been cared for; no such things as homes for the elderly had existed in those days, at any rate not anywhere near the glen. Even if they had, he knew that his parents would never have accepted such a solution.

Once Dan had gone down to the kitchen very late at night for a glass of water; his bare feet made no sound, and he opened the door noiselessly, to find his mother sitting by the fire in her long white nightdress. She was crying. Dan wanted to go to her and put his arms round her; but he did not. He shrank away without a sound. He knew without asking what was wrong. It was a long time before he could get to sleep that night.

Then, an unexpected visit from a cousin of his mother's had brightened all their lives. Alec, a young man in his twenties, worked in a shipyard in Glasgow; he had been ill, and had been ordered by the doctor to spend some time in the fresh air of the country. Coming to the glen, with its ways so utterly new to him, had been like entering a new world; Dan now wondered who had been more astonished, Alec or themselves.

'What do you do for pleasure?' he asked one day. 'Don't you wish you had shops for all the things you need?'

'You don't miss what you've never had,' Rena replied evenly. 'The one thing I do envy you, I suppose, is electric light.'

It was some time before they noticed that the old man had been much more stable since Alec came; he seemed to sense that in the presence of a stranger his outbursts must be controlled. This, and the stimulation of Alec's lively talk, brought back to Dan's mother something of the old cheerfulness. Most of all, Dan remembered, Alec took an interest in her painting. He himself, although not a painter, produced very passable sketches; he was also in the habit of spending hours every Saturday at Kelvingrove Art Gallery. Dan noticed how his mother drank in all that he told her of the great art he had seen there. She said she really must make an effort to go; but Dan knew she never would.

The time came for Alec to depart. He had put on weight and there was colour in his cheeks. But 'the city is in my blood,' he had sighed, when they spoke to him of staying.

They all missed him when he went. And very soon they knew that the brief respite was over. Old Alan began to deteriorate rapidly. It was about Hallowe'en when Alec left; the time between then and New Year was hard. There was a kind of brokenness in the house, Dan thought, as he looked back over the years. His parents on edge: waiting, watching, pretending. Now, when visitors came to the house, his mother would often lead the old man gently up to his room. Nobody ever knew when he would break out either in anger or in grief. And so it was when another New Year was upon them, one none of them felt ready for. Dan watched his mother especially, seeing the strain showing in her face more than ever; as always, his father said little, but Dan was aware that he had become more helpful to his wife, doing jobs like feeding the hens, which normally fell to her lot.

On Hogmanay night, old Alan retired to bed soon after the evening meal. According to tradition, the glasses were laid out on a tray, with the whisky bottle, the ginger wine, and the plate of shortbread; as the night wore on, several of the neighbours came in, and were welcomed into the parlour. Alasdair the roadman, who normally brought his fiddle, had not done so out of deference to the old man, feeling that music would have been an intrusion; but young Iain had had no such reservations, and he soon began to play his melodeon, and Dan could hear the music long after he had gone up to his room. He lay awake for a while; then, as he had done so often in the past, he could not resist getting up and opening his door so as to hear better. There at the top of the stairs, leaning over the banisters, he saw his grandfather; tears glistened on his cheeks, and he looked as though his mind was far away, perhaps re-living New Years of long ago, hearing the voices of those who were long since gone. Dan shivered and went back to bed.

In the morning he awoke very early. Listening intently, he could hear no sound of drops from the roof on to the window ledge; that meant there was frost. The slide would be lethal by now! He had sluiced it with water last night; now, he decided, he would creep downstairs and have a good hour on it before anyone was up. He could hear his father snoring next door. Silently he dressed and tiptoed down to the kitchen; he chewed a piece of oatcake and drank some milk, then wrapped his thickest scarf around his neck and put on his warm mitts. He stepped over the two dogs and pulled open the door that was half-jammed with the frost.

As though he had fallen from the doorstep, the old man, his grandfather, lay there in the snow. His face was turned to one side; he seemed to be looking up to Beinn Dobhran, to the high slopes with their dark woods. A dusting of snow must have come since his fall, for on the back of his hand crystals glistened like diamonds. Dan bent down towards him, awed, looking closely at the face, at the wide-open eyes with their opaque, milky film. The mouth, half-open, reminded him of a trout when it has been landed from the river and is left lying on the bank; but the corners were turned upward, as though with the vaguest hint of a smile. Blood had stained the snow beside his right temple where it must have struck the stones in his fall.

Where could he have been going? What had he wanted? Suddenly Dan saw, lying a little out of reach of his other hand, a single thin log. It was from the rowan tree.

seven

Dan remembered the face of Alan Drummond exactly as it had been on that New Year's morning. Now he shivered in the cold wind; he began to climb the steeper slopes, going slowly and steadily, yet feeling conscious of his laboured breathing, stopping every few minutes to regain strength. Was he, he wondered, becoming like his grandfather? Was there nothing left now for him except ghosts?

No! This was still his land; these were his fields. That was enough. That was the umbilical cord that kept him firmly anchored; he belonged here; he would keep going while he still had the strength.

And he was determined that now, today, he would not return to the farm until he had gone much higher; if he went back now, he knew that Kate would turn a look of triumph on him, as if to say 'I told you so.' He felt a sudden rush of anger. Who was she to invade his world, to assume some sort of power over him? He was well aware that she wanted the farm after he was gone; but she would not have it. The land did not know her; his ghosts did not know her, even although he had to admit she was good with the sheep; she had been well taught. But not here! Her ways were not his. And then he asked himself why it was that he was crossing and re-crossing the fields of the past, today especially? Surely it was because the memories of his own people were a part of him always, like photographs that did not fade. And the centre of the world was Achnagreine; always he had gone from there and always he had returned.

He came at last to the barrow and paused at its base. It was a long, high mound, with three straight pines on the summit. From their branches some rooks flew with raucous cries. Up here he felt the wind keenly; he put his hand up to his cheek and found it icy cold; his fingers, unprotected by the woollen mitts, were almost numb with cold. He stood and considered the ancient mound. Once there had been a tunnel there that led to the graves of men, perhaps the very first men who had possessed this land. Had they too felt the pain that came with age? Had they loved this place and known the dread of leaving, the awareness that soon they would not see again the evening skies as they turned loch blue and shone with a strange light as dusk came on? How beautiful it was! He sat down between two great rocks, and listened to the music of the wind in the pines. As a child, he recalled, he had imagined himself below the rigging of a tall ship, the three trees with their mighty sails ploughing through unknown waters. Now the sound brought a measure of peace to his troubled heart. He was a child again; the same trees still stood, and they held him, rocked him, sang to him. As he sat, more and more and more memories of the past surged through his mind.

Alan Drummond had been buried beside his wife in the old burial ground at Drumbeg. Dan did not go to the funeral, nor did either of his parents ask him to; they were aware of the nightmares which were plaguing him, strange dreams which brought back over and over the sight of that face in the snow, with blood staining its whiteness. But in the end even that passed; and with the return of spring, his favourite season – the delight at the coming of primroses and lambs, the hatching of chickens and ducklings, and nests to be found in the woods and moors – there was healing for him. The weeks went by and soon it was summer.

His father seemed buried in his own silence. Dan would come home from school bursting with energy, longing to run and kick a ball about the yard, eager to make things – from metal, from wood, from anything he thought might be thrown out. He would bounce around his father as he worked, sharing all his ideas – he and his friends were going to ride the river as far as Abercree in a canoe like the ones the Indians had made. Or he was going to make a special trap to catch the pheasants he had seen in the rough pasture at Drumbeg. Or could his father show him how to build a hut? At times he would try to pull Johnny round by the shoulders because he felt he was not really listening. Always the answer seemed to be the same: 'Leave it till later.'

But there never was a later. His father was distant and dark, as he had been in those tense days when his grandmother had been bedridden, before the fire. It was as though he had shut himself away in some walled place, Dan thought, where nobody could reach him. And in a way, he could perhaps understand — had he not lost both his parents within a short space of time, and in tragic ways? It was no use, he would think in the end; I'll never be able to reach him. He then did what he had done before, even though he was older now and his shoulders growing broad; he went to his mother. She had always been his comfort, always a source of strength, full of energy and laughter. With her he would recapture the joy that seemed to have gone.

But it was not there. It was, he thought, as if he had gone running up to the shoulders of Beinn Dobhran in summer, looking for a stream he had known and loved, and found only the merest trickle remaining. Something terrible was wrong with his mother, he realised, with a sense of fear that almost choked him. She looked ill; pale and drawn, she moved about the kitchen with none of her old cheerfulness, none of the songs he used to love. He began to watch her covertly. He would come in from school, and find her sitting slouched in a chair, as if she was too tired to do anything else; no longer would she be baking, or ironing, or making up a hot mash for the hens. And when he asked her to come and see a mallard's nest he had found by the river, or to climb up to the wood because the wild hyacinths were in full bloom, she would say, 'Dan, I'm just too tired,' or 'Your father has to have his supper early; he's helping up at Camus Lurgan with the clipping.'

She seemed to make almost as many excuses as Johnny himself did. Yet he knew, knew with a terrible sinking of his heart, that it was not that she did not want to go with him; she loved all these things as much as he did — indeed, had she not taught him to love them? No, it was simply that she no longer had the strength.

Why had he not noticed before? He had supposed it was the old man who had been too much for her. But it was more, much more. He saw the creamy pallor of her face; he realised that she was tired, drained, at the end of her tether. Not that she showed any less love to him; feeling his eyes on her as they sat together at the kitchen table sometimes, she would pick up his spread hand and hold it, stroking back the wild hair from his forehead with a gentle hand. In a way he thought her even more beautiful, with the grey lines now about her cheeks and her face thinner and her eyes with the dark shadows about them, like deep blue lochs.

But the silence of his father did not help her either. Sometimes it seemed to Dan that Johnny found it easier to show affection to his dogs than to his family; there had been a time when he had been hard on them, saying that dogs were for work — 'Pet them, and they'll laze at the fire all day,' he had said. But now it was different. Dan had often seen him bending down, balanced on his heels, stroking the warm, thick coat of one or other of the collies, the dog's head stretched forward eagerly to receive the caress.

Increasingly aware of all that was wrong at home, dissatisfied with Achnagreine for the first time in his life, Dan took more and more to going out by himself — to the woods, to the river, anywhere at all as long as he could forget his worries even for a short time. That was when he had been about fifteen. School bored him. He would sit at his desk, leaning on one elbow, sleepily hearing the flies on the window pane, longing to be free. He did not know what he wanted — only that it was not this. There was a restlessness in him; he trailed home alone, telling his friends he could not be bothered playing football. After a cup of tea he would often retreat up to his room until supper-time. Then there would be jobs to do, like cutting sticks for the fire; as soon as these were done, he would say:

'I'm going out.'

'Where to?' his father always asked, a roughness in his voice that made Dan stiffen at once.

'Let the boy go, John,' his mother would say; almost always she took his side.

'Has he no lessons to do then?' Johnny would reply gruffly.

Once, his mother had boldly added, 'And what would you have him do? All his Saturdays, slaving away with you on the farm, and from Monday to Friday never looking up from his books. What kind of a life is that? You'd think you were never young yourself!'

Dan had slipped away at that point, his eyes smarting with tears. What was happening to them? Why could they not be happy together? Everything, everything had gone wrong since his granny had died, he decided. And, as he had done so often, he made for the solace of the wood, to sit and be quiet, and hear the soothing wind in the pines overhead.

Sometimes he would go straight up to the barrow without stopping, and lie face down in the soft moss; and he would wonder if holding a woman in his arms would feel as soft as this. Sometimes he would sit and look down at Achnagreine and the weak gold of its light, and then at the other farms dotted along the line of the glen, each with their own stars of brightness. At other times he was so filled with restlessness that he did not stop at all by the barrow, but went crashing on instead into the dark of the pines, hardly feeling the branches against his face; once he even thought, 'If I have blood on my face maybe my father will at least notice me!' On and on he went, until at last he was free, standing there in the beautiful bowl of the corrie on Beinn Dobhran, milk-white and bare, reminding him, as he turned, of a giant's head. All that was in front of him now was a great expanse – loch after loch, round blue-black pools joined by deep trenches of burns. Knee-high heather all around; orchids in summer, curlews crying; all this was his, mile after mile without end. And he was free.

Yet it was not always here he sought refuge on those days when he could bear the house no longer. Sometimes he would start blindly down the field, past the ruins of the Lodge, and on to the road down to Drumbeg. And one night, still clear in his memory, his feet stopped outside the old churchyard, and he had considered; then very quietly he had opened the heavy iron gate and gone in, round to the strange lines of the gravestones with their grey shadows. Nothing but the sound of the river in his ears, and the bleating of sheep from the fields above Drumbeg, and the scent of the trees after the rain. He found his grandmother's grave, and brought from his pocket a single orchid from the moor, its veins delicately traced with mauve, the flower she had loved most in the world. He knelt by the side of the stones; he tried to pray, but no words came. He did not know if he wanted to speak with this God who had taken her away and who now threatened . . . but no, he would not even form his fears about his mother into conscious thought. His eyes filled with hot and bitter tears and he buried his head in his arms.

When he felt the hand on his shoulder, he started up in fear; then through his tears he saw the face of the new young minister, John Maxwell.

'Come on, Dan, back to the manse for a bit.'

Dan said nothing as he went with him, feeling only the wet grass against his ankles, aware of the intense stillness of the evening, the glen seeming to wait for the end of summer and the coming of harvest. The skies were clearing and a pair of ducks went low overhead with their quick wing-beat. He noticed an old man in the doorway of one of the Drumbeg cottages, gently encouraging a little toddler who stomped on uncertain legs on the path. As Dan and the minister passed, it turned its head to look, lost its balance and fell in a helpless pile of frustration. He felt, in self-pity, that he was somehow the same; every time he got up and began to grow, it seemed to him, he was knocked over; one blow came after another. How could there be a loving God? There could not be, he decided. He walked on in silence; the young minister leaving him to his thoughts.

As he was left alone in the study while the tea was made, Dan thought about John Maxwell. There had been plenty of talk in the glen since the old minister had died and he had arrived, only last autumn. The elders did not approve of him, he knew that; they said he did not keep his place, he was too familiar, too much like one of themselves; and in his preaching he was too soft, too ready to understand and forgive the failings of people. All Dan knew was that the dark cloud was gone that had hung over going to church every Sunday; he for one did not miss the stern old man in the pulpit.

'What do you want most in the world?'

John's question startled Dan as they sat by the fire, each with a cup of tea in his hands. He glanced at the minister's face in half-suspicion, but the man meant it, really wanted to know and would respect his reply. All that past year, he now thought, nobody had listened; his father merely told him what to do and became angry if he spoke back; his mother had become more turned in on herself, and because of her obvious weakness he had not felt able to share his thoughts with her as before. But this man was giving him his complete attention; he was looking at him with eyes full of concern and kindness. No one had ever asked him this question before and he did not answer at once, wanting to be sure of his own mind.

'A real father,' he said suddenly, almost shocked at his own reply, looking into the fire and nervously tugging at his hair, adding, 'someone who would go to all the places.' He looked up at John Maxwell: 'There's nobody left . . . my granny used to come when she was able . . . my mother too, but she doesn't any more. And my father . . . ' his voice trailed away. 'It's not the same on your own.'

John nodded gently and kept his eyes fixed on Dan, as if waiting to hear if he had anything else to say. Then, bending down to lay his cup on the hearth, he said:

'I know how you love your land, Dan. Even though I don't belong to the glen I can see, and I understand. But you know, the greatest father you can have is Christ. He would have loved this glen as you do – the Beinn, the lochs, the fishing, all the things you love! He would be up early like yourself, to see the deer in the fields, the otters by the burn . . . '

Now it was his voice that trailed away, as he leaned forward to stretch out his hands to the blaze. Then he sat back and looked straight at Dan. The boy, seeing the warm intensity of that gaze, thought he had never felt safer or more at peace with anyone in his life.

'We all need a real father,' the young man went on. 'You may think I don't, because I'm a minister; that I'm strong, and never afraid. Believe me, Dan, I'm just as lonely as you are. All winter I was alone in this cold, dead old house; I've never felt so alone in all my life. But I couldn't go on living – and I mean that – if I didn't know God as my Father. He's really here, you know, as close as you are now! And on those long lonely nights I could feel His presence. It made all the difference in the world.'

Again he was quiet for a few moments, while Dan struggled to take in what he was saying so earnestly.

'We all need an anchor in life,' he went on, 'when all that is bound by time is uncertain and shifting. The summer passes and the winter comes; those we love are taken away, again and again, without our understanding. Don't turn away, Dan, you have to have faith.'

eight

But he *had* turned away. He could not, would not believe in a God who would take away those he loved most. What kind of a God was that? If indeed there was a God at all, then he, Dan, was angry with him. He had not liked to share these thoughts, not even with the young minister who had an understanding heart. And at times he felt sad – felt that he had been, as it were, shown a door opening into a place of beauty and peace; but he could not go in.

Nor did he particularly want a Creator to thank for the land, for the glen he loved; it was enough that it was there in the morning, that it grew green in the summer, and the colours came in all their glory in the autumn, and in the winter it was bare and stark and still beautiful, and when snow covered everything the beauty was beyond description. Yes, these things were enough for him.

Another spring came and he was away in the hills more than ever. Dougie and Iain, the two brothers from higher up the glen who had long been his firmest friends, hardly saw him now, and he knew they felt he had shunned them. But he could not help it; he had to be alone to think, to try to work things out. It was fine to throw yourself into a hard game of football at school, but after school it was different – you had to have the quietness of the wood, or the rocks down by the burn. He felt he wanted to empty his head of all that was being crammed into it; sometimes he was angry, finding his brain full of alien things, like adverbial clauses and the Latin gerundive and logarithms. What had these to do with his life here? It seemed as if he was sacrificing his life, his real life, for a lot of useless facts, things he had not asked to learn and would never need again. It was his life; why should he waste precious days on things he cared nothing about? As a result of thoughts like these, on some days now he plucked up courage not to do his homework; either that, or he would be out of the house until late at night and forget about it altogether.

'Well, Drummond, what about those geometry problems I set you?'

'I haven't done them, sir.'

Old Murray, whom they called Kaiser Bill, looked coldly at him with raised eyebrows. He got up slowly from his desk and paced slowly to Dan's seat, the immaculately polished brogues scraping on the hard floor.

'This is not good enough, boy.' His voice was ominously quiet. There was not a sound as each pupil leaned forward, waiting to see if Dan would be punished there and then. 'You'll do your work exactly when I tell you to, Drummond,' the master continued, pulling Dan roughly to his feet. 'And come and see me when we've finished for the day.'

Dan was not frightened, not any more. He simply did not care. He had had plenty of beatings from his father in the past; but Johnny Drummond did not beat him any more, not now that he was as tall as himself. Sometimes it seemed to the boy that they faced up to each other like two dogs and then retreated. So now he looked out at the fields around the school, and wondered what the Kaiser meant to do, what he would say to him. He could belt him if he liked. He did not care.

'I'm disappointed in you, Dan.' The old teacher was sitting in his chair looking up at him, and he seemed more sad than angry, Dan thought. His eyes even held a hint of a smile; and he had used his Christian name. 'You want me to believe you're no good at your work; but you know, and so do I, that that's just not true. You have a good brain, boy; there's a lot more in that head of yours than fishing and shearing sheep.'

Dan had said nothing. In those far-away days, Dan mused, pupils were not expected to reply; today it was different – the pupils seemed to be on familiar terms with their teachers. He remembered clearly how he had hesitated even to ask a question about something he did not understand. On that day, he had simply sat looking out of the window, seeing his own reflection, his face thin and dark and resentful. Then he looked back and saw the old teacher's eyes still fixed upon him.

'In a year's time, Dan, there's the bursary examination for university. I want you to take it.'

To his own surprise, Dan found himself saying fiercely:

'No!'

Mr Murray's face seemed to change for a moment; a look of anger flashed, but he held himself in check, and then continued in the same quiet, even voice:

'I'm not going to argue with you now. But at least listen to what I'm saying. Don't lock yourself away. I've seen fine students in this school, with promise and fame so near their hands they could have reached out and touched them. But no – they were as stubborn as you, and they never went further than the market at Abercree, never read a book again apart from the Bible. And aye, they believed they needed nothing else; the glen was enough, year in, year out, good years and bad. But there were some that regretted it, bitterly regretted the wasted opportunities, when it was too late.'

There was a silence and then the old man got up, as if wearily. Dan saw that he looked tired, tired and old; an air of heavy sadness was all about him.

Dan asked, 'May I go now, sir?'

The teacher nodded. But as Dan turned to go, he seemed to pull himself up and in a strong voice said:

'I'll not say this again, Dan; put your mind to your work and you'll go far.'

'Thank you, sir,' Dan replied, in a tone of meekness he was far from feeling. His thoughts were turbulent as he left the building. 'I'll go far, will I?' he muttered angrily to himself. 'The old fool – where does he think I want to go but here? To some horrible town, perhaps, to teach a lot of stupid children and end up old and tired and done like himself? Does he not realise I have everything, everything in the world I need, in this glen?'

Yet he did not forget the old teacher's words. And once he had calmed down, he could not help feeling proud that Kaiser Bill, one of the strictest teachers in the school, should have singled him out and spoken to him as he had.

At home he felt a deeper unease than ever. His mother was far from well; she seemed at times to drag herself around; she was deathly pale and her eyes always looked sleepless, strained. Her face was thinner, drawn, its beauty withering and yet somehow sharper, more striking.

'Go to the doctor, Mother,' he said, more than once.

'I'm fine, Dan, just tired,' was her invariable reply. She would smile gently at him and he would smile back, but his whole being ached with the dread he felt; he had an overwhelming desire to guard her, protect her. And at times a kind of blind anger at his father came over him; he would look at him sitting by the fire, seemingly unaware of the terror that filled his son's heart. It was the silence that was hardest to bear, the silence that seemed to Dan to be made up of their three minds waiting, listening in the shadows of their own thoughts, wondering. Worst of all was the silence at the table as they ate, not looking at one another, keeping their heads down. Once, his mother had suddenly broken down; she dropped her knife and fork so that they fell from the table and clattered to the floor. Then she ran from the room, stifling her sobs. For a moment or two he had sat there, willing his father to go after her. Then, still half in doubt, he stood up and scraped back his chair.

'She'll be all right,' Johnny muttered with his mouth full. 'No need for you to move.'

'I'll go if I damned well want to!' he had suddenly shouted at his father; the words were out before he could stop them. As he banged the door, he heard a muffled shout from his father in reply:

'You dare to swear in this house!'

He took no notice, but knocked on his mother's door and went in. But what was there to say to her as she knelt by her bed crying? He felt awkward, an intruder; the words he wanted to say would not come. As a child he could so easily pour out all the empty promises – that he loved her and would never leave her, that she always would be the closest to him. Now he longed to assure her of his love, but he could not. He still loved her with intensity; yet in some way he was also aware that the umbilical link was broken; things could never be again as they had been in childhood. Knowing her deep hurt, he felt at that moment all the more helpless. His silence was in a sense worse than his father's.

One day he came home from school and knew at once, from the remembered smell of the doctor's tobacco, that he had been there to visit his mother. His heart began to thump uncontrollably with fear; what could have happened? There was no sign of his mother or of supper. Almost at once Johnny came in; Dan knew he must ask him what was wrong, but at first he simply could not frame the words. Each time he tried, his tongue seemed to be frozen. Then the dread question was out:

'What is wrong with mother?' Johnny's back was turned; he did not answer for what seemed like an eternity. Then he turned to face Dan.

'The doctor says it's . . . it's some kind of anaemia,' he said slowly.

'Anaemia,' echoed Dan. 'What's that?'

'He said . . . something lacking in her blood.'

'But that's all right, surely,' answered the boy desperately, 'they can . . . can replace what is lacking?'

'Not with this kind, son,' Johnny replied.

Startled by being called 'son' – it had been a long time since his father had used the affectionate word – Dan looked at his face; what he saw was naked pain and despair. Not knowing what to say, he muttered that he would get some kindling, and rushed outside. Passing the window he glimpsed Johnny; he was slumped at the table with his head in his hands.

'He does care,' he thought in wonder. 'He is terrified to lose her, just as terrified as I am! Then why, why doesn't he show it? Why does he not tell her he loves her? Why does he have to hide away from us both?'

He sat in the barn until his thoughts had grown calmer. Finally he said to himself, 'Why don't I tell her either? I'm just as bad as he is!' In some strange way, though, he felt comforted. When he returned to the house there was no sign of his father, but his mother was moving about slowly, making the supper as usual. She said nothing about the doctor.

It was from that day that he found himself beginning to think seriously about old Murray's words. What he loved most in the world he could not have. He now faced the fact that he was likely to lose his mother; the thought of staying here with his father alone was unthinkable. The farm was not big enough for both of them. Perhaps after all he should prepare himself for the thought of leaving; perhaps one day he should try to find freedom to be himself, to live his life as he wanted it. And one day he would come back, back to the glen and to Achnagreine; and the land would be his, truly his own as his brother had wished it to be all those years ago.

All the same, he did not reach a decision for some time. There were days when he accepted that he would go; and he would almost pluck up courage to seek out Mr Murray and tell him he would sit for the bursary after all. Equally, on other days the very idea of going to the city, enduring the long years there, seemed like utter madness. How could he bear to be away from everything that he cared about? Often he was simply in doubt, trapped as it were in the deep pool of his own confusion. Perhaps it would be better to find work somewhere else in the glen – that way he would not lose everything. Underneath all the uncertainty was one clear thought; he had to escape, even for a time, from the domination of his father. He had to be himself.

Then came a day when Rena, his mother, was finally beaten. Dead tired, weary of the unending struggle, she took to her bed, and slept for several days. Coming home from school, everything seemed altogether empty and cheerless to Dan; the very air seemed strange. In the deserted kitchen there was no welcoming smell of baking. He now had to cook for his father; their meals were eaten in almost complete silence, and Dan dreaded them. His mother ate little, mainly tea and fruit; sometimes, though, she would ask him to cook fish for her.

She did not remain in bed after the first few days; revived to some extent, she got up and, still a prisoner in her room, began to paint again. It had been a long time since she had last touched her brushes; it was as though she poured into the new canvases all of the mingled love and longing and sadness that were bound within her. Rich as the paintings were with detail and colour, there was yet a kind of jaggedness, seen especially in the trees and the skies, that seemed to reflect something of her own inner pain. She moved into Dan's room to paint the view up to Beinn Dobhran, her favourite of all as it was Dan's too. He was not allowed to see it until it was finished; when he did, he could not help throwing his arms around her in sheer joy, laughing with delight, proud of her, amazed that despite her weakness her gift was still so great. As she hugged him, a golden light caught her thin face from the evening sun. He knelt by her side, as if begging a favour:

'Mother, I want you to know something . . . I'm working for the bursary, to go to university.'

Her face lit up and her tired eyes shone as she held him close and said:

'That's wonderful, Danny. And I know you will do well!' Then, after a moment, she gently teased him, ruffling his hair, 'but you'll have to work hard – not so many hours up in the woods any more. It'll be the midnight oil from now on!' She laughed and hugged him again.

What meant more to him than anything else was that they had become close again. Somehow the spontaneous delight which the painting had released in him had also broken down his stiffness; he realised it was he who had made the gulf which had in recent months grown up between them, his growing up which had shut her out. All those years his mother had been there, ready to welcome him when he came home, but he had not properly seen her; he had taken her for granted. Now he determined it would be different. And he found himself doing the things he had almost forgotten – on his way home from school, he would pick a bag of hazelnuts to lay on her table as she lay sleeping. Or he would make her an especially tempting supper, and sit by her, telling her all the day's happenings, while she ate. He spent as much time with her as his homework would permit.

For a time, during a spell of perfect autumn weather, she seemed to rally, to regain a little of her former vitality. Dan was ready to make the most of it. On a golden day of early October sunshine, he persuaded her to come up with him to Donnie's Pool. It was a Saturday, and he had worked hard at his homework all morning; then he had made a picnic for the two of them, with all the things she liked best. It was as though she had become the child, he thought; all she had once given him he now delighted in finding for her.

As they sat there together in the late afternoon light, he had taken her hand and said gently, 'You're a lot better, Mother. By the time spring comes you'll be well.'

He saw her lips trembling. For a few moments she did not reply; then, in a small voice she had said, 'Don't, Danny; don't break my heart by saying such things. I only wish with all my heart you were right. And I had . . . I had longed to see you through university. It was Andrew's dream too, you know.'

She was silent then, and sat holding his hand, while a pain that was almost physical passed through his whole body. He could not answer.

She continued, 'But we'll be good to each other.'

At that moment he thought of his father. He and his mother were now so close; sometimes it seemed as if his father had ceased to exist.

There were times when he could feel sorry for him. He and his mother would spend an hour or more in her room, talking of many things, looking at her paintings perhaps, sharing deeply now that all was well between them once again; then his father would come in, expecting his supper; as always he would seem withdrawn, in a sense threatening. Dan knew that he could never overcome the edge of fear he felt whenever his father was there. He was shut out, a stranger; and while Dan blamed him for it, he still at times could feel pity for his loneliness. After all these years, he still recalled that time, after his grandmother's death, when his father had for once opened up his inner self to him; he could still see him kneeling by his bedside and hear him say: 'Here I am at last, talking to you.'

'Why, why, why,' he cried to himself, 'can he not do it again? What is wrong with him; how did he come to be like this? Is my mother dying of a blood disease or of a broken heart? But then, is his heart not broken too? And whose fault is it but his own?' It was all beyond Dan. He felt trapped, baffled; he would never be able to understand.

Then there was the question of the land. Dan felt that there was another world which was his father's, a world he was not allowed to enter. Although he helped around the farm, and indeed there was often far too much for him to do, he was very aware that in a sense he was shut out; this land, to him more precious than gold, was possessed by his father. He longed for the day when it would be his own.

His father did not once mention the exam; Dan did not tell him about it, but he knew that he would have heard. The thought came to him that his father would think that Dan had given up and was leaving, as it were beaten, driven away; that he, Johnny, had won. Then he dismissed the thought as unfair. He did not really believe it was like this.

So the winter went past; Dan had never known one so dreary. His mother never left her room now; the short-lived improvement was over. As spring came, what hurt Dan most was the awareness that the house was not clean any more. In the old days, he knew, he would never have noticed; now he began to see cobwebs in the rooms, and was aware of a general air of untidiness and neglect. As he came up the glen from school, he could see the housewives busily engaged in the annual ritual of spring-cleaning, and he would recall the joy his mother had taken in her freshly washed blankets and curtains, the spotless floors and polished brasses. His heart felt like lead.

But one day a girl started up the track to Achnagreine. She had two big cases in her hands and she walked slowly, her gaze fixed on the ground. Dan went down nervously to help her, whistling because he was shy and had no idea what to say. He took the cases and then walked a little ahead of her. She was Catriona Morrison, and she had come because Johnny had suddenly announced that the house was going to wreck and ruin. Her parents were from the Isle of Lewis, but after a short time in Glasgow they had settled in Abercree. Dan scrutinised her discreetly while they were having a cup of tea in his mother's room. She was pale, and had thin white hands rather like his mother's. Her long brown hair flowed down her back, thick and glossy. They stood together at the window; Johnny, digging in the garden, looked up and saw them; he raised a hand in greeting.

'Your father?' she asked. In her voice was a kind of music that he did not miss, the lilt of Gaelic.

'Aye,' he answered sharply, not looking at her, annoyed with himself that he had somehow allowed anger into his reply. 'You're not seeing the place at its best yet,' he went on quickly, 'the green's not back yet. The hills are a bit colourless at this time.'

She laughed lightly. 'I know,' she said, 'we have a few round Abercree, you know.'

She wasn't really laughing at him, he decided; there was a friendly glint in her eyes. All the same he felt himself beginning to redden. He was glad to go over and open the door for Corrie; the collie growled ominously on seeing a stranger. But she spoke gently in Gaelic, and the dog relaxed, even let her stroke his head. Maybe a token, he thought, of her acceptance at Achnagreine?

Later, Rena managed to come downstairs in her dressing-gown, to show Catriona the cupboards and drawers where things were kept. After Dan left them, he heard them talking and laughing together as if they had known each other for ages; he felt his spirits rise as they had not done for a very long time. He knew things were going to be better, especially perhaps for his mother. Catriona seemed a quietly confident person; although she must only be a couple of years older than himself, she seemed many years older in maturity.

She was to have the little spare room across the landing from his own. It smelled a little of damp, he noticed, as he set her cases down; but she laughed and said it would be fine for her. Even Johnny came in from his work earlier than usual, put his head round the door and said to Catriona with a shy smile:

'Och, well, you seem to be settling in grand.'

At dinner, she chattered to Dan and his father about Lewis, about Glasgow, as well as about her family and – as she put it – the hundred and forty-three cousins she still had on the islands; she told them how she missed the ceilidhs, how she loved and hated the life all at the same time and never knew whether she wanted to go back or not.

But it was the farming Johnny wanted to know about – how many sheep had they had on the croft, how hard was it to make a living there? Catriona ended by laughing at the seriousness of the questions; Johnny looked at her a little startled, but she told him she had been too young when they left the island to know much of croft life; what she remembered best were the winter gales and the slates rattling, and in the summer going for water with buckets – and finding wild orchids on the moors.

'Do you like orchids?' Dan said quickly.

'There's nothing more beautiful,' she answered simply.

'They were my granny's favourite flower.' He felt himself begin to redden as he spoke, and bent quickly to eat again; there was still a burning at the back of his eyes when he thought of her. He could not say any more.

'Catriona is good for us all,' he told himself as he went to bed that night. First, she would be company for his mother, and would be able to cook dainty meals which he himself could not do properly. It would make his own life much easier too; sometimes he had difficulty getting his homework done with all the extra work; his father, for all his faults never a mean man, insisted that Rena had a fire in her room all the time; that was only one of the jobs which fell to his lot. But the really important thing, he felt, was that she did not seem the least bit in awe of his father – maybe the silent meals would even be a thing of the past.

And so it proved. He no longer dreaded coming home to find the empty silence of the kitchen, his mother lonely and depressed upstairs, his father withdrawn and tense. Catriona wasted no time in tackling the work – Dan noticed the well-scrubbed doorstep, the spotless curtains, the smell of polish on the furniture – and it did his heart good. Before going off to begin his homework he would sit talking to her as she went briskly here and there, preparing things for the meal. She was full of fun, and was forever pulling his leg about housework, telling him with a sarcastic grin how impressed she was at the tidiness of his room. But she wanted to know a host of things about the glen – where his favourite places were; whether there were eagles (she recalled seeing them as a child in Lewis); how much Gaelic he knew; whether he had heard this story or that, or knew certain Gaelic songs. She told him also of her life in Glasgow, of the ceilidhs they used to go to, where most of the people you met were themselves Lewis exiles and knew all the same people. He told her of the bursary he was working for, and she was full of enthusiasm.

'You must go to Glasgow!' she said excitedly. 'It's the best city for Highlanders – and after all you can easily come home for the holidays; it's not as though you'll be away for ever!'

The months went on and New Year came again. A New Year when it seemed to him they were all so happy together that he began to have serious doubts about going away at all. Looking back to the previous year, Dan could now scarcely believe they were the same family. All the old friends came for the celebration – old Calum from up at Camus Lurgan, Alasdair the roadman bearing his beloved fiddle, Jessie and Kirsty Maclean, two sisters who sang Gaelic duets, Iain with his melodeon, Peter the post with his mouth organ. They even cleared the floor and had an eightsome reel. And his mother was downstairs, looking so much better and happier that when he caught sight of her face he wanted to cry for sheer joy. Best of all was that Johnny was sitting beside her, holding her hand. When the glasses were passed round, he did not even object when Dan calmly helped himself to one. He had not felt so happy, he thought, since he was a small child. This was New Year as it should be.

He could not get to sleep that night for thinking of his father. What an enigma the man was! When would he ever understand him? This silent war that went on between the two of them – how much he longed for it to be over. Sometimes he would have an urge to go to him and simply tell him he loved him. But what would come of it? He felt that the answer lay with Johnny himself. It was surely he who had built up this strong dyke around himself, not to mention the precious land which he so jealously guarded, and so only he could break it down. There were times when Dan would pluck up courage to go to him with an idea, perhaps of something they could do together, or someone they might visit; always, though, he seemed to be left feeling that his timing had been wrong; he would vow never to be so stupid again. He would swing this way and that, between hatred and love. At times he doubted whether his father's friendly overture on the night of his grandmother's death had ever happened at all.

'Dan, you need to get away,' Catriona suddenly said to him one day when he was staring out of the window, his thoughts far away. The snow was beginning to melt; soon it would be lambing time again, and he could expect to hear his father's voice in the early dark, calling for him to help. The girl sat down beside him and he noticed the red-gold sheen that lit her hair as she looked at him, her head to one side, her expression half comical, half gentle.

'I worry about you, Dan, you know. Half the time you're away in your own world and you shut folk out. You're a bit like your father, if you ask me.'

He turned round with an expression of horror so that she laughed out loud. 'Och, I said it to annoy you . . . but there's truth in it! You're a right pair, the two of you. It's not easy, believe me, living under the same roof with you both. You're like two strange collies, circling each other the whole time, waiting for the chance to have a nip at each other. No wonder your poor mother's tired out!'

Dan looked round at Catriona sharply, shaken by what she had said.

'D'you blame me too then?'

'Yes, I do!' she retorted with feeling. 'You certainly don't make things any easier. You take your mother's side in every single thing, just because of your war with your father.'

'That's not fair, Catriona. I do it to protect her . . . she's had to put up with him for so long. He acted as if he was God Almighty when I was younger; he thought he could rule us all. I won't let him any more, and he knows it.'

She nodded, her eyes searching his face. He felt a sudden heat in himself, that burned and passed. He must not! But she was beautiful; he had been aware of it from the first day, and told himself sternly that he must suppress the flame in his being. Deep down he knew that he had fallen in love; he was determined all the same not to acknowledge the fact. She was more than two years older than himself; he was still only a schoolboy. How could she possibly take him seriously? Thus he crushed his feelings, not daring to allow them to develop further. One moment he would attempt to deny their very existence, the next he would be desolate to think she had come just as he was about to leave. He had never felt more confused.

He sat the bursary exam. He had worked feverishly, sometimes through the entire night, in the lamplight of his room, until his eyes were badly strained and he was near exhaustion. When he came home that day, Catriona, full of questions, was eager to know how it had gone. He simply could not say; he told her quietly that they would have to wait and see, and he went to lie on his bed so that he might attempt to gather his muddled thoughts. His mother and Catriona. What exactly did he want? Was it worth the price – escaping from his father, to lose them both? Had Catriona been right in what she said, that he was to blame as well as his father? But the thought of leaving here! He would come back, though . . . just three or four years in the city. But would it be too late? He didn't know, he didn't know! If only someone could advise him! If only he could see into the future! Perhaps the best thing would be to put it out of his mind until he knew the results of the bursary.

At last the papers came. It was a Saturday; and for that whole day he kept them unopened in his room, saying nothing to anybody. He had put them into a drawer and in the afternoon had gone away by himself, right up into the corrie below Beinn Dobhran. It was a still day; not a breath of wind, no movement except that of the sheep as they passed below him among the pasture, mainly the grass that grew among the heather. And a single buzzard high above him, come down from the sharp-cut edges of the Beinn, mewing with a cry which surprisingly seemed no stronger than that of a mouse. A long glide as it circled, two wing beats to keep height, then the long glide again. He sat for a time beside one of the dark lochans, trying to find stones that could skip over the water, but all he found was shingle and rough edges of quartz and granite.

'What on earth am I doing up here,' he asked himself, 'running away from the answer?' The question came into his mind before he seemed to have given it conscious thought. What was the point of torturing himself? He had to know! Yet there was a part of him that was scared – for so long he had been at a kind of crossroads, waiting and wondering; now it was out of his hands, the decision made. True, but did he really know what he wanted? It was as though the child inside himself was frightened, not knowing. He got up and started back the way he had come. And as he crossed one of the deep channels that linked the lochs, flowing black and clear as liquid smoky quartz, he caught sight of a young fish darting under the bank. Only a second and it was gone, yet somehow it set him thinking. The fish would go down to the sea, leave the glen river until the water had turned bitter with salt; but it would come back! It would find a way past the nets on the estuary, back to this place, the beginning. He knew before he opened the envelope what his answer would be.

nine

Dan shivered. It was cold here in the trees' shadow, as the wind gusted over the barrow and hissed into the wood behind. He would have to start walking again. There seemed to be so little time; he had taken perhaps an hour to reach this far from the farm. To think how fast he once had run here! But he did not want to leave this special place – not yet, at least; there was too much to remember. And having come so far in his journey of remembering, he was determined to go on.

That day when the bursary results came was still as clear in his memory as if it had been last week. Catriona had danced with him round the kitchen. He had had a great urge to kiss her, but he had refrained. His father had shaken his hand; even he, that day, had been unable to keep from smiling.

'Well, you're the cleverest of the Drummonds,' he had said, 'but don't let it go to your head!'

His mother, who should have been the first to know, was the last. That would need time. He went in to her room, the paper half-crumpled in his hand; he saw her turned away on one side as she slept, heard her soft breathing. Her little paraffin lamp still burned by the bedside; the book she had been reading had slid down to the floor. He looked out of the window in the growing dusk at the field that ran down to the Lodge; the ruins, he thought, were as dead and silent as his grandmother. He knelt softly by the bed and reached for the hand that was curled around the covers. She wakened up slowly, saw him at once and smiled sleepily.

'I won the bursary, Mother,' he whispered.

'Of course you did, Danny,' she said, and opened her arms to hold him.

'I want you to know something, though.' It was not easy for him to speak; he had to fight to get the words out. 'I'll come back, the minute you need me . . . if you . . . if you're not better.' He did not dare say it any other way, but she understood; she held his head between her hands, and made him look at her.

'Listen, Danny,' she said urgently. 'You've been here when I needed you most. All of these years. But when I'm . . . when I'm really ill, I won't be myself any more and I don't want you to see it. It would break you. Please . . . I'd rather you remembered.' Her voice failed and she hugged him tightly to her.

Never had he loved her so much. And in his heart he cried out again and again: 'God, if you're there, if you're hearing me now, listen – don't take her away!'

But the summer came and went and she was worse. The weather was sultry; her room was too hot, and she could get no rest. Dan could see that his father was frightened; he was short with Dan and even irritable with Catriona. He sat far longer than usual at the kitchen table, looking away from them into the yard, his face grey and drawn. Dan suddenly saw him looking much older, his hair almost all white now, the furrows across his brow deep-ploughed. The walls he had built around himself now seemed higher than ever; in his grief he had retreated even further into himself. In near desperation, Dan would think back to that one night when the iron gates had been opened, when he had allowed the light to fall on his inmost soul, allowing his son to glimpse the guilt he felt over his dead mother and Andrew. Yet he had not learned; he was still doing the same things, was still closing himself so that none could reach him. And soon it would again be too late – Rena would be gone.

Dan was at times half crazed with a mixture of pity and frustration. Before he left Achnagreine, he determined to find a way of breaking that wall, for his mother's sake if not for his own. Again and again he had sought the answer and had come no closer. On those hot, airless nights he had lain awake and heard his mother coughing; his thoughts gave him no rest either, and he fell into an uneasy sleep just before it was time to get up. His mother began another canvas but again would not let him see it until it was finished. He had to help her over to the other side of the room and he dreaded this; each time it seemed to take an eternity. As he supported her he would lay his head gently against her shoulder, feeling her ribs, her frail body that was turning thin as a bird's. Once she had run with him into the fields above Balree to pick mushrooms, played hide-and-seek in the woods around the farm and he had believed she would never grow old; she was eternal, strong and full of laughter. Now, sometimes, she could not even summon up the strength to talk to him; she just smiled with a kind of twisting of the mouth, and pain would surge through him as he looked away.

Catriona asked him suddenly one day whether he had found lodgings in Glasgow; his mind was far away and he had trouble in focusing his thoughts. He did not reply. He went out quickly and ran up to his refuge, the barrow at the edge of the wood; in the dark shade of the pines he lay down, smelling the moss, watching the birds moving restlessly among the trees, listening to the running of the stream that had shrunk to almost nothing. And he cried.

At home he began to make preparations for leaving, far earlier than he needed to. Not because he wanted to go, but because he was frightened. He did not know what would happen next; it seemed to give him the chance to have things ordered, to feel himself at least master of the small world of what he had, when all that was inside him had been ransacked and burnt, left in ruins. His mother was clearly getting worse. One day the doctor came and Dan waited down in the kitchen for a long time, cutting aimlessly at a piece of wood with his penknife. When the man came down heavily from her room at last, he touched Dan's shoulder gently; he had known them for a long time.

'Is she any better?' A plea, not a question.

'I'm afraid not, Dan,' the answer came in a quiet voice; the boy turned to look into the fire. There was no more to be said.

But his goodbye had been said already. She had finished her last canvas two days ago, and was happy about it. It was the view down to the Lodge and the hills beyond, with the light as it came in the early morning. He had held her hand and simply sat there, nodding and smiling in appreciation, filled with gladness for her that she had managed to complete her task, filled too with love and grief that broke him in pieces like a leaf in a river's flood. She had tried to raise herself in the bed, but could not; she attempted to laugh but started to cough instead. Then, brokenly:

'This one is for you, Danny. You are to keep it. Always.'

He could not speak. He would never forget her. As she now smiled, she was suddenly as she once had been – the thinness that had changed her beauty was gone, and she was mother, the mother he had known from the beginning.

Now he was ready; it was done. His room was almost bare, a dark shell that possessed him no longer. The two big cases stood there, waiting for him, on the day the thunderstorm came. The fields had turned ill and red-brown, sick with the drought. Between the pools of the burn there ran thin serpents of water, a mere trickle. Dan watched the yard, the rough pasture that ran as far up as the first screes, the grey dome of Beinn Dobhran, as suddenly the darkness seemed to rear like wild horses over the glen, orange and purple masses of cloud as the lightning flickered down and a great roll of thunder went on and on. He opened the window and put his head out; drops of rain as big as grapes soaked it in a moment; he closed his eyes and let the water run down his face.

'Dan!' It was his father, down below. 'Help me cover the bales!'

It did not register with him for a moment; it was as if he did not understand the question. He kept looking down dumbly at the white, upturned face; then his father turned and ran to the back of the yard where the dry bales were stacked. Dan ran downstairs; he opened the back door and stood there for a moment as the huge drops splashed across his hands and shoulders. Then he was running over the ground that was dancing with silver, until he was standing above his father's bent back.

'Father!'

He had not heard; he was still struggling to move the bales.

'Father!' he tried again. He must have heard; he was just not listening to him. Dan could not bear it. Blindly, in sheer desperation, he pulled his father up with all his might, to face him. The face seemed empty; the expression changed to one of utter shock as Dan struck the pale cheek. A red weal spread as he looked with horror at what he had done. But he was past caring now.

'Father!' he shouted again, half sobbing. 'Go, go now – let me do this.

Go to mother, for God's sake! Don't waste another minute; tell her, tell her you love her! Don't leave her as you left granny! Can't you see? There's so little time left!'

He was really sobbing now, broken, the dam burst. Nothing mattered any more except that Johnny should go to her. And when he looked up, he had indeed gone. The drought, the thirst, finished. He heard their voices in her room as he came downstairs with his cases, quiet and close. That was all that mattered.

Catriona was standing by the fire when he went in; she looked startled as she saw the cases and realised he was leaving. He smiled gently at her; then he went over to her, kissed her softly and touched her hair, as he so often yearned to do.

'I'm going, Catriona. Now, tonight, I've finished everything I needed to do. But I'll be back; I promise you I'll be back.'

ten

The old man smiled to himself as his thoughts went back to that day, more than sixty years ago. In the end, he reflected, the circle had been complete; he had gone in peace.

He got up from his seat on the ancient mound, and moved into the shelter of the wood. The streams were choked; it seemed that they gossiped to each other as they flowed down to join the burn that passed the farm and Shian, sounding for all the world like the voices of the old women as they came out of church and stood talking together in their tight black circles.

He had lost the glen of his childhood, he mused as he walked, lost it and then found it again. He had discovered what lay beyond the ring of hills which had enclosed his early world, had as it were reached up to pick his own Eden fruit, and found that it was the trees of home which bore the apple, however bitter, that alone could assuage his thirst and give peace to his heart.

He left Achnagreine knowing full well that his mother had precious few days left. But his farewells had been said; he knew that and so did she. He remembered her as she had been, all that had nourished his childhood. Now there was no choice but to turn away, all the rich memories stored in his heart. He told himself that he must grieve no more; rivers of mourning had flowed out of him already; now he must look to the future. And one day he would return.

Glasgow. As he turned his thoughts to that period of his life, he found a strange thing – his mind would not function in its normal way. Whereas the memories of the glen in his early years were as clear as if the events had happened yesterday, the sequence absolutely fixed in his mind, of Glasgow he could recapture only a kind of kaleidoscope of impressions, with a few outstanding happenings etched clearly in his memory. For example, he could recall little of the journey south – only that the hills became noticeably lower as the train snaked its way southwards. At one point a little boy in the compartment had suddenly noticed Dan opposite him and had shrieked:

'Look at his funny hair!'

The child had been duly reprimanded and smacked; but Dan had all at once become aware of his shabby clothes and luggage, and had shrunk back into his corner, overcome with embarrassment. He remembered too that, as they neared the city, the miles and miles of drab tenements – grey-black buildings where surely the sun's rays never penetrated – seemed to go on for ever. There was so little green left; the few trees looked almost black, and he fancied they fought for breath among all the grime-laden stones. As the train passed slowly by, he remembered catching sight of groups of ragged children watching it, young girls carrying younger children in their arms – the face of poverty as he had never seen it until then.

Of his arrival he remembered little except that all seemed to be bustle and activity – and noise. He never became used to the city's noise, of shouting, trams and motors. A flurry of grey doves, he recalled, had risen up around him as he heaved his heavy cases out of the train. Everyone but himself seemed to know where they were going.

More impressions surged back as Dan began to concentrate his mind on that far-away time. He remembered his room. He had asked for one where he could cook his own food; it was cheaper than the more usual 'lodgings with full board'. In a dingy tenement, considered superior because the walls of the 'close' were tiled, it was up four flights, at the very top of the building, and contained a small iron bed, a table and chair, a large cupboard and a single gas ring. The high ceiling made it seem cold and unfriendly; the only consolation he found on that first night was a tiny skylight on the landing, through which he could just make out the stars.

He remembered his landlady. Even now, after much experience of life, he marvelled that anyone could have shown so little interest in another human being, especially in one so obviously at sea as he had been. She had her own family and was totally immersed in her own affairs and theirs; she found out nothing about him, and came to see him each week only to collect the rent. If I died tonight, Dan would sometimes think, she would never know until rent day; even then, she would care only about the nuisance it would cause. He knew that he had been singularly unlucky; other students seemed to have landladies who cared about them. From time to time in chance encounters, usually in the small shops, he would meet people who exhibited some of the warmth for which this city was generally known.

The loneliness, especially in the first week or two before classes began, almost crushed him at times. He wondered how he could possibly survive it until term ended; then he remembered that he would not be going home for the holidays – how could he bear even to think of New Year in the glen now? That was what he most remembered – the loneliness. And the dirt and deprivation. It was the beginning of the Depression, and groups of thin, hopeless-looking men could be seen standing at every street corner. Pale women carried their babies tightly wrapped in shawls tied around them. Ragged children, many with the leg deformities he had been told denoted rickets, were everywhere.

He remembered the struggle to survive on his bursary. He had in fact been awarded two, the extra one being given to certain students from the Highlands and Islands. In addition, he had a few pounds which a cousin in Australia had left to him a couple of years before. He had been determined to manage without asking his father for a penny; but Johnny had insisted on giving him ten pounds – a princely sum for those days – on the day the news of the bursary came. He realised he was going to need every single penny. All the same, it had not been so very many years since students from the glens used to go to university with a sack of oatmeal to last them the whole term; he was infinitely better off. He determined to live largely on porridge and potatoes; what else after all could he hope to cook on one gas ring? And he must forego the luxury of taking a tram. Yet one of his few happy memories was of a day when he had, in the teeming rain, got on to a tram. It was absolutely empty, and the conductor was standing by the door lustily singing a Gaelic song. Dan, his heart leaping, could not resist joining in, and they finished the verse in duet. The conductor, equally delighted, greeted him in fluent Gaelic. Dan went past his stop in the excitement of finding that Duncan came from Skye, from the next township to that in which his grandmother Eliza had grown up.

After perhaps a week, on a day when he had spoken to no one and felt he could not bear the loneliness another moment, he decided he would go into a pub. The very idea made him nervous; he knew too that he could not hope to eat if he spent money on whisky, but in desperation he shrugged the knowledge off. It was a Saturday night and he sat on his own, drinking his whisky faster because he had nobody to talk to. All around him were voices, ugly voices of working men, arguing, sometimes shouting, looking angrily at him – or so he imagined – if they caught him looking at them too intently. The whisky burned his throat; he did not like it, simply hoped it would dull his pain for even a little. Nobody spoke to him. Suddenly he noticed a man who looked like his father; guilt washed over him at the thought of what his parents would think if they were to see him in a place like this; not only that, but he reckoned the whisky was costing him as much as a week's ration of oatmeal and potatoes. A fight broke out noisily at the other end of the bar; he finished his drink hastily and began to edge out. The bar was closing, and in a tight scrum of feet and sour voices and smoke they were all pushed out on to the street. But he felt warmed and relaxed now; then suddenly, as in a dream, he seemed to see his own feet walking down in twilight from Beinn Dobhran to the yard at Achnagreine. It was a long way home. A hard key in his pocket, to admit him to his cold empty room; girls going home with laughing faces, protecting their hair with shawls as they half-ran in the rain along the glistening pavements. He did not go in a straight line; his hands were stuck into his pockets; his head hung so that the horizontal rain did not touch his face. Nobody could see that he was crying.

Afterwards, he decided that he would not go into a pub again; instead, he would buy a small bottle of whisky – the gill size – and drink it only when things got too bad. He bought the bottle. Then came the day he would never forget. Dan could not remember now how long it was after he had left the glen, only that it was the day before classes were to begin. As usual he had spoken to nobody all day. A deep depression had hung over him from the moment he had wakened up; he had been unable to banish thoughts of his mother for even a moment. Reaching near-desperation, he had gone for the bottle of whisky and drunk the entire gill. Soon after he had finished it, his landlady shouted that he had a visitor. It was Davie Shaw, a boy who had been a year ahead of him at school and was starting his second year at university. He was shy, turning his cap round and round in his hands.

'I . . . I came back from the glen today, Dan,' he said quietly. 'Your father asked me to tell you . . . to say that your mother died this morning.'

How cold and final it sounded! Not that he blamed Davie; he felt sorry for him, having to bear such a message. There was silence as Dan struggled to remain calm. But had he not known all day? Not once had she left his thoughts. So she was gone! All he wanted was for Davie to go and leave him to his grief, but he did not know how to send him away. He felt awkward too because he knew his breath must smell of whisky; not only that, but when the boys at school had laughed at Davie because he was old-fashioned, religious, he had often joined in. Oh, he had been nice enough when they were alone together, but not in the pack. All these thoughts surged through his head as they stood there in what must have been a long silence. Then, keeping his voice as steady as he could, he said:

'Sit down, Davie. And thank you for coming to tell me.'

The boy sat down uncertainly on the only chair. Then, looking out of the window, Dan went on:

'I came away early, you know. It was the right time and I don't regret it. You won't understand, but in the end I was glad. There was nothing more I could have done.'

He knew his voice was slurred; he knew he was concentrating too hard on his words and he knew that Davie knew this. But what did anything matter now? If only he would go! But he sat there looking dumbly up at him, so Dan continued:

'You probably think I'm callous . . . but she began . . . began dying a long time ago – and she was tired.'

For a moment he saw her there, pale and drawn, at the kitchen table; his voice caught on a nail-sharp edge, but he did not break.

'Only at the end I saw it and . . . and I gave everything I had. That was why I went away, Davie; there was nothing left to give.'

He looked intently at Davie and the boy's glance shifted.

'What about . . . the funeral, then?'

Dan turned away and leant his elbows on the window sill.

'You won't understand.' He almost groaned. 'Nobody will understand.'

He was not simply speaking to Davie, but to himself and to all the ghosts who asked him the same question. Perhaps one day he would not understand himself; but for now, at this moment he knew exactly what he was doing, and he knew what the answer must be.

'I'm not going to the funeral. There's no need.'

'But Dan, think of your father!' the boy burst out.

That made him angry. 'For once I'm thinking of myself and not my father,' he said. 'After all the years he hasn't thought of me – no, nor of my mother. He's the one who needs to make his peace with her, not me. I said goodbye all right, not at some empty hole, like on the day my granny was buried, but at her bedside, when she was still alive. Then it meant something. It was telling her I loved her, knowing she heard me.'

He was almost breathless by now and he lowered his hands, and then put his head down on the sill as if in prayer.

'Something of the glen is dead now, Davie. I said goodbye to them both and . . . I'm here. One day I will go back, but the wounds have to heal. I have a lot to learn before then.'

'Don't fail her then, Dan,' he heard Davie say softly, but he did not raise his head. 'Don't lose yourself here, in this dead place. Too many have done that – got lost and never gone back. And Dan – don't lose your faith, for her sake.'

When Dan at last looked up, he had gone. Then he could let the tears come.

He forced himself the next day to go and find his way around the university. Fighting to keep afloat in the sea of misery which threatened at times to overwhelm him, he went up to the quadrangles and the high towers of dark stone; he gazed at the ornate windows, the tall pillars, and felt guilty as he recognised in himself a flash of pride that he was here, in this place of ancient learning. There was even a kind of beauty in the sunlight shining on the pearl drops of rain on the iron railings; he had never thought to see beauty in any city. Later, in the huge English class, he felt poor and shabby again; everyone else seemed so poised, so well dressed. But as time went on he was to meet many others from the glens and the islands, to feel at home in the endless discussions and arguments, to form his own opinions with confidence. But it took a long time.

All these years later Dan remembered little of it, certainly no kind of sequence; the days of his first term were a blur, made up of classes in which he struggled to understand, failed to write fast enough, struggled again at home to make some sense of his notes, tried to feed himself adequately, and had endless cups of tea with a handful of new friends who were as much at sea as himself. He told no one at all about his mother. When the misery became too bad, he drank whisky. It helped at night but made the mornings much worse. And then he was hungry because he dared not spend too much on food.

Once, desperate to see some green, he went to the park. Down from the dark castle of the university and into this strange world with a dirty black river flowing through; he leaned over the bridge, trying not think of another river. Old men looked curiously at him as he passed, he fancied with a touch of fear. He had seen the same look as girls turned away their eyes from him or crossed the street as he came near. He wanted to shout aloud that he would do them no harm, there was no need to be afraid of him. This park seemed to him an unreal place, a world that did not belong to the world of reality. Someone had told him he ought to go there because it was 'like the country'. But not to him. It only made him all the more restless and frustrated; to compare it to the real countryside he had known all his life was unthinkable. It might be fine for them – he thought of the lovers he saw on many of the benches around him. I know what it's like for me – *I am like a foal that is given an edge of grass to run in when it has remembered fields without end.*

The days went on into autumn. Dan recalled a day when he saw a chestnut tree at the edge of the park. The sight of the shiny mahogany chestnuts was almost like a physical pain. There were times when the struggle not to think, not to remember, seemed almost to drain away all the strength he had. And while he could manage to blot out the memories – of his mother, Catriona, Achnagreine and the glen – during waking times, in sleep he was defeated. Dan now realised that he still remembered some of his dreams more vividly than he remembered his life in the city.

In one of these, his father came and wakened him up, smiled, and told him they were going home. They went by train, but the houses went on for mile after mile, so that he began to be afraid that they would never escape. Then Johnny told him to go to sleep; and in the dream he put his arm around Dan, so that he felt secure and happy. When he opened his eyes they had arrived, but strangely they were coming running down to Achnagreine from the hill above, and his mother was waiting for them, waving from the back door.

Another dream had recurred and recurred. Again he sat in the train, a ticket held tightly in his hand on which was written 'Achnagreine'. Suddenly from the window he would see the farm, set in its own place beneath Beinn Dobhran; but all around were roads and tenements and factories. He would beat against the glass to get free, until the picture misted and he awoke. But the horror of it would hang like a dark cloud over him all day.

Although lostness and loneliness were the predominant memories of that part of his life, Dan found that individual acts of kindness still remained. Like the time he had met old Mrs Dean. Of all the people he had rubbed shoulders with as they came and went in his landlady's house, only she had taken any interest in him; the others, like his landlady, had smiled at him and asked him how he liked Glasgow and then listened to nothing of his reply. They talked without listening, looked without seeing. Mrs Dean was different. She asked him about his home, his studies; seeing perhaps something of the isolation he was feeling, she invited him to come for supper the next night. He went shyly; but in the warmth and kindness of the welcome she and her husband gave him, he relaxed. Apart from his cousin Alec, they were the only city people he had ever known.

A letter came from Catriona. He recognised her writing from the shopping lists he had seen her write. He could not bring himself to open it at once; it appeared to him more significant and in a way more dangerous than any he had received before, and he wanted to think. He had heard nothing from his father since he left; he had met nobody from the glen apart from Davie. Since then his world had changed; it seemed that the light had gone. What had his father thought of his failure to come home? What had Catriona thought? Was she perhaps writing to tell him she was leaving Achnagreine? Or had something else happened – his father? He took the letter with him to university and felt it in his breast pocket; he held it in his hands at the lecture hall as he sat alone; he looked at it, as if somehow he could divine its contents. In the evening, on impulse he went again to a pub, taking it with him. He sat at a table by himself, looking at no one, drinking quickly. When after a time he felt as if cocooned in his own world, warmed inside and fortified against possible shock, he at last opened the letter, tearing at it with clumsy fingers. His hands were trembling, his heart beating fast. But there was after all no condemnation; just the prayer of them all that he was well and that he would be looked after and upheld. No empty words to say that his mother had died peacefully, that the funeral had been good, that people had been kind . . . just suddenly . . .

'When the spring comes I'll go up to the wood above Balree and pick some primroses. I know they were your mother's favourite flower; and it's one of the places I could imagine her best, Dan, among the trees in their fresh green and the spring all around. I'll have them on the table in the kitchen, with fresh water each day to keep them as long as possible.'

He folded the letter and held it in his hands and breathed deeply in relief. It was all right! She did not think him callous, did not blame him for his failure to come home. She understood.

He recalled another dream. His mother came to his bedside and spoke to him gently, telling him they would go home. It seemed everything was ready in his room; all his belongings packed and standing in the middle of the floor. Then, as if for an eternity, they were walking through the streets, in all the traffic, the smoke and the noise; his feet were bare. All at once his mother was not with him any more, and he was calling, calling for her above the noise of the trams and the newspaper sellers and the men with their barrows of fruit. But they did not listen and it was no good – she was gone. As he continued to call her name, a bell kept tolling in the background.

He awoke, sweating with fear. It was Sunday morning and the bell of his dreams was a church bell. *The Sabbath!* he thought, as he crept out of bed, shivering; the sky was clear, a single pane of blue edged with gold, the gold of the late year's sun. In the back court, two black trees had frost on their branches; he could not deny something of beauty in the scene. He turned and slipped back into bed, and lay there listening to the bells. Transported back through the years, he was holding his mother's hand as they followed behind his father, going down to the old church in Drumbeg. He remembered that Davie had given him the name of the church he attended; it was in one of his pockets. But he was surely crazy to be thinking like this? He had given up going to church; it reminded him too much of all that he had found repressive in his father's treatment of him. Still, he found himself crawling out of bed. He caught sight of himself in the single cracked mirror and noted the unkempt hair and unshaven chin. *There is no time,* he told himself. The excuse relaxed him and he went back to bed once more. But he could not sleep. Damn it all! He got up again, shaved, and dressed in the best clothes he had. Outside, he began to run towards the sound of the bells. *Why on earth am I doing this?* he asked himself as he ran. *I had decided never to go inside a church again. But I have to admit, I miss the psalms. It will be good to hear the psalms again.*

The singing had already begun when he slipped into the back pew, where an old lady whose whisper smelled of peppermint leaned across to show him the psalm. The swelling wave of strong voices rose and fell about him, a stern tide. Somewhere within, he thought, there is an anchor, made of a strong metal – if only I understood, if only I could find it. What was it that held my mother so surely, that my grandmother trusted in, aye, that gives that strength to Catriona as well? And yet in some strange way, even although he did not begin to understand, it seemed as though some strong invisible hand held him at that moment, a hand he did not fear.

'*I to the hills will lift mine eyes.*' That psalm above all! He looked up to the high beams of the roof as though somewhere in the plaster there was Beinn Dobhran. And he who had not believed for a long time, not truly since he was a child, found himself singing in a strong, clear voice. '*The moon by night thee shall not smite, nor yet the sun by day.*' He had never been more conscious of his need; he felt as if he had at last found pure water amid the filth of the city; he drank in the words as he sang them, and felt cleansed and renewed. He watched in delight a little girl who sat with her mother near him; she swung her short legs backwards and forwards beneath the pew, and pointed things out to her mother in whispers – a twist of silver paper on the floor, a bird high on a branch outside. He saw those small things with her and did not think them foolish; they mattered to her, were part of her small world. They reminded him of the butterflies he had longed to reach at her age, the blooms he could not stretch high enough to pick. And he thought of experiments they did in his biology class; they would take a whole flower and dissect it, so that they could see the cells of the living organism. Yet there was no possibility of putting it together again, of restoring the loveliness that had been. And he wondered if that was what faith was like – seeing the whole, as it were, from afar, taking things on trust; for when one came too near with critical eyes, with eyes screwed up looking for proof, the picture was gone.

All these thoughts tumbled around in his mind as the light of the midday sun pierced through the windows and gilded the face of the minister as he leaned forward in the high pulpit. Dan realised with a start that he had listened to very little of the sermon. They were singing the final psalm; and suddenly he was again standing small between his father and mother in the church at home. Then he had longed to escape; the river and the woods were calling to him to come. Here, he had no desire to face all that lay outside. He decided to linger for a while in the warm church after the folk had gone. Then he caught sight of Davie far in front, just rising as the congregation began to go out. He rose and went out into the knife-sharp cold, realising all at once how hungry he was.

eleven

It was more of an accident than anything else that Dan saved the little boy's life. All he saw was a momentary glimpse of small legs pumping; then he heard a woman's voice raised further away. As he crossed to the other side of the street, there was an impact as a small brown head dunted his thigh. It had all happened in an instant. Then the boy was lying on the ground, crying bitterly, and a young woman was bending quickly to pick him up and soothe him, while the elderly man in the motor who had had to jam on his brakes was shaking his fist angrily at the little party.

'I'm so sorry,' Dan said shyly to the boy's mother. She was quite a young girl, he noticed, who was cleaning her son's face with her handkerchief. She looked up sharply, saying simply:

'Sorry? But . . . you saved his life! He would have gone under that motor. I can't thank you enough.'

She smiled at Dan, who accepted dumbly what she had said. She was not in the least shy or embarrassed, he thought, and spoke as if he had been an old friend. She was capable too; she had the little boy calmed and smiling again, and looking up at Dan with interest, his face red and his eyes bright, the fright forgotten already.

'Well, I'm glad to have done something right for once,' Dan said laughing.

'How can I ever repay you?' Her voice was serious but he heard the gratitude in her tone. 'Come with us, please, and have a cup of tea.'

It was a bitterly cold day. Dan's hands were red and sore with cold, the wind seeming to cut through him as he crossed between the tenements. He was feeling lonely as usual, not having spoken to anyone all day; yet he was shy of accepting the invitation. All the same he felt suddenly warmed and happy, and knew that he would go. He listened to the little boy's chatter as he now skipped at the end of his mother's hand. Dan stole a quick look at the girl; she was pretty, her face almost surrounded by dark-gold curls, eyes that were mischievous-looking, a very dark blue. Her son, he thought, was a small replica of her.

Over tea, they talked. He was glad of its warmth, holding his hands gratefully around the cup. She told him that she had a good job in an office, and worked there in the mornings while the boy went to his aunt's.

'And in the afternoons I am with Daniel,' she added.

'Dan?' he asked in surprise.

'Daniel,' the little boy answered firmly.

She caught Dan's glance and they both laughed. He noticed the dimples in her cheeks and he felt excited, happier than he had felt for a long time. He touched her arm as she looked out of the tearoom window and asked if she wanted more tea. She was doubtful about spending more time there but he persuaded her; it seemed important that they should go on talking. He did not ask about Daniel's father, but framed his questions carefully enough to know that he was not with them now. Her name was Susan Baird, she told him, and she and her son lived in a small flat left her by her parents, who had both died young. Daniel was four. She ruffled his hair lovingly as she spoke, and he got up on the seat and stretched up to be hugged. There was something sad in her, Dan thought, but she was beautiful! He thought that if he were an artist he would want to paint her here, sitting in the corner of the cheap restaurant, the people coming in with their coats buttoned against the early December cold. But he could only paint the picture in the recesses of his mind; and for a second it seemed to him that she had a look of his mother.

He walked home with them, even though he had been on his way to the library and it was in the other direction. Before they left the main street he dived into a shop and reappeared with a bar of chocolate for Daniel. She seemed more pleased than the boy, but it did not matter. He found himself telling Susan all about his course, how lazy he had been from the beginning, how strange it still was to him; she said he was like all other students, spoiled and a bit mad. But her eyes teased when she said it, and they both laughed again. It was so easy to laugh with her, he could hardly remember when he had last found so many things amusing. They reached the bottom of the stone steps leading up to her flat, and Daniel went running up ahead.

'Can I see you again?' Dan asked shyly, suddenly a boy again.

She had started up the stairs but now looked round, and was quiet for a moment.

'You know where we live. I can't stop you.' She went up a few more steps and then turned again and said in a warmer tone: 'Yes, come back; I'd like you to. Daniel and I see very few folk.'

Dan went back to his cheerless room with a deep glow of happiness in him; and he worked hard that night. Catriona was a broken image at the back of his mind but tonight he hardly cared; he told himself that loneliness was destroying him; he just had to have companionship. He had been alone too long already.

But he did not go back for a few days, until the Christmas vacation had begun. He was not going home, but had been to the station and witnessed fifty farewells as his fellow students had departed for their homes. He had gone to all of his term exams, but had not done well. He knew he had not deserved to; he had skimped on his work. Now he could not wait to see Susan and Daniel again. He went back, was welcomed by them both and felt a warmth he had almost forgotten; soon he was on his way to see them at every chance, and as he had poured out affection on his mother, so he began to do now on them both. When he could get hold of a piece of wood he delighted himself in carving, bringing rough-cut squirrels and bears out of it for the little boy. Susan, he soon found, had been used to men who treated her hard; she had known little tenderness at all since her parents had died. She gave herself to Dan because she trusted him, realising that to him this was no game; he was simple Dan, swinging at times between sorrow and a boy's laughter, sincere and vulnerable. They came together because each had known much of suffering; they saw understanding and compassion in each other's eyes.

For the first time in his life, Dan celebrated Christmas; only New Year had been recognised in the glen. They had a festive dinner of chicken and plum pudding, and in addition a tiny tree with tinsel, and crackers and balloons, both a novelty to Dan. Susan laughed and said he was more of a child than Daniel.

At New Year, a parcel came from Catriona. He did not want to open it; he felt sick with betrayal. She had packed little gifts for him – her own cake, a bag of hazel nuts she had picked in the autumn, a pair of warm gloves knitted by herself, even his favourite treacle toffee. From his father there were socks and handkerchiefs. Everything he touched burned him; he felt wretched and hollow and found himself wishing there had been silence instead; it was all he deserved. Or at least, some kind of reprimand in the note that came with the gifts. But there was nothing but kindness and acceptance. He quickly sent back presents for the two of them, with a card but no letter, but his feelings of guilt were in no way assuaged. He did not allow himself to think of the glen, of Achnagreine, when the turn of the year came, and he did not even go to Susan. Despising himself, he turned instead to the whisky bottle and a brief easing of his pain.

Soon, though, he was back at the little flat with small gifts for mother and son. His need of love, he realised, was greater than Susan's. She had steered her life cold and bitter since her small son's birth, content to pour her love into him; men had betrayed her and she had lost her faith. Dan needed her to be there, to hold him and comfort him. She was at least a substitute for all he had once known, and represented home now that home was gone.

The old man came out of the tight enclosure of the wood and was now standing in snow – a long ridge that had been blown by the spring gales and had not as yet receded to show the green alive underneath. He was impatient now to be away from the trees, to stand free on the open moor land. The lochans were above him, in the long saddle that lay beneath the jagged neck of Beinn Dobhran. They reminded him of blue brooches, pinned to the deep heather plaid that was spread all around. He would not reach them today and he shivered as the fear came to him that he might never see them again. Had he indeed come up here to say farewell?

There arose in him a dark panic like the wings of many birds, and he felt his heart flutter against his chest. Oh, for the chance to wind time back and stand here a boy again, his breath strong and his feet ready for many miles ahead! Such days were gone; the tree he now was stood grey and bent and almost broken. A tree must be cut down, though, for the seedlings to grow; but roots, surely the roots may remain for ever, to be discovered by succeeding generations of workers who tend the land. He did not want this place to forget him.

Many a time Dan had fancied that his spirit would linger here after his death. Was that mere wishful thinking? To see the lochs with the evening breeze just right for a cast, the snow as it came over the moors almost horizontal on the wind's knife, the merlins, the soaring of eagles in a clear sky. As a boy he had had the same fearful thoughts of death, the same terror lest all he loved in this glen were to be blacked out in a single moment; but then he had tried to imagine what it would be like to live to be eighty, and had decided that if that time ever came he would be content to say goodbye. Here he was now, having come so far; yet there was not a part of his spirit that did not cry out against the sadness of leaving this land behind. Despite his faith, despite his longing to see again those whom he had loved in life, this was still the truth.

He sat down painfully between two boulders of quartz and held his hands between his knees, for they were very cold. He listened to the curlews as they rose up from beneath him – what more lovely cry was there in all the world? This was the very edge of the cultivated land; he felt that beyond here nothing had been touched or changed since the beginning of time. It was intact, a kind of reconstruction of creation. Now they talked of coming here to make a dam, to flood the upper part of the corrie here to generate power – how long had it been since he had heard Kate mention it? He could not remember, and in any case he could not fight them; they would not listen. They wanted jobs and money and fast lives. Everything was changing. He did not even want to keep up. At least most of Achnagreine was still safe, though the men who had bought the land round the Lodge had put up a deer fence, a shining metal wall that seemed to leer at him when he caught sight of it from the window on the stairs. Was it set up to keep him out?

It was no good, he was tired of thinking of all the changes, all the threats of the modern age. His thoughts returned once more to that far-away time in Glasgow; as he sat in the lee of the boulders, the years he had lost came back to him in vivid detail. What he had thrown away, to gain nothing in return! Or perhaps he *had* found something – in that each day of his years of captivity had as it were prepared the soil of his heart for the harvest that would come later. Never again would he be in any doubt about the things that were important to him.

He had not remained at university beyond a year. By then he had made more than enough enemies among the staff; at first encouraging, tolerant of his excuses for work not done, they had in the end lost patience with him. At the start of the summer term, as his relationship with Susan had grown more intense, he had taken to staying later and later at her flat most nights; things had deteriorated from then on, the gaps between his attendances at the rooms in the quadrangles growing ever greater. Dan even now in his old age could recall clearly how he used to creep downstairs like a mouse in the small hours – Susan was scared lest any of her highly respectable neighbours should complain. He reflected wryly how things had changed; today he might have moved in with Susan and not an eyebrow would have been raised.

But as he thought over the reasons for his leaving, he knew it had not simply been due to the neglect of his studies but, more profoundly, to his conscious rejection of much of the teaching offered; more especially, of the way in which it was carried out. He had become aware that not enough freedom was given to students to argue their own case and his growing convictions were being stifled. Above all he wanted to be allowed to think for himself; yet it appeared useless to attempt to deviate from his tutors' line of thinking.

'I feel the claustrophobia of it all in the very walls,' he remembered saying dramatically to MacKenzie, his philosophy tutor, on the day when he had finally come to the conclusion that it was useless for him to continue.

'Maybe it's a fault in myself,' he had gone on, 'but I never imagined I'd be prevented from thinking for myself. It is as if there is always a choice of answers that have been worked out before, and all I am expected to do is to pick one out, like a parrot. Yet I'm sure we have to go on searching for answers! We can't just stop – we go on and on because there are always doubts and always discoveries.'

How surprised he had been at himself for daring to 'talk back' to a lecturer in this way, remembering how he had looked up at the dark high tower that seemed to stretch up to the sky, reminding him of the Tower of Babel.

'But you simply must go on,' MacKenzie had replied, exasperation showing in his face and voice. 'You have to get over this first stage and then go on into research – the whole world can open up for you then and people will listen to you because you have proved yourself. Undergraduates often feel as you do – the best ones too. Yes, I include you,' he added, almost smiling.

'All these years lost in the city,' Dan had murmured half to himself.

MacKenzie had sighed and let him go. Dan knew he thought him strange; he did not care.

After days of searching, he found a job. It was the last thing he wanted, in a stuffy office five floors up, endlessly filing letters and papers and checking mail; but his money was fast running out, and he was fully aware that he was lucky to have a job at all, in this city of mass unemployment, poverty and degradation. He turned his eyes the other way as he passed the lines of miserable-looking men at the 'buroo'. He told himself constantly that he ought to be thankful, yet he felt the work drowned his spirit. The office looked down on a school playground, and he saw that the children had nothing but concrete and high railings – no grass, no trees, nowhere to run and be free. Somehow he envied them, as he did the butterflies he set free from the window all that interminable summer. He felt crushed. Life had become a treadmill of days to be gone through; trams to his work and back again, miles and miles of dingy streets that seemed to have no end.

His room saw less and less of him as on most evenings he almost ran to Susan's flat. It seemed to him that she breathed on him and the pieces of his shattered self were put together again. He tried to appear strong and buoyant in her presence, fearing above all things that she would look down on him because he was several years younger, still perhaps in her eyes a boy; but in the end he would always break. She was the only solace he knew, in among this seeming maze of concrete and stone, dirt and despair. Daniel too provided balm to his spirit. He took him to the park and pushed him on his favourite swing; the little boy's delighted laughter gave him joy. There were cats to stroke on the way home, raindrops hanging from railings to touch, games of hide and seek to play. Above all he took delight in telling Daniel what life in the country was like. The child never tired of that.

'Tell me more 'bout the glen,' he would beg Dan.

Dan needed no urging. He spent hours describing the farm with its animals, fishing in the river, the woods. Once Susan said quite sharply that he must stop putting ideas in the boy's head. Later, they quarrelled about it; she told him her grandfather had been a sheep farmer in Argyll and had had to come to Glasgow, penniless, after he had lost everything. Daniel probably had farming in his blood, she said, but she did not want that for him. She did not want him to end up penniless. Dan argued back furiously, pleading with her to come to the country with him and let Daniel be happy. She ruffled his hair and shook her head.

'Your head is in the clouds, Dan. There are no roads to your places. You'll see one day when you've gone as far as I have.'

That was by no means their only quarrel. As time went on, Dan began to have deep doubts about their relationship. *Have I stopped loving her?* he asked himself. *Have I ever really loved her? Is it love or simply infatuation? Or is it only that I need a mother?*

Even in Susan's embrace, he would sometimes see Catriona's face. He had tried to bury that memory because of the sense of guilt and betrayal it brought. In his waking hours he usually managed to suppress it; in dreams he was beaten. Again and again he dreamed of his mother; sometimes he would be following her, and then she would turn round, and the face would be Catriona's. When his birthday came, she sent him a cake with twenty candles. He could hardly bear to look at it. He could not write in thanks because he had no idea what he could say.

Back with Susan again, he saw the hurt that lay in her as deep as knife-wounds. Men had abused her; Daniel's father had walked out on her when he found she was pregnant; she had had to fight hard to keep her son and bring him up by herself. Dan recognised the hardness she had been forced to grow as a shell around her; she looked out from the battlements of her world and let only Daniel inhabit that imprisoned place. He saw that he did not know her, that she would never allow him to know her. He could come no closer. They were on guard with each other.

One Saturday he went down to the Clyde. Almost a year had gone by since he had left his studies but he felt much more than a year older. He did not give up his job because times were hard, and he helped Susan a little and barely managed to make ends meet. Now he sometimes found himself envying the students he saw, wishing he could begin again. Today he walked through mean streets he had never seen before. Wherever he looked there was poverty. He kicked a bottle by mistake and it spun round on the pavement; some people arguing at the mouth of a close turned and shouted obscenities at him. A woman was crying inside one of the tenements he passed; he seemed to hear her for a very long time, and her crying seemed to embody all the misery he saw around him. He had a sense of fear; there was a thin mist hanging over the city like a spider's web; it got into one's hair and the back of one's throat. He stood there at last looking at the yards where the great ships were built. He knew that many of them were silent now, with huge numbers of men out of work. He watched the water, dead and still like a huge pane of glass, the cranes leaning over the river like herons watching for fish. But any fish were long gone from here. The water was dead, poisoned; nothing could survive there.

He began to think about Susan. He could see her in his mind as she would be now, getting the supper ready, talking to Daniel, answering his questions. And he realised with a sense of shock that he had run away; he had come here because he no longer wanted to be with her. He listened to the long, low hooting of a tug as it turned and went west into the fading light. Then he began to retrace his steps. But after a short time he knew he had gone wrong; he had no recollection of having taken this way before. In the middle of a wide street with derelict tenements on either side, he saw a gang of youths standing; one of them held a bottle in his hand. He turned quickly and went down a narrow lane; a dog leapt out at him, snarling; a man dragged it away with a curse. An old crippled woman appeared on the other side; Dan started to cross to ask directions, but stopped, fearing she might be afraid of him. He passed a derelict station and, looking through the broken walls that echoed at his approach, remembered the day – so long ago it seemed – when he had first arrived in the city and had looked north to the end of the tunnel. He suddenly saw himself walking on the railway track, mile after mile, the only sure way of reaching home. He felt as if he had awakened from a long sleep, only the nightmare from which he had thought to escape from was reality. He found himself trembling all over. He was in a place from which there was no escape! He began to walk blindly; let him at all costs get away from here. He tripped on something and bent to pick it up. To his surprise he found it was part of a branch; probably some child had snapped it from a tree. Even in the sickly light he could still see the green edge beneath the bark. Suddenly the picture of his father cutting down the old rowan came back to him in vivid detail, the branches being sawn, the bunches of red berries. The thought of the glen became very real to him; and with it came a faint sense of hope. Maybe there would yet be a way back.

A few days later he had the dream. It was after he had had another row with Susan; he had reprimanded Daniel for swearing and she had shouted at him that this was her child and she would tell him how to behave. He accused her of shutting him out; she retorted that he was like every other man she had known – they all wanted women as possessions to hold and control. He said quietly that he only wanted to love her but she was too proud and bitter to accept love. She turned and left the room, banging the door. Not knowing what else to do, he had gone back to his lonely room.

Misery came over him like a cloud. He felt the old fear once more, the fear that he was trapped in this place for ever. If he should die without every seeing the glen again! That meant more to him than seeing any human being, he thought. But there was Catriona – what if he should never see her again? What if she had gone, left Achnagreine, without saying where she was going? He must go home; he must! He knelt by the window with his head in his hands; then darkness came and he lit his lamp, and got out the bottle of whisky and a glass. He drank until his eyes swam, and then he went to bed and slept.

In the dream a man came into his room and led him away, down the stone stairs in his bare feet, through places where he had never been before, until he was utterly exhausted and lost. But they came to the River Clyde and followed it, back out of Glasgow and then away up into a valley and the open country beyond. Dan felt his feet torn on sharp stones but the man who led him never once slackened his pace, until they came to a place where the river was a white waterfall, deep and narrow. He lifted his eyes and saw, far away on the north side, Achnagreine and the hills. He wanted to rush down the last few steps to cross the river, but realised it would be useless for he would be swept away by the strong current. As he turned helplessly to his guide, he saw two tall trees on the near side; both were covered with red berries. The man had an axe in his hand; he approached the trees.

'Don't cut them! Don't cut them!' Dan heard himself crying, though his feet were rooted to the spot and he could go no nearer. He was filled with fear because he knew the trees were rowans.

'Do you not want to cross?' answered the man in a deep voice. 'Then we must cut the trees to build a bridge.' The axe flashed in the air; the strokes fell, regular as the seconds of a clock.

With a start he awoke; the clock in the hall was chiming: one, two, three, four. Sweating with fear, he lay for a few moments and then got up, wincing at the thud of pain in his head.

He knew from that moment, without the slightest doubt, that today he was going home. The certainty was so total, so absolutely clear, that he asked himself almost in wonder why he had not gone before. *It was because of my father*, he answered himself. *I was afraid of him.* But why? *Because I thought he would be angry at my failure in my studies; and more — I was afraid he would gain some kind of power over me when I came crawling back in failure and shame.* And if he *is* angry, if he refuses to accept me? *Then I'll find work somewhere else in the glen, and at least I'll be there — and maybe, just maybe, there will be Catriona as well, and she'll forgive me.* His heart leapt as he began to take it all in; the river was crossed, he was going home!

But first there were things to be done. He determined to leave this place in debt to no one. With trembling hands he carefully counted out his money. Yes, he had enough. Enough for his fare and a bit more, once he had left two weeks' money for his landlady — the rent he owed, plus an extra week's rent in lieu of notice. That was the agreement. He wrote her a note. Then he wrote a letter of resignation from his job. *Nothing could give me greater pleasure*, he thought; *what a waste of all those days!* Here, too, he would have to forfeit a week's wages through leaving without notice. What did it matter? On impulse he added a fervent plea that his job might be given to a friend and neighbour, desperate for a job; he enclosed their address.

Just one thing more. He must write to Susan. That was more difficult; but he knew she would not grieve at his going. More likely she would be relieved. Daniel would cry for him, and as he wrote, tears were in his own eyes for the little boy who had given him so much. In a parcel he packed for him the only things he had to leave him – the cows and sheep and terracotta barns of the toy farm, the present his brother Andrew had given him as he left for France. He hoped fervently that one day Daniel would indeed find his way to the country and become a farmer like his grandfather, although sadly it seemed unlikely.

Then he turned to his own packing. He found room for everything in his two battered cases, left his room spotless, and shut the door behind him. It was still early; he saw no one as he let himself out. He went to the Post Office, which had just opened, and posted the parcel. He then walked to the station, and waited for the first train to Abercree.

twelve

Going north on that morning train Dan seemed to be the only one awake. It was not quite light yet and Glasgow lay shrouded in a yellowish fog. Just a frail light here and there in the tenement windows as the train went slowly past. Dan said a thankful goodbye to the city – to every empty window and street and back-court; he could hardly contain his joy at the thought that he would not be coming back. As though a war had ended and the wounded were on their way home – that was how it appeared to him as he sat looking across at the sleeping faces of his fellow travellers opposite.

Then it was over, the houses left behind. To the north lay the fields and low hills. A sharp ray of sun bled from the east, red and strong, like the single string of a great harp; he closed his eyes and felt the warm light on his face. Now he slept, relaxed and dreamless, as a child might have done. So he returned to Abercree, impatience surging in him as he got out on to the familiar platform. So nearly home, and still not there! Once more he carefully counted out his remaining coins. He had just enough to buy a small twist of tobacco for his father and some chocolates for Catriona – please, please let her be there! Then he met a farmer from up the glen who offered him a lift home in his old Morris; gratefully Dan climbed in with his heavy cases. He answered the man's questions as briefly as was possible; he did not want to talk; there was so much to drink in, and he was half-mad with joy. It was as autumn had always been! The edges of blue sky blown by the wind, the leaves coming like red-gold wings from the trees, the river sparkling with sharp light. He felt as if each place was nodding to him, welcoming him on his return. His eyes flitted from one side to the other, delirious with happiness. And after they had passed Drumbeg, he plucked up the courage to say to his benefactor that if he didn't mind, he would get out a mile or so before Achnagreine, as he wanted to walk the last bit.

'You'll think me daft, I know,' he added apologetically.

The man did not seem to mind, and added kindly that he would leave Dan's cases at the foot of the brae for him. He drove away, Dan shouting his thanks. And then he was walking, alone, looking up at the Beinn above him edged with just a breath of mist, the slopes russet with bracken. On impulse he leapt over a fence into a field where a chestnut tree grew; how good it was to see one again! Would there be conkers? He could hardly contain his laughter as he shuffled among the fallen leaves, stuffing the polished nuts into his pockets. *I'll never grow up*, he told himself; *they'll always give me a thrill.*

Quieter now, he reached the final stretch. He saw the churchyard and stopped, at first irresolute. Then he went in, his feet noiseless on the wet ground. His heart beating fast, he went round and found his mother's grave, saw the stone with her name on it:

RENA MACLEAN, BELOVED WIFE OF JOHN DRUMMOND

Incised at the foot, the familiar words – *Gus am bris an latha* – 'until the day breaks'. He bent down close to the stone, and whispered:

'I've come back, Mother, and I'll never leave again.'

His eyes burned, but this time there was no deep grief, rather a feeling of peace.

He stood and listened. A robin was singing – the sound of autumn. There were seasonal smells too; how well he remembered them! All the years seemed to flood into one, all the impressions and memories that made the rich tapestry of his past life in this place. He heard the river going over its rugged bed. The waterfalls are past, he thought; he had climbed back from the sea to the fresh water, the only stream that could satisfy his thirst. And his mother was in all that grew so richly in this place; she was in all the beauty he loved, which she had taught him to love. He would grieve no more for her now.

Soon he had reached the last part and his heart thundered. Who did he want to meet first at Achnagreine? For the hundredth time he wondered if Catriona would be there, and if she was, would she welcome him? But he had to meet his father first. He had no idea what he would do, what he would say. There had been a betrayal, he knew; it had happened, but it had purified his blood. Now his need of journeying was over, and his father must know that. The long, cold war was over as well; the old juvenile pride had stopped eating at him. A mother and a wife was gone; father and son must surely bear the grief together.

He saw the heavy cases where they had been left at the foot of the brae leading up to the farm but he left them lying. He wanted to run the last bit, to drive straight into that knot of fear inside, to summon up all his strength. He was in bad condition he realised as he came to the crest of the hill; in the old days he could have run twenty times farther and not noticed. None of the dogs was about, so his father did not turn round from the place where he was crouching at the far side, the burn side, of the yard, mixing some paint. Dan went slowly and stood there, seeing the bent back and grey head. Then the sun burst from behind him and cast his shadow dark on the wall. His father turned, then said just one word.

'Dan!'

Then he felt his eyes swim helplessly and he put his arms round his father and was half-laughing, half-crying; as though a sac of poison had burst inside him, he felt bonds released and the clenched fist of his bitterness relaxed at long last. It no longer mattered what his father thought now. He had thrown himself across the wide gulf that had been between them with a whole heart; he had beaten swords into ploughshares. He was back where his heart belonged. And when he looked again at his father, he was smiling with a joy he never remembered seeing on his face before. He was an altogether older man now, Dan realised, older and more weary; the lines in his face, like the rings of a tree, spoke of suffering. But he was still who he had always been, his father, proud and determined. Dan, still holding on to him, found himself muttering:

'The prodigal, Father . . . forgive me.'

Johnny was unable to answer. Dan saw that he was fighting to control himself; he just shook his head and, half-choking, said:

'Thank God . . . Well, no doubt we'll hear all your news in due course,' he finally managed in a more normal voice.

Dan, turning away towards the house, could not help smiling to himself; it might have been that he had been away for a weekend! *It won't have seemed the eternity to him that it has to me*, he thought.

But his father amazed him by adding in a quiet voice: 'Two years and thirty-one days – it's been a long time, son.'

Dan stopped in his tracks, and for a long moment they just looked at each other.

Then his father, smiling again, said, 'Away in then and see Catriona. It's herself will be glad to see you.'

He spoke to him as a boy still, but for once Dan didn't mind; he went swiftly to the kitchen door and opened it wide, stepped over the dogs and stood there, looking at Catriona as she sat at the kitchen table. She looked up, frowning a little as if the light was bad and she was not sure who it was. Scared, uncertain of what to say, Dan found himself adopting a loud, falsely hearty tone.

'Oh, come on, Catriona, surely you can do better than that!' he said, forcing a cheery grin.

He went towards her and then stopped, his smile falling away under the simplicity of her gaze. He felt naked, her eyes boring into his very soul. She said nothing. Then she got up and, calm as anything, walked slowly over to the fire. He felt his heart quaking.

'Catriona! Don't keep me in suspense!' he begged. 'At least speak to me, after all this time.'

Now her eyes flashed at him. 'Aye, Dan, after all this time, indeed! Is it any wonder when you go off and forget folk's very existence? Do you really expect me to throw my arms round your neck and say it's all fine, after what you did to us?'

Her voice rose in anger and she leaned forward, firing her words at him like gunfire.

'Do you have any idea how I waited, Dan? How I wondered every day for two whole years if there would be some word from you, just one word even? And there was nothing – month after month of nothing. And I had really believed you cared.'

Her voice broke and she hid her face from him, crying like a child.

She slumped into a chair and covered her face with her hands. And then he was down on his knees beside her, wretched with the deep guilt he felt; he put his arms round her, kissed her hair and her face and hands, stroked his fingers through the beautiful soft hair.

'I know, I know,' he whispered brokenly. 'I hate myself, Catriona – you'll never know how much I hate and despise myself. I never knew . . . never meant . . . I could never be sure if you could love me. But that's why I did come back in the end. I went wrong . . . I'm not worthy of you, wouldn't deserve you in a hundred years. But I didn't forget you ever; I swear I didn't!'

She turned to him then and said simply:

'Hold me, Dan, and don't go away – don't *ever* go away again!'

It was all he could have asked for, far more than he deserved; and he closed his eyes, smelled the warm fragrance of her hair, touched the soft skin of her cheek. They comforted each other and he felt he was offering her his whole heart, swearing never to betray her again. He would have liked to confess all that he had done, to gain peace of mind; but he knew that would have been to buy his peace at the expense of hers. Then a glow of absolute happiness spread through him; it came to him that only that morning he had been in Glasgow and he had had nothing. Now his hands were filled with a harvest richer than any lord's. Knowing he did not deserve any of it, he felt gratitude well up in him. In the end it was Catriona who pressed him away from her, smiling.

'This won't do, Dan,' she said. 'I've got to make your father's tea – and yours.'

He nodded. 'There's something I have to do anyway,' he answered. 'Don't worry – I'll be back in time. I could eat an elephant.'

He kissed her and went out of the kitchen into the yard, beginning to run. He passed his father but did not stop until he came to the burn. There was still plenty of time, he thought. Up and up the steep sides of the burn he clambered until his breath was coming fast. But it felt good! The blood sang in his ears and there was a cool breeze in his face. Once he tripped on bracken and fell headlong, but he only rolled over, panting and laughing, and then drove himself on mercilessly straight up the steep slope until it levelled out and there were birches and he could see the white tail of the falls. How long was it since he had been here last? This most special place – the place his mother had always loved best for a picnic, the last place they had been together. For a moment he paused, panting; there were ghosts in this place and he could not but be aware of them. He went down slowly then to the wide black ring of the pool. Donnie's Pool. There was still a smudged edge of sun coming from the west, shining in a golden bell on the water's surface. It was mad, he thought, what he wanted to do, but he was going to do it. He threw off his clothes and stood for a moment, shivering, looking at himself in the mirror of the water. He was thinner, he knew, much thinner than he had been when he left; and he felt his face had changed in some way. Then with a great yell he plunged into the deep black pool and he was gasping and blowing, wildly waving his arms and ducking his head under the freezing water. His whole body ached with cold, but he scrubbed his face and hands and dived back under the water and opened his eyes to the pain of the cold. Only then did he stumble back out, gushing streams of water.

Later, dried and warmed after a run around the bank, he sat for a few moments of reflection. He was clean again, the city dirt washed away. Healed, too – at least in part. It would take a long time before he forgave himself, he knew. He thought of the sincerity with which his father had breathed the words 'Thank God'. What about him? Could he believe in this God who was so real to his father – and Catriona? He had found himself thinking of himself as the prodigal returning; I could almost recite the whole story after all these years, he thought; my mother taught it to me so thoroughly. Could I really be forgiven, just like that? Maybe, he thought, maybe.

thirteen

Dan came back down from the moor, Beinn Dobhran like a dark hand guiding his left shoulder. He had wanted to climb higher, but he simply had not the strength in him. The streams chuckled as he crossed them; for a moment his shadow would fall on them, then he was forgotten. Compared with them, he thought, he was a mere child! What was he in time but the quickest blink of the eyes, the fall of a stone? Yet in his mind his life had been a long time, many hard miles of marching.

He would skirt the wood now, come down over the moorland and the lion grass – as his mother had always called it – to the cave, the place of shelter. It was hidden among the rocks, so that many would fail to find it; but not he – he could find it blindfolded. But as he walked on, the keen wind came sharp across his face and a thin mist blew over, covering like a fleece the hollow between Beinn Dobhran and the Tor up to his right. The whole wood was swallowed up and the glen vanished. The breeze was edged with a smirr of rain like tiny pearls that clung to his face and neck. The ground was thick with boggy hollows, and there were but few stones to use as footholds. Often Dan had to stop, precariously balanced, spying out as a hawk might the next place of landing. He kept going right, towards the piled rocks at the base of the Tor where the cave was, but it seemed much further than before. His chest had begun to hurt, and he was forced to stop, wheezing, bent on one knee on a gnarled lump of quartz, angry with himself for his weakness.

Now he felt an edge of fear cutting at his mind – what if he had gone wrong, disorientated by the mist? Surely not! It wounded him even to think that might happen to him, of all people. But he should have been over this ground long ago! Then, without warning, like an owl rising, the mist cleared and he was free, and the glen lay below him bathed in fresh light the colour of golden corn. Even then, he did not at first find his way to the cave. He could not be sure whether it was above Spies' Rock or not. In the end he blundered across it, finding the low entrance sodden with water; two sheep which had been lying near rose on thin legs and ran away. He saw that they were slow and heavy with their lambs.

Shivering, he decided to stay in the cave for a brief rest and get warm again. Thankfully, he crouched there in the semi-darkness, looking around and noting the corner in which his father had found flints and potsherds which had later been found to be of great antiquity. Memories connected with this cave flooded back as he sat there; but he had not yet reached that part of his life, he was not ready to retrace those particular steps. Instead, he began to recall the chapter which had followed his return from Glasgow.

He and Catriona had been married the following summer. At least, he thought wryly, it had put an end to the glen gossip that had driven the two of them mad and which had begun even before he had left for the city. After Glasgow, though, whenever he was tempted to lose patience with the old women who seemed to be forever whispering when they came out of church, he would force himself to remember the frightening anonymity of the city, and tell himself to be thankful for the identity he had here. Folk were simply interested; but it was no good, it still annoyed him! An old lady for whom he was working once asked him how his father was coping with the drought. He had answered that it was a bother getting water from the spring, but that he and Catriona helped. At this the old lady's eyes lit up – like a crocodile's, Dan thought to himself maliciously – and she put down her cup with a clatter.

'Now, Dan,' she said eagerly, 'maybe you can put us right about this. They're saying that you and Catriona . . . that you're going together. Is that true?'

There was a moment of silence as she leaned forward expectantly. He couldn't resist it — he was half raging, half laughing inside as he calmly replied. 'Well, some say we are, and some say we're not; you just don't know who to believe sometimes, do you?' He went home whistling, feeling that a score had been settled.

In any case he married Catriona. It wasn't many weeks after he had asked her that they had the wedding down at Drumbeg. The day they got engaged, he remembered, his father insisted Catriona must go home for a month's holiday, until the wedding; it would not be right for them to be in the same house. Nothing ever changed in the glen, he had thought at the time. Some sixty years before, his grandmother Eliza had been found lodgings with the gamekeeper's family until her marriage with Alan could take place; here was the same thing happening again! They missed Catriona, and fully realised how much unseen work she did, during those weeks of absence.

His father cleared one of the barns, and the wedding ceilidh went on until it was morning and the hills were shaded with August light. Dan remembered with absolute clarity the picture of old Jean Cameron being whirled round so fast in 'Strip the Willow' that she was nearly sent through the wall without an arm. But what he remembered best was Catriona, his beautiful bride. There had been no honeymoon for them; Dan was starting work on the following Monday repairing a drystone dyke for an old man down the glen. Nor did they feel the slightest need to go away. And why should they? They had each other, and everything else they could possibly want or need, at the farm. There was the beauty of the hills all around, and more than enough work to be done. They had a room and a bed to share and took delight in each other. All these years later, Dan's pulse still quickened as he recalled the richness of those far-away days. It was as if they came tumbling one after another like clear water from a well. Never had he known such absolute joy, such deep contentment which filled his whole being.

He worked with his father for a while after his return, but the place simply was not big enough for them both. While before this had been because of the antagonism between them, now it was a simple fact. Dan would have to find other work. Finally he announced that he wanted training in fencing and dyking; since he had at last bought an old and battered Ford van, he could take work wherever he found it in the glen.

So it came about that he was usually away for about three days each week; the extra money was welcomed by all three of them. Dan remembered how he had watched his father carefully at that time, to see whether, and in what ways, he had changed. Certainly much of the old hardness had gone since his wife's death, but he could still be stubborn and at times stern. He still appeared to be chained hopelessly to those few rough acres of land, and it was still almost reluctantly that he showed his care for Dan and Catriona; but both knew that strong feelings ran deep underneath. Sometimes Dan felt his father had become weaker, that he had not the same power either in hands or voice. He moved more heavily and became frustrated when his back pained him, but now there was no anger, no sign of rage or blame directed at either of them, just a silent sadness of which they could not but be aware. Now and then Dan would mention his mother, because he was conscious often of her nearness and wanted her to be kept alive among them. However, Johnny would not join in the talk; it was obvious that it caused him discomfort. His silent sadness was only too apparent to both Dan and Catriona, but nobody could doubt for a moment that he was still master of Achnagreine. Not once did it seem to have occurred to him to allow Dan to take over the farm now that he was married and settled; he clung, in a way almost pitifully, to all he owned there. Dan could never really imagine a time when the land would truly be his own.

All the same, Dan looked back on those early years of his marriage as a time when his world had never been so good. All of his happiness was built round his deep love for Catriona, and with his father too; there was a kind of peace as they sat by the fire together in the evenings after a hard day's work, listening to the wireless. This was a novelty they now shared with most of the glen folk − one which (apart from the nuisance of having to charge the batteries) on the whole had brought them much pleasure. It had brought in something of the outside world, and marked the beginning of many a change in the lives of the people.

One thing which it did bring in a very real way, and one which Dan could still remember all these years later with a sinking of the heart, was the fear of war. How well he still recalled the three of them sitting one night listening to the ravings of Hitler and the frightening roars of the Nuremberg crowds. They said little to each other; but Dan knew that all had experienced a kind of shattering of their peace.

The coming of war. When it came to thinking of this phase of his past life, Dan knew he was reluctant to remove the covers; the pain was buried – let it remain so. But no, he had set himself the specific task of retracing all of his steps; he must face this too. So he began to re-live those days.

What he recalled most vividly – and with the most pain – were the sleepless nights. Nights when he had lain awake, Catriona asleep by his side, thrashing out, over and over again, his confused thoughts about this war. He knew he hated war with every fibre of his being. He hated violence – to man and beast, and it was something he knew he shared with his brother Andrew, the brother he had scarcely known at all, the brother who, hating to kill even a rabbit, had yet gone off to the hell of the trenches of the earlier war, and never returned. And this war? How could he go, leaving Catriona and his father, perhaps never to return either? But how could he not go? The very thought of Fascism and all it stood for was anathema to him. He would have to go. So he reasoned, as the long hours of the nights ticked by on the old clock by his bedside. At other times he decided that he was really a conscientious objector. But how could he be? He was too much of a coward, he decided, to follow that path – nobody in the glen would understand; he simply didn't have the courage. In any case, others were having to go, so why not himself? Iain and Dougie, his two best friends from schooldays, were already in the Air Force. Soon his own call-up papers would arrive. If it must be, he knew he would go.

But the weeks went by and no papers came. He was puzzled, especially when two school friends of his own age were called up. Then one day, a strange thing happened. Dan had been out on a dyking job and had come home early, soaked to the skin. He had gone up to his room to change his wet clothes when he heard the doorbell – an unusual event, since neighbours were in the habit of simply walking into the kitchen. Then he heard voices raised in anger. His curiosity aroused, he pulled on a pair of dry trousers and in his bare feet went down the stairs and stood at the bottom, looking into the kitchen. Catriona was standing motionless by the stove, while his father faced a burly man in uniform who was clearly extremely irate.

'For God's sake, Drummond!' he was shouting, and Dan heard at once the alien English timbre in his voice. 'Surely you didn't think you'd get away with this?'

It was the sight of his father particularly that Dan would never forget. Drawn up to his full height, and seeming to tower over the other man, his face was deathly pale, his eyes blazing with a mixture of anger and distress.

'You tried to take away my land.'

It was as though he did not address this Englishman at all, but someone else, through and beyond him. His voice was deadly quiet and steady.

'You took away my first son,' he continued, 'and he never came back. What did he have to die for? And you took away half of myself. Now you're asking for my other son and . . . ' His face becoming a spasm of fierce pride and anger, his huge hands knotted white and ugly at his sides, 'and, if you do that, you'll kill a man, and his wife, and his father.'

Dan began now to step forward; it suddenly dawned on him that it was *his* life they were speaking of. *This is ludicrous*, he thought.

'I ask you again. Did you receive call-up papers?' the man in his correct English voice snapped.

'I told you!' Johnny seemed to fill the whole doorway with his rage. 'I kept them. I burned them!'

Then, turning to Dan, he shouted in a voice of sheer desperation.

'Dan! Listen! Listen, for all our sakes! Get out of here! Do what George did! Up to Beinn Dobhran and the hills, where they'll never find you!'

Dan met his father's pleading eyes, saw the white, rigid face of the military man, and felt Catriona at his elbow; close and pale the oval of her face.

For a moment, as in a dream, he saw himself in the snow. At the cave on the face of the hill, cutting from the bare rock the very bones of life. Coming down to the house in secrecy to snatch food, and Catriona's embrace; an exile from his own home. It was not right; it was not right. He was shaking his head at his father, then broke away suddenly from Catriona's arms.

'It's no good, Father. You've fought them as far as you could, but no farther. I don't want to go either – Catriona, yourself, the glen.'

He looked back at Catriona for a moment and saw the bare white struggling of her eyes. There should have been a child . . . to say goodbye was the hardest thing in the world. This was his land. Even the soldier seemed to look insignificant now among them, was shut away by the door, pale and ineffectual. It was they who were strong, he thought. Touched hands, proud voices, strong words. Tied with cords that were stronger than death.

And they would bring him back.

fourteen

As he came down the steep scree towards the Lodge, the old man was caught up in a rush of stones and mud, and had to turn painfully on his side so that his hands could find something to grip. His palms were covered with mud, and a deep cut oozed blood through the dirt. There was no pain; he simply lay there for a moment, looking around him, far away in thought. Then, thinking with a wry smile of what Kate would say if he were to return in this mess, he continued slowly down to the burn and, bending, allowed the ice-cold snow water wash away the earth and blood.

Earth and blood, he thought to himself. Earth and blood – that was what the war had been about for him. In Africa, with long desert marches, endless miles and miles of sand, and that huge pitiless sun like a great oven whose coals flamed down as if in a kind of perpetual punishment, until the sudden fall of darkness. Sweat in one's sleep, the smell of bodies – dead and alive – and the engines of the flies, coming on everything like black scabs. Drink, when they could get hold of any, had been like a gentle death; it killed the pain for a little, dulled the sound of bombing, blurred the sight of towns on the horizon burning without reason. He drank to forget, so that the happenings of the coming day might be kept hidden in the darkness of the desert; he drank also to remember, to be able to see the dawn come through the glen, and a wood carpeted with bluebells, and the face of a girl at a cottage window.

Never for a single moment did he feel that he fought an enemy; for him, the enemy was one man, the personification of all that was evil, one who destroyed his own people as surely as he did Dan's. And he did not come to this desert to fight, but stayed with his maps and his plans in a secret room somewhere in Germany. The men he saw dead, they were not enemies. Most of them were no more than boys, with whom he could easily have talked, and shared stories, and exchanged photographs of girls and wives and children. Of course he told these thoughts to no one. How could he tell even his friends that he cried inside when he saw the white faces, the bodies that slept where the shells had blown their lives away. He cried because they would never see their homes again, just as surely as he cried for his own dead, the soldiers whose voices he had known, whose stories he had heard over and over again. The ones who had proudly shared with him the little tattered pictures of the girls they had left behind.

There was the Irishman, Connolly, who swore blind to all and sundry that he had been teetotal all his life but who would get roaring drunk whenever he got the chance and talked nothing but broad Irish Gaelic. Occasionally, he and Dan would attempt to converse in their native tongues, with such an outstanding lack of success that the others would be convulsed with laughter. Davidson, a Glaswegian, kept Dominic, a pet rat, in his pocket and brought it out at meal-times, saying that it had to be kept fit and well to survive this war as it had been a present from his wife. There were some pertinent comments about this from the company. In the end Davidson went out on a night patrol and did not return; he was never found, nor was Dominic.

He had letters sporadically from Catriona; never from his father. Sometimes he would write a few words at the top of a page, but never more – not that Dan had expected anything else. It worried him greatly to think that some of Catriona's letters were lost. When one arrived, he would open it with trembling hands. At the beginning he would laugh out loud at remarks in the letter, sharing them like a child with those around him, certain of their appreciation. After a time he stopped; as the months passed he was only too aware of the dangerous silence some of the lads were experiencing from the wives and girlfriends they had left behind. So occasionally he kept a letter all day, reading it avidly at night in the light of the lanterns. He wrote back to Catriona spasmodically. He would have no heart for it, the days rolling by in one long battle for water, for rest, for whisky, for peace; then one day he would wake up very early with a physical ache of longing for her, and he would write madly, telling her how much he loved her, assuring her that the war would soon be over and he would be home. Of the war in the desert he said nothing; he asked about the glen, about the farm animals, about the driving test she was planning to take. At times he really believed the war would end soon, but then it seemed to be stalemate and he would feel he was stuck there for ever and that he could not possibly go on.

It was during one such low time that he happened to be out alone and found the German. Of all his war experiences, this was easily the most vivid in his mind. He had gone out with Edwards, a Londoner with whom he had struck up a friendship. They had then gone in different directions. Dan had brought out his water bottle and put it to his lips – and then stopped dead. A man was lying on the ground near his feet, looking up at him; blood oozed from his chest, and his hands too were red with blood. Dan had heard shooting earlier, and now saw one of their own soldiers lying with his head half-buried in the sand. The German was breathing badly; his hands twitched and he tried to rise, but he was clearly badly wounded and could not move. All the time Dan was aware of his eyes fixed on the water bottle.

At first Dan stared stupidly at him; he could not, he thought, have been more than eighteen or nineteen. He saw the flies as they sizzled and boiled on his wounds, and the half-open mouth called out with thirst, but the noise that came out of it was a kind of rattle, the sounds of an old man. Dan kept staring at him in fascinated horror; he felt a fear beyond anything he had ever known. He had seen death, had even grown used to death, but this was something far worse, a land between two worlds which was like hell itself. But he did not leave; he was locked together with the dying boy at his feet. And in the end he bent down, and with quaking hands tipped water feverishly between the gaping teeth, and saw the drops that were not swallowed run like liquid gold over unshaven cheeks and chin. There was a bad smell from the German's mouth and Dan longed to go; but he could not, he could not; he stayed, watching the eyes, listening to the throat as it began to utter the pathetic cries of a young child. *Oh God, let him die, let him die!* A hand suddenly reached out like a claw for his own, but he did not want to hold this hand; he did not want this man's blood on him. But he held it all the same; he did not know why, but it did not matter. Then, of all the strange things, he found himself singing softly the song his grandmother had sung to him long ago when he used to go and stay overnight up at Balree and would call out in the dark in fear. The Gaelic words came easily to his mind and he sang with assurance. He closed his eyes and he was singing for himself as well, for all that was beautiful and good, and somehow for a few moments the darkness was shut out, and a kind of peace came. There were still things to love and praise.

He opened his eyes and saw that the mouth had closed, the head had fallen away to one side and the terrible sound from the chest was ended. Edwards and another soldier were approaching, shouting to him and asking what the hell he was doing there; and Edwards had a bottle from which he thankfully accepted a slug.

He and Edwards were joking together, two days later, when they hit a mine. Etched in slow lightning, he saw Edwards' body coming down, torn apart. Dan had been on the outer side of the explosion and only one side of him caught the blast; an electric length of pain was injected into his left leg, and he was dimly aware of someone screaming – and then that it was himself – before the light was turned off and a bliss of blackness overtook him.

Dan woke in one of the field stations, seeing a woman's face swim before his eyes, and he was not sure if it was a dream. He drifted off into darkness again, and then the woman seemed to be speaking to him from a long way off. He felt desperately sick and wanted to be left in peace, aware of himself again being washed away by the tide of darkness. A long time later, or so it seemed, he opened his eyes and found himself in a large ward. The window was open and he could hear birds. Everything was very still and he lay there drinking in the cool air, and watching the sky which was the finest blue. There was a slight movement beside him and as he turned his head slowly he saw a young man sitting by the bedside, smiling, a white coat over thin arms.

'Hullo! You've had a long sleep, haven't you?'

He patted Dan's good leg and grinned.

'Well, the good news is that you'll walk again. We've had quite a time of it trying to save your leg – pretty smashed up it was when you came in here. But you'll get there OK now.'

'And what about the bad news?' asked Dan weakly, trying to raise himself and failing.

'A good deal of pain, I'm afraid. In your arm too. But you'll be going home soon – that should help! Not many days now.'

Going home! He couldn't take it in. He opened his mouth to ask 'why? when?' but the doctor had moved on and he lay back, wild with thoughts. It was so sudden, he hardly felt ready. He slept again, and in his dreams he was back at Achnagreine. The dream seemed to go on and on, sometimes Catriona was there, sometimes his mother, and sometimes he was back at Balree with his grandmother. Then he would be setting off for home all alone, trudging across the sand, with the sun like a cross on his shoulder. He would awake frightened and distressed and then, overjoyed, he would sleep and dream again.

At last they got him up and soon he was stamping around the wards, seeing those who had lost legs and arms, feeling their eyes boring through him as if in envy of the wholeness he still had. He felt almost guilty then, longing at times to be back among the lads he had known so well, the ones he had not said goodbye to. Amid all the sweat and blasphemy and cigarette smoke, they had shared a kind of terrible companionship, even love; they had cared about each other without ever putting it into words. He missed them. Ordinary men, come here to survive and go back together. One night he dreamed that he had found his way back to the camp to say goodbye, and all the lost dead were there. He saw each face, heard their voices and laughter, and in the dream he felt it was all right now; he could go home.

But it never happened – there were no goodbyes. One day he arrived in England after a long journey, and a huddle of people on the quay greeted the soldiers on a grey day of rain. There was black smoke over the flat land, and he felt nothing, nothing, just an emptiness inside him; or maybe, rather, a hard lump of poison, a knot of misery that never went away. Eventually he was on his way home at last, and he limped through the half-empty streets early one morning and waited nervously for a train that would take him north to Edinburgh. Everything seemed so quiet, so normal; suddenly he felt a kind of rage at these people who were going about their business, with nothing to worry them but their ration cards and coupons. How safe they were; they did not have to live with the smell of blood! He wanted to scream at the crowds on the station platform; he felt sick inside.

Once inside the train, he leaned his head against the side of the carriage, shutting his eyes and forcing himself to be calm and imagine the glen, and the river, and Achnagreine. And Catriona. *I must pull myself together,* he said to himself a dozen times, and as he came nearer to home, he somehow believed that a change would come over him, and he would find the skin of his old carefree self lying waiting for him to put on again.

At long last he came to Abercree, yet still he felt nothing but emptiness inside. He could not face going any farther – he went past the Black Watch Inn and then turned back, with the thought that a drink or two might put some strength into him. He stood alone with his whisky in the corner of the bar. Someone was playing an accordion; all eyes were on the player and nobody took any notice of Dan, nor did he want to be noticed. He felt like a complete stranger, a dead man come back. Why would his hands not stop shaking? He slammed down his glass and ordered another drink. As he sat in a corner, other voices, other faces came into his mind. He saw the playing cards in Edwards' hands, heard Davy doing his well-worn impressions, saw Davidson feeding the rat Dominic pieces of cheese. All kinds of memories came rushing back, tiny things that he had grown used to from day to day as the bonds between them all had strengthened. He had a sickening feeling of having betrayed them all; should he not still be out there?

Suddenly he had a vivid picture of Catriona's face and knew a far sharper sense of betrayal. What was he doing here when she was up the glen waiting for him? He almost flung down his glass and made for the door; soon he was walking with his head down in the rain. There was no one about and he knew the chances of a lift were slight. Well, he would walk. He crossed the old bridge that led towards the long miles of the glen road. In a short time he heard a car, but did not slacken his pace. The car stopped. It took him a moment to find the handle and fumble his way inside, and then to focus on the face of the driver.

It was Catriona.

fifteen

In the end it was all right. There *was* a way back. And eventually, after a long hard haul, she brought him there, carrying in her arms the pieces of him that were broken.

For many months he had an anger inside him that could be triggered like a gun. In the middle of the night he would waken up shouting, his body drowned in a sweat that seemed to come from the desert's own heat. There had been those early words of his father.

'Now you're back where you belong.'

And he had raged at the lie.

What do you know about it? he said to himself, not once but many times. *You never saw them, did you? You never had to wonder if they'd be there the next day! And they're still out there getting blown to bits. No one even remembers them, least of all the ones that sent them. They've got to stick it out while we live here nice and easy and talk about prices and markets, and worry about the weather. It's rotten to the core, that's what it is. Rotten!*

Rages like this wore him out. There was sand in all his clothes, but in the end nothing remained. Just a long expanse of desert in his mind, a place of silence for the ones he had lost.

Only Catriona saw it. She did not ask to be admitted there; but she called, as it were, from the outside, and with gentleness and patience brought him out from the grey walls in which he was imprisoned. Afterwards he wondered what would have happened to him if she had been other than she was; he did not like to speculate. Not once did she reproach him, nor turn aside from the anger he hurled at her; never at any time did she even mention the nights when he had not gone to bed but had sat at the fire, thunder in his eyes and a mouth foul with whisky. One night he had gone to bed early for a change, and then came down around midnight; she was sitting quietly mending his socks. He marvelled at her patience and forbearance. It was never in her nature to make a fuss about anything, he remembered after all the years. Nor did she ever try to tell him what to do. But there had been a single, remarkable exception.

One Saturday afternoon when he was sunk in a deeper depression than usual, she suddenly said, 'Dan, go and see the minister.'

He looked up, startled.

'And who is he?' he asked – he had not gone near the church since his return, and expected to hear it was a stranger.

'It's still John Maxwell,' she answered. 'He had to go away as a chaplain, but he was invalided out like yourself and he's back.'

Dan did not reply, but later in the evening he said, casually, that he would take a walk down to Drumbeg.

'Take the van,' was all she said.

But he replied that he felt like walking.

He never told anyone of his talk with John Maxwell that night. It had been in a way like rolling the years back, to that other time fifteen years ago when he was grieving for his grandmother and terrified of losing his mother. This man had offered him the road to faith then, and he had turned away. This time it was different, though; he was desperate, cold and dead inside. The sac of poison inside had to burst, or he was finished. He could not, could not go on living like this. He knew that and so did Catriona, for all she said nothing and bore everything.

No great light shone, he remembered. There seemed only to be enough light to see by, but as he walked home under a sky ablaze with stars, he felt for the first time a sense of peace, a kind of security he had despaired of ever knowing. He went in and found Catriona sewing; he said nothing but gave her a hug. And next morning he came down dressed not in his dungarees but in his good clothes, and she looked up with her eyes alight and they hugged each other hard again. One day, he thought, I'll really come back to Achnagreine having laid the soldier I was in a grave far away.

And so it was that, always with Catriona's quiet help, his healing slowly began. She made him rest his leg as much as was possible and had him beside her in the warmth of the kitchen. She chatted to him about all kinds of things to take his mind off the war – about her driving, the time she had knocked over a pheasant and managed to slip it into the back of the van to make a rare addition to the meat ration; about the vegetable plot she had worked so hard on, and the family of rabbits she had watched very early one morning taking her carrots but didn't have the heart to chase away. She described how several children had started coming on Saturday mornings while he was away. She was teaching them to bake, and how to look after hens and help with the lambing. And about the time a pine marten had come on to the window ledge one morning and had tried to lick out an old honey pot she had left there.

He improved steadily under her constant care. He had relapses, times when he could have screamed, even at her, and wanted nothing but peace and quiet. He would bang the door as he went out; and, as he had done before, make for the wood or the ancient barrow. At times he found himself talking at her, trying to make sense of it all.

'I miss them all so much,' he would say. 'If only it hadn't ended as it did. Just to have had the chance to say goodbye . . . I just wasn't ready. I wish I could have gone back, just once.'

She came and leaned close to him and the scent of her hair was fresh and sweet, her hands gentle as she held his face and looked deep.

'You can't go back, Dan. It's finished. They're gone.'

And after a time the ghosts themselves began to die; like weak and flickering lights they burned out one by one – Edwards, Davy, Connolly, Davidson. He would never forget them but they ceased to haunt him; only from time to time in an unguarded moment a spasm of pain cut him like a knife.

The lambing in the spring played a big part in his healing. Dan could do a little by then, but he still could not walk far on the steep ground without the pain in his leg beginning to rage. Catriona helped with the work, and more than once he found she had got up while he slept to help Johnny when things were especially busy. He felt her come back into the bed very early one morning, cold and shivering. He turned to face her and ran his hands gently through the soft hair.

'Oh, there was one wee angel,' she whispered, her eyes dancing as she looked at him. 'Just legs made of jelly, footballers' socks on him – and something else, only you'll be mad if I say it.'

He shook his head lazily, smiling back at her. He was safely sleepy. 'He had such a look of yourself, Dan!'

He roared with mock anger and rolled over to grab her as they laughed together. Holding her, he then said shyly:

'Are you wanting lambs yourself, Catriona?'

She looked at him steadily, not blinking. Just nodded, and went on holding him. But no child came to them that summer or autumn.

In the winter something happened that was to change a great deal in their lives. Johnny Drummond was fixing some of the slates on one of the outhouses' roofs, and fell. The grass there grew sparsely in ground that was rock-hard with the frost, and it was his back that took the worst of the fall, for he had come down twisted; and he was a heavy man. So it was that Dan had to drag him upstairs; and on each step he remembered the times when his father used to find him as a child, fallen and with blood on his knees and roaring, and how the big arms had carried him. Now the positions were reversed; it was his back, his legs, that now had to bear the strain. They had, indeed, as it later proved, silently changed places, although neither knew it at the time. Dan was given the chains of office; it was his load now to bear. But all he thought about at the time was the agony his father must have endured on that long afternoon, an agony far deeper than any pain in his back – his fallen pride, his broken power.

Johnny lay in bed twisted and turned away, refusing both food and comfort; his eyes were black like a beast's, or so it seemed to Dan at the time. He never called them, never made any requests. And Dan pitied him and longed to say something to show his concern and, yes, his love; but no words came. Only his inner voice cried to the man who was his father and hoped he heard and understood. But aloud he said nothing; he felt helpless and frustrated and dumb.

All that winter it seemed to rage and batter at the windows as if reflecting the anger locked up in Johnny Drummond's head. Dan now had the farm to manage, so there was no longer any question of his accepting any outside work. So much to do, he thought at times almost despairingly; there was a hole in the barn roof and more than one of the dykes needed repairing; a blizzard came and three sheep were suffocated in the snow. He floundered around the fields wondering how he could ever cope with it all, how indeed his father had ever done it. At times he panicked and felt that he needed far more time – there was so much to learn; he and his father had worked together so little over the years. What he needed was for Johnny to become strong again. One evening, as Catriona was placing buckets inside the back door for the leaks and the rain was lashing against the windows, the doctor came. Sitting with them at the fire afterwards, he quenched that hope.

'No, Dan,' he said, 'that back of his is finished. He's had it fine and strong all these years – few around these parts could compare with him for sheer strength – but you can't go on putting that kind of strain on a back for ever. I'm afraid it just had to give in the end. He should have been slowing down over the years, you know, not lifting the kind of mountains he was.'

There was silence for a moment while Dan and Catriona digested this, and then the doctor added:

'I mean, he'll *walk* again all right, but he'll never do another lambing.'

'You haven't told him that, I hope?' Dan queried anxiously.

The man lifted his hands helplessly.

'He asked me to tell him the honest truth, Dan, and I owed him that – as a doctor and a friend. After all, he had to know sooner or later.'

'This was surely sooner,' Dan muttered half to himself, wishing fervently that there had been another way. So much had already been taken from him! Just to have had some hope would have make all the difference. He knew his father so well; certainly he had asked for the truth, but was it not, deep down, more likely to be told what he most wanted to hear?

Dan said no more to the doctor, who left soon after to face the storm. For a while they sat, in silence but for the clicking of Catriona's knitting needles.

'I'll get him dressed and help him down to the fire – make him feel a bit more normal,' Dan said.

After a struggle, his father consented, and they sat listening to the storm for a while.

'Come with us to church tomorrow, Father,' Dan then dared to suggest.

Johnny turned slowly towards him and the darkness in his eyes caused him to shiver.

'We'll make you comfortable in the back of the van; you'll be all right,' he continued.

'Ach, leave me alone, I'm finished,' his father said hopelessly.

Dan did not argue. What was there to say? He understood what his father meant. The last lightning had struck, and for him it seemed there was nothing to get up for any more.

'Father, let us help you back to bed,' Dan said at last when it was late and they were both tired.

Johnny did not reply; he just sat, his big arms hung over the chair. Catriona said goodnight and went upstairs. Dan lingered. He bent down beside the chair, his head lowered. Now, or perhaps never; what was it he wanted to say? Say it, say it! All the things. All the times they had passed by on the other side of one another, dumb beasts that had lost their speech. Far apart, locked in different worlds, yet forever joined.

Then: 'I see it, Father. Don't think I don't understand. To be broken like that – in a single moment. To feel you can't go back, that there's nothing left. I can hardly bear it for you, and that's the truth. But maybe there's still a chance.'

His father turned his head sharply. Dan waited, half-expecting the mouth to fire at him as once it had done, to tear him in pieces. But there was the strangest hint of a smile and the eyes were wet.

'No, Dan, it's no use – it's the end for me. Maybe it's better this way than slowly going back, losing hold – I don't know. Anyway it's yours now; that was the way your brother wanted it; Achnagreine's your own. And there's no better place on earth, son, no place that could haunt a man more than this land.' He smiled and ruffled Dan's hair gently. 'Just promise me one thing – you'll never let this land go to an Englishman!'

Dan shook his head, laughing, but at the same time his throat was choked. He put his arms round his father and hugged him hard. When his voice returned, he managed to say:

'Aye, Father, I promise!'

He helped the old man up to his room and then went to his own, but did not light the lamp so as not to waken Catriona. Instead he went to the window and opened the curtains a little; he looked out at the thick waves of snow that came round in drifts and circles; already it had made a thick white covering. He was cold, but he did not want to sleep. Like a child he stood there, watching the endless world of fragments carried on the northern wind. It was beautiful; this land was always so beautiful.

He woke up early that Sunday morning. The frost had come and the skies were brittle blue. He turned over lazily and realised Catriona was not there. He would go back to sleep, he thought; it was warm and quiet.

'Dan!'

She was at the door in her nightdress, the pale oval of her face white against the dark hair.

'He's not here – not in the house! Oh Dan, where would he have gone?'

He got up quietly, although her words had shaken him. He held out his arms for her; she was shivering, and he could see her breath in the cold air. He nodded, searching her face.

'He knew, Catriona. You saw as well as I did that he worshipped only one thing in the end – take his land from him and you'd kill him – didn't we always know that? It was the same when mother was alive. Take his land from him,' he repeated, 'and you take his heart out. That's what happened, love; and no wonder!'

As he dressed quickly, he said to her, 'Don't worry about breakfast for me. Go yourself to church. I'll more than likely be away for hours, but don't worry about me.'

She protested that at least he must have his breakfast, but he said he wasn't hungry. Down in the kitchen she put rolls and cheese in a bag and pressed them into his pocket.

'You'll at least take these. And you just look after yourself, Dan,' and she flicked his cheek with a finger, 'I don't want to lose you as well!'

They kissed and he went out, wrapped up against the cold.

He took one of the dogs, Donnie, with him and stood there in the yard, in that gold and blue breathless light which chipped the hills perfect and clear. How many hours had he been gone? Had he indeed ever gone to bed at all? He must have managed the stairs somehow, and perhaps gone out in the blizzard. Surely then they would have heard the old door on its grumbling hinges? He found tracks in the snow, but they were smothered, indistinct; there had been a good deal of fresh snow on top of them. But he could follow them all the same as they led down to the burn and across, and wound drunkenly up and on towards the edge of the wood. Once there, he lost the prints among the thick trunks of the alders and pines where only odd freckles of snow lay.

He went on, to the very edge of the wood. Far beyond, the empty moor suddenly came to life when six greylag geese heard him and flew upwards with the sound of bagpipes in their shivering wings. But here there was nothing. Across the expanse of snow that was a foot deep not one living creature had passed. It was an unbroken land, untouched, and for a moment Dan only gazed over it, marvelling, forgetful of why he had come. In the distance was the first of the lochs, shining blue and deep, a skin of ice reaching out across the few yards of its surface nearest to the shore. It was like a stained glass window set in the holy sanctuary of this wild horse-shoe between hills. It was moving beyond all words.

He stepped back and wondered *Where now?* The tracks he had followed, they must certainly have been his father's; but beyond the edge of the trees, where could they go? Suddenly he remembered the ancient mound; he had not looked there. So he went down over the hard ground and the deep layers of frozen leaves, and once more surveyed the glen below, and Achnagreine. But here, where the first men had made their abode, there was nothing but the whispering of the tall pines and the quick flight of a tiny wren. He was wrong again. Where would his father have gone? He must think, he must think. How far could he have got in the snow? But then he recalled the hours after frost came, and how there would have been light from the snow and clear skies; the old man would have found his way all right. It came to him then as distinctly as any picture and he nodded, breathed the word, and was off at once up through the wood and on by the other side, the western edge, towards the scrawny neck of the Tor.

Sure enough he found tracks, weaving across the white, frozen land. On and up he went, searching, searching. Then all at once he was at the cave, that haven of men before history; and the search was abruptly over. There lay Johnny, his face to the sky; and as Dan bent to feel uselessly for the pulse he knew already he would not find, he saw that the eyes were closed and the mouth still, not set in anguish. It was as though he might have been sleeping.

Dan sat down beside his father. He did not feel that he should weep. Indeed, a taut string inside him seemed to break; almost as if something rose up and was gone, and there was left an emptiness; but he did not mourn. He sat unmoving while his mind ranged far, back over the years it went, seeking for answers to many questions. Had Johnny ever really known happiness? Perhaps, perhaps. In the days when he himself was an infant, when his mother was still young, and sorrow had not yet touched them? But then the wounds – they had come, one upon another, until it must surely have seemed that God was punishing him. And always there had been the land. The legacy of Alan, Johnny's father – a few poor acres of sheep farm on the rough slopes of Beinn Dobhran. Acres strewn with streams and boulders, scant enough pasture for the beasts, a place exposed to the fury of the winter winds. Could this man really have given his heart to such a land? Or had it simply taken possession of him, stolen him away from those who loved him, and in the end led to his death in this lonely place?

The fear then came to Dan that he too was in the same danger; might he not be swept away by the same obsession? After all, the same blood flowed in his veins; could it be that he, now that he was master of Achnagreine, would turn fallow and in the end be overcome? *Let it not be so!* He breathed the words like a prayer. He whispered them again – 'let it not be so!' He had seen what his father had done to them all, year after year, regretting only when it was too late. Many a time Dan had sworn that he would never forgive, never forget the years of betrayal. Yet forgive he did – the old man whose grey head he had held last night and kissed, who had at last in a moment become real, become his father. What if he had not managed to say the words of sympathy, of reconciliation? How different it would have been for him at this moment if he had not!

They buried Johnny three days later beside his wife Rena and his parents, John Maxwell conducting the service with sincerity and simplicity. To Dan's surprise, for Johnny had had few close friends, most of the glen came to the funeral. Perhaps they had found him hard to understand; but they had respected his integrity, and he was one of them.

In the hush after the coffin had been lowered into the earth, the single fluting note of a curlew was heard, high and sad. Dan lowered his head, feeling an overwhelming sense of peace. There was nothing to add.

Tomorrow he would begin again. Perhaps there would soon be children to run about the yard and help with the feeding of the orphan lambs. How blessed they would be – Catriona would give them the world!

After all the people of the glen had departed, he and she sat in deep peace together, looking out at the darkness rolling down, avalanche after avalanche, from Beinn Dobhran. Dan had no idea how long they sat there. And as they went at last to bed, he looked up at the stars burning high above, and the ring of dark hills all around, and he knew he had come home.

sixteen

It began to snow. Small crumbs of wet ice at first that touched the hands and broke into water. But then larger and whiter flakes came circling down, and Dan felt the cold and the dark weigh down upon him. He knew that he should go back to the shelter of the house; the warm orange glow from the kitchen window drew him; but he did not want to go back. This might be his last day and he did not want it lost. If he went down to the barns, Kate would be sure to come out, tell him he would catch his death of cold, scold him as if he were a child, tell him it was time he took his pills. No, he was not going to go inside.

Now the snowflakes were thatching the wild white hair, so fast they fell. He began to make his way down to what had been the ruins of the old Lodge – now splendidly rebuilt for the new owner. His sight was not good and he slipped on the wet ground beneath the trees; he stopped for a moment to recover his breath and then found the old path. His thoughts were far away; as he came around the side of the house, it was the Lodge as it had been long ago that he was seeing; his heart could still miss a beat as he recalled that day of horror in his boyhood when the flames had taken it. And his grandmother, she had seen it all; why had nobody listened to her?

He was startled out of his reverie by the sight of the figures on the lawn, a large, gleaming vehicle parked nearby. Who were these people? He did not want to disturb them; in some confusion he turned away. But one of the figures detached itself from the little knot of people, and a clipped English voice said briskly:

'I'm terribly sorry, but this is private property.'

Dan thought that he did not sound the least bit sorry!

'I really must ask you to go.'

The old man looked closely at the speaker. He saw a tall man with a moustache, fine clothes and a cravat beneath his jacket.

'I had no idea there was anyone at the Lodge,' Dan said in bewilderment, speaking so quietly that the other man had to bend towards him to hear the words.

'Ah well, yes, my name's Turner. We bought this place recently, intend to run it for shooting parties – Germans, Americans, you know the sort of thing. But now I really must ask you to leave; it's private property and I'm sure you'll understand that we can't have everyone who's passing simply walking over the place.'

Dan looked at him, confused, trying to focus on what he was saying, trying to take in the words. He could not think of anything to say. Anyway it was too late; who would listen to him, what did he have to say that anyone wanted to hear? His time was past; all decisions were out of his hands, everything slipping away. Like the trout in the burn, he thought; where once he had guddled them in the deep pools, now they would slip through his fingers. He could not hold on to anything any more. He turned slowly away, not knowing where he should go. The man Turner had returned to the other figures on the lawn, and they all moved towards the Lodge. The snow was beginning again.

He went down in the end towards the road, past where he remembered the flower beds used to be; he would go along the road a little way and then up through the trees, skirting the Lodge. And then on up to Achnagreine – as his grandmother had done, when she was banished from the Lodge all those years ago. His journey in memory – the thoughts of the past that had come crowding in on him all through today – where had he left off? His mind wandered so easily! He must think; he must return to complete the memories of the years. Now he remembered! The death of his father.

The years since then, and they were many, had been good. Hard, but good. He and Catriona had never had a child. How much that had broken her, and for so long, nobody would ever know. How often he used to pray that a child might come! And for all her secret tears, the prayer had never been answered. There had been no small hand to lead to the places they loved.

For all that, Catriona had not turned away; several small figures could often be seen making their way up the brae to Achnagreine over the years. One or two had lost their fathers in the war; one belonged to a single mother who worked hard to provide for her child; others came simply because they loved Catriona. She was an angel to them all, he thought; she would turn the kitchen into a playroom for them, and when he came home he would find her baking with them, or modelling with plasticine, the floor covered with a jungle of animals. It used to break his heart to see her say goodbye to the little party as they set off down the road again, waving at every turn. She did not once complain; but he could feel his chest contract with pain for her.

He had taken up the fiddle again. He recalled how he had thrown it down in frustration at around the age of ten, and it had been banished to the attic along with paintings and old chairs and a rocking-horse their father had once made for Andrew. Dan had got it down and dusted off the layers of time, and polished up the wood that was like the colour of a chestnut newly broken out of its shell. He smiled as he remembered how Catriona had winced at his first notes; she had laughed and said the dogs would start howling if he went on playing like that. So he removed himself and the fiddle to a spare room and practised for an hour each evening. Then, when she had at last admitted he was becoming quite good, he dared to ask the boys up. New Year had been the first time, he recalled; after that it became a monthly event, when they produced a lively medley of marches, strathspeys and reels, in an evening of sheer enjoyment. Word got around, and from time to time they were invited to play at a ceilidh down in Drumbeg. Not, of course, for money; nobody had bothered about that in those days. And then he had persuaded Catriona to begin singing again. For a while she did nothing about it, but then one day she came in with a whole pile of music and dumped it on the floor beside him, having been to Abercree to spend the day with her folks.

'Well, it's your own fault,' she said laughing. 'Don't say you weren't warned.'

He had put on weight and blamed it on her baking. They were at ease with one another, always with so much to share, happy in each other's company. There were times he used to see her like his mother – the gentle joy in small things, and yet the stubbornness that could at times lock him out and render him helplessly weak. Never did he understand her fully, nor what it was exactly that he longed for and found in her. It was the same, in a way, with the land; all the parts shifted and changed in the light – you could never say what the whole meant, could not capture the words that would paint it and set it fast, as it were, framed. But you found yourself going back and back again; the thirst inside you would be quenched for a moment but returned, stronger, different; and the water was never the same twice, nor the colour of the light.

Sometimes he had to admit to a measure of selfish relief that they had no children. How could he ever have shared her? And yet . . . and yet the heaviness of it weighed him down too. Not only because of the wound in her which he knew would never heal, but because there would be no boy to follow him at Achnagreine, to take the reins of this land, and learn to ride and steer it. It was at times like a knife in him to think they would be the last in this place.

The people of the glen were dying too. He saw it year in, year out; faces he had known from early childhood, now gone; folk who had had their corners of hillside and were written into the names of each homestead – it was as though a river had swept them away. But it was not simply the loss of the old which caused him pain; it was the loss, in a different way, of the younger ones who were taking their place. When had the changes begun? When was it that they had started to lose their heritage, to prefer the songs of America to those of their own race? When had they turned from their own language? Not a single child now could understand Gaelic; the songs lived only with the old, who could no longer sing them. When had it all begun, Dan asked himself again; why was it that nobody, including himself, had seemed to notice or take any action? He could not think, could not understand. Now it was too late; he was too old and too tired. One thing he did know; some changes had come about through the intrusion of alien ways of life – by television, and by people of other lands. But there was more; there was a change within the people themselves.

One year they had found gold, on the other side of the glen, in one of the larger burns. A nugget of gnarled yellow metal that had quickly brought people eager to try their hand at finding riches for themselves. They came with caravans and loud music, and they threw their rubbish by the roadside. One night they returned drunk from down the glen, and young Iain from Camus Lurgan was killed when their van careered into a rock-face. Dan remembered how the whole glen had mourned. Four weeks later, though, the gold hunters had moved on – it was said that not enough gold had been found to make even a wedding ring.

After that, a kind of normality had returned for a while. However, there were always new dangers, always more erosion of the old way of life. Oh, he knew fine that these were the conclusions of an old man, one who clung to the familiar patterns of life; but were these not the best? When, for example, had the young ones ceased to find fascination in the land, in all the beauties of the glen which had delighted himself and his friends? Did any of the boys even know these days how to guddle trout? He could not think of a single one.

His memory was not what it used to be; he could no longer remember dates and times other than things that had happened long ago. There had been the new hotel built at the mouth of the glen, and a new music had come, beside the voice of the river. Then there had been the dam up at Loch Lurgan, to bring electricity. It had been good to have the light – how his mother would have appreciated the freedom from the daily tyranny of cleaning the row of paraffin lamps! But in the end the dam had stood there, cold and sharp and alien, a concrete wall incongruous among the hills. Had that perhaps been one of the things that had turned the thoughts of so many to making money, to acquiring fancy houses and fast cars? There was a day, he thought, when it would never have crossed one's mind to notice what kind of a house anyone had. We were all equally poor, but our lives were rich; rich and satisfying in spite of all the hardships.

There was another thing. When was it that people had started locking their doors? Had this – at one time unheard of in the glen – perhaps started when people had begun to turn away from the church? Nowadays it was half empty! In the old days, everything had stood open: barns, houses and coalsheds. Loads of potatoes or peats, yes, and parcels from the grocer – or indeed the jeweller – could have lain for a week at the side of the road; nobody would have touched them. The honesty of the glen folk had been proverbial. How well he remembered the time his father, tired after a long day's work, had insisted on walking all the way down to Drumbeg one night to return an extra shilling he had been given in change by the postmaster! There was nothing unusual in that incident, he mused. But now the character of the people was different.

He decided he must stop these ramblings, and go on with his journey through memory. What was to be gained by an old man's opinions, now that nobody listened to him any more? He thought back to the time when he had begun to be aware of growing old . . . tired and old. He fell asleep in front of the fire after supper, when the wireless was on; he would even doze again after Catriona had wakened him with a cup of tea. Catriona. She too had grown older, her hair turned grey and her face filled with the lines of the years; but still his Catriona. Her laugh was still the same, her eyes the deep pools which he could never quite fathom.

He had begun to need more help with the sheep − more than the normal assistance from neighbours at the dipping and shearing. He had had to cut the size of his flock; and it hurt him like a wound. Time was biting; the winds were stronger, Beinn Dobhran steeper. And then all of a sudden Catriona fell ill. It was such a shock to him that he felt as though the house had been struck by lightning. Oh, she had been ill before, of course, but she had always struggled on, and in a day or two she would be as right as rain. This time it was different. He came home to a cold and silent house, with only the old clock breaking the silence in the kitchen. It was in the middle of the busy lambing season too; at times she went from his mind as the hours went by in hard work, and tiredness pounded in his head. Then he returned to the house to find nothing but the dogs whining at the fireside. He would go up and sit with her, even when she was sleeping; and he would offer to go for the doctor, but she would say it was only a pain in her chest and she would be fine after some rest. In the early mornings he often lay awake by her side as she turned restlessly, uncomfortably, asleep but not rested. And he would say to himself, 'Next week she'll be better; she'll be out with me to see the new lambs, to feed the two small orphans in the barn.'

Then one night he came in and she heard him and turned her face to the light. It was no longer pained, he noticed, and her eyes were shining.

'Are you better, Catriona?' he asked with rising hope, hushed, and kneeling by her bedside. But she had just shaken her head, smiling.

'Dan, tell me a story,' she had said unexpectedly, her voice sleepy, half-muffled by the pillow. He looked away out of the window at the moon over Beinn Dobhran, searching his mind for a story that would give her pleasure. They had done this together many a time, mostly in the early summer mornings when the sun woke them and they could not get back to sleep. So many had been told; he must find a new one. Then it came to him – a story from his grandmother, from almost as far back as he could remember, in the days when the road up to Balree had seemed to go on for ever.

'All right,' he said gently, stroking her hair which was splayed all over the pillow. 'Close your eyes and think of the first lochan beyond the wood, away up on the shoulder of Beinn Dobhran.

'There was once a house there, long, long ago; even the stones of it are gone now. But a young lad lived there, with his folks who struggled to scrape a living from that poor soil. One winter it was so cold that the loch froze solid. The skies cleared and the light was clear as glass. Anyway, the wee boy had always longed to skate. But they would never have had enough money to buy him skates; he knew that fine, and it made him very sad. Soon the ice would melt again and his chance would be lost, he thought. What could he do? One night he thought of a lassie he had always had a liking for; she lived in a fine house down in Drumbeg, and her parents were rich. Surely she would have skates! Next morning, off he went down to her house and shyly knocked at the door; he asked her, and sure enough, she had skates. So back she went with him to the corrie, and he watched impatiently by the lochside while she showed him how to skate. But as she went close to the far edge of the lochan – crack! The ice broke, and she fell into the freezing water and was lost from view. The poor boy was grief-stricken; his mother and father were both away at the croft and nobody was near at all. There was nobody to help and he could not even swim. And do you know what he did? He just crouched there by the side of the loch and cried, hour after hour, until the evening came and it grew cold. And he never stopped crying and his eyes were so full of tears that he couldn't see what was happening to the ice. But in the end all the tears melted it and turned the water warm! Suddenly the wee girl rose to the surface and cried out for him to help her to the shore. And happy he was indeed. Even to this day they say that lochan will never freeze for the sake of the wee boy.'

He looked at her closely as he finished; her breathing was soft and easy, and he thought she had fallen asleep. But she opened her eyes and said softly:

'Thanks, Danny.' In a moment she added, smiling up at him, 'and now, a psalm; sing me a psalm.'

'Which one?' he asked.

'What but the 23rd?' she answered. 'The shepherd's psalm.'

He got up from the bedside so as to be able to sing more easily, and began:

'*The Lord's my shepherd . . .* ' but she stopped him at once.

'No, no, in Gaelic – it's so much better in Gaelic.'

So he sang the whole psalm, the words coming back to him without effort. When he had finished, he knelt again by the bed and saw that this time she really was asleep.

He did not dare move lest he should waken her, so he slept on the chair beside the bed, in his working clothes. He was cold during the night, for there was a hard frost, so he woke early, long before dawn, but there was light in the room, a light that came through the uncurtained windows and drew from the shadows the chest of drawers, the clock, chairs, and a painting of his mother's over the bed. He looked first into the yard; something fell from the little shelf beside the bed as he brushed it with his elbow. There was a clicking sound from below and he saw three roe deer, sculpted in velvet, leaping away into the field.

Then, very quietly, he bent down towards Catriona and saw her still lying as she had lain the night before, the marble light etching her whole face. But now she was no longer breathing.

A black cloud crossed his mind as he re-lived the utter desolation of that time; he could feel the knot of bitterness which had come to lodge inside him, the emptiness and loneliness nothing could assuage. A whole year, he remembered, had been filled with that bitterness – a year in which he had silently fought his own battle, allowing no one else to come near or comfort – not even John Maxwell, although he had stood by quietly all the time, waiting to help. He had lived in a kind of daze, eating and sleeping when he needed to, working on – Achnagreine, his sanctuary and his all. His heart was like a stone; every place she had loved he could not, would not, see and he shut them out of his mind. On the Sabbath he could not go to Drumbeg, for her face would be there before him. The words of her death were cut from cold stone in the churchyard; how could he ever bear to see them? He might as well have been dead, he told himself often; what was left for him here any more?

The months went on, arid and bare, until one day a little boy came running up the track, legs stocky, hair tousled straw, a little bunch of primroses clutched in his hand. He burst out:

'These are for Catriona!'

And the cold war was over, the dam at last burst. He bent down to the small head, put his arm gently round the shoulders, and cried. Cried for himself and for his dead, wooden heart, and for Catriona who had been for him the stream through which all his joy, his laughter and song, had flowed. But the world, he saw then, had not ended. He saw her in the faces of the flowers, smiling, as in the wren-bright eyes of the little boy who had loved her too.

And from that day he had allowed the blood to flow back into his veins, had allowed friends to come near him, had gone back to church and found a spark of faith again. Slowly, healing had begun. In a sense, the darkness did not grow any less, and the loneliness would be there always; but the small lights along the way began to make it easier to bear. As the years went by, there was fiddle music again at Achnagreine; and old friends came back, to share good talk round the fire in the evenings. He needed someone to help in the house; that was when Kate came, with her son Roddy. Although the boy was strange and liked best to be on his own, it was good to have him about the place. As for Kate, her back was strong and her sight far better than his own, and she was good at the farm work. At first she was quiet and withdrawn, and when they sat at meals she hardly said a word, and sometimes her eyes seemed to flash at him as if she was nervous. Perhaps, he thought, she had heard stories of him, after his year of silence and anger? But maybe it was not that; maybe it was that she was self-contained, confident. She seemed to fear nothing; she made decisions quickly and stood by them. She grew frustrated by his slowness, and in the end he let her go off up to the top fields, while he himself worked away at the dykes down to the track, where he had peace and time.

Then when last winter came he had felt the cold as never before. He would lie awake in bed, listening to the wind, becoming fanciful, his eyes seeing in the half-light his mother and father and Andrew . . . and Catriona – always Catriona. The photographs that were fading.

Dan had come full circle. He climbed wearily up through the wood and saw Achnagreine ahead of him, on the little ridge. Now he was tired and the darkness coming fast. It would be good to sit by the fire again.

He did not see the deer fence until he was only a few steps from it. Towering over him by several feet, it seemed in his imagination a giant that stood in his way. Confused, he stood looking at it, his eyes searching for a way of climbing, but the mesh stretched up, shining and impregnable, held by the posts as if by a line of sentries. Maybe the gaps in the mesh would be wide enough to hold his feet? He went forward, reached up stiffly with both hands outstretched, placed his left foot unsteadily on the wire; then he swung up with his right. When it came to keeping both hands taut in that position, however, his strength failed; he attempted to step back but instead fell backwards, badly twisting his ankle. He tried to move but could not; he could only crouch there, on the ground that was covered partly with snow, partly with the mixed leaves of autumn, now frozen – leaves of birch, alder and rowan.

He turned round to look at the Lodge, his eyes just making out the empty shape of the lawns; nobody was left there now. Hopelessly he shouted for Kate; his voice was lost in the wind. Flurries of snow came and went; how cold it was! He began to shiver uncontrollably. He closed his eyes and listened to the bleating of sheep and lambs in the distance. It grew darker still and now he could see nothing, nothing but the glow of the light of Achnagreine through the wire of the fence. He wished then with all his being that he could go home, home to the light, to the place of his people. But he could not get up now; he could not move an inch. Sleepy, he turned on to his side and curled up in an effort to keep warm.

After a long time he heard a voice. His heart leapt. It was Catriona, of course; she had come to find him! He talked to her, and asked her to take him home . . .

seventeen

The funeral was over. Kate had found the service strange, the long psalms tedious. The minister had spoken of a seed having to die in order for life to be born; she had found her thoughts wandering. A scattering of glen folk, most of them old, had walked away afterwards, some with sticks, some arm-in-arm with others. She walked quickly past them. Her shoes were dirty from standing in the graveyard; it was thawing fast and the trees were dripping. She must get back to the farm.

How dreary the kitchen was! It needed some bright new furniture, a better rug at the fireplace. She looked round for just a moment and then, her heart beating fast, went up the stairs two at a time and into Dan's room. Her hands trembled. She had seen the envelope in his spidery handwriting; here it was at last.

On the outside she saw the word 'Daniel'. What was this? Certainly a mistake – he had been confused for the last while, of course. She tore it open and began to read the single sheet of paper, her lips moving fast over the words:

My dear Daniel,

I have at last found your address and have arranged for this letter to be sent on to you when I am gone.

Many years ago when I was studying in Glasgow and you were just a little boy, I loved your mother. It is even possible that you still remember me from that time. In the end I left to come back to this glen and my own people. Before I went, I left behind for you the gift my own brother had given me when he went to the war, a set of toy farm animals. That was all a long time ago. But now I want to do what may seem a very strange thing – I want to leave you something else – this farm, Achnagreine, and its land.

It is the thing of most value that I have in this world, not because of its riches or a soil that will bring in much money, but because it is a precious piece of land, to me more precious than gold. Your grandfather was a sheep farmer in another place in the Highlands, and I believe you have inherited his love of the land. Perhaps you even remember from all those years ago how you loved the stories of this glen I used to tell you, and how you would say you wanted only to farm the land. You were as a son to me then, Daniel, and I have had no son since.

I do not want these fields to die, nor do I want their use to be changed. I ask you to come here, and your sons after you, to live in this place; to find in these fields both the living and the dead; to guard the land.

There's a new rowan tree I planted by the barn last year where one grew long ago – see that it grows good and strong!
May you always be blessed in this place.

Dan Drummond

THE SUMMER IS ENDED

For Richard Campbell,
and also to the memory of Richard Leaf,
who died long before his time

one

Cam was still far away in his dreams when his father came to waken him. It was something to do with Rosie; he seemed to be chasing her through a thick wood and he could hear her laughing the whole time . . .

'Cam! Cam!'

In the end he turned round and looked up mistily at his father who was smiling faintly, the grey edges of his beard almost tickling his face. The boy frowned in the bad light of the room. It could hardly be more than six . . .

'Cam! I've found something! I want you to come down and have a look at it.'

Cam swam through deep seas, struggling to keep his eyes open. He loathed and detested the early morning; it was the very worst thing about living on a farm. Rain danced against the window panes.

'Will it not wait? 'S only dawn, Dad!'

'Och, come on.' His father's eyes twinkled in amusement at his son, lazy as ever. 'It's worth getting up for, I'm telling you, boy! Good practice for university as well!' he added with a wink. 'I'll see you down at the bottom field, Cam. Put your boots on.'

The door closed. Cam sighed and dunted his head back into the pillows. He'd better go. He would die of curiosity if he didn't, and he was more or less awake now anyway. He flung back the bedclothes and got up, feeling the nip that was in the air now. The summer was over all right; not long now till the frost would be here. He stumbled blearily towards his clothes, shivering, and began to get dressed.

Cam passed his brother Robert's room and was on the point of going in to waken him. His hand was on the doorknob and his heart thudded with a wicked joy, but at the last moment he turned away. Robert was older and stronger; Cam had lost every fight there had ever been, and he'd be sure to get a good kick if he went in and woke him for nothing.

Robert had said hardly a thing about the place at university, in fact nothing at all. Cam thought about it now, mulling that over in his head. Rob had never even wanted to go to university himself; it would have taken ropes and horses to drag him to a city, let alone make him study there. Ardnish was all that had ever been in his head – the hills, the fields, the house, the land. Not that he would ever have said so, but he was fiercely proud of it. Maybe he was thinking of Annie again, whether he had a chance or not . . . Maybe that was why he was so sullen and dark these days, Cam thought.

He clattered down the stairs, deliberately making a lot of noise. After all, if he was up, why should the rest of them get two hours' extra sleep? Misty was in the hall; she stretched and wheezed when Cam came towards her. His dad must have taken Fruin instead. Misty was getting old and lazy.

'Aye, you like your chin being tickled,' Cam whispered, and bent down for his boots. All of a sudden, a picture of Fleet came into his mind and a shadow of pain went through him. He'd loved that dog like nothing else on earth. He could see her yet, the big yellow eyes like marbles, so wise and gentle; she was the only dog that had ever been his own. When Corrie had had her puppies he had been allowed to choose one for his birthday. He remembered it so clearly – hadn't it been his fourth? Fleet had lain at the bottom of his bed for ten whole years, big soft lump that she was. Cam bent to untie the laces of his boots – he must have kicked them off without bothering the night before. He yawned, and his stomach made hollow noises; he would make sure of a good breakfast when he was back from the field. Misty looked questioningly at him as he got up, and his hand passed over the tip of her nose.

'No, you stay here,' he said gently. 'Lie down! I'll be back.'

He opened the door and went out. He dug his hands into his jacket pockets and stopped in his tracks, looking out to the west at the whole world, the breath suddenly knocked right out of him. Far off he could hear the sound of the curlews, maybe a dozen or more of them; it was like the strangest singing, as though they were women, mourning lovers who had gone off to war and would never come back. He'd listened to them often enough; he'd heard that song through the bedroom window as he lay trying to sleep, but just at this moment it seemed different; it meant more than at other times. In a week he wouldn't be here any more; he'd be away in Aberdeen in a new life, surrounded by streets and night life and folk from every part of the world. It was what he had wanted, wasn't it? It was what he had worked for. Yet just at this moment he wondered.

He suddenly felt as if he would be going into exile. But that was stupid; he could be back here as often as he liked. All the same, a sort of panic came over him, a feeling that nothing would ever be the same again, that things would happen here while he was away, and he would be outside of it all. He imagined his father dying, the farm being sold, a huge hotel being built down by the shore, looking out towards Shuan. Och, he was being stupid, paranoid; likely as not there'd be no great changes at all. But for a second he found himself envying Robert, with his complete contentment here, his ability to shrug his shoulders at anything but Ardnish and the life he'd always known.

I'm too restless, Cam thought to himself, I've always been my own worst enemy. He sighed, shivered slightly as a cold edge of wind came from the shore; he told himself firmly that he had a whole week left before going away and he would go round and look at things, and remember – not because he was really afraid of losing them, but simply to try to see this place as it was, instead of just blindly going round fiddling away the days . . .

'Are you coming before Christmas?'

Cam turned and looked down the field to the solid figure of his father. He smiled and started down more quickly towards him. The mist was lifting off the sea, moving away in white curls that were like the wisps of hair on an old woman's head. He passed the edge of the barley field and on into the next one which was under grass for hay. His father had been working away on a great mound of earth that was plumb in the middle of that field – a wart of a thing it was, with great slabs of rock sticking out at odd angles, and a strange lump of grassy ground at the top. Duncan

Mackay had always told his sons it was just a heap of rocks the first farmers had dumped there to be rid of them; now he was tired of forever going round it with the machines. It was like an itchy spot on his skin and he wanted it away. A lot of the big stones had gone already; Cam had seen him staggering under the weight of slabs that must have weighed more than a hundredweight before heaving them on to the shore.

Now Cam felt an edge of excitement inside him. When he was very young he would look out of his window at that place, his eyes hovering over it; somehow it always fascinated him, almost as if he knew without being told that more was buried there than just huge slabs of stone. To him it was an ancient secret place; he could remember hiding there from Robert, crouching down like a hedgehog when they were playing hide and seek, or when Robert was on the warpath for some reason or other. It was almost as though in a funny way it was the centre of everything at Ardnish – not the house at all. But he'd never said any of that to anyone; these were just odd thoughts that filled his head now and again like thistledown, and then blew away.

His father was bending over the grassy mound, except that now the roof of it was gone, as the top might have been sliced off an egg.

'See what I've found you, Cam Mackay,' he said with a kind of boyish pride. 'This was worth getting up for, I'm telling you!'

He gestured with his head towards the mound and Cam bent down, and then involuntarily drew in his breath as he reached out to touch the thing. Clearly delineated in the earth under the top of the mound was a harp. It was still buried, but the rim could be seen, as well as the strings that stretched across it. On the surface of the wood there were the most wonderful knots and curls, with a complicated interwoven pattern which the eye followed with difficulty. The ground there was peaty, black as pitch, so rich that its scent filled the air all around. Cam gingerly touched the harp with one finger, almost as though it might crumble at his touch like that bunch of flowers they'd found in the Egyptian pyramid. But the wood was strong and smooth, as if it had been fashioned the day before. Cam just looked up at his father and stared, not knowing what to say; for a moment he even wondered whether the harp had been planted there as a kind of joke. Duncan Mackay just laughed, a delighted chuckle that expressed his pleasure at finding this treasure, and on his own land too.

'No one's taking that away to Edinburgh anyway,' he said firmly at last. 'So you'd better keep it under your hat when you're in the village. It's old all right, no doubt of that. And it'll still play! Run your hand over it, Cam – harder than that. Look! The thing's held its tune for maybe a thousand years; imagine that! Now that's better than the things they churn out in Japan, eh?'

Cam was hardly taking the words in as he crouched there; to tell the truth, he was still half-asleep and almost believed he was dreaming all this and would waken up in bed. But the wind on his face was real enough, and the wood of the harp was solid and didn't melt away when he touched it.

'You could get Martha to try playing it,' he heard himself saying, as he dared at last to pluck the strings, and the sounds were at once blown away by the wind. His father's eyes lit up like lochs in sunlight.

'That's an idea all right! Of course, Martha's got a clarsach. I'll give her a call.' He turned to go.

'Dad, have a heart – it's only six,' Cam said weakly, with a hint of reproach.

His father nodded and bent to stroke Fruin; the dog was lying on the other side of the mound, looking for all the world like a bored pupil waiting to be allowed out of school.

'On you go and get some breakfast,' Duncan said more quietly. 'I'll be in in an hour or so. I've another stone to lift.'

Cam hesitated and then said, 'It's great about the harp, Dad. To tell you the truth, I'm jealous. Wish it had been me!'

His father grinned, his pride restored. Cam turned and started back up the field towards the house.

He had been going to go up to the plantation seeing he was up anyway, but the smell of breakfast from the kitchen was too much. He kicked off his boots and went in to where his mother was standing with the frying pan, basting the eggs with fat.

'Is that all for me?' he said with huge eyes and leant over her shoulder. She shook him off, but her eyes shone with pleasure at his teasing.

'I haven't seen you up this early since the days Rosie used to come for the eggs! What on earth have you been doing?'

'Dad'll tell you soon enough,' Cam said firmly and sat down at the table. Robert appeared in the doorway now, his dark hair tousled and his face puckered with sleep. He glowered at his brother.

'You made a noise like fifteen elephants going downstairs this morning. I could've murdered you.'

Cam smiled angelically. He had been the early bird just for once, and victory was sweet. His mother put a plate of sausage and eggs in front of him and he ate greedily, suddenly eager to be off on his own again. The first real sunlight burst through the kitchen window and shone like silver over everything; he was thoroughly awake now and there was a restlessness in him like an ache. He would go up into the larch wood and then on. He wanted to use the day, to draw from it the last drop, and he was suddenly glad that his father had wakened him so early. He could hardly have borne to miss these first hours when everything was just starting to come to life. He scraped back his chair.

'Thanks, Mum, that was great. I'm going out.' Already he was half through the door.

'Will you not even have some tea?' she called after him but he shouted back, 'No thanks!' and was out into the bright magic of the light. The rain had gone off, and he looked away east, beyond the track and the plantation and the village to the low blue skies and the sun. His father was coming up from the field with strong, steady strides, and in his arms he carried the harp, as though it was a child he had found, a precious and beautiful child he was bringing home. Cam waved but he didn't see him; he was lost in his own world. The boy turned and began up towards the track that led into the larch wood.

The scent was what came to him first, that fresh, deep, green scent as the branches moved together under the breeze sounding like a great sea. The track now turned a corner and all of a sudden he was hidden by larches; the house, the sea and the fields were all swallowed up and no longer existed. Only the trees were left, chaffinches flitting away in small groups, and the sound of a pheasant whirring up into the air in its ungainly flight.

There was one place Cam wanted to go more than anywhere; had he remembered correctly, was it past the pool or did he go off to the right farther on? He stopped at the pond for a moment and looked at his reflection. Once he didn't have to bend at all to see his face. Now he was nearly as tall as his father, and taller than Robert – something that did not please his brother one bit.

He bent down and put his hand into the water. It was like breaking black glass and the cold reached up to his wrist in sharp knives of pain. Over at the far side, the burn tumbled down into the pool the colour of crystal; it came from the moor and one of the hill lochs, finding its way through the deep carpet of larch needles and quartz boulders to this place. Cam recalled the boats he used to sail here; he would spend hour after hour playing with them, pushing them round the rim of the pond, building islands of stones to which his ships voyaged to find treasure. He had made up his own stories, a world of legends, and narrated them aloud just as long as neither Robert nor any of his friends were within earshot. Once a few of them had hidden in the larches to watch him; they had burst out laughing at one of his stories. Mortified, he had pounded down the path to the house with hot tears on his face, buried himself in a pillow and refused to be comforted.

A group of pigeons flew from the treetops and Cam looked up, his thoughts forgotten. He had been wanting to find the glade anyway; he hadn't meant to stop here at all. He walked now on a thick carpet of moss, feeling tiny edges of damp seep through his shoes, for all the ground by the pool was black and wet. It took him longer than he expected to find the glade, but he broke in there at last, and stopped, breathing hard, squinting up at the sunlight as it strummed down in arrows through the thick green boughs. They were like the strings of the harp, he thought. He recalled what had once happened to him here . . . had it been real or just something he had wished would happen? He couldn't even recall how old he had been . . .

His mother had been in the habit of reading tales of Scottish history to Robert and himself: stories of Border warfare, of cattle rustled and prisoners set free, of battles for keeps and castles. She read them when the curtains were drawn and they were cosy in their beds, and he would lie awake long after the light had gone out, wishing he could have known those days.

One morning – it was probably a Saturday – he had wandered up into the larch wood, most likely on his way to his grandparents' place, when he was waylaid by the sight of a deer; he turned aside and went crashing through the larches after it, to find himself suddenly in that strange glade, timeless in its silence, the finches fluttering about in the held breath of the air. He half-remembered lying down there to look up at the canopy of the branches and the way the sun was spliced by the larches, when there came a sudden drumming, the echo of strong hooves, and the passing of that great black horse with its rider, a flag in his armoured hand, his head bent as he galloped on without a glance to left or right.

It was as though he had been in a nowhere place, as though all sorts of curtains of time had rushed together to allow him to see through, into something that had happened long, long before. Somehow he had been aware that the rider had been a messenger, that he was coming from a battle; but Cam had never bothered to find out more, to look up any book that would have helped him to identify the rider and place him in his context and time. Half of him kept the memory of that strange happening; perhaps the other half did not want to find out.

But today there was nothing, just the sound of the wind among the branches; he felt strangely disappointed by the place. It was not as he had imagined it, not as his memory wanted it to be. That thought almost frightened him – would he perhaps remember everything, when he was in Aberdeen, as his mind painted it, and then come back expectantly only to find an illusion?

Abruptly, he turned away, going back among the larches and letting the soft green boughs with their rain-wet edges brush across his face. The rain was back again now and he stopped by the pond, arguing with himself as to whether or not he should turn back. His bed wouldn't be really cold yet; it was a strong temptation. He decided to give the skies a chance; if the rain cleared a bit he'd go on over the moor to his grandparents' place; if not he'd find his way back and make a start on his packing. The thought hit him like a sharp slap as he began circling the pool to go on through the wood. Up to now, his leaving had seemed vague and distant; now he had to think in terms of suitcases, fees, bus passes, rent. For a second he had a vision of Union Street, with many feet going past and buses rushing as the same rain fell on the grey stone of the pavements.

If only, if only Richard were going! His eyes hurt with the thought. Richard, the best friend he had ever had; if he could only come back! But he was gone, and only the wind came like the touch of a hand on his cheek. Cam did not allow himself to cry.

All of a sudden he was out on the other side of the wood. Four grouse went bubbling away and he couldn't resist lifting an imaginary gun to his shoulder whilst making bangs with his mouth. Robert wouldn't have let them off so lightly, he reflected; he had an eye like a merlin's and a rock-steady hand. The number of dead things that had come home from that moor! Robert wasn't interested in them once they were dead, either, it was just the shooting of them that seemed to matter to him.

Cam looked up and over the moor. There, a little over to his left and far off, was the strange pyramid shape of Ben Luan, its sides of steeply-angled scree. His eye travelled round from the sea and the Ben, over the moor, to an old track that wound its way indistinctly over the heather, and then became lost. His heart lifted. That was the way to his grandfather's. Before he left for Aberdeen he was going there. He had to say goodbye to its ghosts.

Between Ben Luan and the track was a long, low, dark line along the brow of the hill. That was where Cameron Mackay, the grandfather after whom he was named, used to cut his peats every summer. Cam screwed up his eyes and looked through the steady drizzle at the place; he saw the shadow clearly enough, bent over the peat cutter, methodically, patiently measuring out the next piece from the bank as the cutter went down and his left foot pressed it home. Cam could almost hear the thud of the peat as it was laid perfectly on the bank, ready to be stacked now in readiness for the long course of the winter. He saw himself, half the height he was now, running up through the larches with a flask for his grandpa, saw the old man turn, lean on the cutter and wave. He was always singing some Gaelic song or other to himself, humming away cheerily and singing so quietly that you couldn't catch the words. It was like getting a station on the radio when it was bad weather so that the voice is frayed and drifts away and you have to keep your ear close to hear it. That was how the songs had been; that was how his grandfather was now – just a station he occasionally found by chance, and remembered, and tried to listen to again.

Cam thought then of the peat bank and of the harp. It seemed to him that it was like that with memories; you went through layer and layer of them, back to the very beginning, and in the end you sometimes couldn't be sure what was a memory and what was a story. He felt himself cutting away at the years, sifting through each place for the people and the stories. And in that peat there were harps and there were gemstones, and maybe knives and coffins as well; he wanted to find all of them, wanted to be sure.

But now it had turned again to rain in earnest and he didn't have the heart to go on. Grey-black curtains had swept away Ben Luan and were smudging the peat bank and the old track.

Cam turned and started for home.

two

'Rosie's here for the eggs, Cam!'

He was already up and dressed; he'd been trying on different sweaters to make sure the blue lambswool was the best. It had one tiny hole in the left elbow, but if he pulled the sleeve round far enough . . . His hair was all flat now; he'd combed it in five different ways before he was satisfied, and had gone into his parents' bedroom on quiet feet to help himself to some of his father's aftershave. His hands were trembling a bit and he'd been to the bathroom twice, and had even practised his smile in front of the mirror.

Now he went hurtling downstairs and his mother, having exchanged a word or two with Rosie, vanished into the kitchen, giving her son a knowing wink as she went.

'Both of you come in for lemonade and biscuits when you're done,' she said, and the door closed behind her. Fleet snuffled and lay down.

'Hi,' Cam said and felt his cheeks going on fire.

'Hi,' answered Rosie, and there she was, the gentle bob of her dark brown hair, the rowan of her cheeks, the big brown eyes that caught his heart and sank him every time he saw her. His heart was drumming in his chest and with every second that passed his legs were more like jelly.

'So, can I have some eggs?' she asked, and there was the slightest hint of a smile on her lips. He came to and fumbled with his boots, nearly losing his balance, and she laughed, not at him in an unkind way but just for its own sake and because he amused her. She was in the class above him and was taller than him, and she could run like a wild hare.

'Fleet, go in!' he commanded in an uncommonly severe voice which somehow restored his self-confidence. 'I'm only just up,' he muttered, moving off towards the hen-house. 'I didn't realise the time.' Then after a small silence, 'Richard and I are going for chestnuts tomorrow.'

Her eyes lit up.

'Aw, are you? Lucky things!'

'You can come if you like.' There, he had said it; he had actually got out the words and his heart, which had been going like a blacksmith's hammer, went quieter, the worst over. Cam was gaining courage by the second; something was pumping round in his veins that made him almost dizzy, and he felt taller and stronger.

'Aye, we're going to get them off that big tree in Mr Fraser's garden – you know, the one behind the hall?'

'He'll kill you if he finds you!'

'Och, we'll be all right. We'll come round for you about seven.'

They went into the darkness of the hen-house. It smelled of straw and warm air and dung; one or two swallows flitted about in the rafters and the hens conversed in a low clucking, for all the world, Cam thought, like ladies over their tea at the Women's Guild. It took them a moment or two to get used to the dark; he moved quickly and brushed his hand against hers, and for a moment their eyes met and he muttered 'sorry' and blundered away. The eggs in the nesting boxes were still warm, one or two of the shells slightly blotched with green dung, and they squeaked as he placed them carefully into the polystyrene box that Rosie had brought. His hands were trembling; he simply could not help it.

'Will you be a farmer one day, Cam?' she asked gently, and she was completely calm as she looked at him. He was taken aback and did not know how to answer; he was only just fourteen and he'd hardly thought yet.

'Robert'll get the farm,' he said automatically, for that was what he always heard his parents say. He put the sixth egg into the box and tried to close it tight. 'Maybe I'll go exploring in Africa.' Then it flashed across his mind that he was excluding her from his plans and he back-tracked hastily. 'Course I want to come back and live here. Wherever I go, it'll only be for a while.' He climbed down and gave her the box and she thanked him. 'What do you want to do yourself, Rosie?'

'I want to be a designer,' she answered, and there was real feeling in her voice. 'I want to be really rich and go all round the world.'

He nodded, not knowing how to reply. It was as if she was a princess and miles above him; he looked down at his grubby hands and his confidence left him altogether. A kind of bubble rose up within him, his heart began to hammer again and he wanted . . . he knew he had to say it, now or never again.

'I'd be really sad if you went away. I really like you, Rosie.' And madly, wildly, he bent in a storm of feeling and kissed her cheek, except that he missed and got instead the lock of hair that came down about her ear. He was so dizzy he felt almost faint, and yet there was a wild elation in him too because he'd done it, he'd found the courage in the end.

She smiled at him and her voice was soft, not much more than a whisper.

'I like you too, Cam.'

He was standing at the window that evening, on the same day his father had found the harp, remembering Rosie, wondering about all that had happened since the day she came for the eggs. At first it wasn't clear in his mind at all; whole years of Saturdays seemed to have run into one. He realised nothing was left even to prove to himself the strong imprint she had left – no letter, no gift, no picture, not even a Valentine card. He looked out to the water and saw the tide far, far out, the shore grey and bleak in the foreground, and somehow the two things seemed the same to him; and yet she was like a flower growing deep down in some place in his mind. She had been his first love, and at the time she had meant everything to him.

He opened the window wide, lifting it so that he could lean right out into the early evening. There was a beautiful scent in the air; he did not know what it was. The low sun was weaker now, weak enough to look on full, and it came in a buttery yellow across the fields and the moors, changing and shifting, as elusive as a running child or a summer butterfly, searching and searching without ever coming to rest. He could hear the curlews again from down near the shore, though he could not see them, and he watched four oystercatchers fly over the shingle with their fast wingbeat, as if escaping from an enemy. Sometimes, when he was like this, intent on all the beauty about him, he knew that he feared death; he wanted never to lose hold of all this that was so precious to him. And because of all the memories of Rosie that had flooded into his mind again that day, at that moment he wanted her to be there too, for she was part of that world.

His mind would not stop thinking of her now – had they ever got the conkers that day? He thought hard. Now he remembered; Rosie hadn't come with them in the end, but Richard had fallen off the wall, and then a light had gone on in Mr Fraser's house and they had crouched down, hardly daring to breathe, until at last the light went off again and they had packed every pocket with beautiful chestnuts, polished so that they looked like mahogany.

After that, Cam remembered with a pang, he had neglected Richard badly. He had held Rosie's hand and she had written his name on her jotter with a red felt-tip pen; and every Saturday she came for a longer and longer time. She had helped him build the last of the den up in the larch wood and they talked there about a million things. They played tricks on his big brother; they put a frog in his bed and seaweed in his wellington boots. They went up into the loft of Ardnish house when it was raining, and opened up old trunks and played endless dressing-up games. And they had had some terrible arguments too; most of the time they were best friends but when they argued they did it in style. He had no idea now what it was they disagreed about. Sometimes Rosie would get very angry; she kicked things, and she nipped him. Once or twice, he remembered, he had kicked her too and that had made things much worse. It was usually Cam who said sorry first, very, very reluctantly, but he always had to drag any apology out of her. All the same, they never seemed to stay angry for long.

But then, one holiday time, everything fell apart for good. Cam's cousin, Beckie, who lived in Campbeltown, came to stay just after Christmas. The snow had come at last and there was enough in front of the house to get the sledges out and spin down all the way to the burn. Cam had shaken Beckie's hand rather icily when she first arrived; he had played compulsory games with her and then tried to sneak away as often as he could. She had freckles and glasses, and she liked maths at school, which made her, in Cam's eyes, a monstrous kind of figure, quite beyond the pale.

Then they went sledging. He found she was absolutely fearless; she would go backwards on the sledge, or she would stand on it and hurtle down the most terrifyingly steep inclines. Cam was quite bowled over; he forgot his cool front and became excited as a puppy with her, bounding about as he chatted.

'Aw, you should see the hill above the manse! It's miles long and if you get up a really good speed you go right over a bump at the bottom and straight over a fence! It's really scary but you'd love it, I'm telling you!'

That was the Saturday, the last one before they went back to school. Rosie was puzzled that she hadn't heard anything from him that morning, so she bumped along the farm track with her sledge, all muffled up in her winter gear. She came round the back of the farm just as Cam and Beckie had toppled over together in the middle of the top field and were lying in a heap, roaring their heads off and nearly crying with laughter. Rosie looked from one to the other and in an instant made up her mind as to what was going on. Her face crimson, she shouted at the top of her voice, 'I hate you, Cam Mackay! I don't want to see you ever again!' And she stamped away as he sat there looking at her with his mouth half open, and new flakes of snow twirled out of the heavy, grey skies.

Three days later Beckie was away on the train and school had begun. The snow had melted, and the pool of ice under the pear tree had gone, but Rosie walked past Cam as tall and frigid as an icicle. Worst of all, she chose to sit beside the boy he most detested in his class, Mitchell Simpson, and shared his lunch. He watched them in anguish. His whole world seemed to have collapsed. He pushed his food around his plate and seemed hardly to hear when anyone asked him a question. His mother watched him quietly, not knowing how to help; she said nothing when Calum, Rosie's brother, came the following Saturday for the eggs. Cam was still in bed.

After the boy had left, she crept upstairs and stood in a pool of morning sunlight, holding her breath as she listened outside her younger son's door. He had been crying so long that he hardly had the strength to sob any more; his red face was buried in the pillow. He felt desolate and completely confused, above all angry with himself for having lost her. He told himself that he would never, never fall in love with anyone in his life again, but remain distant and lonely and full of bitterness. He sobbed heavily and then turned to face the wall as his mother came very quietly into the room and closed the door. He had known she would come but he didn't turn round, and buried his face in the pillow again.

'Cam?' she said softly and sat on the edge of the bed. 'Cam, I think I know why you're so upset, and I just wanted you to know that I understand.'

He moaned in frustration. There was nobody in the world who could understand! His mother thought of taking his hand but then thought better of it. Cam was growing up and maybe it would remind him even more of Rosie.

'I'll go if you really want me to,' she said then, 'but I thought you might like to hear a story. Would that be all right?'

In reply he gave a kind of whimper which she couldn't translate, but she decided to stay anyway. Afterwards she would cook sausages for his dinner, and invite Richard over as a surprise.

'There was once a man who lived in a Highland glen,' she began, 'away up in the very far north of Scotland, in Sutherland. He had a hard life all right, cutting enough peats to see him through the winter, and getting milk and cheese from his two cows. He was always very lonely during the bad weather, for it blew like a hurricane from October till February and at times it was nearly impossible to walk a step on the road outside his door. Now and again his nearest neighbours, who lived maybe three miles away, would send word that they were going to have a ceilidh, and he would excitedly get down his old fiddle from the wall and march along the road, no matter what the weather was like, and they would have songs and a lot of good talk, and sometimes a dram as well, and plenty of oatcakes and cheese.

'Well, one night when he went to their house there was a girl there who was the most beautiful girl you could possibly imagine. She had long golden hair and eyes that were the colour of moorland lochs, a kind of deep blue-black. She laughed and she danced, and when she smiled at the man it seemed to burn into his very heart. He found out from his friends that she had come to look after an old relative who couldn't manage on her own any more, and when he heard that the man's heart began to beat very fast, for he wanted so much to see her again.

'But then his heart failed him because she was so beautiful and everyone seemed to like her, so how could he possibly believe she would ever look at him? So he did nothing, and the spring passed and then the summer came, and he was miserable because he didn't know what to do. Soon she might go away again and he'd have lost his chance!

'So one night he plucked up courage and asked if he could keep her company on the way home from the ceilidh, and she agreed. And as they stood outside her door he said shyly the thing he'd wanted to say for so long.

'"I know that I love you. Would you . . . could you ever be my wife?"

'But she just laughed and then held his hand lightly in hers and looked away over the land, and her eyes as he looked at her seemed to be filled with the stars. And then she said quietly that she did not yet know what it was she wanted, that she needed time to think it all over. Then the door closed and she was gone, and he was left alone in the dark emptiness of the night.

'Day after day he waited, hoping against hope for an answer, but she never came to the house. Then again there was a ceilidh, and every man there wanted to dance with her and it seemed to the man that she was like a kind of golden sun among them all. Once more the faithful man guided her home and dared to ask her again if she had thought about his question and if she had an answer for him.

'"Oh, I will think about it, I really will," she answered. "There's been so much in my mind lately, I never have had time, but I will, I promise."

'So he took her at her word and once more he waited; he waited right through the long winter. But still there was no sign of her as the snow ran off the hills and the first lambs began to appear in the fields. Several times more after that he asked her, until after one ceilidh that went on and on until after the dawn she stood on the doorstep and laughed and said:

'"When you've made me a wedding ring from the gold that's in the river, then I'll promise to marry you."

'She did not really think what she was saying; the words did not mean a thing to her, for she was too happy with all the men around to want any of them at all. But the farmer believed that this was a real test she was setting him, and he went out at dawn the very next morning and began panning the river for gold. He dug down deep into the silt and found tiny winks of gold, thin as paper, left in the bottom of his pan. Each piece he kept with the utmost care; sometimes he would find slightly bigger pieces, so that the time came when there was almost enough. He was so desperate to win the girl he loved that he neglected the work of his own farm and spent every minute of his time searching the river pools. At last he melted what he had into one lump and knew then that he needed only one tiny nugget for the work to be done.

'So, one day of snow and gale, he went out again to search. He felt sick with the cold and soon he was drenched with the blizzard, but still he kept on. On the afternoon of that day he found the last precious piece he needed; later the ring was made. That very night he trudged through the snow to her house and knelt at her feet to offer the ring she had asked for. Her face turned white as ash.

'"But I never meant you to do it!" she cried. "I need more time; I need to think! And I really will, I promise."

'But the poor man was broken. He rose up from where he was kneeling on the stone, and he did not say a word. He knew now that she could never love him, and he turned and went away, as pale as a ghost. And they say that soon afterwards he died, for his heart had been broken.'

Gradually, Cam had come to listen. By the end, he had his head on his elbows while he stared out through the window, not saying a word. His mother smiled as she finished, and dared to take his hand and squeeze it.

'It's a hard road you have to travel,' she said after a silence. 'But one day you'll find the right one, and just don't go and make wedding rings till you're sure they'll keep them.'

In spite of himself, he smiled – at least, his mouth twitched and he turned away, because he didn't want to look happy too quickly.

'It's just that Rosie misunderstood,' he said sorrowfully, and then found himself blurting the whole thing out. 'She saw Beckie and me together in the snow and thought we were going out together and I was two-timing her!'

Cam's face puckered again and he cried as if his heart would break, for the loss of Rosie, for the poor man and his ring, for the hopelessness of everything. He let his mother gather him into her arms and he soaked her shoulder . . .

But all that had been years ago. Now they were older; it was all water under the bridge. Cam was still standing by the window, in the same room where he had cried his eyes out for Rosie, and it made him feel strange to think about it. He could never tell her, not even now, not as something to laugh about. Too much pain was still in the memory. Oh, he had picked himself up all right, and by the time that spring's lambing was over he had almost forgotten the snow and Beckie and all the trouble she had caused. Rosie's winter passed too, and by the summer her frosty mood had melted enough for her to say hello to him, very carefully and quietly. Mitchell Simpson had abandoned her long ago and was at least three girls farther on, and maybe she was beginning to miss the old days herself. But her pride had been so hurt that day in December that she could not allow herself to forget. She saw well enough that when Cam walked near her he went like a wounded fawn, but she wanted him to suffer; she wanted him to know the pain she had been through. One day she might let the walls come down, but not yet . . .

Where was she going now? Oh yes, somewhere in Edinburgh, a management course in one of the colleges – a far cry, he thought, from her old dreams of fashion designing in London! She had a boyfriend in Fort William who came every weekend on a wasp of a motorbike; she smoked now and was much louder, and like most of them couldn't wait to get away to the city, away from 'this boring place'. Somehow he wished he could go back in time, back to that first time he'd met her at the door, on the day she had come for the eggs. Maybe he could have made everything different, if Beckie hadn't come, and they had stayed together. But what was the use of thinking like that? It was too late to change anything now.

The sun poured down over the sea in a shining circle and it was like a golden ring, a ring you could never catch. If you took a boat out from the shore you could paddle for all your worth and never get there, never reach that magical ring.

He would meet a sea of girls in Aberdeen. He smiled to himself and imagined for a moment – in a few days he would be there! But afterwards the experience would be tarnished, and he didn't want that either. But maybe his mother had been right, and there would be one who would take his gold forever? He didn't know. It lay in the sun coming up tomorrow and although he wanted to know the answer, it somehow excited him that he didn't; thinking of it now was like hundreds of butterflies in his heart.

Tomorrow, he decided, he would go to the croft. It would be a lovely day tomorrow, and that was exactly where he wanted to go. A picture of his grandfather flashed across his mind. If only he had seen the harp. If only he'd lived to see it!

three

As Cam went across the moor, struggling against the tug of the wind and the driving rain (his weather predictions had been completely wrong), he heard the raven's deep croak. It was a sound made out of coal; the raven itself was made of coal. He stopped walking and looked all around intently; the cronking gave him a strange prickly feeling down his spine. There they were, just one pair of them on the moor; there was nothing else at all to be seen between them and Ben Luan, nothing but the mist. Then the ravens went over a rocky knoll and were lost to view. Cam was alone now, and he felt the better for it.

He was following the ancient track to his grandfather's croft, and the big metal key to its door was in his pocket. He had been half-reluctant to leave because of the rain, and his mother had fussed over him, insisting that he take this and that before he went. With Robert in a bad mood and his father annoyed at having to fill in a lot of forms he had been glad enough to leave the house.

'I'll try to be back in time for dinner but don't worry about me if I'm not,' he told his mother. 'I've known the road since I could walk, remember!'

Now he felt bad that he'd been impatient with his mother. She always got caught in the middle when he and Robert fell out with each other, or when his father was annoyed about something. Anyway, he was sick of the constant rows with his brother; Robert hadn't even looked at him when he had passed the shed where he was working.

Now the rain was getting heavier. He looked back and saw that

Ardnish was completely blotted out, and so was the sea. Now and again bits of Ben Luan loomed out of the mist, making it seem as if a huge pyramid was there, towering over the plateau. He began to think of the First World War, in which his grandfather had fought, and he found himself wondering whether the two landscapes might have seemed to him quite similar; the land was pock-marked by craters which you could imagine had been made by shells; without difficulty you could make yourself believe the mist over the promontories was enemy gas. Cam could even see a ragged line of grey men coming from behind a ditch and then being lost in the mist. He pulled himself together and laughed at himself for being so fanciful.

The track was now gone. He had to stop and look about him, frowning, to make sure he was heading in the right direction. Where was the single pine tree? As a wee boy, that was the thing he had always looked forward to, the one tree in all that emptiness, its branches all keeled over to the east, flattened so that it looked like a man being beaten and cowering under the whip. He really needed that landmark, for on such a day as this you could have wandered on for ten miles and more through the mist, only to find yourself hopelessly lost.

Toberdubh. The place where his grandfather had lived all on his own after his wife died. She had gone suddenly, the summer before Cam was born; a stroke had taken away her speech, they told him, as well as the power from her left side. Before that she had been as strong and busy as a woman thirty years younger. But after the stroke Peggy fell away to nothing; she became gentle and she cried a lot, and she had no will to live at all. In that way, they said, it was a blessing she had died; that was what Duncan, Cam's father, said himself.

After that, somehow, Cameron Mackay had gone on living at Toberdubh alone. Cam thought about it now and wondered how he had ever managed to do it. His mind went back to his very first memories of the place; they were in black and white, and fragmentary. When, for instance, had he tasted whisky? He remembered the smell from the glass, the hot burning taste. It had put him off the stuff for life!

Now memories came crowding back. It was before he'd begun at school, or maybe during his first year at primary; he wasn't sure. Anyway, he had gone out to see his grandpa and it had rained in rods all day. He'd gone running to his favourite place on the ridge above Toberdubh, a peat-bank where he could hide in under the walls and pretend it was his own house. It was beginning to get dark when he heard his grandfather shouting for him, and he scrambled out of the peat-bank, which was filled with mud like chocolate, to see the single yellow light above the back door of Toberdubh and his grandfather in the doorway. The rain was heavier than ever and Cam bolted like a rabbit down the heathery ridge, his mind full of thoughts of tea and the fire, when down he went into a bog. He gasped for breath, utterly taken by surprise and up to his neck in black mud.

'You'll be out in a minute,' old Cameron chuckled. 'That'll teach you to run like a train down the hill! You'll have to learn to look where you're going, boy!'

Cam remembered bursting into angry tears; he was cold, covered in black clammy peat, and shivering. Suddenly he wanted to be back at Ardnish with his mother more than anything in the world.

'Wheesht, laddie! You'll be home soon, never fear. Now, a nice hot bath and a wee tot of whisky and you'll be as right as rain again, you'll see.'

The bath was good, right enough, and Cam enjoyed lying in comfort listening to the rain and wind hammering on the window, but he was still a bit sorry for himself. So his grandfather wrapped him in a massive towel and carried him downstairs and sat him down beside a roaring fire. Old Balach the collie was banished to a corner, and then a small glass was put into Cam's hand, with just a thimbleful of gold liquid which caught the reflection of the flames.

'Go on now,' said the old man. 'You won't like it, I know, but it'll keep you from catching cold.'

Cam put his nose into the glass and then sneezed violently. He looked quizzically up at his grandfather who was shaking with mirth; at last, to please him, he ventured to take a sip. Immediately he started to cough; he made a face and spluttered: 'It tastes awful!' Nothing would make him take anther drop after that.

'Och well, I think I'll tell you a story,' old Cameron said then, 'and I hope you'll remember it well. Then you can be off to your bed and you'll sleep like a top. It's a story of how the devil first got the taste of whisky.

'Now the devil lives in a horrible deep den, away far down inside the earth, right at the very centre where everything is on fire and it's just fearfully hot, like an oven. Well, a long, long time ago he was sitting down there when this strange smell came into his nose and he couldn't think what it was or where it was coming from. In the end he was sure it was coming from the earth above him and so he came bursting up through all his dark dens and caves until at last he reached the place where the smell was coming from. He wandered around for a while; it was cold and wet and miserable. And then who should come out of his hut, playing his bagpipes, but a man called Fraser Campbell. He got the most fearful fright when he saw the devil and ran back into the hut and slammed the door, but the devil soon got in; he knew fine it was from there that the wonderful smell was coming. Inside was a whole array of bubbling glass bottles and tubes, filled with this strange yellowy-gold liquid, and on the table stood a glass full of the stuff. Without even asking, he went over and drank it, and it warmed him up all through. So he took away as many bottles as he could carry, and off he went. The man was glad to get rid of him, but it wasn't for long – every now and again he was back for more, and there was nothing he could do about it.'

Cam was half-asleep by the time the story was finished, but he had completely forgotten about the bog and the cold, and how miserable he was. He remembered his grandfather picking him up and carrying him upstairs to bed, but he was asleep by the time they reached the top of the stairs.

Every time he even sniffed whisky he still recalled that night long ago, and the weird story his grandfather had told him – strange, he now thought, that the old man should have told him a story like that. But in their family stories always played an important part, especially for taking your mind off things that were troubling you. So his thoughts ran, recalling old memories of this place, until he stopped in his tracks and his eyes burned as he found himself looking down again at Toberdubh from the ridge. Even now he missed the heathery grey tuft of smoke fluttering from the old chimney. In the old days, he thought, one of the dogs would have been up by now from the fireside and out to the door, barking away at the scent of the approaching visitor, and his grandpa scolding it for making such a noise, as he tramped out toward the back door. At one time, the walls had been as white as scrubbed clam shells; now there were big damp patches stretching down from the roof, and loose slates clacked in the wind. For a few moments he just stood there, looking down at the old house; it seemed to him that it was itself a ghostly thing, filled with the sadness of departed spirits. It was like going to tend a grave; this was the real place where his grandparents were buried rather than the graveyard down by the church! But the rain had come on harder than ever and pulling himself together, he began to slither down the steep bank and reached the back door at a half run. He searched for the big key and let himself in.

Something fell from the shelf in front of him and made a ringing noise as it rolled across the floor – a candle, still in its enamel holder. He went into the sitting-room and it was gloomy, cast into shadow by the dark of the afternoon outside; the wind seemed to roll about the house, tugging at its foundations so violently that the place felt a bit like a boat whose anchor was straining to keep hold of it. The house was still furnished, for now and again Cam's father let the place to folk as a summer cottage, or to shooting parties in the autumn. The trouble was, as always, that whenever Cam came here he saw his grandfather wherever he turned; if he looked outside, he could see him working on the walls, or maybe digging in the overgrown garden, or inside he would be kneeling by the fire, making a good blaze.

Why had he come back? Why was he here now, putting himself through this torment when nothing in the world would bring the old man back? He thought about it as he searched around for some kindling to light the fire. He found himself wishing that his grandfather had known he'd got the place at Aberdeen.

'You stick in at your lessons now, boy! You've a good head on you, Cam.' His grandpa had known, of course, that Rob would be the one to take over Ardnish in the fullness of time. There wasn't enough work for the two brothers to share the place, so Cam had always known he'd have to make his own way somewhere else. No one had ever actually talked about it; it was just something that was understood and taken for granted in the family. Often the old man would come back to the subject, asking him if he'd thought what he wanted to be, maybe a doctor or an engineer? 'I don't know,' Cam had replied with some irritation one time. 'I've no idea what I'll do. I've plenty time to choose yet.'

'Aye, but see you stick in at your work, Cam. You don't get many second chances in this life, you know, and you may regret it . . . '

'I'm sick of grandpa going on at me about my school work,' Cam remembered complaining one night at Ardnish. 'He goes on about it the whole time. I wish he'd give me some peace! Can you not tell him to leave me for a bit, Dad?'

'Come here and listen.' His father's voice was gentle but strong. He was wearing his glasses as he sat there at the kitchen table, accounts and forms spread round him like autumn leaves. 'When your grandfather came back from the war his nerves were shattered; he couldn't concentrate on a thing. He'd been brilliant at maths and science and he never got a chance to use them. When he got back here all he could do was work the croft, and by the time he had got a bit better he had a family on his hands – no chance of university for him in those days! And Cam, try to understand – he's only human, and maybe he's just a little jealous. Wouldn't you be, if you were him?'

That was all. His dad had turned back then to his work and never said another word. Cam felt his cheeks flame with guilt. He went over to the window and looked out at the last of the sun, and saw away over the moor a faint trail of smoke that might be from Toberdubh. Fool that he'd been, he thought now; he'd just taken it for granted that the croft was all his grandfather had ever wanted. Next time he'd remember, and be more understanding.

He couldn't help thinking of it all again years later, back here at the old house, kneeling by the grate to get the fire going. How proud the old man would have been to know of his place at Aberdeen! Suddenly he had a picture of himself running over the moors to Toberdubh with the piece of paper in his hand, desperate to tell the old man his news as he always did when anything exciting happened. There would have been a celebration, and certainly a dram!

When the first flames rose and lit the hearth they somehow threw the room into greater darkness. Cam got up, went to find the power switch and flicked on a light. He returned to the sitting-room and there, for just a moment, he fancied he saw the old man stretched out on the couch, his eyes on him, the white hair splayed out behind his head.

'I got the place,' Cam whispered to him. 'I'm going to Aberdeen, but I'll be back! I'd never go away for good.' Then it seemed that the blue eyes were lit, and he smiled as he said: 'Mind you stick in when you're there, then.' But the couch was empty again, and the wind came round the house howling like wolves, and the boy shivered.

Now he became uneasy; he recalled what old Cameron had told him of the strange light that appeared on the shoulder of Ben Luan. It was not a bright light at all, and it didn't keep to the one place; nor was it that all the folk in a village like Findale would see it at the one time, but it would appear to one here and there, as though it shone only in their direction. There was old Murdo Fraser who had gone out in the night from Crossallan, determined to search out this mysterious thing, not sure if it was perhaps some poor soul who'd gone up to climb the hill and been benighted there. At any rate, his grandfather said, he was back by morning, weak and weary, having found not a thing – he lost the light after wandering for a while over the screes and got nothing but a cold for his pains. And when the lambing snow came a couple of weeks later, Murdo was dead and gone.

Chrissie Bain had seen the thing too, according to the old man, not many weeks before she passed away. Oh, there had been plenty . . . By now Cam had got himself really frightened; all of this was like a kind of marsh in his mind over which he was afraid to tread. He was thirsty, and he wanted to brew up some tea, but he had become like a child again, frightened of the unknown thing that might be round the corner. What if he, when he looked out of the window, should catch a glimpse of the eerie light? What if his own grandfather had seen it just before he died? By now Cam's heart was hammering in his chest and he was becoming so afraid that he didn't even want to move . . . He should go home, he should go home! But the rain and the wind were blattering on the windows and roof so fiercely that he dared not set out with the feeble little torch which was all he had. He would have to wait until morning, when he could find his way without any trouble.

When the outer door opened suddenly he nearly died of fright; he leapt up, his heart hammering. It was his father who came into the room, a strong torch still lit in his hands.

'Aye, you picked the night for coming here all right! Your mother said you'd no torch and she wouldn't rest till I came to get you.'

Why did she never stop fussing? Wouldn't she ever allow him to grow up? These were his first impatient thoughts. In a moment his foolish fears were gone, the other, fearful world at once shut out. He got up and filled the kettle, saying in casual tones to his father, 'Thanks for coming, Dad. I'd have been fine. I was going to stay over and come back in daylight.' His father hardly heard him; he was checking cupboards and running his hands over the walls.

'The place is still in fairly good shape. The Fothergills or whatever their name was have left things pretty well. Just a mug of tea then, Cam, and we'd better be off. I've a pile of things to attend to before I get to bed.'

That was all. So that was all this place was to him – a letting house for holidays! He, Cam, couldn't go round the back without seeing the old, dry ruins of the well and imagining an old bent back working at lifting a bucket of water; he couldn't stand by the door without remembering the black beehive of peat that used to stand there against all the winds of winter, every turf made of effort and life. He wanted to turn to his father and look him straight in the eyes and ask if he didn't feel the presence of the old man here yet – was he so soon forgotten? Was a life so easily scrubbed out and lost, washed away by a strong river, leaving no trace? Maybe his father did remember . . . maybe he had just become too good at hiding it.

They walked home together through the wild night, hardly talking; the silence between them was comfortable. In places the track was under water; streams ran off the slopes that rose towards Ben Luan, showing white even in the darkness. Now Cam felt strong, unafraid of his grandfather's eerie tales; he looked across towards the Ben and inwardly challenged it to show any light, but there was nothing, nothing in all the wide expanse except the nodding beam of his father's torch, nothing to be heard but the wind, and the heavy thud of their boots as they trudged on towards Ardnish. In the end Cam reached the point where he marched without thinking; he no longer felt the ache of his calves or the cold of his fingertips after the unceasing, drenching rain. His feet led him but his spirit was far away.

He thought of his grandfather's last days and how quickly the old man had faded in the end. There had been so little warning of the final fall that it came as a shock to jolt them all, and even sent tremors through Findale and far beyond. It was as though a stout ship that had had no accident all its days had suddenly gone on to the rocks, to be wrecked within hours. That last summer old Cameron had still brought in the peats to Toberdubh, although Rob had helped a good deal with the cutting and had done most of the stacking too. He had seemed much the same as ever – maybe a bit more stubborn and at times quick to flare up. But then he fell. He went over on his ankle and lay helpless half a day before one of the local shepherds passed by chance and managed to get him up to the house.

After that, his son Duncan made no bones about the fact that he was coming to Ardnish whether he liked it or not. He didn't like it, of course, and he came with bad grace, and was put into Cam's room. The two brothers had to share a room for the first time in years and agreed to it dourly, as suspicious of each other as a couple of strange sheepdogs.

But the old man went down very fast. Maybe it was a mistake to uproot him from the croft that had been his home ever since he married Peggy; it was the only world he knew. Ardnish was maybe too loud, and too young, and he felt out of joint there. The fall had twisted more than his ankle; in truth he had suffered a first stroke, and in no more than a handful of days he slipped from their grasp so quickly that they could only watch helplessly as the strong man went downhill and was soon lost to them for ever.

It was strange that during those final days he talked nothing but Gaelic; he wasn't really with them any more. On his face, Cam recalled, there was a kind of shining look of complete serenity. The strange thing was that when Duncan went the next day to Toberdubh he found a clock fallen from the mantelpiece; he couldn't understand how it had happened, but it seemed as though time itself had stopped.

Now they came to the larch wood and heard the whispering of the branches as drops of water fell among them and ran through the boughs. There seemed to be a strange kind of warmth in the trees after the open wildness of the moor. The two of them went quickly down the last yards towards the back door of the farmhouse. Rob's light was still on and cast a pale yellow reflection over the ground below; from behind the window came the sound of loud music and Rob's own voice singing along with it. Cam's mother was fussing about the kitchen, picking up nothings from beside the stove, as the two of them went in.

'You should have started back earlier, Cam,' she said accusingly, looking at him with sparking eyes. 'Your poor father . . . '

'Och, Mum,' Cam said, going past her towards the far door. 'Can't you let me go? I'm not a child any more.'

He looked back at her as he opened the door to go up to his bedroom and their eyes met. He saw a sadness in her face that he had never seen before. For a moment he wanted to go back, to say he was sorry, and take away that loss from her eyes which he knew would haunt him; but he didn't. He shut the door and went heavily up to his room, and then opened his window and listened to the sea far off.

He would go down to Shuan, for Richard's sake. Not just yet, but certainly before he left. It was one thing he simply must do.

four

During the night Cam dreamed something that he was to remember for a long time after. He was restless in his sleep, waking first because the window was banging as the rain came in many fingertips across the glass. He saw the moon rushing through cloud like a silver coin, before he crashed back into bed, shivering with cold. He was thinking about his grandfather as he went back to sleep, soundly this time. In his dream, he was going over the moors in front of Ben Luan; at first Richard was with him and afterwards he was not. At any rate Cam found himself at the edge of a lochan that seemed to be covered in specks of white. To begin with, he thought these were snowflakes, but as he drew nearer he realised they were water lilies, their heads half-closed as they bobbed on the surface of the water. He knew he must pick one at once, no matter how cold the water might be, no matter how deep; he was also aware that if he got one, Rosie would be his again – he would give the lily to her and she would be his forever. His clothes seemed in some magical way to flow from him and in a moment he was down into the black water, right up to his thighs. As he went deeper and deeper, the cold was worse than anything he could have imagined, like knives of steel through every fibre of his being. He could see clearly the very lily he wanted; it had a beautiful golden heart within its petal sheath. He stretched out for it with his fingertips; the water now rose up to his neck, the dark tendrils of the lilies beneath caught his legs making him flounder, dragging him down so that he could not breathe . . .

He woke up terrified, with the wind tapping at the glass like a teacher on a blackboard. For a second he was sure there was someone else in the room; he held his breath in fear, but then the wind was quiet and he dared to look up, and there was nothing except the moon splaying down brilliant milky light on to the floor. He recalled the dream in vivid detail but could not understand it; he had a strange feeling of somehow being at war with himself. He wondered why this should be; perhaps it was because recently Richard had been so much in his thoughts.

He saw that it was a quarter past six. Soon it would be time to get up; it was Saturday, and he had promised himself that he would begin his packing in earnest today. But he did not want to start. Fear gripped him from time to time that the whole thing was a dreadful mistake, that he was being a complete fool. Surely anything would be better than throwing away this place he loved so much – he could easily get a job in Findale instead; he could stay on at home . . . But it would not be as he dreamed of it now. That was the worst of both the future and the past – they were always pure and unspoiled. In the end they did not really exist. Only now was real.

Suddenly he found himself wishing with all his heart that Richard was still there – to talk to, to argue with, to understand. He wanted him back, so badly that it hurt him physically, like cramp in his stomach. Richard was dead; Richard would never come back! Cam lay there in bed as the wind howled outside, hot and angry tears running down his face. Why, why did things have to be so hard? He felt like a child, lost and out on his own, reaching for the lily that he could never, never hold.

'Can I borrow that new shirt of yours? There's a party on at Camas tonight.'

Robert was already halfway inside his younger brother's wardrobe, searching for the precious shirt Cam had got last Christmas. He had wakened up with a start when Robert began talking, and he hauled himself round in the bed to see the time. Ten to ten! His head was heavy and still thudding with sleep. Robert had the shirt now and was taking it off the hanger. Cam got up furiously and snatched at it.

'I never said you could have it, right? At least have the decency to wait for an answer! I want it for Aberdeen next week so you can't have it tonight. Give it back!'

He was still tugging at the sleeve, half in and half out of bed, really rattled now by the way Rob had just barged in to help himself to what he wanted. He was only doing it to see how far he could push Cam; there was a kind of triumphant look on his face as he still kept hold of the shirt, scoffing, sure of his supremacy.

'What're you going to need this for next week, huh? All you're doing is studying. Might as well take your school blazer and uniform with you! You're too young even to be allowed in a pub.'

'Just give me back that shirt!' Cam realised he was whining, which made him madder than ever. The roles were as they always had been. The door opened abruptly and his mother put her head round.

'Rob, give it back to Cam! Your dad's wanting you to help him.'

Cam ripped it back with righteous indignation, still looking daggers at his brother. Rob went over to the door, grinning like a jackal.

'Cry baby,' he said scornfully over his shoulder as he left. Morag's eyes passed over Cam after Rob had gone out but she did not say anything. She had taken sides too often in the past and Cam had rebuffed her last night for interfering. The house was filled with the smell of fresh baking; her shoes clacked as she quickly descended the stairs. Cam still raged within himself. What a fool he had been to think he could ever stay on in this house! He hated his brother and couldn't wait to be free of him. He bashed his fist into the pillow and lay, face down and eyes closed, until he felt calmer, his turbulent thoughts quietened down. But he found he couldn't lie in bed any longer so he threw off the bedclothes, got up and looked out of the window. The fields shimmered with rain. Still, he had made up his mind to go to Shuan; later, perhaps, he would go.

He saw his mother at the far end of the kitchen as he went in. Her head was bent as she kneaded dough for bread. Silhouetted by a sudden ray of sunshine from the window, it might have been that she was praying. She had not heard him come in, and for a moment he stood quietly watching her, thinking of how he had distanced himself from her the night before. He allowed his gaze to wander around all the familiar things in the room; everything seemed to be black and gold in the light. Misty and Fruin lay stretched out like a couple of hearth-rugs; his father's boots stood drying after the soaking of the previous night.

A black ridge of cloud then passed over the sun and the room was plunged into shadow. Cam looked up at the long prow of cloud and it reminded him of something from childhood, a time when he had believed a strange hobgoblin rode such clouds as these. Sometimes he could actually see the high cape around the creature's shoulders and the outline of the black mount on which it galloped across the skies! And once, he recalled, he had been so frightened that he had run down from his room, scared that the hobgoblin was real.

'I'll do a final wash for you today, Cam.' His mother's voice interrupted his reverie. 'Bring anything you need done.'

Cam looked at her. She sounded tired, as though she hadn't slept well the night before. Most likely she had been up since six too. She turned and began to shape the dough.

'Thanks, Mum,' he said as gently as he could, really meaning it and wanting to make amends. 'I dunno how I'm going to cope with everything on my own.'

She put down what she was doing and came over to him. 'Och, you'll be fine, Cam. No doubt you'll be home often enough with plenty washing!'

He wanted to tell her that he didn't even know that he wanted to go, that he was scared of leaving Ardnish and all that was familiar here for the first time ever, that he would miss her. But his mouth seemed dry and he didn't know where to begin, and his hands knotted helplessly on the wooden table; he simply stood looking at her as she now went round the kitchen gathering things to be washed.

There was always so little time in this house. Were other families like this? It was nobody's fault, but it was everyone's. They were always so busy doing their own things; they talked instead of listening. When they were children, he and Rob had talked to their mother much more; then, there was no fear of embarrassment, of being seen to be weak and foolish. He wondered how long it was since all that had changed. Now the room was back to silence and he didn't know how to begin. It was as if he held many broken pieces in his hands and he did not know which one to bring out first. Angry with himself, he turned and went up the stairs to the attic without having spoken another word.

He thought of how often he had raced up the steep stairs, two steps at a time, the echoes sounding round the house as Richard or some other friend came after him. The place had a low ceiling, and set into the sloping roof were two small windows that looked east. Cam went over to one of them, still breathing hard after having run so fast, and down and away to the right he could see the grey smudge of Findale, the church steeple poking the sky like a needle, the hills and woods beyond. The mist had almost gone; the last of it was like thin stretches of wool, drawn now over the low ground around the river.

He dragged himself away from the window and forced himself to think of his packing. He had come up for a trunk, to take all that he would need for his first term, but he had no heart for it; he simply had no wish to start. His eyes grew accustomed to the dim light; there was dust over everything. At one time, he remembered, he and Robert would be up here every single day; whenever there was rain, their adventures automatically moved in from the fields and the shore to this secret place. Cam spotted something metal shining on the floor and bent to pick it up. It was a Redcoat soldier firing his musket. He smiled, remembering how at one time their war games had stretched from one end of the attic to the other, and how the battles had gone on for days. Cam looked at the soldier and turned it in his hands. The war games had ended a long time ago; it was real conflicts with Robert that went on now! A sadness fell across him for a moment and he let the little soldier fall. What was the point of it all in the end?

As a child he had loved nothing more than rummaging through old boxes or trunks, that had maybe come from Toberdubh, or from an old uncle who had been a ship's captain and had sailed round the world. There was always the hope in him that he'd find something really precious, perhaps a gold coin that had been passed over, or an ancient letter unread for centuries. He picked out an old tin box, easily side-tracked both by memories of past joys and the desire to stay up there out of Robert's way, and in a place where there was complete peace.

He didn't find much in it. This was one of the boxes he had stowed away years ago, full of things he'd been made to clear out from his bedroom. There was an old rusted bit of metal he'd once dug up in a field which he'd been quite sure was Roman; an assortment of shells that had come from a white eternity of beach on the Island of Harris; various old buttons of odd shapes and sizes with which he had played for hours on end when he was small. At the back of his mind, though, as he sifted through the collection of junk, was the hope that he might come across something given to him by Rosie. She was gone now, of course, and he had no thought or hope of regaining her, yet the memory of her was still inside him, part of all the memories of this place, and somehow he didn't want to forget. But there was nothing.

Then, from the bottom of the box, he dragged out a scruffy white feather; as he twirled it in his hands he realised that it was a quill. Somehow it touched off an old memory; he set his mind to thinking hard what it was, and gradually it all came back to him. Richard had taken him once to a weird, barrow-like hill down on the way to Shuan and the sea. It was a place Richard said he loved; there were tall pines like ships on top of the hillock, and hundreds of these white feathers which must have been pigeons'. Cam could now clearly recall Richard bending down, picking up some of the feathers with a strange, wondering look on his face and saying, quite seriously, 'You know, Cam, I used really to believe that angels came down here once a year, at midsummer, to moult. I always thought they were feathers from angels' wings!'

Now it came back to Cam where the quill pen had come from and he sat there, going over it all in his mind. It had been that year they had gone away for Christmas, far from the coast, to stay with relatives. He remembered how his mother had wanted to visit an ancient library in what seemed to him a weird bit of countryside, low and sunken, as though it might have been under water. There seemed to be hundreds of rooks and jackdaws everywhere, and a smell of bonfires in the air. It was not a place that appealed to him at all; he remembered the car dunting along the single-track road, and how he had had the feeling that something strange had happened here. It was no one place in particular; it hung over the whole area, and he was glad that he was not alone. The farm windows were lit like pieces of amber all around, for their visit was in a late afternoon in the winter dark. They came to the library and an old woman came out of her house, unhooked a great iron key and walked with them down the track to the ancient building.

It smelled damp and fusty and bats flitted about in the shadows, and he and Robert played hide and seek. The adults were fascinated by the old books but he knew that he had not liked the place at all; it gave him the creeps, and when at last they left, he looked over his shoulder several times to make sure no one was following them.

Outside, the air was filled with soft feathers of snowflakes, and his uneasiness had vanished in the joy of having snow; maybe they would get stuck, maybe they'd be snowed in and would be unable to get home for the start of school! The old woman was very kind and friendly to them and she asked them in for tea.

The room was bathed in a warm glow; there was a huge open fire giving out a wonderful heat. The woman's husband came in; his gnarled hands looked to Cam as if they were carved out of wood, and he wondered at the thinness of them. They sat and talked while they had tea and hot scones round the fire, and Cam's eyes kept looking out to see if the car was covered yet with snow; he could hardly have borne it if the snow had stopped. The old man then asked if the boys would like to see something special, and he took them over to his desk in the corner and brought out a penknife and two beautiful goose feathers. And he said something Cam could never forget: 'this is the last real penknife'. They watched in fascination as he cut a quick arc of white to make the nib of the quill, and then sharpened its edges with fast, practised strokes. He wrote their names in beautiful flowing letters on a sheet of paper and gave them the quills, one each, and Cam remembered how he had felt this was the most exciting gift he had ever received. His parents too had been impressed. They had left, the good wishes of the old couple following them, as the darkness came in earnest; the snow had changed to a fine mist and the stars shone above like pieces of broken glass. The boys had waved and waved although they could not really see or be seen, until the strange place was just a red glow through the car windows.

Cam turned the quill in his hands and saw that the nib was broken. He felt sad; the old people would no doubt be dead by now; someone else would be looking after the old library. And the man had said his penknife was the last in the world, and Cam had believed him; nobody nowadays made quills out of goose feathers. Somehow he wished with all his heart that he had taken care of the special gift, that he hadn't allowed the nib to get broken. For now he did not know the way back to that place; it was in his mind like a lost Christmas on an old map that had long been discarded.

He looked up and saw that it was raining, but the drops fell through an edge of sunlight that made them look as if they were snowflakes instead. Strange, for the moment it was Christmas that was in his mind; he realised that what he missed was the bigness of childhood Christmases – would there ever be a Christmas like that one again? The bigness of everything seen through a child's eyes; that was gone forever too.

For a moment he felt he wanted to escape from all that was filling his mind from the past; he needed to get it out of his system. Why not go down to Findale with Robert that night, get someone to buy him a drink or two at the Arms? He wanted to be free of his melancholy. What was it that was bothering him anyway? He hadn't been able to shake off his underlying sadness all day. Then he knew it; he must go to see Richard's parents. As soon as he had thought of it, he recognised that he would have to go. It was never easy, but he would do it right away. He drummed down the stairs, still holding the quill in his hand.

The place was always a shock to him. There on the edge of Findale, with the tall oaks round it, a long grey mansion, and a silver car on the driveway in front. He stopped for a moment and looked up at Richard's window, and at once a flood of memories washed over him; he could see Richard's face at the window, could hear his voice calling to him to hurry, that there was something he wanted to show him. How many times had he, Cam, gone along that drive like the wind! There was a giant eel they had trapped and they needed a net; there was a huge ship out at sea and they needed binoculars to see if it was Russian; there was . . .

He closed the gate and the wind sighed in the fence with a queer whistling sound. Before he was halfway to the door, Barley, the old fat Labrador heard him; he struggled out on to the front steps, barking as though he had heard good news. Then Mrs Brennan came out and joined him, wiping her hands on her apron. Cam's first thought was that she had become much older-looking.

'Oh, good to see you, Cam! Come on in.'

He didn't mind the cultured English of her voice; somehow it was all right, even beautiful. If he'd heard someone in a shop in Findale speaking as she did it might have been different, perhaps, but he had long ago become used to the Brennans' voices. Richard had even begun to acquire quite a Scots edge to his tongue; Cam had taught him phrases, sayings, and had made him repeat them till they sounded acceptable to his ear. They had had many laughs together over their differences in speech. But Mrs Brennan was different, and he accepted her as she was.

'Tom's out just now, I'm afraid,' she said, taking him into the living-room after he had kicked off his boots in the vestibule. 'You have to take us rather as you find us and Saturdays do tend to be somewhat busy.'

'Oh, I'm sorry,' Cam said at once, sitting down and stroking Barley's silky ears.

'Oh no, no, not at all!' she exclaimed, throwing up her hands in horror. 'I'm truly glad to see you, Cam – the place is really lonely when Tom's away. But I'm happy to see you at any time, you know.'

For a second their eyes met, and he saw the shadow that passed across her face, and looked quickly away. His own cheeks burned, but she steadied herself; she did not let the mask break, but instead began to scold Barley for all his moulting and apologised for the state of the carpet.

'Let me get you some tea,' she said. 'Or will you have coffee? All right, just make yourself at home and I'll be back in a moment.'

Now he could allow himself to look at the picture of Richard on the mantelpiece, the smiling face, the hair blond as straw. There was another one of him in his school uniform, beside the big brass clock that kept up its stern beat. Sometimes it was just impossible to believe he was gone; often during the past year he had wakened up, sure that he had heard Richard's running steps on the path outside Ardnish. It seemed like no time at all. He was so far away in his thoughts that she had come in without Cam's noticing, and his eyes were still on the picture; he knew she had seen and was mad at himself.

'Do you know it'll be fifteen months next week?' she said in a brisk voice, pouring the tea and not looking at Cam. And then very quietly: 'D'you still think a lot about him, Cam?'

He nodded as she handed him the cup. He could not speak; he did not dare to say a word. A big black wave seemed to roll at the back of his head, and he strove with all his might to keep himself above it. If he lost control he would never forgive himself. Perhaps she knew; perhaps she saw the strange shining in his eyes as he nodded, and she understood. She must surely have seen it before.

'And you'll be going off to university in the next few days, won't you?' she continued brightly. 'What a change after Ardnish! Aberdeen, isn't it?'

How could she do it, Cam wondered; how could she say all these things so easily? He had been her only son; he'd have been going to university himself at this time, to Aberdeen too perhaps! He didn't want her to go through all this; her mask made it all the worse. But he couldn't say. He didn't know how to tell her to stop pretending, to let down all the elaborate defences she had constructed to keep out the darkness. Why, why had it ever happened? Why had Richard to die? Why were others allowed to have long lives – and Richard had everything to live for? Then he heard himself babbling: 'I'm nervous of going. I've never really been to the city and I'm not even sure what I'm going to study! Seems stupid after all the work for exams and everything, but I suppose I've still plenty of time to decide . . .'

She interrupted him, leaning forward, her face very serious.

'You have to let the people become the grass of the city.'

It was almost as if she hadn't heard a word he had said. 'You were just the same, the two of you – two of a kind. Richard loved everything that ran and sang and leapt. He adored this place from the very first day and he'd have hated to leave it again. I think you'll feel lost at first, Cam; I really do. You may feel it was the maddest thing you ever did, and you'll miss the farm and all the things you love here so badly that it'll hurt. But you must just stick at it. As I said – let people become like the grass you miss. Then in the end you'll be all right.'

five

It was Sunday morning and they were driving down from Ardnish to Findale at a terrible rate of knots. The track between the house and the main road had seen better days, and occasionally Duncan swerved to avoid a particularly deep pothole, causing Robert, in the back, to groan as though in pain. They were on their way to the kirk, and as usual they had left the house with only a few minutes to spare.

'Have you remembered your collection, Cam? Well, where did you leave your jacket last night . . . Are we ready, then? Well, let's go.'

It was always the same, Cam thought gloomily. It was his mother who saw to it each Sunday that the family went to church. Even Robert, nineteen and broad as a hay bale, seemed to become fairly meek and submissive as she rushed around on a Sunday morning getting them all ready. She sat in the front now, in the passenger seat, checking her hair in the mirror and looking round to see that her sons were reasonably smart. Duncan swerved to avoid a sheep and Robert groaned again. He was in anything but a good mood, Cam realised.

In fact Robert had not had a good night at all. He had gone to the Arms and found a crowd there celebrating Sheila's twenty-first birthday. He wasn't all that keen to stay once he'd arrived, but Annie was there and he was desperate to know if there was any chance of winning her back. He had had a drink or two first, but had drunk fast so as to build up his courage, and then he had dared to draw up his chair beside Annie's and begun rather nervously to prattle on about music, and sheep, and second-hand cars . . .

'Leave me in peace,' Annie said finally, enunciating every word very clearly and coldly. He was taken aback and at a loss to know what to do next, so he returned to the bar after finishing his pint almost in one gulp, and ordered another. Stubbornly he went back to his chair beside Annie, and this time interrupted her talk with Sandy across the table to say: 'I'm going up to Fort William next week. You can come with me if you like.'

'Right, that's it.'

She turned and very calmly poured what was left in her glass into his lap. In a second he was stone cold sober; in a second too everyone there had seen what happened and loud laughter broke out around him. He did not linger for a moment after that. Miserable, humiliated, he went home, feeling he would never show his face in Findale again; far worse, Annie was lost to him for good.

Now he sat in the car wincing at every dip in the road. Worst of all was the fact that he well knew his young brother was gloating; Cam knew fine he had a hangover and was not going to let the occasion pass unnoticed.

'Feeling rough this morning?' he asked sweetly, leaning across to slap Robert on the shoulder. Rob slumped forward and turned venomous eyes on him.

Cam yawned and left his brother in peace. He let his mind wander to the night before, when he had returned from visiting Richard's mother; he had walked by the river, watching the water that splayed down from the falls in wide, white curves. He missed Richard so acutely that it was a physical pain; he wanted to cry out, to vent his sorrow and anger in some way. Again he asked why, why, why had he died? Why did others live to be old, when Richard, so full of life, had been taken so young? There was no justice in it at all! And here he was, next morning, on his way to worship the God who had seen fit to allow this to happen; there seemed to be no sense in it, no sense whatsoever.

The sun came down like a huge net on the glen as the steeple rose out of the trees, and they were there.

'The harvest is past, the summer is ended, and we are not saved. For the hurt of the daughter of my people am I hurt; I am black; astonishment hath taken hold on me. Is there no balm in Gilead; is there no physician there? Why then is not the health of my people recovered?'

The words of the prophet Jeremiah flowed sonorously through the church; the building was filled with grey-blue light, and Cam felt as if the words were a great tide on which he was being carried along . . . and always, inevitably, carried to the place where Richard had died. For him at that moment, the summer that had ended was Richard; that he had ended was a horrible, inescapable fact. Nothing in the world would bring him back, no doctor, nor all the great spring tides of the Atlantic. In his mind's eye he saw great thick snows coming down over Ardnish and Crossallan and Findale, huge clouds of wet snow on a land that had been drained of all the colours of autumn. He saw himself, as it were, standing at a window looking out at all these deaths – his grandparents', Richard's, even the loss of Rosie was a kind of death to him – and he looked around at the men and women in the pews, many of them quite elderly; one man's hand shook where it lay so thin and old beside his hymnbook. For many of them, the summer had gone. How many of them would be gone before he sat in this pew again? Even his own father was growing old – the eyes were the same as ever, but the face had changed; it was wintering. Soon Robert would have taken his place; the land would pass to him.

Cam felt frightened by all of it. He was suddenly reminded of the phantom horseman whom he had once seen in the larch wood, riding and riding without slowing his pace for a moment. Even as the minister was talking his heart began to speed in a kind of panic; it was like those nights long ago in childhood when his door was shut and the lights were out and he would begin to think of eternity. For ever and ever and ever and ever . . . fear would grip him and he would want to shut off the thoughts, but could not. Now it all washed over him again; guiltily he realised he hadn't heard a single word of what the minister had been saying.

Then normality returned as his father passed him a sweet; his whiskers tickled Cam's face as he pressed the mint into his palm. Once it had been his grandfather who had done that; now the custom had passed to Duncan. Cam felt almost as though his father had somehow heard his frightened heartbeat and had found a kindly way of wakening him from the panic. What a fool I am; why am I allowing this melancholy to take hold of me just now? He forced himself then to listen to the sermon.

The minister's voice was beautiful – an English accent which somehow had a calming effect upon him at this moment. The Reverend Francis Pearson. Cam remembered the parodies of that name at school assemblies; indeed he recalled the very first time the young minister had stood behind the lectern in the hall, facing two hundred children with hearts like ferrets, ready to pounce, ready to find and pierce the slightest chink in the minister's armour. But they had come away disappointed, able only to pick on his name as a kind of revenge, for he hadn't stuttered once; his voice, then as now, flowed strong and confident, as beautiful as the luminous green water of Avainban Bay.

Richard and he had become curious about the minister. There were all kinds of rumours going round the district about him, mainly because he was unmarried – that he had his eye on this girl or that, or that he had been seen with so-and-so. But the Reverend Frank remained alone in the manse for a few winters, and the gossip began gradually to fade away. Cam's mother maintained that he was a writer as well as a minister and spent much of his time at his books and articles, which was why he had not managed to do half of the visiting his predecessor had, among the elderly and sick. Rumours about him at school tended to be both wilder and nastier; but the one thing that was true was that he was regarded as an outsider and he seemed to have nobody in the community who could be called a close friend.

'Why don't we go to the manse?' Cam suggested to Richard in the attic one evening. It was autumn, with the early dark just beginning.

'Boring,' Richard replied; 'What would be the point?'

'Apples, that's what!' said Cam, taking the catapult from his friend so as to get his full attention. 'Anyway, why don't we spy on him? See what's going on – see if he really is a writer, or what. Come on, Ricky! We could stay at your house. It's Sunday tomorrow . . . '

For once, Richard had taken quite a lot of persuading, but in the end Cam wore him down and got his dad to take them into Findale in the car, dropping them off with their bags and boots. It was smirring with rain and almost completely dark by then, but once the red lights of the car had been swallowed they began running up Victoria Road towards the manse.

It was set in a large glebe and almost entirely surrounded with tall sentries of trees and gloomy, high walls. Richard heaved Cam over after him and they both landed with a dull thud on the other side.

'Apple trees over there!' Cam hissed, and they crept through the long grass as the branches of the trees were lashed by the storm above their heads. Cam glanced over his shoulder towards the big house across the lawn and saw a lemon light shining from one room. They sank into the bushes for a long moment to be sure nobody was coming and then prowled on until their eyes made out a tree groaning with fruit; they ran over, and leapt wildly until they managed to catch hold of a bough and ripped off half a dozen huge apples. Cam took a giant bite out of one but in a second his face curdled, and the apple fell from his grasp; he gave a kind of groan of disgust and spat, whispering to Richard: 'Ugh, they're cooking apples!' This rather took the edge off the entire adventure, but they had come this far and certainly didn't feel like turning back.

'Let's go up and see what the minister's doing,' Richard suggested, and they flowed up over the lawn, two black shadows in the vague silvery light of the evening. They reached a gravel path and tiptoed along it, hushing one another urgently when a heel snapped a twig or a step was too loud. Then they came into the lime glow from the open window and shrank down as low as possible, peering now at the man who was seated at his desk, clearly working on the last of his sermon. It was all so ordinary and somehow disappointing. Richard was all for going.

'I'm cold,' he grumbled. 'You promised we'd get back for nine and anyway I dunno what the point is . . . C'mon, Cam, let's go.'

'Just a second!' hissed Cam, beginning now to feel bolder. 'I'm going to give him a fright, just to see what he does.'

'Cam, you're crazy!' Richard hissed back. 'Anyway, how d'you mean?'

'Throw a pebble, of course.'

Richard was absolutely against the idea; Cam called him a chicken and at the same moment took a pebble and lobbed it so that it banged the glass. Richard lost his nerve and went shooting along the path like a frightened rabbit, while Frank Pearson dropped his pen, began rattling the bolts of the French window and looked outside.

Cam was still crouched on the ground with no idea of what to do next, when the French window opened and golden light spilled out over him as he looked up blindly into the minister's face. 'Cameron,' he said in surprised tones. (He had been up to Ardnish to visit the family and arrange with Morag Mackay about harvest thanksgivings, and knew the boys well enough.) On this occasion Cam was tongue-tied. He could have invented some kind of story but for once his lively imagination deserted him; he simply looked dumbly up at Frank Pearson, his mouth slightly open and his eyes blinking and blinking in the light.

The minister chuckled, relieved.

'Well, I'm glad it's only you,' he said mildly. 'I came out thinking an eagle had crashed into the window! You'd better come in for a mug of cocoa – it's a good time. Are you staying in the village tonight then?'

Ten minutes later, the Brennans rang up to apologise for their son's inexcusable behaviour and to ask that Cameron Mackay be sent along to the house as soon as possible. Frank Pearson seemed only amused by the situation and came back with cocoa as he had promised; the two of them then sat in front of a rather cheerless gas fire. Although the man was so friendly, Cam had so far managed only to mutter monosyllables.

'Ah, it's a good excuse for me to get away from my desk,' the minister said brightly. 'I never seem to have a minute's peace, you know. I've still got to prepare what I'm going to say to you lot on Monday morning. It's actually going to be a story I made up myself. You see, Cameron, I write books, mostly for children, so I can test you all at school with them – a bit like guinea pigs!'

Cam took a sip of cocoa and looked at the man again. A writer of children's stories! He dropped his guard and couldn't help but feel interest. He began to relax as the minister drew him out; he found himself telling all about his grandfather, and how he had always told them stories when they were small boys.

'Well,' the minister said at last, 'seeing you're so keen on stories you can listen to this one as a punishment! Then I'd better let you go to the Brennans or they'll wonder what on earth has happened to you. Anyway, the story goes something like this:

'There was once a man who lived in a very big city. He had a very fine house of his own and a good job as well. Every day he got up at five past eight and each evening he was home by twenty to six. The most precious thing he possessed was a little silver key. It locked his front door, it opened his office at work, and it unlocked his safe as well. One morning he got up as usual, went out on to the street and searched for the key. But there was nothing! Just the long metal chain to which the key had been attached. The man was bewildered. He looked down drains and he searched under flower pots, he emptied every pocket in a fever of anxiety and he went running up and down as if the moon had fallen from the sky. He would have asked his neighbours for help at that point but he didn't know any of them, and they just peered at him darkly when he tried to look in at their windows. But that was no use anyway because there was no one who had exactly the same key as himself. And it meant he was shut out of his house and his work as well, and he had no idea what in the world he was going to do. So he just wandered through the streets until dark, and then he crept miserably under a bridge and huddled there wrapped in his coat until morning.

'That's about the end of the story really, Cam!' said the minister. 'Not my most cheery one, I'm afraid. But can you perhaps guess something of what I'm trying to say in it?'

Cam just looked blank, so he continued: 'Well, it's like this – first, you can't just live for yourself all your life! Life is so much more than simply doing a job and having possessions. It's about finding God; he's the real key. D'you know where I got the idea? Well, it was the first year I was here in the village, and the house – and everything else – was still strange to me. I sat here by the fire one night and I must have fallen asleep and dreamed the whole thing. It was one of those dreams you're sure is real because you remember it so clearly.'

It was strange, thought Cam now, how often that odd little story had kept coming back into his mind over the years. In the end, the minister had not used it at assembly after all – maybe he was the only one ever to hear it, or maybe it had been put into a book? But he, Cam, had as it were carried it around like a strange stone he might have found on a beach and could never quite bring himself to chuck back into the water. Sometimes he would think of himself as the man who had lost the key; he saw himself running through the streets of Aberdeen not knowing a soul, and having no idea of how to get home. But he wasn't even sure he had a key to begin with . . .

The sermon was over and the sunlight had passed through the old church. There was a sound as of many leaves being blown across stone as the congregation turned up the final hymn in their hymnbooks. Robert staggered to his feet – more like an old man than a teenager, Cam thought unkindly – but a moment later, against his will, he felt a slight pang of pity for his brother. After all, Cam had lost Rosie and knew what it felt like, and Robert had been nuts about Annie. Women, he said to himself, are a difficult breed; I think I'd be better off staying clear of them. Staying single would mean a far less troublesome life.

But when Fiona Stewart smiled at him on the way out of church he forgot all of that pretty quickly. He'd never really bothered about her at school because she was so popular; still, a smile like that . . . Robert had managed to pass the minister without having to shake hands, but then it was Cam's turn.

'All the best for Aberdeen, Cameron!' Frank Pearson smiled as he pumped Cam's hand. 'And see you behave yourself. I've got any number of spies stationed there, you know!'

Cam thanked him warmly, and really meant it. Ever since Richard's death, and that last service which must surely have been one of the hardest ever, he'd believed in the man, even felt real affection for him. He had really seemed to understand how terrible it was for him to lose Richard. Maybe it went back even as far as the night of the apples, Cam thought; he wasn't sure. At any rate he tried to thank him sincerely at this moment; he even stayed longer than he needed to and talked a bit more while Fiona walked away, looking back to see if Cam was coming but then shrugging and giving up on him. He forgot about her almost at once; it didn't matter after all. But it mattered that he talked to this man who had been a good friend to him – the man who was still regarded as an incomer, who was still alone in the big old manse, and still, Cam felt, misunderstood years after he had first come to Findale. It mattered that he didn't go away from here without thanking him.

'I'll get back myself,' Cam said to his mother as he stood with the three of them beside the car. He had made up his mind what he was going to do.

'Och, Cam, you're missing a good dinner!' she lamented.

'Rob can have mine,' Cam said nastily, and got a crocodile's grimace from his brother.

Now it was time to be on his own. He wanted to go down to the shore, maybe over to Shuan. The days were going past so quickly; I have to be ready, I have to be at peace with myself. And then aloud:

'I'll not be all that long. It's just that I have something I must do.'

His mother still stood by the car, reluctant to give up.

'Let him go, Morag,' said his father, easing himself into the driving seat. 'But remember, I'm not coming to find you!' he added in mock anger as he started the engine.

Cam stood still until they had gone out of sight, hands in the pockets of his jacket as the wind came at him, tossing the wide branches above his head. The remaining groups were walking away down the sandy track; he could hear their voices and the sudden plumes of laughter although he could make out none of their words. The minister must have gone back into the church again so the place was empty, and Cam was glad. He ran down the shore road through Findale and got on to the path that would take him most directly on to Shuan. With any luck the tide would still be far out and there would be time enough.

Far above his head he heard a buzzard mewing; he stopped at last to search for it, shielding his eyes from the glare of the sunlight. Ah yes, there it was far above, streaming through clouds like a strong branch, circle after circle. It could see the whole of the land – moor, settlement, field, sea, all of them at once. For a second he felt a stab of envy; he could see only one part at a time; he could not put them together. And then he realised how different those he had been thinking so much about were from each other – his grandfather, Rosie, Richard. They were all such different pieces and he did not know how to fit them together. He thought once more of the minister's key; he found himself wishing that he possessed some key that might have solved the puzzle, brought all the broken pieces together to make them one.

He lost sight of the buzzard and turned away, taking the steep path that led to the sea.

six

Far ahead of him, Cam could see the outline of Shuan Island. At low tide it was no island at all; a narrow strip of pearl sand curved out to it from the mainland. But where he stood, the coast was still rocky, indented here and there by tiny cuts of bays, most of it overshadowed by great black buttresses against which the sea came in loud booms. He was looking all the time for Rockdove Cave, a tiny place at the bottom of a deep gully to which there was only one frail, green strip of a path. He knew he had to keep his eyes open for the great quartz boulder, and for the glen on the far side – there it was now! He looked away down and saw the place where Richard and he had gone so often.

I'm wearing all the wrong gear for this, he thought; if I fell here they wouldn't find me for fifty years! The grass was wet and the soles of his shoes smooth – absolutely useless for walking – but he started down all the same, gingerly enough, hanging on to rough rock noses and bits of ledges so as not to rely too much on his feet. Gulls screamed over his head; guillemots and razor-bills went wheeling away to their ledges on the cliffs. Out to sea, in the tiny gap between rock buttresses, Cam saw the long outstretched necks of two cormorants flying low over the water.

Drops of crystal water seemed to be dripping from all the rocks. The noise of the sea was now muffled by a huge rock which sheltered Rockdove Cave, so that he stood in a strange kind of chamber with basalt walls rising sheer on every side, and only a single window of sky above. For a second he panicked, fearing that perhaps his shoes would be too slippery to allow him to climb back to the top again; then he realised he was being foolish, and the ascent was nothing like as hard as it looked.

He began to clamber over the rocks to the narrow strip of beach and the black porthole that was the entrance to the cave. For a second he stopped and just stared at the place, not sure whether he had even been back here since Richard's death. The echoes of our voices must surely be in every rock, he thought; hour after hour, summer after summer they had been here. A vein of sunlight burst through forbidding skies and flooded over the waves so that he turned round, shielding his eyes, suddenly finding his thick wool sweater too hot.

All of a sudden he decided to do something mad, something so mad that he would never tell anybody about it. Without any further thought he began tearing off his clothes, throwing them down on the stones at the top of the beach. He had no trunks and no towel, but if he stopped to think he wouldn't do it at all, and he knew all at once that it was simply something he had to do. Straight out into that searingly cold water, his arms hugging his chest, stride after stride until the grey Atlantic was up above his knees; and then he was biting his lips so as not to cry out with the sheer pain of that cold. He glanced in sudden fear around the tops of the promontories, half expecting to see someone watching, imagining for a moment with a brief flicker of amusement what his mother would say if she were there . . .

'Cam, are you out of your mind? You'll catch your death of cold!'

But he was doing it for his own reasons, which probably neither she nor anyone else would understand; he was doing it in some way to remember Richard. In the end the water was up to his chest and he was breathing fast, feeling the knives of pain that still drove through his thighs and hands. His feet were numb now so that he felt he was staggering on rather as a penguin might have done; the water reached his shoulders and he began to splash about, and then lay on his back and kicked high spray with his feet. He turned and put his whole face under the water, looking about him at the luminous green world, and he scrubbed himself, almost as if he were peeling away a dead skin, an old layer of time, and a past that was gone for ever. Not so as to forget, but that the pain which lingered in his very bones might somehow be healed.

At last he could bear it no longer and he clambered out, slipping on the wet stones and streaming water, shivering in the chill of the wind. He crouched in the entrance of the cave and wished he had had the wit to bring matches, for there was any amount of driftwood for a fire scattered all around on the beach. He dashed about for a while letting the wind dry him, and then, though still damp, struggled into his clothes.

Shivering, he moved deeper into the cave and smelled the musty darkness, the rank smell of pigeons' droppings. He remembered vividly the time Richard and he had thundered down from the ridge above and Richard had blundered into the cave, terrifying a scattering of birds that flapped out from the blackness; today there were no birds, just thick, dark emptiness stretching for some twenty or thirty feet. But he was out of reach of the wind and he settled himself there, sifting memories from the darkness like uncut gems, holding them as it were to the light.

The darkness reminded him of Hallowe'en – an October night that smelled of bonfires, decaying leaves and wet grass. He remembered the sense of excitement there had always been as the great day approached; bonfires were finished off, apples picked, parties arranged.

He began to smile as he remembered the year his parents had had the party up at Ardnish – to smile, but at the same time to cringe. Richard had been there, of course; it was a couple of years after the Brennans had come to live in Findale. A good number of his parents' friends had been there, and it was the time that Rob had just started going out with Annie, so her parents were there to meet the Mackays for the first time.

The bonfire had been lit down at the bottom of the lower field and a mighty stack it had been too, since his father had had to cut down a rotten old tree and great chunks of it were piled among the branches. There was hot punch in the kitchen for the grown-ups, and hot orange and toffee apples for the children; Cam remembered how the two of them had run about here and there, shouting and laughing, nearly out of their minds with excitement.

He recalled running up to the larch wood just to get a good view of everything. The fire had been lit by his father and was a tiny orange ball in the gathering darkness; up above, the stars were sparkling like fires themselves. Maybe that's what they were, Cam used to think, great fires beside which giants crouched in the skies, watching the earth. On a night like that, dark things might happen, magic and secret things, beyond explanation. He shivered and looked at the grey shadow of the rocks up in the top field and wondered again how they had come there. The world was not explained; the teachers at school had not explained it. To him it was strange and wonderful, filled with the most intriguing secrets.

All of this was before the guests had begun to arrive. The hours had gone by like tortoises, but at long last people started to come. He left his outpost and went down to the house; the first sparklers splintered silver in the hands of children; a group had gathered beside the bonfire, talking and laughing. A number of older children from Findale trooped up to Ardnish, all dressed in weird outfits and with swinging turnip lanterns; they sang two verses of a song, forgot the rest, and were rewarded with nuts, apples and cake. Then Richard arrived.

'You have to see the den – I finished it today!' Cam had shouted excitedly, dragging Richard away at high speed up to the larch wood. They reached the trees and then crouched to enter a low tunnel, all covered with branches which Cam had taken from the tree his father had felled; this led through to a domed cell hidden at the back of one of the larches. He was as proud as if he had personally built St Paul's Cathedral. Richard had been suitably impressed, but was cold.

'Listen!' Cam said then, getting up suddenly in excitement from where he was crouching, 'Why don't we sneak back and get a bottle of wine from the cellar? That would warm us up all right. My mum's been using it for making the punch. We could come back here and make a fire – it'll be hours yet till the fireworks start!'

Richard had not been too sure. 'They'll kill us if they find out!' he said.

But Cam was up and on his way. 'There'll never be a chance like this again,' he shouted as he ran down the hill. 'Come on, it's a brilliant idea!'

They got down to the cellar and Cam grabbed a bottle. Who should they meet just as they were coming out of the basement door but Robert, involved in a long kiss with Annie. For once he was not interested in Cam, and the two boys slunk away to the wood and dived gratefully into the den. They set about making a fire, using nearly a boxful of matches before it was lit. Then they poured themselves a couple of glassfuls, clinked them in mid-air, and drank.

'Don't notice any effect,' said Richard in disappointed tones after a few minutes, taking another slug in case he had missed something. Cam remembered trying to sound professional.

'Hm, not bad,' he had pronounced after a critical sip. 'Pour me some more; this is good stuff,' he added later. The bottle seemed to last an unbelievably short time.

All of a sudden they heard a terrific bang and the two of them jumped like startled rabbits as a shower of red and purple sprayed the sky.

'Help, the fireworks!' Richard breathed in horror; Cam started to his feet, but the ground came up to meet him and he fell in a heap. The two of them began to giggle uncontrollably; then Richard got to his feet more cautiously and very gingerly the two of them started down the hill, trying hard not to stagger. The harder they tried, the worse they got.

The whole crowd was arranged in a semi-circle on one side of the bonfire whilst out in the stubble crouched Duncan Mackay, setting up a line of fireworks. Head after head turned as the two zombies tripped and staggered their way towards the fire. Rob stepped out from the rest, holding Annie's hand, leaning forward to make sure it really was his brother. Then, 'You're drunk!' he said in a loud voice; every head turned, and suddenly somebody gave a loud chuckle, and the whole lot of them started to laugh. His father didn't bother to light the next firework; he turned round to see what was going on and saw the two swaying Hallowe'en ghosts.

Cam laughed to himself now as he crouched in Rockdove Cave. He recalled the many lectures the two of them had been given on the dangers of alcohol, and how Richard had been banned from Ardnish for long enough afterwards. They were never allowed to forget the episode, he thought ruefully; whenever people talked about Hallowe'en or bonfires, you could be sure this was the first thing they'd mention. And he and Richard were never allowed anywhere near the cellar again.

'Och, we were good for them!' he found himself wanting to say aloud to an invisible Richard before the familiar stab, the awful sinking feeling, came once more. How was it that he could still forget, still imagine they were doing something together? It was bad enough in dreams, when his presence would be so vivid . . . Then he shook himself mentally. Why am I tormenting myself, going over all this? What does it matter – these are only childish pranks which mean nothing to anyone else? Why don't I just go, get on with the next part of my life, be at peace within myself? And then he seemed to answer his own question: it does matter. Richard was wound tightly round the first part of my life; I can't just go away as if he'd never existed.

And then, all of a sudden, a darkness fell upon him and he felt desperate to get away from the place; it was almost as though Richard's dead body had been carried on the water into the little cove. The shadow of death fell like a folded kestrel, and Cam felt fear, real fear as he began to scramble up and away, back over the slippery stones, up and up until he had climbed the steep face safely and was standing breathless on the ridge, shuddering as he stared back down into the cove. Had it been his own imagination? If only he hadn't been born with such a vivid one, as his father so often told him! Or had something really come at that moment, something dark and terrible?

He shivered and broke away over the headland, letting the wind that drove up bitter cold from the sea blow away the blackness of his spirit. He knew he was going to have to hurry if he was going to reach Shuan before the tide changed and the sands were cut off from the mainland. It would take him a good half-hour to get up that far and he was going quickly, pounding along the jagged ridge that extended along the length of the coast, wishing he had something more suitable on his feet than his best shoes. He was suddenly very hungry and thought longingly of the good Sunday roast his mother would have served by now; he searched his pockets but found nothing – not even a scrap of chocolate.

It was as he came over another bit of ground and turned inland for a moment that he caught sight of the dragonfly. He stood stock still, forgetting his hurry, wide-eyed with amazement. Often enough he had seen dragonflies around hill lochs in the middle of summer, looking for all the world like tiny helicopters, nudging the reeds and droning low over the surface of the water. But never before had he seen one so close, landed motionless on a clump of dead heather. Carefully Cam leaned forward, making hardly a sound as he tried not to breathe at that moment; every second he expected the beautiful creature to fly away, but to his surprise it remained, until he was right over it and had his hand out, trembling, to allow it to clamber aboard. It was like the bar of a brooch, a tropical blue, kingfisher blue even; as it moved up on to his finger he saw that the four wings were made out of hundreds of tiny panes, all of them shining like the paper of Chinese lanterns.

What a tale he could have invented, if Richard had been here! They used to bounce ideas off one another, sometimes making up new games, sometimes telling a story, hungry at the end for encouragement or praise, awarding marks on a carefully constructed scale. Cam sat down gently on the heather; the dragonfly still clung to his hand.

'I will make up a story!' he said aloud. 'It'll be about you, and I'll try to think of some of the things I know Richard would have thought of.' He let his mind wander, spinning out ideas in a hundred directions, like a spider's web, to trap mad thoughts.

'All right. There was once a young boy who was kept prisoner by Fan, the horrible king of the underworld.' Richard had invented Fan; there was even a cave near Avainban Bay which had been identified as the entrance to Fan's lair. 'He was miserable the whole time; he missed the sun, he missed the colours of flowers and leaves and ferns and seashells. One day he felt he couldn't bear it any longer. He went and begged Fan on his knees to let him out for just one day so that he could see the spring again. Amazingly, Fan finally agreed. The boy ran as fast as he could, up and up through all the tunnels and chambers of the underworld, until at last he came up into the early morning sunshine. The sun was just coming up over the sea and everywhere he looked, green things were beginning to grow after the long hard winter.

'The wee boy went running around like mad, running and laughing in the sunshine, determined to see as much of the beauty of spring as he possibly could. He went on drinking it all in and the day passed far too quickly; suddenly he realised the sun was starting to go dark in the sky and it wouldn't be long before the night came. He knew with a sinking heart that he had to go back to Fan's horrible kingdom but he wanted to take something with him, just one special thing, so that he would never forget that wonderful day. Away over in the west where the sun was about to set there was the most beautiful bit of blue sky and the boy stretched up on his tiptoes, took enough to fill his hand, and put it safe in his pocket. Then he ran the whole way back down into Fan's prison.

'He thought and thought about what he should make. And in the end, he took the piece of sky and smoothed it in his hands until it was long and thin. Then he got a bit of shiny metal from the cave where he was kept and he hammered it out until it was thinner and lighter than a feather. He shaped all the wee bits for hours and hours until he was quite satisfied with them and then, very, very carefully, he put them on to the piece of sky and fitted them exactly. Then he held what he had made gently in his hands and blew softly. Sure enough the creature took off into the air and went humming round his head. The boy was absolutely thrilled; he jumped and sang for sheer happiness.

'But then Fan came in to see what the noise was all about and he shrieked in terror; he couldn't stand anything made of light. He covered his eyes and began to make strange whimpering noises whenever the bright creature came near him; it began to fly round and round his head, and gradually Fan just crumpled into a ball, and he seemed to melt away. And in the end there was nothing left of him at all.

'The boy could hardly contain his joy; he called to the creature and it came and landed on his hand. He wanted then to give it a name, but he found he had forgotten what things in the real world were called, and the only thing he could think of was that there were huge fiery beasts at the centre of the earth which kept the ovens of Fan's kingdom alight. So he decided he would call the little creature a dragonfly, and he carried it all the way up to the top of the world before setting it free.'

Cam found himself unconsciously looking over at the next tussock, almost believing Richard was sitting there listening to every word, eyes narrowed in judgement; Cam imagined him rocking gently back and forth as he had done a hundred times, the smallest edge of a smile on his lips as he grudgingly nodded: 'Not bad, not bad.'

The dragonfly suddenly lifted off from Cam's hand and thrummed away through the air till it was lost to view. He found himself wondering whether it had really been there; it was as if he might have imagined the whole thing.

Now he realised how much time he had wasted; he must get down to the beach at Shuan and across to the island without any more delay. He would be mad at himself if he had missed the tide now; he had only a few days left and most of his stuff was still waiting to be packed. All his time was precious.

Cam remembered how Fleet used to cover this ground with the two of them – for all the world, he thought, like a black and white waterfall as she flowed through the heather effortlessly ahead of them. He recalled clearly the only time they had lost her; it was when she had decided to go off and roll in a dead sheep on one of the ledges high above Avainban. What a stink there had been! Richard and he could hardly bear it; they had had to carry her to the first rock pool they could find and dump her in it to get rid of the worst of it. Even after that, though, she wasn't exactly popular when they took her home.

As Cam looked across the last headland he could clearly see the long white spar of land that curled out to Shuan. There was maybe an hour or so left before the waves came over the narrow peninsula and covered it again. Nobody now lived on the island; all that remained of the only house was a grey hump of rubble and an area of grass that might once have been a field. Richard and he used to declare that they would build a cottage there one day; when their talk grew wild and bold they would dream of all kinds of things – they'd have a boat to explore the coast; a diving bell to find the wreck of the Spanish galleon; a summer house of their very own on Shuan. They knew every inch of the island; they had made maps of it over and over again; they would put in all the place names they invented from each new visit. In Cam's eyes, Richard's names were always better than his; he recalled how he had often felt he stood in his friend's shadow and had, in a sense, needed to fight to be an equal. But then it was also true that he, Cam, had been the bolder and stronger of the two. There was nothing he wouldn't jump off, or be the first to creep in and explore.

He came down to the shore and five oystercatchers took off, screeching at him in panic. Away in the north he could see the dim outline of the hills of Rum and Eigg; fantasy peaks they were, when the clouds were thick and grim as that one on the horizon. His nerve nearly failed him now, but as he looked across the strip of sand towards Shuan he saw the shadow of a boy with straw-blond hair, calling and waving to him, bringing him across.

'Come on, Cam! The tide's nearly turning, and there's starfish and flounders everywhere . . . '

seven

Cam started across over the ribbed patterns of the sand, and then bent down and took off his shoes and socks so that he could splash through the pale water. The whole of his view was taken up by Shuan now – the red-gold rocks that ringed its outer limits and the main dome of darker stone that made up the centre. Around that hill, in little glens and coves, were buried stories. They were like fossils, different ages, the memories of long summers. He wanted so desperately now to reach the place that his heart began hammering in his chest. Once he had been round the island in a boat, but that was all; when Richard died, a book had, as it were, been closed, a book that he could hardly bear to read again. He had never come back. Yet here he was again; now it seemed to him that he longed for this special place with all his heart, and that it did not matter what happened, just as long as he got across to Shuan again.

Looking all around, it seemed that there were signs of storm everywhere; yet, in the very eye of it, brightness burst upon the water so clear and white that it almost hurt his eyes as it was reflected. The wind rushed over the shallow pools at the edges of the sand-strip, ruffling them and changing their colours, yet Cam felt no cold at all. He kept to the sandy pathway, hardly making a sound as (from time to time) he drove his feet through the grey pools. There were sudden booms of sand as flounders, almost the very colour of the sand, swept out into the safety of the deeper water. There were shoals of minute sand-eels too, colourless mini-snakes swaying together in their hundreds, thousands, turning like perfectly trained soldiers to surge away into a new place. He marched for a time in step with a green crab as it thudded its way out to Shuan. Around him and above him countless white birds screeched continuously – gulls, terns and shearwaters. Further out at the northern end of the island he saw other birds rising into the air and crashing straight down like white bombers; as they hit the sea, great plumes of spray rose up, tall geysers of water. He smiled to himself as he realised there must be a good shoal of fish off the island to attract such a multitude of gannets.

In the end he got over to the island. The strip of sand now curled round wide to the left, making a long arch of beach on which there were tidemarks of miniature shells – scallops, periwinkles and cowries. But Cam did not stop there, much as he loved to pick up tiny, perfect specimens, particularly of cowries, his favourites; instead he walked on and up among the huge boulders of rock that were like giants' dice, stones that had obviously once rolled down from the slopes of Cruachan, the highest hill on Shuan. In among those rocks, he recalled, that's where we found the treasure!

He couldn't remember now whether it had been early spring or late autumn. At any rate, he knew it had been a fierce day, with the wind hurling about their heads and the rain seeming to come from every direction into their faces. Richard and he had decided to go over to the island because of the high seas there had been in the last few days. Now and again they would find the oddest things washed up on the beaches – a broomstick, a globe, even a coconut. And they were determined to go to Smugglers' Cave.

'Now be careful you two, when you're going over to Shuan,' Duncan Mackay warned them as he laboured with the bales of hay. 'The waves are as high as a horse; it's a wicked day.'

The two of them made their way down to the beach and across like the wind, but as they rushed up among the great shining black boulders Richard, who was ahead of Cam, stopped and pointed down to the edge of the sand.

'Tea bags!' he said then in disgust. 'A whole load of them must've been washed up – look.' He clambered back down, hands deep in the pockets of his anorak as it was so cold and wet. It was hardly worth looking through really, just a burst-open sack it seemed, containing nothing more valuable than tea. Cam was kicking over the sodden heap when all of a sudden he turned something up and jabbed at it like a gannet.

'Ricky!' he shouted, squatting down among the mess of bags. Richard came over at once, his eyes searching through the driving rain to see what Cam was holding. It was a tiny cotton bag, for all the world like just another tea bag, only whiter. Around the four sides it had been precisely sewn up. And inside there were tiny stones.

Cam allowed his friend to hold the bag, passing it over with hands that trembled.

'Maybe it's diamonds,' he breathed as he turned his wet face up to Richard.

'Maybe it's drugs,' Richard said as he examined the minute package. He was unbelievably jealous that it had been Cam who found the treasure. And then: 'Let's open it and see.'

'No!' Cam nearly ripped the precious cotton bag from his grasp. 'No! I want to wait till we get home!'

They went round to the cave after that, but their hearts weren't in it any longer. Cam kept turning the bag in his hands and wondering, wondering all the time. They were stones all right, but what kind of stones? It was almost more exciting not knowing, just hearing them patter over one another as he tipped the bag back and forward between his fingers. It was like a strange pillow, this tiny bag that had floated over the waves.

'Tea comes from Sri Lanka,' Richard mused as they sat later, hunched inside the cave, while the rain continued to come down in sheets outside. 'There are lots of gemstones there, my dad says – sapphires and topazes, emeralds too. Maybe they were a gift to somebody, the person who was getting the tea? Maybe they were a kind of secret sign that something was going to happen, a deal between mafia agents . . . '

Cam let Richard go on using his ever-fertile imagination; at the moment he didn't really care all that much about the story; one day it would perhaps become more important than the stones, but not yet, not yet. All he wanted to know was what they were, for this was his treasure, the first real treasure he had ever found.

'Let's go home,' he said suddenly and stood up to go.

Even now the early darkness was beginning and as they crossed the spit of sand, the world seemed grey and dead around them. They plodded along like a couple of hedgehogs, withdrawn into their anoraks as they splashed back the long miles to Ardnish. But Cam was far away in his own inner kingdom; a proud drum beat in his heart. Tight under white knuckles he clutched the precious cotton bag.

Now, years later, he looked down once more at the place where he had found it. There was nothing left of the consignment of tea, nor of the sack which had contained it. He couldn't avoid the thought that came to him – Richard was gone as well. And he would have given all the treasure in the world to bring him back.

The stones had turned out to be opals. Tiny things they were, and milky, but with a strange reddish hue in the heart of each. What mattered to him was that he had found them; they were treasure.

Cam started up now from the beach, and soon reached the bottom of the hill. The path was scarcely visible among the great mauve clumps of heather, but he did not hesitate and climbed quickly; after about a hundred feet he was warm, and his breath was coming quickly; as he rose on to the shoulder of Cruachan the breeze began to cool his face and hands. An occasional startled grouse exploded near him out of the heather. On and on he climbed until at last he stood panting on the summit. The sunlight fell in an orange-gold path over the sea; he looked away out as far as his eyes could reach, and there was nothing, no sign of a ship, no land. Nothing between here and New York, and it felt awesome, terrible, huge and wonderful all at the same time. Then he looked down to the western shores of Shuan and to the tiny secret beach of Camas and his eyes began to burn with unshed tears; and, despite himself, the tears came and he rubbed them away angrily, even although there was nobody to see him.

Last June it had happened, at the very height of the summer. The days were so long that they seemed to run into one another; the nights were blue and filled with the sound of the curlews and the breathing of the sea. The holidays had just begun, and he and Richard had planned out each day months before; it seemed as if they had been wishing and dreaming ever since Christmas. That particular day was no different; Ardnish looked and sounded just the same; all the windows of the house were open and there was sand on the kitchen floor.

At six in the morning a stone cracked against Cam's bedroom window. He had had a bad dream, though he couldn't now recall what it had been about, and his head was heavy after too many long, sun-filled days. And it was Saturday. After a few moments he stumbled out of bed, still more than half asleep, and swam through the blue shadows of his room to open the curtains; a blast of steely light caught his eyes. He shoved the window open and, half-blind, peered down at Richard.

'I'm going over to Shuan, to Camas! It's perfect for swimming, Cam!'

Cam groaned. 'Not yet!' He ran his hands through his hair. 'It's early and I want to sleep!'

'Lazy old sheep!' Richard taunted. 'C'mon,' he begged. 'It'll be brilliant; once you're up you'll not feel tired. You promised, Cam, remember!'

'I'll be over later,' Cam said finally and started lowering the window; he crept back to bed, already feeling a bit guilty. He had said yesterday that he wanted to go over to Shuan early in the morning to swim. It took him longer than usual to get back to sleep; Robert was crashing about in the next room and then in loud conversation with his father. At last silence descended and he slept without dreaming, dead to the world.

In no time, it seemed, his mother was shaking him and calling his name, and at first he thought he was dreaming.

'Come downstairs,' she was saying. 'Come down right away!' And he heard her crying; he could hardly remember such a time, except for once when Rob had been brought home by the police . . .

His head seemed to be full of cotton wool and he staggered about trying to find his clothes; he saw it was after twelve and could hardly believe it. He got on a shirt and trousers, and raced down the stairs; ever after, he could remember how his stomach had been churning with fear, and the awful taste in his mouth. Always, at the thought of that terrible morning, the sickness returned, and the memory of stark fear. In the kitchen were his mother and father; they were hunched over the table, their arms folded as though their stomachs hurt. The room was filled with blue light and birdsong and warmth, but in the atmosphere was something of doom.

'What is it, what's wrong?' he asked, thinking first that he had done something dreadfully wrong. But they told him that Richard was dead.

Attie Duncan, a fisherman from a house near Findale, had been out that morning laying creels off Shuan, when he had seen something bumping the rocks beside Camas beach, and found the body. It had been about ten in the morning.

After that everything was confusion, a kind of haze in Cam's mind. He remembered how he had just gone on staring and blinking, saying nothing, feeling as though the room was swaying about him. He did not break down. His parents held him; even Rob's hand was there, but they were all distant; he seemed to see and hear them through blue water. It was like having a fever; it reminded him of times when he had been ill as a child and the pillow would seem to bury him and the ceiling was huge and far away. It was as if he had been wrapped in cotton wool and he did not know how to get away from it.

After that, the days seemed to run into each other like the carriages of a crashed train. He did not go out; he was stranded in his own small world, as if he too had drowned and would never come back to life again. But five days afterwards, he went downstairs when everyone else was out, and there, sitting on the table, was a photograph of Richard and himself, taken by Mr Brennan the previous winter. When he saw it his eyes welled with tears; a stone wall cracked within him and he realised, he understood, he knew what had happened. He cried as though his heart would break, until he was too tired to cry any more. And guilt ate at him; he had failed to go with Richard as he had promised, and the awful thought came to him that perhaps, if he had gone, it would never have happened at all. When he had stopped crying he went outside, trembling and weak as an invalid, but he could not get away from the awful truth; the face of Richard was in everything he saw.

Fifteen months had gone by and now he looked down on Camas. Never again would he swim at that place which had been specially theirs; it just was not possible.

Nobody ever really understood why Richard had drowned. A blue, still morning with almost no wind, but little ridges of waves coming in to the shore, gentle and luminous. Perhaps, they thought, he had tried to swim out to the cluster of rocks away over to the west of Camas, and had been taken by a sudden cramp. Perhaps he had lost his footing when clambering over the outer rocky shore, and had fallen and injured his skull, for there had been a wound to his head, a deep cut at the base of his neck.

In the weeks and months that followed, speculation went on and on; there were new articles in the local paper following the inquest; there was always talk in Findale. Sometimes a well of anger would rise in Cam; none of this mattered, for nothing would bring Richard back from death. The Brennans shut themselves up in their own world, and did not come out until the reporters had grown tired of the case and had found a new story to dismember. Only when the winter came at last, and with it the snow, did it seem to Cam that something was washed away; the first colours came back with the spring.

It shocked Cam after that how quickly he began to forget. He would be in the middle of doing something, carried away, when all of a sudden his face would be slapped by guilt. He felt it was a kind of betrayal. In time, though, even that passed; it was simply a fact that his world was changing, and it was no longer one that had known Richard. New experiences came; soon he would be sitting his last exams, soon he would be away at university. In a way, Richard was now younger than himself. He was growing away from him and could no longer be part of the same world.

Nonetheless, Cam felt Richard's presence strongly on such a day. Here, in this landscape they were equals, and so it would always be. This place they had shared completely, and if Cam felt him to be anywhere it was surely here – in the clear water, in the caves, on the moors. Sometimes he did not know which was worse – to forget, or to remember: both had their cost, both hurt. He had not come back to Shuan since that day in early summer last year; until now he could not face it. Even now he was not sure whether he had the strength to remain. While he had been climbing he had promised himself he would go down to Camas and the cave, but now he did not feel he could, not yet. He despised himself for his weakness, but it was no good; in the end he turned away and began the fast descent to the shore as the tide was turning, and only an hour remained until the sea would cover the path again.

He thought of the weird dreams which had begun to plague him in the weeks after Richard's death; as he remembered, cold fingers of fear descended his back. The minister had visited Ardnish several times to talk to him; he had listened with understanding to Cam's fears, had heard of the deep guilt he felt through having failed to go with Richard on that morning. Although it helped to talk of the sickness that was deep in his spirit, his head was still full of thoughts and imaginings, and for a long time the dreams still came.

For some reason they were not of Camas itself, but rather of the other side, the gap between Shuan and the mainland. Always the land on both shores was very high and forbidding, like the shoulders of giants. It always seemed to be twilight, unclear and full of dark shadows. Each time he, Cam, appeared to be waiting right at the edge of the shore as a strange boat carved its way through the water towards him. It was a large craft, with a metal gangway descending into the water as the boat drew closer. There on the deck stood a single figure, a man with his legs planted wide and his hands on his hips. He looked straight at Cam and his eyes shone white, like strange dead moons in a night sky.

In this recurrent dream, Cam would always wake up before the boat came to land. All the same the dream scared him; on one occasion, he remembered, he was strongly tempted to go through the house to his parents, but he didn't go, terrified that Robert might find out or his father and mother think him silly. He was not as close to them as he had once been; he felt he did not know them so well. But in the end the dreams passed and did not return. And Frank Pearson came for a last time to Ardnish to talk to him.

He wondered how it would be in the future. The sand between Shuan and Avainban was growing less and less as he walked across, and no doubt it would be just the same with all the things he remembered; bit by bit they would be covered. The time would come when he would struggle to think of Richard's face, or to remember the way he laughed; the thousands of words, the stories they had shared, would fail and become only the bones of things, nothing more than names. But still there was a sense in which Richard would be with him for ever! Somewhere deep inside him a certain special feeling was aroused when his name was mentioned, an inexplicable sensation that would not, he felt, ever die or diminish but which was always there, strong as the scent of bog myrtle over a moorland, quick as the taste of salt from a high-kicked wave of the sea.

Soon, dark would come. As Cam reached the top of the ridge on the far side, he caught sight of the bar of light – like a bar brooch shining gold – that was Findale. It was a long walk yet, but he did not mind. In a way he did not really want it to end at all, not, at least, until all the tangled threads had been brought together in his mind, and he felt he had made some kind of sense of them.

The darkness fell as a weight across his shoulders. Time frightened him these days; he was conscious as never before of its passing, of so many journeys and changes, of his own powerlessness; he had reached a landmark, the end of the first part of his life. A whole new era lay ahead. As he walked back to Ardnish with the rain now falling spearlike against his face, he felt in a strange way that Richard was somehow to be envied. It had only been in the last year, the year since he died, that Cam had felt older, more threatened, almost as if a load had been placed on his back. The load comprised many things to do with responsibility; before, he had never given a second thought to danger, the passing of time, or the possibility of death. It was as if he knew their names, but they were far too remote to be of any consequence to him. Then, before the end of that summer, Richard had died, and his perspective had suddenly had to change; now he could no longer run away from reality. Once again the enormity of it all struck Cam. Richard had gone out barefoot and carefree in the wild beauty of that summer morning, and had run without thinking, without fear of danger, into the sea. But in a strange and terrible way, Cam felt, he had perhaps died in time, he had died before it was too late.

He stood stock still as this thought, which he scarcely understood himself, came to him; he was on the edge of a sharp ridge, looking down on the white anger of the sea as it rose in storm; he could look inland from here too, out over the rough pasture land towards Ardnish, with all its memories of his grandfather. Maybe these thoughts were mad; maybe they were his own way of accepting Richard's death without becoming twisted and bitter in the face of such terrible loss. He did not know. He was tired of trying to make sense of it all, tired of trying to square so many circles . . .

All at once, the strange story the minister had told him all those years ago, about the man who lost his key, came into his head. Frank Pearson had said that God was the real key, that everything else fell into place when he was at the centre of one's life. Maybe he was right; he would have to think more about it. But not now; the emotions of the day had exhausted him. The weather was worsening all the time. As he steered his way home through driving rain and wind in the gathering darkness, he felt for all the world like a battered ship heading for port, knocked off course from time to time by sudden big waves.

He would not think any more, he decided. His father had always told him he took life far too seriously; he was aware that this was true, but neither knew how to change, nor really wanted to. But perhaps he should try to do what his father said – let time shed the old skin and make him a new one.

At last he swam into the warmth of the lights and shivered gratefully as he thudded the mud from his boots. He opened the back door and stepped inside. There was no one in the kitchen; he walked across and opened the far door; from the other end of the house there came the sound of singing and a fiddle. Wet through as he was, he slushed through the house in his soaking clothes and opened the door of the sitting-room. Half a dozen faces lit up with smiles.

'Welcome home at last, Cam!' It was his good friend Danny, the postman. 'We just decided on the spur of the moment to come and give you a bit of a ceilidh, boy, to send you on your way!'

The tiredness seemed to leave him in an instant; the warmth of the fire reached him, and burned his freezing cheeks.

'Great!' he said. 'Just give me a few minutes to change and I'll be with you!'

He was glad; he was really glad. They would never know how much it meant to him.

eight

The music went on until three in the morning; it seemed to go on to a timeless place where all that mattered were the songs themselves, and the singing. When the last of his friends had gone Cam went outside to still his racing thoughts. The stars were glittering like cut gemstones on the dark back-cloth of the sky; there was no moon now, but the skies were intensely bright. He stood there in silence for a long time; he didn't even have a sweater on, but just went on standing there by the back door, getting his breath back, getting his balance back, feeling almost as if it was music and not blood that coursed in his veins. Into the songs he had poured all his despair over Richard; the best songs were the sad ones, he always felt. But at the same time he was aware of having also poured into them the celebration, the thanksgiving. In the end he began to realise that he had ceased striving to make sense of it all; deep inside of him there were at last the beginnings of peace.

'Are you going to bed now?'

He turned abruptly round and saw Robert standing there in the kitchen, a black expression on his face. He had left the ceilidh hours before.

'Some of us have to work tomorrow, you know,' he added sourly.

Already he had turned away and Cam couldn't think of an answer. It had always been the same, ever since he was a child; when anyone came out with some accusation, no matter whether it was true or utterly false, he could never manage to think in time. The words would haunt him for ages afterwards and by then he would have a hundred answers flying like bees around his head; but it was too late, it was always too late.

'You'll be glad to know they're all gone now,' he wanted to hurl the words indignantly at Rob's back, but his brother was already disappearing up the stairs and Cam had no wish to waken his parents. He sighed, went inside and shut the door quietly; the joy of the night had been smashed by Rob. There had been no need for him to speak like that! Had he not seen Cam's friends leave? But of course he'd only done it to annoy; he'd timed it perfectly so that Cam had no chance to answer. Now his heart banged within him, frustrated and enraged. Always, always it had been like this; always he had been the loser. At that moment he felt he really hated his brother – not for his action just now, but for all the past years of things, the triumphant words and expressions, the winning of countless arguments, time after time. He had always been not simply the younger brother but the weaker brother.

He could not go to bed yet; tired though he was, there was no point – he would never sleep. He went back into the sitting-room and put another couple of logs on the fire; better here in comfort than lying awake with all the worms of past memories writhing in his head! The thing was that he didn't really want revenge on Rob; after all, the two of them were grown-up now – Rob was nineteen. Maybe he felt worse about it now because of his memories of Richard; maybe he was frightened because he now realised things could happen so fast, without the slightest indication. Death sent no warning. Richard had been taken away in a split moment, and for ages afterwards Cam had blamed himself bitterly for having let him go alone to Shuan. He had suffered remorse over the death of his best friend; how much more would he suffer if anything should happen to the brother who was his enemy?

In a way he knew it was crazy to think of the possibility of death like this. The chances were that Rob would still be stomping around Ardnish in his eighties! But the thing was, nobody could be sure. Cam knew that once he had trusted life, had trusted it blindly, taken everything for granted. It was true of course that his grandfather had died, so he had known death; unconsciously, though, he had linked it with the old. Then Richard had died, and suddenly all that was turned upside down. Nothing was safe.

Now he began to think how much he wanted to heal this rift with his brother before he left, for his own peace of mind as much as anything. All he asked for was an end to the war, nothing more. But he did not see how to accomplish this; there seemed to be no way. He looked round towards the window and his attention was caught by a flutter of something white against the pane. Must be a moth, he thought. He got up and went over, to see that out of the darkness tiny flakes of snow were drifting down. It was almost beyond belief – this early in autumn! Mind you, the seasons had been so weird of late that it wasn't perhaps all that strange, and it had certainly been cold enough earlier. Probably by the morning it would be gone and forgotten.

It brought something to mind, though, and he smiled. Ages ago the whole family had been to some ceilidh or other – maybe it was the year they had gone to the ancient library and had been given the quill pens? He wasn't sure. At any rate there had been plenty of snow about and they had had the most awful job to get the car down the farm track to the place. What he recalled vividly, though, was the quality of the snow – it was that wonderful kind which came so seldom, flakes like feathers from the wings of snowy owls, huge and fluffy, perfect for sliding and snowballs. He remembered how madly excited he had been, asking if they were likely to be snowed in, while his poor father kept scraping the snow from the windscreen as well as having to get out and clear the middle rut of the track so that the car's undercarriage would survive.

At last they had arrived and Cam remembered it as a big building built around a central courtyard. The lights from the low windows were a beautiful orange-red colour and they made him shiver with anticipation. Inside there were maybe a dozen or so folk in a room that appeared to be on several levels. He was the youngest there, and was allowed to sit on the floor right in front of the fire, so that his cheeks burned with the heat. Then began an evening of songs and stories and talk; he became more and more uncomfortable there on the floor, not sure whether it was better to cross his legs or to kneel or sit with his back to a chair. He kept trying to catch his father's eye to tell him it was time to go, but Duncan was far too carried away with the night's entertainment, and eventually Cam gave up in despair.

Then he simply had to go to the loo, so he made his way out at the end of a song, balancing carefully between feet and instruments till he had reached the door and then found his way upstairs. As he returned to the room he stopped and looked out of the window to monitor the snowfall. The wind had died away to almost nothing and the flakes by this time were very thin, as fine as threads. Darkness had fallen and a great silver back of moon was rising from among the trees. It was then Cam had the most wonderful idea; he leapt to the front door, hauled it open and brought in two mighty handfuls of snow. With a tremendous sense of triumph he put one into each of Rob's boots, just before their hostess came out of the room to guide him back for the final songs of the evening.

By now it was fairly late; Duncan Mackay, carried away as he was in enjoyment of the entertainment, remembered the clock at last. Cam could scarcely keep a smile of triumph from his face as the family moved towards the door and he had to be sharply reminded by his mother to say thanks for the evening. He was careful to be first out as Rob roared in agony and rage at the discovery of the snow. He hopped about the yard, hurling bits of snow at his brother, but unable to walk properly because of the sheer discomfort of his feet. Cam was unable to contain his joy; it was all he could do to keep a few steps away from his enraged brother; he was out of breath with laughter. For weeks afterwards Rob would hardly speak to him. It had been for Cam one of the very few victories that went some way to making up for months, years even, of defeats.

Cam looked out of the window and saw that the snow had already stopped. The little that had fallen was already beginning to melt; by morning there would be no memory of it on the ground. The logs he had put on the fire were more or less burnt out, and the room was turning cold and grey as ash. He put the guard on the fire and went softly upstairs, his feet making no sound at all; he knew those stairs so well, knew each tread that squeaked, as though an unwritten map of them lay in his head. Would he have begun to forget all the details of home, he wondered, before he returned?

He went to bed, but although he was dog tired he didn't sleep for a long time; he seemed to be always on the edge of it but half-thinking, half-dreaming. In his mind he kept hearing what he thought were curlews crying, although he knew it was not the time for them; some old story came back to him that the crying was a mourning for loves lost long ago. And it seemed to be the name Rosie they were crying, until gradually they seemed to go further and further away and he lost them altogether . . .

'Is it breakfast or lunch you're wanting?' his mother said with a twinkle as Cam eventually lumbered blearily into the kitchen. 'You're certainly practising for your student days, I can see!'

'I have to finish my packing today,' Cam said as though it was a promise. 'Where are dad and Rob?'

'Mending one of the fences. One of the sheep got tangled and made a right mess of the thing,' she replied. And then added: 'Was it a good ceilidh then? There was enough noise from you all anyway – I don't think I slept till about four.'

Before Cam had finished eating, his dad came in and announced that the fence was done.

'Come out when you're ready, Cam,' he said, changed into another pair of boots and disappeared upstairs. The boy was not sure what he meant, but he finished his breakfast and put on his boots and an anorak. By now the rain was coming down in earnest and the fields, when Cam looked out, were enveloped in mist.

Duncan came downstairs and they went out together to the barn. There were bales of hay stacked in the far corner; one of the new calves was tramping about its pen in the semi-darkness. After a few moments Cam's eyes became adapted to the gloom; he picked out the huge stack of logs over to the left that were ready for the winter, and the old implements from Toberdubh hanging now from nails in the stone walls. Then he saw it – there at their feet the harp was lying, cleaned now and beautiful, as if it had been made the day before. Cam looked at it with awe; he bent down involuntarily to touch it, stretching out reverent hands to feel the strings, to run his fingers gently over the wood, with the strange curling designs woven into it. It had been so lovingly restored by his father, polished so that the wood shone – no wonder he was looking so proud and glad, smiling at Cam. And then:

'I want you to have it, Cam,' he said quietly. 'There's plenty Rob'll get from here, but somehow I reckon this will mean more to you. As long as you don't go and sell it!' he added with a laugh.

'Oh Dad, thanks . . . thanks so much.' He looked up at his father, overcome, grateful beyond words, but not sure. Rob wouldn't like it, he knew; Cam was not certain that it was the right thing for him to accept. Yet he did not want to hurt his father by saying no. He was silent for a moment. 'It's amazing,' he finally said, running his hand again over the shining wood. 'I just wish Richard could've seen it, you know. Anyway, don't worry, I'll look after it all right!'

'Are you wanting those sheep brought in from the lower field?'

The two of them turned round in surprise at the sound of Rob's voice. He was standing there in the entrance to the barn; maybe he had been there all along. Cam's heart hammered in his chest. He got up at once while Duncan Mackay began to tell his older son what he wanted done, and Rob started towards the house. Even by the way he walked, Cam was somehow sure that he had heard, sure too that he was angry and hurt by what his father had done.

'Rob!' Cam called lamely as they came back to the house, but his brother stormed inside, kicked off his muddy boots and banged away through the kitchen and upstairs. Morag Mackay turned round from the stove, her face full of questions; Cam didn't stop but followed Rob up to his room.

'Let me tell you this,' Rob said harshly, 'dad can give you whatever he wants but he can't give you Ardnish, see? This place is going to belong to me and there isn't a thing you can do about it. Once you've been to your nice little university you can go off and find some high-powered job somewhere and you'll soon forget this place ever existed. Anyway, you'd better, 'cos you won't be coming back here!' Incensed now, he made a grab for Cam's shoulder, but the boy ripped himself desperately from his grasp.

'Just leave me alone!' he found himself wailing as he escaped through the doorway and went battering back down the stairs.

'Cam?' said his mother anxiously as he went storming through the kitchen. 'Cam, what on earth is going on?'

But he didn't answer; he wouldn't stop, but pulled on his boots at speed and ran out of the door and on up to the path heading for the larch wood. His father caught sight of him from the barn and knew at once that something was wrong; he went back into the house to find out what it might be.

On Cam went at high speed until he reached the cover of the larch wood. He hoped his mother had not seen that he was crying; now he stopped and wondered what he should do. The rain was not as heavy as it had been, but fine now, like soft down. Every inch of the land was green and shining; the trees loomed out of the low mist and it seemed as if the whole world had been wrapped in cotton wool. As soon as he sat down on his favourite flat rock in the wood Cam let himself cry in earnest. He cried in anger and bewilderment, but above all because of the sheer injustice of it all. What had he done, after all? Why should Rob try to punish him for something which was not in the least his fault? It simply wasn't fair! But he was crying too because he loved Ardnish and it was a thought too terrible for words that he would be kept from his own home. This land was where everyone would be buried! All the ones who mattered to him. And he wasn't just thinking of their bodies – he meant their stories, their laughter, their lives! It was as though Rob meant to put up some huge electric fence around his beloved Ardnish to keep him out. It was unfair, it was unfair! Surely he couldn't mean it? But then, what would be the point of coming back if his brother hated him that much? How could he ever be happy here like that? Once his parents were dead, Rob would be master here and no longer afraid of what he could say or do.

He thought of himself in Aberdeen, watching from a window the slush of traffic through grey streets, knowing that he could not go back, that he was a prisoner of the city. Surely Rob had no right to do such a thing to him! Yet the worst of it was that he knew deep in his heart that his brother would indeed have that right one day, that there was nothing at all he could do to stop him.

Cam got up from where he was sitting and began running again, not knowing why, but feeling he could not bear to sit still any longer. He did not want to see Ardnish, that much he knew; he could not bear to see it at this moment. He crashed through the trees and into the glade he had loved so much as a child and for a second he remembered the horseman; he was the horseman, ploughing on madly without any thought or care about where he was going. Abruptly he broke out on the other side of the wood, and in the bad light did not see the bank dipping away beneath his feet. Down he went, and hard over on his ankle; he gave a single cry as he landed and lay on the muddy bank, his hands splayed out behind him. For a second he did not move; he was too shocked to do anything. Then he shivered and tried to move his ankle, to raise himself, but pain at once jagged through his whole leg.

Now he wept again, for Ardnish, but also for his own misery; he wept because he felt as helpless as a child. The wind chilled him as it whipped round from the edge of the trees. At last he picked himself up carefully from where he lay and crouched over in a ball in an attempt to keep warm. The pain that seared through his ankle when he so much as twitched it seemed unbearable; he felt he dared not risk trying to walk. But what was he to do? The tears came again as waves of self-pity washed over him. His father would come to look for him in the end, he felt sure, once they all realised he had not returned. He wanted to be found and he did not. He was not sure any more what he really wanted. As he lay there miserably, rain lashed down and wind whirled through the larches; he closed his eyes and shivered.

Into his mind there came a picture from childhood. It was of a father standing outside a house with his arms thrown open wide, while a younger man, his son, toiled towards him from far away. The picture had been strange and wonderful all at once, filled with the bright colour of fruit and the hot light of a distant country. It came from a book his mother used to read to them of the story of the prodigal son. Then he thought about himself again – was he one who would go away and squander his inheritance in the city, he wondered bitterly? He might just as well, perhaps, for there would be no forgiveness or welcome home for him once his father had gone! He fell for a moment into the frame of that picture and saw himself running over the dusty track, there under the hot blue skies; but the doorway was blocked by the figure of his brother, and there was neither mercy nor love in his eyes.

'You won't come back here!' He heard Rob's words over and over again in his mind; each time he flinched from them. They were like a physical blow to him. If only, if only his father had never said anything about the harp! It had been that which sparked off the whole thing. His father had found the harp; it was his, and he had no wish to fight over it with his brother. But the quarrel was, he knew, about far more than that; it was about the land itself; it was about pride and honour and rights. There was something in him that was jealous all right, he had to admit that; he wished he had been the elder brother. But there was no way on earth the two of them could have shared Ardnish, no matter the number of its acres.

Maybe he should have been glad he was leaving, washing his hands of the whole sad quarrel for ever. Yet somehow that was not what he felt in his heart; that was no real answer, else he would not have wept so bitterly over Rob's harsh words – nor ended up here in the mud! The truth was that he had no heart to fight; it was not the way he wanted things at all.

The cold became worse as the wind blew in from the moor with another fierce barrage of rain. He must somehow manage to move into shelter or he'd be soaked to the skin in no time. He began to drag himself along, using his hands to propel himself, up the bank and into the shelter of the first of the trees. They splattered great heavy drops from their branches, but right up against one heavy trunk he was protected from the worst of the new rain. It was strangely warm too, he noticed, and he was reminded that it had been the same on the night he had tramped wearily back from Toberdubh with his father.

It was for just the very briefest moment that Cam saw the figure, so brief that he would never be sure whether his eyes had played a trick on him, or that it was all a figment of his imagination. For just that second, away over on the far side of the path something caught his eye, a flash of silver and a raised axe, the small dark man with the cloth about his shoulders. The really odd thing was that although the man was striking at the tree, his eyes did not seem to be on the blow; instead Cam had the queerest feeling that their eyes met, just for a brief second. And then nothing; Cam was left peering though the sheer grey curtain and the larches, seeing nothing but their dismal shadows and the white slicing of the raindrops. He was startled, but the thought of fear had never crossed his mind; that was what seemed so weird. It had happened so fast that he had had no time to think of being scared. But maybe it was because he did not feel that he had seen a stranger. The man had been grey, etched as it were out of flint, ancient as the peat itself; Cam was sure of that. He was surely one of the first folk, the new breakers of the land who had come after the ice slid back and the earth warmed. He had been the first to make fields out of soil that had previously only grown trees. Yet there had been in him something of the look of Duncan Mackay – even of Cameron Mackay! It seemed such a stupid notion, one which he would never dare to say to anybody, and yet that had been his immediate thought as he caught sight of that face. Maybe it was because he had been thinking at that moment of his father; maybe it had all been imagination, a trick of the eyes, of the light? All the same, this wood held something of strangeness; he could never quite forget the horseman, and maybe other shadowy figures too, half-remembered from distant days of childhood – or from dreams? It was as if a curtain of time slid back now and then to a place between the worlds, where the people who had once stood there came back and were for a brief moment etched again.

He thought and thought about the flint man, and the more he did the more he felt him to have been their own ancestor, the very first one, perhaps, to name Ardnish, to mark its fields. He shuddered again at the strangeness of it and felt suddenly afraid and lonely; he did not want to look back there again in case the apparition should return.

He shifted his foot and it hurt so badly that he gave a moan in frustration and despair. The tears welled in his eyes and the trees blurred into grey mist. He longed to go home, but home seemed to be the one place he could not go. Perhaps it was a long time after that, or perhaps it was hardly any time at all that Cam heard the sharp crack of a stick, and looked up startled to see a dark figure coming through the trees, jumping over the rocks at the side of the pool and walking up the path towards him.

'I'm here!' he called feebly from where he crouched under the larch, and the figure stopped, turned round and then spotted him and came up close. Their eyes met. It was Rob.

nine

Strange that it should have been his brother who helped him back to the farm – strange, and more than a little uncomfortable. Cam felt strongly that he didn't want to be that close to him, to have to lean on his shoulder like that. Already, many times over, he felt himself to be the weak one, the inferior; it certainly needed no reinforcing! The two of them spoke little on the way back, nothing at least that did not have to do with the immediate business of getting back to Ardnish. The mist was rolling in again as they came slowly and drunkenly out of the shelter of the larches; Cam could see the white rolls of cloud driving in from the sea, so that even the bottom field was smudged and unclear now, on the edge of fantasy.

Every time he felt himself in danger of crying out with the pain of his ankle he bit his lip, closed his eyes and uttered not a word. It was as much as his life was worth, he decided, to make the slightest fuss about it. At any rate his pride was at stake.

He reckoned his parents must have sent Rob out to look for him. That must mean that the whole affair had come out before he left the house; he thought of this with a certain grim satisfaction. Most of the time, he knew, they took his side, and if Rob had been honest about his side of the story, Cam had no doubt his dad would have been wild as a bull about the whole thing.

'Out there and don't bother coming back until you've found him!'

Cam could well imagine the scene that had probably taken place; it wasn't often that Duncan Mackay got mad, but that was just the sort of thing he hated. And on the rare occasions when he and Rob fell out, they did it in style.

It was all very well, though, being satisfied that Rob had probably been drummed out of the house to find his brother, but it did nothing to heal the rift between them. If anything, Cam thought miserably as he hobbled the last yards to Ardnish and went inside, Rob would be all the more bitter with all the world against him. The warmth of the kitchen hit him at once and he realised how cold he was.

'Away upstairs and get that foot washed!' Duncan Mackay scraped back his chair and got up from the table, taking in the situation at a glance. 'See his heater's on in his room, Robert, and then come down here. Your mother's away into Findale.'

He winked at Cam as he went past him to the door and thumped a kindly hand on his shoulder. Things were pretty well just as he'd imagined they would be, thought Cam; he could hardly help but smile. Negotiating the steps up to his room was a nightmare, and he imagined he must have bitten off about half his tongue by the time they made it to the landing, but he survived.

'I doubt they'll amputate,' Rob suddenly said at Cam's door and shot a glance at him, his eyes sparkling for a second. Then he went ahead of Cam into the room, got the heater on and the curtains closed, and one of the bedside lights switched on. He then came back and helped his brother over till Cam collapsed a little melodramatically on to the bed. The rain was hammering like nails against the window. Cam half-expected Rob to turn and go at once, glad that his duty was over. But instead he squatted by the side of the bed all of a sudden, looking at his finger nails, not at Cam, frowning uncertainly.

'I'm sorry about what I said to you earlier,' he said in a rush. 'I didn't mean most of it – you know that.'

Cam looked up sharply from where he was lying, taken altogether by surprise, his heart beginning to throb in his chest with the shock of what Rob was saying. It hadn't been like this . . .

'Maybe it's just that dad's so often on your side,' his brother continued, still not looking at him. 'Mum as well – I feel I'm always somehow on the outside. And you're the one who's going to university; you were always the one who did well at school. I dunno, maybe I feel this place is all I've got – the thought that one day I'll be able to farm it, do it as I want . . . '

His voice trailed away and he moved, uncomfortable as he was on the floor, still never looking at Cam but clearly thinking, thinking hard. His brother's heart was still racing sixteen to the dozen, his head quite dizzy with the sudden strange turn of events; it was so unexpected. He wanted desperately to say something, to show that he was really listening and that what Rob was saying mattered, mattered indeed more than he could say. But his mouth was dry and he just sat and looked at Rob, dazed – like a stuffed goldfish; that was what Rosie would once have said.

'I always felt a complete failure,' he managed at last, shifting on the bed. 'I was always really jealous, Rob, 'cos you were stronger than me, you could do everything better round here, and you were popular . . . School and stuff, well, that was different; it never meant that much to me. I don't even know if I want to go away, to tell you the truth!'

Rob sniffed and looked up at that, and the two of them smiled.

'Maybe we were jealous of each other the whole way along,' Rob said quietly at last. 'Kind of stupid really, when you think about it. As mum always says, life's too short as it is.'

They went quiet then, but Cam wanted to say something nonetheless, though he didn't know if the had the guts. It pounded in his head and he rehearsed it before daring to speak.

'About Ardnish, Rob. I know it'll be yours, of course, but . . . it means an awful lot to me, you know. I might . . . might need to come back. I . . . I just don't know what I want at the moment, what I may do in the future, but I love this place.'

Rob looked him full in the face now and then nodded, understanding in his eyes.

'I didn't mean what I said, right? All that was just rage, after I'd seen you and dad in the barn, with the harp. D'you really think I'll be out with a shotgun, waiting for you to come off the main road, ready to blow your brains out?'

Cam giggled in spite of himself at the thought.

'Just because I'll be running this place doesn't mean you can't come back; get that into your head! There's no way on earth we could share this place, but . . . it'll always be your home too, no matter what happens.'

Cam was so glad that he felt his eyes blurred with a sudden warmth.

'Thanks, Rob,' he said – and almost immediately regretted it, for his brother threw him a black look at once.

'Nothing to thank me for,' he muttered as he struggled to get up from the floor.

Cam could have kicked himself; of course he knew how Rob would hate to be thanked for something like that. He tried at once to redeem the situation.

'Going down to Findale tonight?' he asked. Rob rolled his eyes and looked away.

'Not after the fool I made of myself on Saturday night! Annie won't speak to me in a hundred years. No, there's plenty to be done around here, after all the time and sweat I spent trying to find out where you'd run away to!'

He turned round and glowered at Cam in jest.

'I'll look in and see how you're doing later, then. I'm not carrying a big hulk like you down to dinner, I hope you realise that!'

They laughed and Cam was glad. He laughed because of Rob's joking words, but he laughed even more because he felt warm inside, because things were all right; they were healed. It would not always be like this; he knew that well enough. But somehow it didn't matter; what was important was here and now, and for that he was deeply grateful.

'By the way,' Rob said as he turned round at the door, in no real hurry to go, 'I wouldn't want that harp anyway – not after hearing that old story of grandpa's.'

Cam frowned, all the pain of his ankle forgotten.

'What story was that?'

'Och, come on, you must remember! I'm sure you must have been there too? It was one of those times we begged to stay up there at Toberdubh instead of coming back here at night. It worked a few times! The old man was trying to scare the daylights out of us with all sorts of stories about weird lights on Ben Luan, folk wandering off and never coming back – all that kind of thing.'

That story about Ben Luan was certainly clear enough in Cam's mind. Had this one been told too on the night that Rob was remembering? He couldn't think of it for the life of him.

Rob came back then and sat down at the end of the bed. He wasn't exactly one for telling stories, not this kind at any rate.

'Well,' he began, 'as far as I can recall it was all to do with the devil and the start of the world . . . Don't laugh at me, or I'll thump your ankle!'

'I'm not laughing!' Cam protested even although it wasn't exactly true. He was just happy; he was really wildly happy and he couldn't help himself.

'Anyway, according to grandpa, the whole floor of heaven is made of ice. Well one day the devil, who was at this time still a good angel, was walking away out on the edge of this ice, where nobody was supposed to go. He was carrying his harp with him and some kind of brand – a torch I suppose. Anyway, he got right to the edge in his pride and fell right through the ice, down, down the whole way to earth, till he landed up, according to grandpa, bang in the middle of that mound of earth out there, right between the two fields.'

Cam was smiling suspiciously at all this. Rob was far better at making up stories than he'd ever imagined. He raised his eyebrows but said not a word.

'I'm only telling you what I remember!' Rob protested. 'I'm not asking you to believe the whole thing! Anyway, I forgot to mention the brand. When the devil was falling out of the skies he let go of it and it landed somewhere away to the north, right in the middle of the ancient forest, and just about the whole of it was burned. At any rate, that's how the harp landed in the old mound there, and it's best left where it is, if you ask me . . . it's an instrument of darkness.'

Rob's voice ended in a melodramatic whisper and Cam laughed until it hurt.

'That last bit at least you added!' he said. 'Whatever else grandpa actually told, you put in that bit about the harp, Rob! Come off it!'

'I'm only repeating word for word the story I remember,' his brother countered innocently, standing up to go. It might have been that there was just the tiniest edge of a smile on his lips. 'If you don't want to believe me, that's up to you. But you have been warned . . . '

He looked round a last time from the door and showed the whites of his eyes. Then he disappeared.

Cam felt the silence after he had gone. Yet his sadness was gone as well; instead, he felt the warmth of the house about him, was aware in a new way of its security and peace. It was growing dark; he could see the edges of black between the curtains. He got up and struggled over to the window despite the pain of his foot.

At times on evenings like this he felt the strangest melancholy, as if the blackness itself came over his spirit, with mist clogging his chest, making it an effort for him to breathe. It was a nowhere time, this period between the end of summer and the beginning of winter, seemingly bleak and dead. Maybe these days were something that only Scotland could produce; perhaps the nature of the land itself, beneath these skies, added to the gloom.

Even tonight he felt the air stuffy, so he pushed up the window and a hint of the coldness of early evening came into the room. Almost at once he heard sounds, very muffled at first so that he was not quite certain what they were; perhaps Rob was out at the car, or something was being mended. They were like squeals, high-pitched and very far away, the intervals between them were so long sometimes that he felt that whatever was making them had gone. Yet now they came again and were closer; they seemed so near, just over the house maybe, that he had the feeling that he could have raised his arm into the darkness and touched their flight. For now he knew: they were wild geese – the first geese returning from Iceland after the long summer days.

A flood of childhood memories washed over him – so many nights when he had wakened up and heard a skein of them dragging overhead. They always made his heart leap, although he never quite understood why. As a child he had felt strongly that it was a terrible thing to shoot one of these wonderful birds which had toiled long and hard to reach this sanctuary of land after a perilous journey across the sea. Once, when he and Rob were very young, his father had gone out with a gun, and they had begged him not to shoot any; they had gone on badgering him until he had reluctantly lowered his gun and come slowly inside, resignation written all over his face. Cam still felt the same now; the geese were to be welcomed, of that he was absolutely sure. He had had no reason ever to change his mind.

Geese would often get lost on just such nights as this. Lone birds could be heard crying in distress above the rooftops, searching for a way back to join the rest of the flock; orphans deserted by their companions. The mist apparently caused their disorientation, destroying their vision as it swallowed up the land. Time after time, he would lie awake in the middle of the night, willing them to break free and escape, sharing in the distress he sensed in their cries. It would be like that tonight, he feared, if there were many coming in over the sea in the first wave of arrivals. And just for a moment he felt himself to be like one of them, wandering in a mist, not sure of the path ahead, struggling to hold on to faith in the face of uncertainty.

But now, as he waited by the window, a stronger breath of cool air came into the room; he saw that a wind had got up and was filling the trees, and he was glad, sure that by morning the last of the mist would have been blown away, and that the geese would be able to find their way back to their well-known haunts.

It comforted him to reflect that some things never really changed; if he were to go down now to his dad and ask him on what day the geese had come back for the past ten years or more, the reply would be that it was always the same. The same day of the same month, crossing the vastness of sea and land, to return to the same fields! It was as if there were unwritten cycles that were never broken but kept on, year after year. The living things that traced these cycles did not understand what they were fulfilling. Nor did they ever question them. Perhaps he was in his own cycle, far too big and strange for him to begin to understand, but one that he should not question, but learn to take on trust. Although it comforted him it also disturbed him, for if that were true, then how much freedom remained his own? It became too much for him to think through; he yawned, pulled down the window, shut out the mist and the voices of the geese, and hobbled back to bed. He did not want to think too much about anything; the day had been too long, too confused, already. His head was whirling as it was with all that had happened. He grimaced as he remembered that he was no farther on with his packing, and in a couple of days he was due to leave.

There was a rap on the door and his mother came in.

'Are you warm enough, Cam? We still haven't seen to that ankle of yours and you've been in for half an hour! Here, I've made you some bacon and eggs.'

He smiled at her as she laid the tray on his lap and then went round the room making sure the heater was on, closing the curtains carefully where Rob had not bothered; she came back and sat on the very edge of the bed.

'Now I don't want to be nosy, Cam, but I just hope you and Robert have made up. It was silly of him to make you run off . . . '

'Mum, it's all right,' he interrupted gently. 'We got it sorted. And my foot'll be fine, don't worry. And thanks for bringing this up.'

'I remember doing it often enough for you when you were a wee boy,' she said. 'Those times when you would have an attack of asthma in the middle of the night, and one of us would come and read to you until you were better. I could always tell when that was, because you'd always ask for tea! I used to go down, feeling so relieved, to make you tea and toast.'

He smiled, remembering too, remembering small things. He used to have a huge bear sitting up on the dressing-table, and in the night when he was scared he could see its shadow and that comforted him. The times when he had had asthma during his childhood were all rolled into one now in his mind; he could clearly recall the terrible toil of trying to breathe in each time, as though he was climbing a sheer mountain. And the air he breathed never seemed to be enough; it was more like wool than anything else.

'Didn't you used to tell me stories too, Mum?' he asked. 'I'm trying to remember.'

Morag smiled.

'I think there was only one, ever – you know I'm hopeless at that! But that one I used to tell you over and over again, desperate to take your mind off things. Poor wee soul, I don't think you ever minded; you were most likely too busy struggling to get better. Och, what was it now? Some silly thing about a boy going into a wood and finding a balloon, a basket balloon, and flying off to the end of the world . . . '

'That's it, I remember now! And wasn't there some old man in a tower?' said Cam.

'Aye, that's right,' his mother smiled. 'He found some magician at the very far north of the world in a white tower, and he could ask for just one wish . . . '

Cam nodded.

'I can remember my wish all right – I always just asked to get better! And I did in the end. I can't even remember the last time I had asthma. But it wasn't a silly story, Mum; it used to mean a lot to me.'

His mother said nothing, but her eyes were glad.

'Well, I won't be able to look after you once you're away in Aberdeen. I just hope you find good friends before too long, Cam; that'll make all the difference. Now I'm going to go away and leave you to eat. Then you should try and get a good sleep.'

She was mothering him again and normally he would have protested, pulled her up for treating him too much like a child, but this time he didn't. He thought of the many times when she had given up her own night's sleep for him, coming in to read when his breathing was bad or when he had been afraid. He thought of the long years he had been at home, and all he had taken for granted. Now was no time to rebel against that closeness and love; there would be time enough for the distance to come between them, all the weeks and months when he'd be away. These were last days for her – the end of one part of her life and the beginning of a new one. It was no easier for her to see him go than for him to leave.

'Thanks, Mum,' he said instead. 'I'm glad I'm here.'

She slipped out of the room putting the main light off as she left. He heard the television on downstairs, the laughter punctuating some programme like clockwork. Only two more nights would he be in this house. At that moment he did not want to be going anywhere; he would have been more than happy to remain and forget that his university place ever existed. He finally put the light out, even though it was still quite early and he was not really ready to sleep. At the back of his conscious thought was the muffled sound of the television, but in the end he didn't know if it was real or just his own imagination. He slowly drifted asleep, but not very deeply, so that when the noise came at the window he was not surprised, but looked up without fear to see what had made the sounds.

Although it was dark, the whole window shone silver with moonlight, and he knew that the mist had gone. He struggled out of bed but the strange thing was that he felt no pain at all in his foot. He looked out of the window and there below him he saw Richard, just as he had seen him on that last morning in the summer dawn.

'It's all right, I'm all right,' he kept saying, over and over again. 'You have to come with me, now! Climb out of the window!'

Cam wanted to speak but somehow he could not. He jumped down to the grass, and again he felt nothing in the foot he had hurt. Already Richard was gone; he was running away fast over the ground in the direction of the sea, and Cam ran after him; he ran like the wind. Away in the distance over the sloping ground he saw the weird hill, shaped like a barrow, with all the pine trees on its summit. Richard, he knew, had loved that place more than anywhere in the world, more even than he loved Shuan and the Camas shore on the far side. It was there he had found the hundreds of pigeon feathers lying under the trees: the place where the angels came to moult.

At last they reached it, Cam a bit later than his friend, and they stood on the summit. Richard didn't look at him; he was craning his neck to look right up above him at the skies.

'The northern lights!' he kept saying. 'Just look at the northern lights!'

So Cam looked up and saw the fires playing in the skies, leaping and chasing each other so fast that your eyes could not follow them.

'If you whistle they'll come to you!' Richard said. 'Didn't you know that? They're wild horses, not lights at all. You can ride them if you can catch them!'

Cam tried to whistle but no sound would come at all. He kept looking up and wishing he could, for it seemed the best thing he had ever heard. But, when giving up at last, he looked around him, he saw that Richard was no longer there; he was running across the last fields towards Shuan, as fast as any horse, and he was growing fainter and fainter all the time.

Cam tried to call for him to come back; he opened his mouth in anguish; but it was too late, and the world went dark.

ten

The next day passed uneventfully enough for the most part. Cam finally got down to the last of his packing, lugging things from the attic as best he was able with his bad ankle, sorting out the new piles of clothes his mother brought for him. Outside it was raining – the colour had drained away from everything – and the house was filled with a heavy, grey light. Rob stayed in his room, the walls thudding with his music; even Duncan had been forced indoors for much of the time, his mood seemingly as bleak as the weather. The rain chimed and sang, it came in at cracks and formed a pool on the pantry floor. Morag was busy with cloths, going here and there in a house that had its lights on all day, for the grey cloud was so heavy that it seemed the sun had vanished for ever.

By the time their midday meal was over Cam was sick of the whole business. Three huge cases and several bags stood ready on the floor of his room and he wanted no more of them. He banged down the stairs, clutching the banister for support, and went into the kitchen to find Misty and Fruin stretched out on the floor, and his parents at the table.

'I'm going out,' he announced, stroking Misty's forehead as she slept.

'You must be joking,' his father said. 'Have you looked out recently by any chance?'

'What about your foot, Cam?' added his mother anxiously. 'Do give it a chance – give it time to heal.' She left the letter she was writing and came over to stand beside him, her face full of concern.

'I'll be fine,' he smiled at them. 'I'm not going to get gangrene or anything like that! Anyway I just want to get out of the house, and my ankle's a whole lot better since Rob helped me to strap it up. I've almost finished my packing, believe it or not!'

Duncan returned to his newspaper and Morag accepted Cam's going once she had seen him wrapped up in his oilskin and he had assured her he'd survive a monsoon. She slipped a huge sandwich into his pocket, all the same.

'And here's a mug of tea before you go!'

He went out of the house and just stood in the porch for a moment, listening to the hiss and rattle of the rain. Thank goodness Rob had come up the track to the larch wood the night before or he would still be lying there feeling sorry for himself! He felt a bit of a fool now for having run away as he had done; the quarrel with Rob now seemed so far away, his fears of last night foolish and exaggerated.

He was keen to go down to Findale, if only his foot would allow him to reach that far. There was something he thought he might do there, and anyway the walk would clear his head after the hours of packing. He set off fairly slowly down the uneven farm track, still wincing if he happened to hit the wrong side of a stone and pain shot through his ankle. The pools in the road were like liquid chocolate; he remembered so well coming along here with his mother when he was a child, Rob dragging at one hand and himself at the other, both wearing wellingtons and making the most of the chance to splash in the puddles as hard as they were able.

A few hundred yards along the track the rain suddenly came on heavier than ever. Cam looked back, his head hunched deep down into his oilskin and his hands buried in the pockets, seeing Ardnish lit like a honeycomb. For a second he felt lazy and toyed with the idea of turning back, but then he remembered his half-formed plan and felt this would be his last chance. He would go on. And if he kept up a good enough pace, he could be back before six.

He went on, still walking with care, until he reckoned he should be coming within sight of the gate and the main road. The mist was so thick that he could barely see twenty yards in front of him, so that even following the track was a trial at times. As he looked ahead and to his left, a boulder seemed to loom out of the grey, maybe one of the great chunks of stone left there when the track up to the farm was built. But as he watched he saw the thing move, and then another shape moved out of the mist, and he realised these were not boulders at all but the backs of stags and hinds.

He stopped stock still, becoming aware that he was now off the main artery of the track; he heard, rather than saw, the beasts in the poor light, heard the sound of many hooves clicking over the rocks then digging down into the marshy ground below. However, they weren't going away from him at all, but rather coming closer, shyly, their eyes wary and never still, lowering their heads and looking round, hinds and yearlings, and the stags with their full crowns of antlers further away at the back.

'Hallo there,' he said very gently. 'What d'you want then?'

He stretched out his hand warily, but too quickly, and there was a drumming as the nearest backed away in fear. Yet they were curious and came edging back, closer all the time; he wondered why they had come down so low this early in the year. There surely can't have been all that much snow on Ben Luan a couple of nights ago? It seemed unlikely that the cold had driven them down. He was really puzzled but forgot his questions when the nearest and bravest hind lowered her head so that she was only inches from his own face, her breath steaming up into the mist.

All of a sudden he recalled the sandwich his mother had stuffed into his pocket before he left the house; he'd had a mighty breakfast and hardly needed to worry about food for a long while yet. Very carefully he raised his hand to his pocket and managed to bring out the bag without a crackle. The wet noses strained in curiosity.

'Now, only one bit each,' he said sternly. 'Ladies first.'

The soft muzzles came one after another to take the pieces of bread he offered. Their mouths were like wet mushrooms, the kind found in the fields early in the morning following a night's rain. After a little he dared to reach up and stroke the hard fur on their foreheads; only one or two jerked back frightened. So they came eventually to form a warm ring round him, misty and faint on the edge of the thick mist, as the rain continued to drum down and a swollen burn crashed noisily beside them on its way to the river.

In the end they moved off, reluctantly and not in fear. Cam felt honoured, as if they had chosen him, trusted him. It was as though for a brief time there was no longer that sad gulf between the world of men and theirs, the wild kingdom. In the mist he seemed to have stumbled over a boundary into a place where fear and the gun did not belong, but perhaps that was only wishful thinking on his part. At last they were out of sight in the blanket of mist, and, but for the dampness on his palm, and the last crumbs of the sandwich, it might have been that they had never existed at all.

It seemed to take him ages to get back on to the main track. Because he was near the river and the woods, mist steamed even more densely into the air and with every yard it seemed harder to be sure of the way ahead. Once or twice he slipped on a deep rut of mud and his ankle throbbed with pain; he felt he would never reach the main road when all of a sudden a car slushed down quite near to him and he was there, only a mile from Findale.

The place he was aiming for was nearer than that, though. A long time ago, up on the hillside just outside Findale, and nearer for folk who came down from places like Ardnish and Toberdubh, there had been another church. At its back was a graveyard where the stones were very old; Cam used to think of them as being like an old man's teeth. But there were one or two fairly recent stones as well, despite the fact that Craig Church was now in a semi-ruined state and had held no religious services for close on fifty years.

It was a queer place really, steep above the road on the right-hand side, so high you could look out west from it and just glimpse the blue rim of the sea through the trees. You had the feeling that the place was much older than the grey kirk itself, which was probably young in comparison with whatever else had been built on that sharp rock.

Cam went along the main road at a reasonably fast pace once he had reached it. Sandy's dad passed him in a car, doing about fifty down the brae, but he screeched to a halt to ask if Cam wanted a lift into Findale. Cam just grinned and shook his head, then waved as the car shot off – far too fast for a day of mist, Cam decided – towards the village.

He got to the Craig and went through the rusty gate that protested creakily as he opened it. A huge black scatter of crows took off from the yews and rowans that grew around the hillock, reminding Cam of flecks of ash as they disappeared into the mist. The path was silver with water, indeed the entire hill was literally streaming with the rains of the past night and day, so that it took him all his time to reach the top and go round the back of the old church to the graveyard. A robin sitting on a wall looked at him, its head on one side, almost as though it had been employed to vet the visitors and couldn't quite make up its mind about Cam, who stopped and smiled as he looked at it.

'All right if I go in?' he said, but the robin darted away. He glanced over to his left, down and through the trees, but of course the sea was gone today, swallowed by the dense mist. He went on quickly, the faintest edge of fear in his heart, right up to the far left-hand corner . . .

RICHARD BRENNAN

The stone was small and simple, and there were new flowers there – his mother never failed. Cam wasn't sure why they had chosen this place rather than the regular graveyard down at Findale; perhaps it was because they could come here more often and remain undisturbed. Or perhaps because it was within sight of the sea, and Richard had loved that more than anything.

Cam crouched down and felt strange; there was no feeling that Richard was here as there was out at Camas, or at the barrow hill. He lowered his eyes and shivered as the rain came down harder than ever.

'I'll be back,' he whispered, feeling all the same that he was talking to himself. 'I'm going away, but it won't be forever, for plenty of reasons. I won't forget.'

He straightened up and looked round somewhat furtively, afraid lest anyone else might have come in behind him and overhear.

Then he thought of something and went back towards the gate for a moment. There were pigeons up in the trees, and as he came out on to the path they fluttered away with a grey whirring. There on the ground, sure enough, were some feathers, and Cam smiled to himself as he gathered up the very whitest he could find and turned back again, shutting the gate behind them. He laid the feathers carefully in front of the grave, his mind going back to that day with Richard long ago and the strange ancient hill.

'I hope the angels come here too,' he said, and turned away for a last time.

He had intended going back to Ardnish after that, but he didn't. He was wet as it was and his foot was bearing up better than he had expected, so instead he headed down into Findale. Rain came in huge drops from the trees on each side of the road and he walked hunched up – like a dwarf – to avoid the splashes from the branches. The river seemed to be growling like a dog at the end of a leash; through the grey light he could see it well enough, leaping down in white curves in its final run to the sea. Everything was glassy and shiny, rhododendrons massed on one side of the road, mist coming like steam through the foliage.

Cam came into the village, over the bridge and into the main street. He took a look through the window into the public bar at the Arms; there was only one man inside with his elbows folded on the counter, slumped over his beer. The place seemed warm and alluring and Cam looked longingly at the roaring fire in the big stone fireplace which cast a warm glow over the room. He wished he could go in; then he thought of Rob, and the whole saga of last Saturday night – if by any chance Annie came in, he would have no idea what to say to her. He turned and went on.

Without thinking he found himself going up Sinclair Street and smiled; this was the way to Rosie's house, at one time so familiar. How many times had he begged his dad to take him down here on a Saturday to visit her, his heart thumping with excitement! It was mad to come here now, but still he went on; he was wandering without thinking and he carried on right to her house, which was the last on the left-hand side.

Her room was round the side, but she was sure to be out; he walked quietly up the driveway, seeing no sign of life from the house. To his surprise he saw a faint glimmer of light from her window and heard the thud of music – she must be up there after all! He stayed, watching, rooted to the spot as he thought back to the days in the past when he had come here . . . The times they had hidden behind a bush in the garden and kissed, the times they had climbed into a tree and annoyed the neighbour's dog, the time they had thought a cloud was a flying saucer, the time they had fished a goldfish out of the pond . . . Then there was movement up above and he awoke out of his reverie, scared that someone might come out on to the porch and find him here like this.

All the same, he didn't want to go away without saying goodbye. He had loved her once, and there was an empty place inside him now because of that. It would do no harm. Cam bent down and picked up a chip of stone and chucked it up at the window. His aim was good enough but it only glanced against the pane and clicked down again on to the drive. The second hit the glass properly and startled him; he waited for the window to be pushed up but as he held his breath there was nothing, only the beat of the music and the steady rain. He turned to go; the idea had been daft in the first place . . . The noise of the window going up made him jump; there she was, leaning out now with the glow of a cigarette in her hand, searching the semi-darkness to see who was there.

'Hi, Rosie, it's me, Cam! Did I scare you?'

'Cam! You nearly gave me a heart attack, that's all!'

She turned round into the room for a second and screamed for the music to be turned down.

'Liz and Jenny are here for the night. My folks are away in Fort William. Are you coming in? C'mon, there's heaps to drink!'

He heard screams of laughter in the background and wished heartily that he hadn't bothered coming; but it was too late.

'No thanks, I'd better get back before it gets too dark. All the best for your course, though, Rosie – I hope you get on well.'

Already he was beginning to move away. Now there was a confusion of folk at the window and another gale of raucous laughter. Somebody wolf-whistled.

'See you then, Cam!'

'Yeah, see you,' he answered, and knew in his heart he didn't mean it. Cam the boy and Rosie the girl were dead, in a way as dead as Richard. All that was left was a garden deep inside his head and pictures – a whole lot of pictures that were faded like those in an old album. Now it was closed, but there were fresh pages in his hands, photographs that had not yet been taken. These were the ones that mattered now, he thought; these were the ones he should treasure.

Limping, he reached the main road through Findale and suddenly felt overwhelmingly tired. He wished he had had the good sense to turn back after going up to the graveyard; he would have been home by now. Slowly he made his way to the old bridge and leaned over it, listening to the loud crash of the swollen river as it tumbled in white falls over the rocks on its way to the sea. He would go on Wednesday he decided. There was no point in putting it off any longer; he had piles of books to buy for the start of term and plenty of things to organise. It seemed like a weight on his shoulders; he stood up, sighed, and resigned himself to the long walk home, hoping his ankle would stand it. A car was edging its way along the side of the road; in its lights the rain lashed down at an angle. He wondered for a moment if someone was about to ask the way. By the time he reached it he realised it was their own car and saw Rob behind the wheel.

'Your mother was worried about you,' Rob said dryly, rolling the window down. 'She was sure you'd get frostbite and die all alone on the moor.' He opened the passenger door and Cam saw that there was a hint of a smile on his face.

They hardly talked on the way home, but it wasn't a jagged kind of quiet as it might have been, Cam thought gratefully; not the sort of silence there used to be so often between them after a row. This was more of a contented peace, a companionship which did not need any words.

The car went splashing through the flooded parts of the road but Rob didn't drive fast, not as he would have done if Annie had been in the car. Cam was content to sit and look out into the darkness. He was tired and his ankle was strummed by pain; he was glad he hadn't had to face the whole walk back. He listened to the thudding of the windscreen wipers and sleepily half-closed his eyes until the lights of Ardnish stabbed him awake.

Despite his tiredness he did not go early to bed. Instead, he repacked one of his cases, found an old box of letters and sat for ages reading them. Rob and his father were talking downstairs about some new building or other; Cam heard snatches of the conversation in between finding things of interest from the past. There were several letters from Richard dating back to a time when the Brennans had gone down to England for an entire summer. He wondered whether he should keep them; in the end he stuffed all of them back into the box; they were still precious in their own way, with stories in them that he did not want to forget.

After a while he heard his father coming upstairs and only Rob remained in the kitchen. Cam felt cold in his room and went down, calling goodnight to his parents who were talking softly in the next room.

'So when're you away?' asked Rob, turning round from where he was sitting at the table.

'Och, Wednesday morning, if anyone'll be so kind as to take me to the station.'

'I doubt it'll be a problem,' Rob said severely, 'that phone has been ringing all evening with volunteers. No, I'll probably be able to take you myself; it will get me out of here for a bit. Have you much stuff?'

Rob sat till eleven, then banged around the house looking for this and that before finally going up to bed. Cam still sat by the fire, his feet cushioned by the black and white curve of Fruin. He was in a pensive mood and for some reason his thoughts tonight kept returning to Cameron Mackay, his grandfather, and especially to the final days he had spent in this house before his death. Sometimes, as now, Cam found himself wishing fervently that he had asked him more about the old days, about how it had been to live at Toberdubh after the war. How many stories were left for him some day to pass on to his own children? Precious few; if only he had thought while there was still time! Those memories were of great value, like flecks of gold panned from a river. But he had lost his chance. His grandfather had always been there, as familiar and seemingly as permanent as the single pine tree that had stood out on the moor beside the old house at Toberdubh. But the tree had been blown down in a storm, and all that was left of it was a few poor branches.

Cam pulled down the radio from its shelf and stood it on the floor beside him. Somehow he wanted to hear human voices; he felt the oppressive silence of the house; he was aware of the intensity of the night outside with the mist, miles and miles of it. It seemed as if Ardnish was the only thing alive in the darkness; out of every window there was nothing but blackness. He clicked on the radio and rolled the dial on and on. There were sudden flickers of language – a woman speaking German with such clarity that she could have been sitting in the room with him, a French song, a report in a language which he thought was probably Russian, something else that came and went in waves which in the end he recognised as Spanish. Then a very precise voice told him, in English, that it was a quarter to twelve.

There were all these languages, but there was no Gaelic. It had never occurred to him before, but now the thought of it made him really angry.

In all of the darkness out there he couldn't hear so much as a word of Gaelic! And yet up there to his right was Toberdubh; farther over was Crossallan, and out ahead of him the Hebrides – all of them places that had at one time been filled with the sound of Gaelic. It was as if his grandfather and his like had been shut out, pushed away and forgotten by the modern world.

He put the radio away and went to look out of the window again. In the darkness he could clearly hear new skeins of geese coming in across the land. They triumphed over the dark! He pulled open the back door and stood there in the light, straining upwards to listen to their voices. They would come back; year after year they would come back, no matter how many guns tried to blast them from the skies. And maybe, too, the language would survive, maybe it would come back before it was too late. If it did not it would be a death, like the death of his own grandfather. He saw him now as he had been in weakness during his last days in the house; in him was a language and a way of life, both dying with him. And he was suddenly aware of how precious and fragile life was.

eleven

During the night the weather cleared. The rain stopped a little after midnight and the clouds drove inland, for all the world like great chariots or the ramparts of castles. The wind went too, all of a sudden, so it was dead still, as if the land held its breath. Stars crackled overhead; the grass stems became edged with frost diamonds so that they looked like jewelled swords. And out of nowhere the moon came, a wobbling shape like a balloon filled with water, very pale at first. The stags and hinds looked up towards Ben Luan, their eyes filled with gold, but then they took off across the moors, their brittle hooves clicking against the stones; the only other sound was of rushing, as the water in the full burns careered from the shoulders of the hills, white and foaming. The sheep lay close into the dykes, their fleeces long now and ready for the hard bite of winter ahead; they were like boulders in the lee of the rocks.

And in the sturdy house of Ardnish the people slept. The work of autumn was almost done; what remained was to tie up and secure all that was precious against the onslaught of the winter storms which would surely come. The house lay dark and small beneath the moors, like some sleeping wildcat with its eyes shut.

Out at the back, in the old barn that smelled of hay and dung and dust, the moonlight fell through the thick beards of cobwebs that muzzled the windows, down across the ancient harp that lay against the wall. At times, as the beams shifted, it was almost as if invisible hands lifted again and played the strings that had been silent for perhaps a thousand years.

'Ca-am! Come on, Cam, wake up!'

He moaned his way out of deep sleep and dragged himself awake. Somewhere up in the grey light was the face of his father. Why did he have the conviction that it was only about half-past six?

'It's a grand morning. Thought we might take a walk over to Toberdubh, Cam. I'll go down and make a cup of tea.'

Cam was still unable to put a whole sentence together, but his face spoke volumes. He looked at his father with such anguish that Duncan, afraid he might burst out laughing, went over and pulled back the curtains, remembering how Cam, even as a little boy, had always hated getting up in the mornings. Steel blue light flooded the room as Cam sat up at last, shivering in the room's cold. He tried to dig up the memory of the previous night and recalled the pelting rain. How was it possible? He shuffled over to the window and looked with wonder at the sharp blades of sunlight scything the fields, diamonds glittering on the grass and a white frost like the breath of an ice dragon. Below in the kitchen he heard his father singing something unbelievably cheery. With very bad grace he pulled on old clothes and stumbled downstairs.

'Are you all ready for tomorrow?' his father asked when they were at the table. Cam nodded, his hands clasped round the hot mug as he drank his tea.

Outside, the ground was rutted with frost. The cold hit Cam's face like a slammed door, his eyes ran and his nose felt pinched. There was ice by the back of the barn, ice that squeaked as their boots passed over it. Somewhere very high up there was yet another arrowhead of geese; Cam could hear their faint cries, but although he searched the skies above he could see nothing.

Wisely his father gave him time to become human again; he walked with an easy stride a few steps ahead as they climbed to the level of the larches and began the walk through the wood, golden in its autumn colours. His father knew well that if you began talking to Cam too early in the morning you might easily have an argument on your hands.

At last they reached the far side of the wood and began the trek over the moor. They walked together now, both with hands buried in the pockets of their anoraks. Cam was barely an inch shorter than his father; he would be taller yet. Duncan put a hand on his son's shoulder and pointed up into the sky.

'Hen harrier,' he said, as a pale-coloured hawk took off from the heather and began crossing the hilly country on slow and regal wings. Cam was impressed.

'Wouldn't have noticed,' he admitted.

'Reminds me of a time I was up in Sutherland,' Duncan said suddenly. 'I may have been there with my father – aye, that's right; we were spending a couple of weeks on the coast in the summer, staying with a cousin of his. Anyway, this day he and I were going out over the moors and it was blazing hot and very hard going. I think I'd gone for a swim in one of the hill lochs (there's about as much water as land there) and we were on our way home. Well, this big man popped out of the heather and he was like a cartoon character – you know, tweed coat and trousers, huge general's moustache, gun under his arm. Just glared at us with flaming eyes and shouted, "Get off my land!"'

'What did grandad say?' asked Cam.

'Well, that was the great thing. I can still remember being scared out of my wits, but he just took my hand and somehow that made me feel braver. He simply looked steadily at the man for a minute, holding his gaze. Then he said very quietly: "I'm not going anywhere." The man looked as though he'd burst a blood vessel any minute; his face was purple. Then your grandfather went on: "My people were Mackays. They were thrown off this land once – their own land. But I'm not going to be. I believe I have more right to be here than you have." And he walked straight on with me, head held high, not proud, just keeping his dignity. Left the man spluttering, raging his head off, but he never looked back once!'

'Brilliant!' said Cam, smashing an ice-covered pool with evident satisfaction under his foot. They chuckled happily to themselves until they had passed the pine tree and were within sight of the chimneys of Toberdubh. The boy was warm and at last fully awake and he felt good; he felt strong and suddenly happier than he had done for days. He just wished that on a morning like this Cameron Mackay were still alive and that they were about to see him. He wished it so fervently that the back of his eyes burned, and he couldn't answer his father when he turned to him and asked him something about the key of the house.

'You still miss him?' Duncan asked unexpectedly as they stood at the door. All Cam could manage was a nod; he felt a fool as he fought his tears.

'I miss him too,' said his father as they went in to the cold of the sitting-room and smelled the edge of dampness there; the dark silence. Duncan said no more but searched for matches and lit the old paraffin stove. Their breath fogged the room.

'I wanted to bring you here for a reason, Cam,' Duncan said. 'This land is yours too; never be afraid of standing up for it. I'm a fortunate man having you and Rob to follow me – most of the young folk in the Highlands today can't wait to get away. Just look at Rosie, the girl you were so fond of – they're all bored stupid in the country and desperate to be away in the city. I'm glad, and very grateful, you're not like that. Oh, I know you're going to university in Aberdeen; I understand that all right, but what I'm saying is, don't ever be afraid of coming home.'

There was a knot in Cam's throat and he couldn't say a thing. He just nodded, feeling as if a heavy sack had just been lifted from his shoulders.

'It can take long enough to know exactly what you want,' his father went on. 'Maybe you'll find it in the city, but maybe you won't, and there's no shame in coming to a point when you say you were wrong. I know fine how torn you are about leaving Ardnish, Cam. Rob knows it too. But don't think any of us feels we're saying goodbye to you forever. There's next autumn's tatties to be done, for one thing,' he added with a wink.

They stayed in the house for a short time; then Duncan decided it was time he was getting back to his work. At the back door, Cam looked up at Ben Luan and he hardly remembered ever having seen it so sharp and clear, a grey pyramid with its granite slabs shining eerily in the steely light, standing out majestically against the brown of the moor. You could see so far that morning that Cam thought he might have glimpsed an eagle flowing through the blue skies half a mile up, or perhaps a flicker of deer. And then he recalled the strange happening of the day before, when for some reason the shy beasts had seemed to lose their fear of him; he would never understand either why they had been so low down at that time! His reverie was interrupted by his father, turning the key in the lock and saying quietly:

'You could always have this place, you know. Rob will have Ardnish all right, but if you were willing to take on Toberdubh you could have it and welcome. At least you know that.' He began to move away, swinging the key up and putting it in his pocket.

Cam felt overwhelmed.

'It means an awful lot to me, Dad,' he said at once, meeting his gaze. 'I can't tell you how much. Just to know it's there for me. I keep wanting . . . keep wanting to go and not wanting to go.'

His father smiled and ruffled his hair.

'That's been the story of this country since the beginning of time,' he said.

Together they started back to Ardnish.

The big cases stood near the front door, along with a little bundle of extra things that had been forgotten.

It had been a big meal, a memorable meal and Cam's favourite, and Morag Mackay had fluttered about the kitchen serving and clearing, her face white and drawn. Cam saw clearly what lay behind her eyes and wished he hadn't been so hard on her in these past days, that he could have sensed earlier her pain in letting him go.

For this special occasion there was wine on the table and Rob and his father were in hilarious mood, roaring with laughter over some story about a Dutch landowner over at Crossallan. Cam hadn't seen his brother so cheerful for a long time; he hoped that perhaps he was beginning to get over Annie at last, and that he wouldn't pursue her any longer after all that had happened.

They finished their meal and pushed the chairs back from the table. The kitchen was still warm after the hours of sunshine that had been pouring in the whole day. The sun was almost gone now, an orange bonfire blazing through the trees above Findale. It would be some view from the top of Ben Luan, Cam thought, and for one crazy moment he actually wondered whether he could go and climb the hill and be back in time to leave with Rob in the morning. But he knew that his ankle still flickered with pain if he happened to put too much weight on the one side, and if he were to fall on a shoulder of the Ben at this stage . . .

'Don't go and sleep in, now,' his brother said, punching him in the stomach. 'I'm up at quarter to six, so down here no later than half-past, sleepy head! I've got stuff to see to upstairs. See you in the morning.'

Three friends rang up after dinner to wish Cam all the best and remind him to work hard. He felt a bit as he had once done while waiting for a piano examination – a pit in his stomach, a kind of emptiness, a fear of what his new world would be like. He saw himself running up ancient stone steps, books and folders under his arms as groups of students moved towards doorways and towers. What if all of it was beyond him? Butterflies invaded his stomach and he felt his heart panicking. Deliberately he calmed himself; after all, even if all of it went terribly wrong, even if it turned out a total disaster, he could still come back; his father had said so. He didn't want it to be like that; after all the hard work and all the waiting, he really wanted to succeed.

'I've made you up a packed lunch,' his mother said, taking him out to where his cases waited and presenting him with a folded plastic bag.

'Mum, I haven't an inch of room,' he whined at first, and then hating himself, thanked her for it and stowed it away as best he could. He would look like a pack animal arriving in Aberdeen. Better make up his mind to face the expense of a taxi.

'Well, don't stay up too late tonight,' Duncan told him and put out the main light. His mother came over and hugged him hard for a long moment.

'See you in the morning,' she whispered.

He nodded, feeling a hard knot in his own throat. For a time he crouched by the fire, fighting for a place beside Fruin. The room had gone cold after the sun's dying and he chucked another log on the fire so that the flames leapt up like hungry wolves at the dry wood.

'I'll miss you, Fruin,' he said as he rumpled the collie's glossy black and white back; the dog stretched and yawned. 'Wish you could come with me, but you'd hate it – there isn't a sheep within miles!'

Once he was warmer he went over to his father's old desk in the corner and sat there. Maybe he should stay longer; he still didn't feel ready. The time had passed so quickly! Yet what more was there to do? He had said goodbye to everyone and everything that mattered; the only thing that was not ready was his own scared heart. It was a bit like standing on the edge of one of the rocks out from Shuan, waiting to dive into deep water but not daring, not quite having the courage. Still, he had done all the important things.

He put off the light over his father's desk so that the only brightness now came from the fire. In those flames he could find all the faces – his grandfather's, Richard's, Rosie's. For a second they were there, like single photographs; then they were gone. The fire was falling grey again and there was no more wood.

'Remember what I was telling you earlier today.'

He jumped and turned quickly to see his father standing there. Duncan sat down in one of the armchairs and tickled Misty's throat as she immediately padded up for attention.

'It's not about success, you know, Cam – it's about finding your own way, what's right for you. I mean, if I had wanted a vast amount of money the last thing I'd have done was to try and dig it out of the soil at Ardnish!'

Cam thought about that and nodded in agreement.

'I know that, Dad,' he said, with a hint of indignation. 'It's not a danger I really worry about.'

'I know, but you should,' his father said; he leaned forward, his eyes bright. 'All I can say is that plenty of others have fallen for it before you, plenty of others who'd made up their minds they wouldn't go for money, no matter what it cost. And I'll tell you what made me think most about all of this, Cam. It was something that happened ages ago, when I was about your own age, down in the Borders. You know I've told you how I went to work on an estate down there when I was just out of agricultural college – it belonged to a man called Colonel Perry. Anyway, I really hated that place, couldn't wait to get back to the west coast! Colonel Perry himself was all right, but his wife – you should have seen the poor soul; she had no life in her face at all. She used to walk round the grounds as if she was sleepwalking, her eyes just full of sadness. Honestly, it used to haunt me; I could hardly bear in the end even to look at her. I'd go out of my way not to meet her; I'd feel this black weight come down on me.

'I don't know what was wrong with her; I suppose she suffered badly from depression. But d'you know what used to frighten me most of all? Looking around the place, I would think that she surely had everything in the world you could want! A beautiful mansion house, these amazing gardens, hills all around, their own stretch of river. A family too. You'd think someone with all that would have to be happy, but there she was in that sad state. It was as if she couldn't see one bit of it, was completely blind to the whole lot.

'It was terribly sad for her of course, but in a way it was really good for me – it made me think. Och, I had friends who were frantically chasing money; some were going to the cities, some in Scotland, some to London or abroad. There was one girl in fact I particularly didn't want to see going away . . . '

'Was that Peggy?' Cam smiled. He had heard stories about her all right.

'Aye,' his father said simply. 'Well, at one time I was tempted to go the same way. My dad was always on to me about work and how I should get on, and not be stuck on the land like himself. It was as if it was some great shame to be a farmer! But after that, once I'd thought over everything having seen that poor lady for a whole year, I learned something; I learned to value what I had, what was important in life. I knew that more than even Peggy, I loved my home. Maybe I could have been a merchant banker in London, but every night I'd have been looking out of the window to catch a glimpse of the moon on Ben Luan! And if I couldn't have seen that, I couldn't have been happy. That's how it seemed to me, anyway.'

Duncan became silent; he wasn't a man given to such long speeches. Maybe he felt he'd said too much.

Cam just sat for a few moments staring into the fire, sorting out in his head what he wanted to say.

'It's a funny thing, Dad,' he said at last, 'but all these last days I've been thinking such a lot about stories. Different stories I've been told, by you and grandpa and mum and even Richard; all stories that have made up part of my life in different ways. It's as though all the important things are made up of stories, the things that matter to me. And I get this strange feeling that in a way they are all buried here, all around. D'you understand what I mean, or does it just sound daft?'

'Aye, I can understand, Cam. Maybe we need stories to explain life, to make it easier anyway. But I don't think they're only here. The reason you feel like that is because this is the only place you've ever lived! But there'll be stories in Aberdeen, stories beyond that, on and on; they won't go away, or cease to be, just 'cos you're leaving Ardnish! In a way they're like the folk you meet – some of them are good and some bad, and you have to choose which you want and leave the others behind. No one will take the ones at Ardnish away from you, that's for sure.'

Duncan struggled to his feet and yawned.

'I'd better get to my bed or I'll be good for nothing tomorrow! You come as well, Cam; your trouble is that you think too much – you were made that way, I suppose.'

Cam didn't answer, just smiled and said goodnight. The fire was down to nothing now, just a few blinks of orange in among the ash. He was hardly tired, but that was perhaps excitement more than anything else. He went over to the window and looked out. The fields were deathly still; you could have lit a match and with so little breeze could have held it until it burned out. Quietly he opened the back door and went out on to the steps, not bothering with his jacket or even his boots although the stars were thick in the sky and it was freezing hard again. So cold, and still only October! At that moment he didn't feel split, but at last ready to leave. It was time to go, and he felt excited, even glad. He loved this place to death, but it would be here all right when he came back, and nothing and nobody could take it away from him.

Over the past few days he had done what he wanted to do, and he had made peace with himself. A harp had been found; he thought of it as a heart, a core that was beyond time, that would not decay. Once again he looked up and over the wood to Ben Luan, and seemed to see on it a strange light, a fire burning. But this time he was not frightened, for it was a long, long way away and was not calling him. He felt at that moment every yard between there and Ben Luan was a year, that his life stretched on unbelievably far.

And one day he, too, would be as a story, written into the land and remembered.

WEST OF THE WORLD

For Finlay, who carries his island inside

It is blowing outside; it's blowing a mad storm. The windows are rattling so that I cannot sleep. It is as if the darkness has trouble harnessing my memories; they are blowing right across the Atlantic into this coast, into America. Every one of them from St Kilda.

I used to know a man on the island who would get his tunes that way, straight off the edge of the wind. His fiddle was that old, it was nearly falling to bits; the wood had turned black, with all the fingers that had held it. His tunes blew right in through the cracks in the windows. He always seemed to get them in the winter, when the sky would be black and boiling for six whole months without end, and the windows would be rattling all the night long.

Then, in the summer, he seemed to go dry. His eyes would turn listless, like pools without any water in them, and he would have no heart for playing at all. The fiddle would be just lying there, like another piece of driftwood brought up from the shore, with its dark wood shining like sallow cheeks. Hector would just be waiting for the winter. He would be drumming his gnarled fingers on the edge of the table, as if his spirit was clean gone from him and he was barely there at all.

That wind!

There was a time when I wouldn't even have noticed it. There was never a day without it. I remember how it would always be tugging at your hair, or driving like a steel blade at your face. Now, in this place, I notice a wind as much as anyone; I go out into the morning and I feel a breeze, and I can tell a change in its strength and direction. But never then.

Tonight, though, it's a comfort. If I switch off the light, if I close my eyes and listen, I could be back there, back in the very middle of childhood.

I am standing in the kitchen. There is the smell of rancid butter; there are three flies crawling over a cracked plate at the edge of the table where my sister is eating. She is flicking them away all the time so that they are making an angry sound, but they keep coming back.

My mother is bathing the baby. Its skin is the colour of parchment and it is bent over in the tin basin so that its stomach is wrinkled. That is Iain, the baby that nearly killed my mother. Now he is about three months old and he is just getting the first dusting of hair on his head, very soft hair that makes me think of a downy peewit chick. His big eyes move slowly and he furrows his brow so seriously that my sister Morag starts laughing and she goes over to the basin and splashes water over his tiny feet, because she cannot keep her hands off him.

I do not like Iain myself. I am tired of everyone always coming in to see him, praising him and touching his fluffy head. You would think there was never a baby before this. They have forgotten about me. They have forgotten Morag as well. Even my father is forever coming in from the fishing and the birds, to rock Iain in his arms and watch him and chuckle at him.

I am standing there at the corner of the table looking towards the fire, looking at my mother bending to wash this lump of soft flesh in the basin, looking at my sister waving her hand another time over her plate, her eyes always on the downy flesh. It is in my mind to do something to Iain. I am wanting him to be away forever, so that my mother is able to see me again, so that she will hold me as I sit on her knee, so that she may sing to me, and tell me stories about the seals, as she used to do. And I want her to let me have a bit of the new cream.

As I am standing there and listening to the splashing of the water and seeing the baby's chest shining with silver drops, I start to make a plan in my head. It is growing clearer and clearer and my heart is thumping because I am sure it is one that cannot fail. No one will ever find out.

The next evening, as the late light turns the low stone walls of the house the colour of butter – sharper even: the colour of pearl and diamond merged together – I am ready. My father is away at Stac Lee; he is on the cliffs, because it is fine enough for climbing and getting birds. Morag is with my mother, helping her to fold the clothes; I can hear their voices rising and falling.

Iain is there, in his bed of blankets. His eyes are so tightly shut; he looks to me like a kitten before its eyes have opened. He makes little noises in his sleep, tiny milky noises; his tightly clenched fists lie on top of the blankets. My hands have already reached out twice, ready to pick him up in my arms, and twice I have drawn back. The awful thought has come to me – what if my father comes home early? What if my mother or Morag finishes with the clothes and comes back into the kitchen? But then surely I could make up an excuse easily enough?

In a moment, I have snatched up the bundle in one quick movement. The downy head is lolling over my arm, and my nostrils are filled with the sweet, thick smell of the baby's clothes, and of his skin itself. I stand then in the doorway for a moment feeling the wind in my face. I look this way and that, along the row of houses, and there isn't a soul to be seen at all. The sun has gone in and the clouds are heavy and *gruamach*. It will rain soon. Suddenly, I begin to run; I mean to try to cover the ground quickly up over the grassy brae behind the houses. But soon I am finding it hard to do more than walk, for Iain is so heavy. I never thought a baby could be so heavy! He is still fast asleep in my arms, beneath the blankets, far away in his milky dreams.

I see them now down at the shore, a small gathering of men beneath the horseshoe ring of the hills, but they are nothing more than black shadows, like posts, strung along the edge of the tide. If a voice had spoken at my back then, I do not believe I would have taken any notice. I am making heavy weather of it now, struggling to get up over the edge of the hill and then away over to the cliffs.

I look up for an instant and my eye is caught by the outline of Stac Lee, like a single tooth standing there, in the midst of the great heaving of the sea. Around it are the ledges full of nesting birds and even from there, even from Hirta, I think I can see the misty swirling of those birds, and hear their shrill cries.

I start then to go downhill and my feet make slapping noises as I go through pool after pool of brown peaty water. Then the baby is awake; his round face opens into a wide wail and he starts struggling as if to escape from me, tugging and stretching as if he is aware of what I have in mind to do. I hiss at him to be quiet. I have a feeling of panic, as if he might waken the whole village, as if my mother might even hear from where she is with Morag and come running to find us. But the more I try to quieten him, the more he struggles and wails.

And now, at last, I reach the edge of the cliffs. The wind is coming in and is starting to buffet me like a mad thing, tugging at me in strong gusts so that I have trouble holding on to the baby. Out to the west the sun has broken apart; like a fire in a huge grate that has gone down to the very embers, full of vivid orange and red and the whitish-yellow of ash. I look down and see the water coming in from the Atlantic and rubbing over the rocks. It is all smashed and white as snow, or like milk that has been spilt over a slab at someone's door. It creeps away and goes back before the next great wrinkle pulls up from the grey and splits like silver.

By this time Iain has quietened; he looks up at me with his huge blue eyes and then seems to follow the movement of the big birds that hang in the wind above us. I think about how long it will take for him to be washed away by the tide, and for a moment or two I panic again and think of what I am doing. I almost change my mind, but harden my heart again and remember that there will be no more Iain, nothing left of him at all, and my mother will be sorry for what she has done, for her neglect. And she will cry and take me back on to her knee again, and sing to me.

Abruptly a huge hand grabs hold of my shoulder. I look round, into the face of my father.

All that night I lay awake, my face sodden with crying. I was sore all over; whichever way I turned, to try to sleep, I felt the marks of the belt. I was aware that I was whining like a dog, but I couldn't help it; if I had cried out loud, my father would have come in and beaten me again, he was that angry.

Morag wasn't sleeping either, I knew. One time she had come over and knelt beside me, her long hair straggling round her white face. She stroked my face as if I was a puppy and laid her cheek gently against my own wet one. For a minute I held tightly on to her as I stared into the empty darkness and listened to the wind pounding the walls of the house.

I had the feeling that my mother had not wanted him to hit me; or maybe that was what I wanted to think. But it seemed to me that she understood more than he did. The moment she saw Iain safe and sound, I thought that something in her expression had no anger in it at all; I remembered the brown wideness of her eyes as my father hauled me away. But she said not a word to stop him.

My father was not a cruel man; no, there was no cruelty in him at all. But if he was afraid or upset, he could change like the wind or the sea. And well I knew that he had been nearly out of his mind that day, fearful that something had happened to Iain. Oh, I knew all right what he had been through. He had come back from the cliffs early, to find my mother and sister torn with grief, and he had gone hammering out of the house, racing away – but in the right direction so that he came upon me in time.

I can remember listening to the sounds Iain himself was making that night; his cradle was creaking as he tossed about. Maybe he was having nightmares? And then he would cry out and my mother would get up and go to him. I cried because of that most of all, because I did not believe she loved me any more. She loved him more than myself, and now, after what I had done, she would never love me again. My throat and my chest and my face were sore with crying; I had reached that point where you are pressing tears from your eyes although they have long since grown sore and tired and dry. All the time my thoughts would keep going back to my mother; and in the end I thought that perhaps she did understand . . . in that moment when she had turned to look at me, I thought, I hoped, that she had seen why I had done such a thing.

I had been the first and I had been the favourite. She had called me her own Roddy.

'I happened to see a light on in your room, Mr Gillies, and I felt I should look in to see you. By rights, you know, you shouldn't have your light on so late because you need your sleep. Now, come on back to bed and you can finish whatever you're writing in the morning. That's it, up slowly, and I'll help you over to bed once you're on your feet. D'you hear that wind out there? It's been blowing a gale for the last twelve hours and it doesn't look like it's going to let up for a while yet. Now, hang on to me – that's it. No, you don't need the rail; I've got hold of you. There we are now; you'll soon be cosy in bed. You could've caught your death of cold sitting over there by the window in your night things – these windows are terrible for draughts. Whoever built this place didn't know a lot. What's that – I didn't catch what you said? Ah, he certainly wasn't a Scot. No indeed, you're right there. Haven't lost your sense of humour, have you, Mr Gillies? Now then, here we are. I'll just plump up the pillows for you; tuck your feet right down, that's it. Now go ahead and get a good night's sleep, and no wandering back to that desk to write; d'you hear? Otherwise I'll have to tell Nurse Johnson and you won't like that, will you? All right now; sleep well. See you in the morning.'

I remember I found a lamb once; it was in the springtime. It was the strange smell that stopped me in my tracks; later I knew it was the tang of blood. I smelled it as soon as I stood in the doorway of the shed, where I had gone to look for my knife. I was going to go away, but then I heard this shifting, this wee noise, so I went into the darkness, blindly. I couldn't see a thing and I just groped my way with my hands out in front of me. And then the sheep moved away and as my eyes began to get used to the dark, I could see it on the far side and the lamb not near it at all. I bent down to touch the lamb; I could feel it trembling and the whole of its back was sodden, like bread soaked in milk, except that this was sticky with the blood. The poor little thing was afraid of me; its eyes turned up towards me, glowing big and afraid, full of distrust and fear. It was breathing heavily and its chest was heaving. I wanted to do something to help it, but I didn't know what. I couldn't go for my father because he was away at the fishing. I could hear the mother sheep shuffling about, not far from my feet, maybe trying to get back to her lamb, but I didn't move, I couldn't move, because I was full of fear myself. And what was making me afraid was the thought of death. I was remembering Iain and how I had been ready to throw him from the cliffs, and it was the thought of the blood that filled my mind – how Iain's blood would have splashed on the rocks and dyed the sea. I thought this little lamb was dying and I didn't want it to die; but I felt so helpless, as if there was nothing in the world I could do to prevent it.

And it seems to me now after all the years that, in a way, I am like that lamb myself. I am breathing fast and staring into the darkness, not knowing what lies beyond. The wind is howling outside, battering the stone walls of this retirement home in America where I am ending my days. Who would have thought such a thing would happen to me. And I am no stronger than a lamb. In my mind, though, I am as young as in the days when I would be springing barefoot through the meadows, on my way with half a dozen others to gather shellfish from the low-tide rocks. In the inner world of my mind I can hear, smell and touch each thing from the island. All of it. Every single thing is intact in my mind. It is like a sword from a battle, dropped from the hand of a fallen soldier, that lies buried under the peat for two hundred years and more, before it is recovered and brought out sharp and clean, unscarred by time. I think to myself that my body is no different from that of the soldier; it is brittle and has wasted away to uselessness. But my mind – my mind is not like that at all; it is as sharp and clear as the sword.

I want to survive as badly as that lamb. I am breathing fast and urgently in the darkness, clinging on to what remains of my life. I want to order my thoughts; I want to leave a record of the world I once knew, before it is too late. None of the other St Kildans did such a thing. There were many I knew who died, barely after their feet had touched the mainland. For most of them it was an exile they just could not bear and they faded, like trees uprooted from a soil they have known for centuries and then put into strange ground.

I want to remember all of it. I want to go back there, if only in my mind, to gather together, thread after thread, the torn garment of it.

It lies dead east of here, far across the water. I go towards it like a mist, to encircle and recover it.

I am back in the church.

'And as we are gathered here today in the sight of Almighty God, we have reason to give Him thanks, for He has preserved us from many snares. He has preserved us from the wild and tempestuous raging of the sea, and let not one of his children be harmed by the winter's violence. Even as He stilled the waters of the Sea of Galilee and preserved the lives of the fearful disciples, so He has stilled our hearts and brought us peace. Yet we would not be unmindful of the manifold blessings He has bestowed upon us in His grace, even in this place in the midst of the turmoil of the ocean. For He has filled the sea with an abundance of fish, and has given the soil that it might bear fruit and sustain our bodies. For He is mindful that we are but frail flesh, that we are as Adam: of the dust, raised up for but a season and then returned to the dust.

And, Oh Lord, this day we would remember before Thee in Thy holiness those iniquities which darken our souls . . . '

I am trying to follow Mr Munro's prayer in the grey shadows of the church, keeping my eyes closed for fear that my father might know if I open them, and would be angry. But my left leg is full of pins and needles; it is as if a hundred thousand ants are crawling up and down, their feet scratching and tickling. I want to stamp my foot hard on the floor, but I cannot, for if I do so my father will be sure to look up.

The wind is gusting outside and a draught sweeps like a ghost against my side, making me shiver. The whole of the island community is sitting here; there is no one absent except for Mary MacQueen, who has been ill a whole month and who may not live beyond the New Year. Mr Munro is the missionary, as if we are some distant African or Indian colony whose souls are being won back from darkness. But then in a way that is how we are regarded – as the last out-post on the edge of the world, a huddle of half-savage and half-starved beings, the relics of a primitive society.

I am frightened by the church. The building and the words are like one another; they do not seem separate to me at all. The church is crumbling; it is filled with damp and blackness, and it is as if gradually the wild ground outside is reclaiming it. The minister always speaks of the realm of darkness, and of the Church being as a light, which must not be extinguished. But to me the church and the words of Mr Munro seem dark; they run cold hands down my spine and make me afraid in the night. I think of eternity and what it means; I think of heaven and hell and am afraid of them both, because they go on without ending. I am powerless to shut out the horrible whisper I hear in my head: 'for ever and ever and ever and ever and ever and ever . . . '

My father brings down the Books to read each evening. Iain looks as though he has been modelled from wax; his eyes are always shut impossibly tight and the lamp shines on his face, turning it to the colour of a tallow candle. Morag and I sit together but we never say anything, nor do we look at one another. We bow our heads when our father says, 'Let us pray,' and keep them tightly shut until he has finished. But often it is then that I escape in my mind; I am running down by the shore in my bare feet looking for driftwood, or I am up by the well looking out towards Boreray and the Stacs.

My father's voice becomes one long, deep sound; the words run into each other and are no longer distinguishable, but I can smell the clover and hear the sound of summer waves plashing against the rocks. It is as if I have slipped out through the door without anyone noticing.

When my father reads, he moves his finger over the words and his voice is slow and uneven. Sometimes he hesitates over a word, and moves in his chair uncomfortably. My mother has a beautiful voice, but it is my father who must always 'take the Books.' And anyway, she is holding Iain.

After my father finishes the prayer, I open my eyes and feel unbearably tired; I do not understand why it should always be like this. Morag and I say goodnight to our father and I can hardly wait to reach my bed, I am so filled with weariness. The fire has gone down by then to a round red-gold light so strong that it hurts to look into its heart. Up in the chimney the wind is moaning, or sometimes howling like some wolf spirit, it seems all year and every year. There is never a time without wind at all.

'This bed is damp, Mr Gillies. I warned you about this before. Why didn't you tell Nurse O'Neill that you needed to go to the toilet, hmm? That was naughty. I have a busy morning as it is and this doesn't need to happen – and you got up to sit by the window. Was that after you had been put to bed? Look at me when I'm talking to you, please, Mr Gillies. I think it was, wasn't it? You know that you shouldn't get up again after you've been put to bed. The only time you can get up is when you need to go to the toilet and that is what you should have done, right? Now I'll have to change these sheets. Is it wet on the other side too? Oh yes, it is. I'll have to change the whole bed and these pyjamas will have to go into the wash at once. Do you hear what I am saying to you? I don't want this to happen again. Now don't move one inch until I get this bed changed . . . '

There was a time I'll never forget, when we went out to look for someone who had fallen from the cliffs. We went out in the boat and I was maybe fourteen or fifteen at the time. My father was there along with three others. The village street was buried under mist, I remember – clenched fists of it. The sea was bucking and heaving the whole time, tearing this way and that, but never tiring. I kept getting great cuffs of water in the face. At first I tried to keep them from drenching my neck, but in the end I just gave up. They were shouting things on the boat and pointing here and there, but the wind was dragging away their voices all the time, tossing them into the air, so that I couldn't make out a word at all. Stac Lee was bouncing up and down on the edge of the horizon, a huge grey standing stone between miles of grey water under an endless grey sky. I held on to the wood of the side until my hand was orange-red, until it seemed to have been soldered to the wood itself, and all the feeling had drained from my fingers.

I could no longer move or even think. I had come running out of the house when I heard that Ewen had been lost, full of fear and urgency, but all of that seemed gone now. Even the other men and my father had fallen silent. Their hair and beards were drenched with water; they stared ahead, hungry for the shore and home; the sea now empty and dead.

I felt so sick that I hardly cared any more whether we reached land or not. The boat was lurching into the air and then thudding back into the waves, over and over again, so that in the end I did not even know in what direction Hirta lay. I was drenched to the skin. I had stopped shifting on the boards to escape the thrash of each new wave that rose high over the boat; water was slapping and banging all the time around the inside of the boat, as high as my ankles.

Then all at once my eyes rested on my father. I saw his head lifted; saw the profile of his face and his chin jutting against the sky. His eyes were not closed; they were fiercely open and yet it seemed to me that he was praying. I cannot describe how he looked to me then; it was as if his whole body was clenched in prayer.

Only a little after that a promontory rose out of the mist like the head of some vile sea monster and we were there. The air was loud with shouts and orders, for we were indeed about to be impaled on the rocks. An arm seemed to wrench me bodily into the sky; I toppled and swallowed a huge mouthful of salt water, rose choking and dragged myself, broken and exhausted, up among rocks, every step an agony. As I went, the freezing wind flayed my face and my ribs.

Somehow or other, then, we came home. They were all waiting in the village street. In my mind, even now, there is a picture of them, each face with the same expression all along the whole line, whether young or old. But our eyes carried the loss of Ewen.

By then I was past caring. I have to confess that I thought only of myself, for the uncontrollable shaking of my whole body. It seemed as if the wind had got inside me and was storming through my entire frame, tearing me violently. I remember seeing Iain's face for a fleeting moment and the fear in his huge eyes as he looked at me before hiding himself against my mother. I think I was afraid myself then, afraid of what I must look like. I remember the clothes being taken off me, as if I was being skinned; I remember standing there thin and white, shaking violently with the cold. And then at last I was in close by the fire and wrapped in warm blankets; my shoulders and back were dry at last and the heat of the fire was burning my face, my chest, my feet. A blessed warmth spreading right through my body.

There seemed to be no one left in the room at all but my mother; everyone else had faded away. And I could hear the wind outside, still chasing along the island, wrapping itself round the houses and shaking them, rattling the doors and shutters. I just kept staring into the heart of the fire, saying not a word; I couldn't keep my eyes from the dancing of the flames. And always in there, struggling and writhing as if striving to escape, was the form of Ewen.

Years later, they would always be asking me where the name St Kilda came from. For long enough I didn't care. I would tell them that we had always called the island Hirta and they had to make do with that. Certainly there was never any Saint Kilda, whatever anyone may say. Eventually, I came to play their game, and to give them what they wanted I would tell them of how the Norsemen arrived on Hirta. At first they knew nothing of the island. All they would have seen from the western skerries of Harris would have been a couple of ghostly crags scarring the skies – surely the most inhospitable sight you could imagine.

'But now, imagine a longship coming out of the west of Norway, on its way to northern Scotland, and think of it being shaken about on the sea like a rat in a terrier's mouth . . . The storm lasts a day and a night, and the longship is blown off course. This storm is different, not, as it almost always is, coming out of the edge of America, but one that's swept out of Norway towards the Skagerrak and has turned to thunder along the top of Scotland.

'When the mists are drawn back like great grey curtains, there's not a thing alive on the sea. The water is as calm as glass and the Hebrides seem to have been blown away by the wind. The Norsemen are by this time both bewildered and afraid; half of their precious supply of fresh water has been lost, and what is left will last only one day longer. The fear of thirst begins to burn in their minds.

'Then, all at once, an oarsman half-rises at his place, his arm stretching towards the south-west, and a cry on his lips. The rest of the ship falls quiet; the oars hang in the grey air, drops of water silvering their wood. It is land. Not the land they have longed for, gentle and easy with green glens and hills softened by time, but a jagged, black mass that might have been broken out of their own homeland, unforgiving and harsh.

'For a moment they see it and are silent; their eyes take in those shattered remnants of rock, disbelieving that their salvation can ever lie in their barrenness. But it is their only hope. One after another the voices rise, the ship sets its course and they are steering directly, desperately, towards the place.

'When they reach the island, it is as if the cliffs have been ranged round it in order to keep them out. They listen to the wild screaming of the cloud of seabirds that sounds in their ears like mockery, and wonder where on earth in all this dark kingdom they can hope to find sanctuary. Thirst is burning in their throats as they drift around the edge of the coast, to find themselves staring at the great horseshoe of the bay. With a ragged cry of relief, three men have already plunged forward into the water as the longship prow daggers towards the beach.

'One of the three, the youngest and the swiftest on his feet, is already preparing to start across the island in search of fresh water. He pounds against the contours of the hill and struggles amongst the stones and scree to gain the high ground of the island. By now, as he turns to glance over his shoulder, the longship seems no more than a toy boat dancing on the waves' edge, the white ovals of the sailors' faces indistinguishable from one another.

'At last he reaches the summit of the hill where the breeze is fresh and cool on his brow. For the barest second he pauses, overwhelmed by the vastness and power of the surrounding ocean; from his vantage point, the other islands around rise like the backs of whales from the grey water. For a moment, too, the memory of home, his own island far out on the Norwegian coast, floods his spirit with longing and he curses the stony wilderness. Then he remembers his own thirst, and that of his companions, and his eyes scan the plateau of the island with the accuracy of a merlin. He listens intently for the slightest chuckle of a stream and there, in among the grey boulders and mattress of heather, he finds the bubble of fresh silver water. He cannot help but throw himself down and drink as though worshipping the very ground from which this blessed freshness springs. It is clear and satisfying, and cold as the snow that covers the highest hills.

'His thirst quenched, he rushes over the island plateau once more to hurtle down the scree so fast that he is in danger of snapping his ankle. Laughter and delight shine from his face as he shouts to the others eagerly, "*Kilde!*" Fresh water.'

'There's someone here to see you, Mr Gillies. Come on, let me help you sit up so you can see. Now, I'll just open the curtains and let in the morning for you, though heaven knows it isn't much of a day. Kevin, you draw up a chair for yourself or sit down at the end of the bed, won't you? Don't be shy now. How's school? I hope you're working real hard? Not being distracted by the big bad city? All right, I'd better get on to the other rooms now and leave you two in peace. If Mr Gillies needs anything just give me a shout, Kevin, and if you want some coffee it's in the day room, second on the left down the corridor. See you before you leave.'

Mary MacQueen never got well again. She was so thin, there seemed to be nothing left of her face. She looked like the skeleton of a ship, its ribs left high and dry on the beach months after the water has worn away the sides. Her breath rattled as if her chest was made of brittle wood that would snap at the slightest touch.

Her husband, I remember, watched over her but never seemed to grieve. A strange kind of winter had frozen all that lay within him; only his breath kept up, as constant as the coming of the waves. The wind battered at the shutters and doors, and rattled in the lungs of the dying woman. Until one morning. Her husband remained beside her, but he had fallen asleep. His cheeks were hollow and the closed lids of his eyes almost luminescent. For a whole week we were not allowed to run or laugh; it was as if we were being punished for her death.

'I brought you these apples, Mr Gillies. I know you don't really like the food in here, so I thought I'd bring you some. I took a break from school to help my mom and dad pick the crop. We've a whole field behind the yard and, what with the storm and the rain, they figured we ought to get them in early. I sure hope you like 'em. Mom said you weren't keeping too good. I'm sorry . . . you look a bit better now, though. Stronger.

Were you kept awake by the storm? Boy, that was some wind; I was fast asleep and I woke up with this terrible crack – we lost two trees. Lucky they didn't hit anything. Anyway we got the rest of the apples in this morning and I guess we can use the wood from the trees for burning some time. Gee, dad was real mad they came down. He's crazy about that orchard. You can't drag him away from it sometimes till after dark. I kind of miss it myself when I'm here in New York – you know there's not a thing to see from the window except buildings. It takes me ages to get to sleep the first night after I come back. I lie awake for hours listening to the traffic. Didn't you find New York crazy the first time you saw it, Mr Gillies? After coming from the kind of place you did, I mean? I'm not sure which would be worse, coming from there to the big city or the other way around, if you see what I mean.

'Listen, I'd better go find Nurse O'Neill. She told me I could talk to you for five minutes but that was all. I don't want to tire you out or anything. I'll be back, though. In a week or two to see how you're doing. Anyway, I'll see you before your birthday. All right. You go ahead and enjoy these apples. Bye.'

I remember once I had gone over to the north side of the island. My father was away fowling and mother was outside, working hour after hour at her spinning. There was a ship of tourists over from the mainland. The women were pecking and gabbling like a bunch of fat hens as they took pictures of the street and squeezed into the Post Office in a hurry to buy postcards. The great thing was to get them franked with the St Kilda postmark, of course. Often, we children would hang about, hoping for coins or maybe a few sweets from them. I have to confess the coming of the tourists had made us all greedy. That day, though, I remember only that I wanted to be away from it all. I think I was beginning to realise even then what it all meant, what it was doing to us – we were a kind of spectacle for them to stare at, and laugh about. It all seemed to have a dark air about it, threatening. Morag was sitting on a raised bank with Iain on her knee. Sitting with wide blue eyes, swinging her legs and looking at peace with it all. I remember feeling angry with her as the tourists began moving down in a herd towards their ship and, after looking to left and right to make sure nobody was there, I stuck my tongue out at her. I felt victorious; felt that what I had done was somehow stronger than any words. I started up the hill, past the graveyard and aiming for the top. I had to fight against the wind and by the time I was up, I was right out of breath. With each step down the easy slope to Glenn Mor, I recovered my calm, my eyes fixed on the clear sweep of Glen Bay with its fortresses of rock guarding each side. It always stilled my thoughts to look at the rocks.

The water was driving into the shore sheer white, I remember, as pure as a gannet's wing. The waves roared as they piled in over the grey shingle and hissed as they were sucked back out to the Atlantic. I ran to a promontory of rock and stood on its summit, standing as tall and still as I was able, with only my hair moving in the wind. Soon the wind gutted me and I climbed down and began walking along the very edge of the shore. Out beyond the western-most head of Hirta, the Cambir, lay Soay. From where I stood it was impossible to tell where the one began and the other ended.

I was scrambling among the rocks, thinking of nothing at all, when I spotted the bottle. It was a moment or two before I took in what it was or thought to pick it up, but as I bent down at last another wave frothed in and I had to scramble backwards to escape it. My hand closed on the bottle a second time and I carried it out of reach of the waves. I am not even sure why I bothered with it at all, for it was no strange shape, just an ordinary straight-sided bottle with a cork in it. Maybe even then, though, I had caught a glimpse of the piece of paper that was stuck inside.

I went up into the lee of some rocks and crouched down low, my heart drumming with excitement as I contemplated the mysterious bit of paper. The bottle was as dry inside as a bird's nest and the paper crackled against my probing fingers, but it was hard to get it out for it was stuck down tight below the neck. I stretched and squeezed my fingers until I was in danger of getting them trapped, so I removed them grumpily, as a bear might when he couldn't reach a hive's honey. I was so excited about the message, sure that it held something of great interest. I went back to the rocks and hunted about to try to find the thinnest piece of wood. It was difficult to find any, every scrap that was beached on St Kilda was precious to us; what was of no use in the house or for the work was gratefully kept for the fire. The only thing I could find, I remember, was a strong bit of seaweed, a twist that had been thrown clear of the water and dried by the wind. At last I was able to catch an edge of the paper and drag it up. With trembling fingers, I carefully smoothed the crumpled sheet. It was a letter, as I had dreamed it might be. I cannot now remember, after all this time, exactly what was written in it, but it seemed so important at the time that it was a letter. And I felt so important, felt that it had really been written to me.

Of course, the idea of a letter in a bottle was nothing new to us on the island. For many years, what were known as 'St Kilda mailboats' had been sent out – missives placed in bottles, or in syrup or cocoa tins, with a float made from a sheep's bladder attached. They were picked up, too, as far afield as Norway but usually on the western isles, and the government even gave half a crown to the finder. But I had never heard of it working the other way round, and that is why it meant so much to me – the first letter I had ever received in my life.

I had to calm myself to read it. It was from a girl, a girl called Ina, and she lived in America. I read it through a dozen times, I'm sure, and I felt like shouting and singing there on Glen Bay. I sat for a while in the lee of the rocks, watching the last white edge of sun break and spread among the long ranks of cloud. I knew that under that light lay America, somewhere so far away that I could not have seen it even if Hirta had possessed the highest mountain.

I kept thinking to myself that it was a miracle. It made me feel humble to know that a bottle with a letter had come all the way from America to me, Roddy Gillies. I thought of how Moses had received the tablets of stone from God, and now I had my own miracle.

After it had grown too cold to sit there on the northern edge of the island, for the wind drove in like a knife from the sea, raw and cruel, I strove back over the headlands until at last I stood on the summit, looking down towards the village. The last little flotillas of boats were making their way out to the ship in the bay; soon Hirta would be quiet again, nothing changed except for a little more silver in the homes of some of the people. Mother would probably have sold some yards of her fine tweed; there would be a glow on her because of the compliments that would have been paid for her work. But my father would not be in a good mood, I knew, because he would have had to answer far too many questions – the same questions over and over again. About what it was like to climb the stacks and what were the Gaelic words for this and that, and how did we ever manage to survive the winter with all the gales. Oh, the tourists meant well enough, but they could be trying, and men like my father seemed to feel it most. Morag and I knew better than to disturb him in the evening after a tourist ship had been in; he would be sitting like a storm in his chair, not saying a word, just staring. Even my mother would be fluttering about here and there, anxious at his mood, unsure of what to do to please him.

But on that special evening, I remember, as I stood there looking down on the little boats and the final procession of folk going down to the shore, I had a glow in my heart. The letter was safe, deep in my pocket, the letter that had found its way from America to me. I saw the girl Ina all the time in my mind's eye; I had already talked and laughed with her. I had a strange bridge from this island on the edge of the world to the wider world, and something of the isolation and the loneliness I had ever known I felt, passed away.

Yet the curious thing was that in the end I never did reply to the letter. I hid it at first, in case anyone in the house might find it – especially my father. I don't know exactly why I should have been so afraid of him seeing it, except that he always seemed to hate anything out of the ordinary, and small things, things which seemed nothing to the rest of us could annoy him. Like the time when young Duncan brought the wireless set from Harris. My father wouldn't even speak to him or look at the set at all. And once when Iain walked hand in hand with a little girl, on a day when the tourists were on Hirta, my father saw them and hauled Iain away and gave him a whipping.

Of course there was nothing wrong about the letter, there was just nothing in it at all, but there was something alien about it all the same, and I could not be sure what my father would think about it. So I hid it under a box beside my bed, to make sure that not even Morag would stumble upon it.

I thought a lot about the answer I would send in the first few days; ideas would keep going round and round in my head. But then I started to wonder what I could really say to this girl in America. What was my life made up of, after all? There was school and there was work, and in the evening there was sometimes a bit of free time before the Books were brought down from their shelf. And on the Sabbath we went to church. When I thought of it like that, my life seemed grey and empty. I looked out of the tiny window at the curve of the Bay and the long promontory running into the sea, and all of my life seemed hammered out of that bleak rock.

So in the end I came to see that I just could not write back to a girl like Ina after all. I was too ashamed of our poverty, our simplicity; and probably I was afraid too of making mistakes in my English and spelling. As time passed I forgot about the letter altogether. It lay there under the box during all the bang and clatter of the winter storms. When the summer returned, and with it the tourists, I took the letter out and sold it for a whole penny to a boy from England.

The night is so cold now. I can hear the nurses' voices far off in their room, sometimes with shouts of laughter, coarse and loud. The wind has gone, it has blown itself out. All across New York State, so they tell me, the apples have been blown down. I see them in my mind's eye, with the leaves lying round them in crimson and gold circlets.

Kevin has gone away. The apples he brought are still lying on the shelf above the cupboard. The curtains have not been properly closed and the moon sometimes peeps out from behind the clouds and spills into the room, curving around the apples and making them look as if they have been beaten from pure silver.

His gift has brought so many thoughts to me. I never saw a tree at all until I went to the mainland. Oh, I saw plenty of pictures of them, but I never really imagined how they would be – a drawing in a book captures nothing of the real thing. Nothing of the wonder. But fruit – I loved fruit more than anything. It was a great luxury to us on the island. I would marvel at the colour of oranges; I knew nothing that was so bright, so vivid. It would seem to me that a whole tropical sun had been distilled into perfect miniature droplets, warming, transforming that dark kitchen on Hirta.

And still to this day I will take fruit in my hands and marvel at it, feeling a kind of gratitude whenever I touch it. Kevin would think if he saw the apples lying there that I did not appreciate his gift. He will hardly know why I have not touched them, why I will keep them and look at them for a long time.

Long before we left the island, things had been going wrong. Everything seemed to be a struggle. My mother seemed tired all the time, I remember, as if it was all too much for her. I had the feeling that although she never slackened in her work – and constant work it always was – her heart had gone out of it. Every day was a fight – against the wind, the damp, the dark. I remember so well one day I really looked at her and my heart seemed to leap into my mouth. She was standing near the fire, her hands busy with cleaning, and as I looked I suddenly saw her not as she now was, but as what she would become. It frightened me so badly that I turned away with a shudder. The deterioration was already beginning.

The passing years were bringing change to my father, too. He may not have looked much older, but I was aware that the iron strength of his legs and arms, strength of which he was always proud, was melting. Once I watched as he lifted a sack that had been landed by boat on the shore. He heaved it as he had always done on to his shoulder and began the ascent towards the village bent almost double. But then, as I looked again, I saw him pause; I saw his shoulders heaving as he laid the sack down in an effort to catch his breath. He glanced up towards the houses, afraid perhaps that someone might have noticed his weakness, for always before he had taken pride in making the journey in one.

But the truth is that it wasn't just my parents who were failing; the whole life of the island was in decline. And, young as I was, I couldn't help being aware of it. Oh, I knew it had always been a struggle for survival. How many times old Hector next door would tell his stories of the old days, of stormy times and hardship and scarcity of food, and of all that the people had learned to endure. But he would tell me much more about the good times. Somehow they seemed to have kept going, to have succeeded in the struggle in a way we were not doing now. He would tell me how the seabirds, the gannets and fulmars and puffins, were the great mainstay of life; how their oil, dried carcasses and feathers would find ready sale on the mainland, along with other items like cheese and barley and wool. But times had changed so now you could say that the tweed – and of course the tourists – were our only source of income. Hector would list at length the many things being brought into St Kilda nowadays; things that we had never thought of needing before.

'What it comes down to,' he would say, 'is that we are living on charity now, and the heart has gone out of us.'

I would have liked to argue with him, but I knew he was right. From the day I had seen my father falter in carrying that heavy sack, I watched him closely, aware that he was beginning to fail. And his weakness enraged him. I had seen him angry often enough before, but there was generosity and even gentleness in his spirit also. This anger was at himself. It was a bitterness which began to eat into him. He would test himself with heavy loads and old challenges and when he failed, it maddened him. On the days when tourists came over from the mainland he would insist on ferrying more than any other islander. I could never understand this, for he had no love for their cameras or their questions. He seldom spoke to them, I knew, on those journeys out to the ship, but would just sit there with his eyes fixed on Conachair above.

I think, looking back, that I forgave him for his hardness. I could not judge him, because I understood something of what he was feeling. I saw the sacrifice of his life and the little he had been rewarded with for it. But I believe that even then, Iain hated him. He had never been an easy child; even his birth had been near death for my mother, but there was ever in him some kind of dark shadow that would rise blackest against our father, struggling and defiant.

I was too old for the belt myself and too wise to earn it, but Iain felt it across his hands on many a day. The anger and resentment of their conflict seemed to lie dormant in both their spirits; but they kept an eye on each other all the time. Morag was almost always on Iain's side. Sometimes she would dare to defend him with incredible bravery, her hands trembling with emotion as she stood up to my father. I had my own conflicts with Iain, of course; because of the battle he was waging he had become harsh and suspicious so that he would imagine I was cheating him. Gradually, I spent less and less time in his company, often glad to be away from the house altogether when the chance came, although indeed that was seldom enough.

My mother was burdened and tired; the conflict between Iain and my father only served to weigh down her spirit the more. The house was too small for us; it was impossible to escape for any length of time and only the hours of the night seemed to offer any respite.

It was at this time that my father began to rebuild the wall. It was an old wall that ran down from the house towards the sea, and a section of it had toppled when a ram charged against it. The stones were already there for the task; it was not that he had to bear them from the shore or the higher hillside. I think some of the younger men probably saw something of the struggle that was beginning to buckle him, for they gathered around him at once to make sure that the labour was shared.

But he must have sensed the pity in their eyes; he was adamant that it was nothing, that it would easily be done before the Saturday morning. In vain they tried to dissuade him and when they would not leave him, he grew angry; the red spots I knew so well above his cheeks widened and his jaw set like stone. He told them one last time and they nodded and quietly left him.

The autumn was beginning. Another summer had passed. We had already felt the tilting of the earth and knew that winter was not all that far away. The blue skies of the mornings had a yellow-white brightness where the last stars lay like pearls. The wind was sharp; it could be sore in the face as it drove up from the shore against the village.

I think I was afraid for my father even then. All that Thursday he laboured. I can remember so clearly watching him from the window, his dark silhouette bending and striving hour after hour. It did not rain on the island, although white clouds smudged the sea more than once, and a little piece of rainbow shone like a ribbon above the place where the mainland lay. Out to the west the long dragon tail of Dun was all but buried in mist; around its black shores the waves leapt, flash after black flash.

It was one of those days which never grows entirely light, but remains grey and *gruamach* till nightfall. I had seen him at work when I was going down to the schoolroom, and I saw him with a stab on my way home. I wanted to tell him to give up, to come home now and rest. Perhaps I even stopped on the track, but I said nothing. Only I know my heart thudded as I made my way up between the houses, watching him bend and rise, bend and rise. He never saw me at all; he had withdrawn to another world altogether, and was blind to everything but the rubble round his feet. By the time I reached the door, I desperately wanted him to finish, to come home, for I was truly afraid of what I saw in him, this frightening determination not to grow weak, not to fail. Because he had started to feel his age, he wanted to push himself all the harder, as if to restore by sheer brute force all that his body had possessed before. I found myself unable to stop watching him in a kind of horrified fascination as the darkness started to fall and the mist crept like wolves from the edge of the sea.

I wanted him to finish and yet I did not. There was in the house a delicious quiet I had not known in long months. My mother was folding yards of tweed with the patient accuracy she had always had and at that moment there seemed a contentedness about her eyes that had been absent for many weeks. Morag and Iain were sitting at the little table writing; the scratching of their pencils and the occasional quiet sounds of the cloth being folded were the only sounds in the whole house.

It was the next day it happened. There was to be a service later that Friday and my father wanted the wall to be finished in good time for it, perhaps so that when the men filed down towards the church their eyes might be drawn to the wall and they would wonder, *has John Gillies completed such a task in that time?*

There was a section of it, though, that had rolled away in the night, for he had tried to finish too quickly. The largest boulder lay rolled over on its side in the grass – a mighty, misshapen thing that would have been the weight of a sturdy calf. My father must have lunged at it, his back bent the wrong way. All I know is that I remember the sound of his cry to this day; I can hear it as though it had lingered in the air there, with all the pain and struggle and fear of defeat in its echo. My mother flew out to him. I dived towards the window and saw him lying in the grass, his face turned up towards me with such a look on it that fear flooded my whole being. The cry seemed to remain; it seemed to stab me like a dagger so that I was rooted there, looking out on this frozen painting, my father like a child on the ground and my mother bending to hold him . . . for a moment. Then she was shouting for me to call the nurse. Morag and Iain were around me with questions and I was dragging on my boots, shouting things wildly and running, running with all my strength.

I think what I felt most at that moment was sheer fear that somehow or other I had wished my father's accident to happen. I tried to tell myself that I had willed no such thing, that such a thought was madness; yet standing at the window the night before I knew I had imagined what life might be like were he no longer there. Tears of anger and remorse burned my face as I found the nurse at last and brought her back to where he was still lying.

He was about to be helped inside by the men. All his anguish must have been multiplied tenfold by the humiliation of being carried like a child into his own house. He was clutching at his chest and side as if he had been stabbed, and his eyes were rolling round, big and afraid as he caught sight of the nurse. Behind him, the wall remained ruined, the stones at one place scattered over the grass, a foretaste of the falling of all the walls that was to come, the walls of the houses and the byres, and of the very church itself.

At last the men left. Only the nurse stayed. She was with my father and we could hear their voices as we sat motionless in the other room. We looked round in surprise as he hobbled towards the fire, the nurse in the wake of my mother. 'I will not go to the mainland,' he said, and his voice was deadly calm, the words accentless and flat – the way he always spoke, I thought, when he had come to a decision and would not countenance changing it. The nurse stood there pale and awkward, her eyes sombre as she sought desperately to convince him.

'Surely you see the importance . . . ' she began, her voice brittle with frustration. She turned round to my mother, to implore her. But the nurse was not one of our own people; she did not understand, nor could she ever. My mother just looked at her stolidly; there was neither grief nor empathy in her expression. She met the nurse's gaze and gave no ground. John Gillies had said he would not go to the mainland and that was an end of it. The nurse looked at both of them again; her eyes seemed to flash between them, then turned and without another word, went out and closed the door behind her.

'I have to go to the service,' my father said, and my mother went out at once to fetch some food for him, having understood.

The pain got the better of him all the same. He was like a ship whose side had been staved in by the rocks. He retreated in the end to bed like a creature that has been wounded, ashamed and alone.

I used to catch sight of him sometimes as I passed the door to his room. He would hear my steps, of course, and look up to catch my eye sometimes if the door had been left slightly ajar. I would pause, almost against my will; his mouth would be half open as he struggled to get breath and as he stretched up time and again, like a climber on a rock-face pulling himself to a ledge. It was his eyes I could never escape; around them, struggle and bleakness had made his temples gaunt and the skin that stretched over them yellow. But in the darkness of his eyes was a hollowness I could not bear; all the strict worship of his God, the keeping of the rules, had been in vain, leaving him in the end broken and bitter, his soul a clenched fist.

He still gave orders from his bed, though. He told his wife what he wanted and he told his children what was to be done. He tried hard to cling to the world he had ruled and refused to admit defeat. He lay like a shadow in the end of the house; when he was silent I was still aware of his presence; it would not have been possible to forget.

Then there came the day when he heard that the crops had been a disaster. He heard it and he looked up slowly, his eyes stone.

'If the harvest fails, then we fail.'

'It sure is a beautiful morning, Mr Gillies. There was mist in the fields as I drove into the city this morning – you know the kind that lies like scarves at this time of year? I had the window open and you could smell the apples and hay in the car. It's a kind of strange time of year, you know, when you feel anything could happen . . . I don't know; it sort of reminds me of being a child, going out to collect nuts in the woods, and then later watching for the first snow coming. It's really beautiful now. The mist's cleared and the sky's completely blue – wonderful, after that storm. D'you want to come over and see? Wait a moment, I'll help you up. We'd better do it quietly, in case Nurse Johnson hears us. Lean on my arm. That's it, I've got you, don't worry. There you are now. Watch your step, I spilt some of the water from the vase when I came in. Did Kevin bring in those apples for you yesterday? Aren't they just beautiful? Almost too good to eat. Yes, that's good; you're doing well, Mr Gillies. Can you see the light? Isn't it just incredible? It's so blue, you wouldn't believe it. Lean by the desk there for a moment.

'Y'know, it's almost clear enough to see the sea today. If those buildings weren't so high I feel sure we could. You know I remember playing in that garden when I was a child. Yes, really! My grandfather was very ill with tuberculosis and they sent him here, to this very Home, to recover. I remember being so afraid. I used to cry whenever we came to see him. I used to bring the old folks presents from home – fruit, nuts, anything at all I thought they'd like. I believe that was when I first thought I'd like to be a nurse . . . Oh, I remember what I meant to tell you, and then I'll have to go or I'll have no job left! I'm getting a sheepdog for my son Billy and I thought I might manage to smuggle him in some day. You must have had sheepdogs on your island. Billy will go wild when he sees him! All right now, you sit at the table and read for a while. I'll slip back again when I have a minute.'

My father's spirit had been broken. The fall had crippled him, true enough, but it was the knowledge that the island harvest had failed which crippled his spirit, and for that there was no healing on earth.

He knew the hearts of the people. He knew they had suffered too much poverty and disease and storm during these last years to endure much longer. The mainland was growing closer and closer all the time. Once, it had been beyond the limits of the sea, a world they could condemn from afar because of the tales of wickedness and indulgence brought to them – stories scattered down like a sudden silver shoal of herring. But it had grown closer every year that passed; with the tourists had come little pieces of temptation, small glimpses of a different world. It was like an advent calendar, every window opening on to a brighter, more alluring scene. Who was to know if the things they were told were true or not? Maybe the visitors were telling lies; they were from a corrupt society, so their motives could easily be corrupt as well. Yet the stories seemed to hang in the air. And with every ship-load they grew more plentiful. One by one they fell into the hearts of listeners like a strange seed, and they did not die. When the people were trailing up from the shore with half a hundredweight on their backs and a wet north wind in their face, they would be remembering them all right. When it was six in the morning and the fire had gone out and there was little food in the house, they would be thinking of them then. It was no longer enough to condemn the stories as nothing but the temptations of the flesh. Hirta had become an old, sick beast. With its storms and terminally harsh life, it seemed to hate its children, and they in their turn had begun to hate it. At the very least, they had to discover if the stories were true or not, if there was anything in the box sitting so tantalisingly close.

After the news, my father failed very fast. He seemed to shrink inwards in just a handful of days; in no time at all the broad shoulders and strong calves thinned to sag on his bones. And the house was so quiet when we came home from school. Once it had vibrated with his commands, been busy with the feet of neighbours coming to ask about beasts or plan business. Now when we walked in my mother would be working by the fire, mending and sewing, the only sound that of the wind eternally chasing through the chimney. All of us were quiet – Morag and Iain and myself – each deeply aware of the silence; listening to it, because it seemed like a glass waiting to be broken. We waited for that all the time. We were apprehensive and wary until at last we wanted it broken. I can remember so well lying in the darkness, fearing what would happen and yet wishing it on. I prayed; my lips would move in the dark and I would be asking for help and understanding, until at last I fell into a fitful and uneasy sleep.

But I do not think it was as simple for Iain. He had feared and almost hated my father's tower, and now that it had suddenly been weakened, in a scattering of days, everything was changed. He took food on a board to a feeble man, he helped him out of bed, he supported him as he walked with the weakness of a newborn lamb through the house. He saw how the dwindling strength of the body was echoed by the collapse of the mind. In the beginning, my father would send out commands from his bed. But day after day his hold on the world beyond his door seemed to grow less. A ball of wool was unravelling. It seems strange to me now, but what was very clear to me at the time, I remember, was this thought – that as his power and spirit drained away, they filled the body of Iain. The boy began to grow at that very time: he increased in height, his shoulders rippled with new muscle, and his very face changed as the round boyishness took on the features of a youth.

He could lift my father easily, sweeping him up in his arms with a confidence that I myself envied. If my father called, it was often Iain who went, not saying a word; I had the feeling that this new order fascinated him, that he was enjoying it. I sometimes thought my father could hardly bear to thank him; it must have cut him to the quick that so suddenly this son he had raged against for years should now be the one to carry him for washing.

It was on one of the very worst nights of winter storm that he died. I remember being hungry and going down to the shore to see if there was anything to glean from the tide. I found nothing except a handful of half-broken razor shells and the bright blue curve of a mussel. I went up towards the village again with a gnawing in the pit of my stomach; I kept thinking of hot stewed meat, however much I pushed the thought from my mind. Even then the storm was brewing; curtains of mist hurtled eastwards over Mullach Sgar; Oiseval reared in and out of cloud like some strange horseman. Cold drops of rain splattered my face and my hands soon swelled to red lumps. I did not care. If someone had told me there was food on the summit of Conachair I think I would have climbed it without a second thought.

As I came round the top of the village I saw a black shadow flapping away from one of the stones in the graveyard. It turned round in the air, croaking. For the briefest moment the sound echoed like horrible laughter and I had to shake off the feeling of gloom which came upon me. I went inside but could settle to nothing. In contrast, Iain appeared relaxed, even happy. Morag was bent over a book; her index finger still followed the words intently, although I knew she did not need such help. I felt the silence oppressing my spirit; it was so strong that it hammered against my temples.

Instinctively, I felt drawn to the other room; I was conscious of the shadow of my father there and looked down on him as he lay propped up against the pillows. Pillows, I thought to myself, that were filled with the feathers of birds he had plucked from the cliff face of Stac Lee. It struck me then that his own life weighed no more now than one of these feathers, that it might blow away just as easily. His eyes rolled round to look up at me and I think there was just a flicker of a smile on his face. Perhaps he was glad that I had come.

'I won't be coming with you,' he said suddenly, and the toneless words were so completely solid that I was left dumb and speechless like a child. Already it seemed it was a certainty that we would be leaving to go to the mainland. There was no question any longer. It was simply a matter of when it would happen.

And then: 'Come here,' he said, in the voice he had used so often when I was a child, a little gruff and imperious, but with something of real kindness at the back of it as well. He took my hand, and suddenly I found myself kneeling there at the bedside as the wind and rain howled against the windows. 'In the Name of the Father, the Son, and the Holy Ghost, may blessing be yours.'

There was nothing else he could give me, nothing within those four walls that was so precious it might sustain me in the years to come. There were things to live by, of course – for making butter, for cutting meat and stone, for hanging and drying and loading and carrying, but what value were they when we did not even know what kind of life lay before us. And so it seemed to me at that moment that this gift was the most precious I could imagine. He had told me he loved me – something he had never done – and a dry, brittle wall crumbled inside me.

That night, when we went into the room to give him the Books, we found him dead. He looked as if he had aged twenty years in the short time since the hurt that had felled him. I think that, of us all, it was Iain who was the most shocked. He seemed almost to lurch as he stepped forward; then he stood biting his lips, staring all the time as with a horrible fascination. I went at once to fetch Mr Munro, late as the hour was, and I remember feeling a deep sense of relief to be free of the house and in the midst of the fierce winds.

The strange thing was that I did not grieve at all then; I can remember clearly instead a sense of release. I walked at first, my feet sure of every inch of the way, and the wind felt uncannily warm, in spite of the lateness of the year. There was even a tune inside my head, and although it seemed like a kind of blasphemy that it should be there at all, yet it would not leave me. That was the night indeed that one of the Ferguson brothers got his fiddle tune; he said that it seemed to come right out of the air to him.

I brought back the missionary and I remember he spoke to each one of us in turn. Gradually, we were joined by others as the news of the death went round the homes. I recall standing wearily at the window, seeing that the skies were lightening, blowing in the grim, grey light of the new day. I believe my father's body lay a full two days in the house, watched over by ourselves and our neighbours. I was with him all on my own during one of the nights, and the room was cold and poorly lit. I kept falling half-asleep, tired out by the anxiety of the past few days; sometimes I would be imagining that I saw my father's head turning on the pillow to look at me, or his hand stretching out towards mine. In those moments I would hold my breath in blind terror, unable to move a muscle for fear that something worse might happen. But then I remembered his final blessing and whispered it over and over to myself, and I grew calm.

In two days the coffin was completed. The task was never an easy one on an island with wood in such short supply, but at last it was ready. The procession to the graveyard was terrible. The whole island was there, the black clothes of mourning flapping in the wind. They were the only sounds I could hear on the steep road to the graveyard, together with the drum of feet on the sodden earth and the slap of black cloth as the procession neared its destination. I glanced back once to look at the long curving line of folk slowly and solemnly making their way up the slope, and was reminded in that instant of the ominous sight of the raven I had seen fly away from the tombstone on the night of my father's death. I shivered, looking with apprehension towards the hillside, but there was nothing at all except the thin trails of mist drifting across Mullach Mor.

The weeping at the graveside was like a terrible moaning, with one voice after another joining in so that it became like a wave which never ceased. All I could think of was hell, with its eternal suffering, and a horrible fear grew in me for it seemed that the crying around me rose out of the very depths of hell itself.

Everything became confused in my mind. I was so weary that I did not believe I could remain much longer on my feet. And I began to see that this intense mourning was not only for my father but for the island itself. Our island was dying and we, its children, were mourning its loss. Only then did it hit me what that might mean. I looked as it were from afar on that tattered group of men, women and children, wondering what we had become.

It seemed that we remained there hour after hour, until I could no longer feel my legs at all. Iain and I stood one on each side of my mother, supporting her, and I noticed as I looked across at him that he was taller now than me. For a second I hardly recognised him at all, for he seemed to have grown and broadened out in such a brief space of time. And all the time the rain went on without ceasing; it might have been that the skies were weeping also except that the elements had never loved us.

Nurse O'Neill did not come back, although I heard her steps somewhere along the corridors. I cannot stop thinking back to my father's death. I see the wrecks of ships which would be washed up on Hirta, disgorging their wood for coffins.

I had seen death before, of course, for in a situation like ours birth and death are no more remote than the sea or the sky. Here in this place, though, death is sanitised; the nurses are afraid of it and the relatives would rather not think about it. When someone dies here the room is scoured – the walls, the floors, even the cupboards. Not a thing remains; everything is left a shining white, smiling bright. But it is all a lie, a huge deception; underneath there lies a hollow and empty darkness, a gnawing void. Covered but inescapable.

Sometimes, in a very old face here, I will see someone from the island. I fall then to imagining that they really are the person I remember, and I talk to them when no one is listening. I pour out stories of St Kilda, all kinds of things which remain clear in memory. At times indeed I feel an urge to rehearse my memories for fear I may be losing them, for fear of the void that will be left without them to hang on to.

And I do the same with my Gaelic. I repeat many words, sometimes strange and obscure, to make sure I have not forgotten them. But most of all I keep the language alive in me by reading in my mother's Gaelic Bible; not only does that bring back the language but it strengthens my own faith at the same time.

Now it is cold, night is falling. The sun has been broken and seems to me like some injured creature, its blood stretching along the rims of the clouds in vivid fires. I, too, am not the same as I once was. I have closed the doors on the world that was once mine. In many ways I feel that the child inside me has never grown up, but is only as old as in that final year on Hirta. In a sense, the boy never left the island at all.

After my father died, I used to have nightmares about him. He was trying to get into the house; I could hear him shouting to me, but I wouldn't move. The dreams were so vivid that I would sometimes waken in the morning to wonder whether they were real or not. But I never saw his face, I remember, just heard his voice, always desperately crying to be let in. I know that often I didn't sleep well because of hunger. I never seemed to have enough to eat, and my mother always favoured Iain. There were hardly any supplies coming to Hirta because of the huge seas, and at times it felt as if one endless day drifted into the next. Often Iain and I were at each other's throats like a couple of dogs; there was nothing too small for us to fall out over.

I remember one Saturday I was down at the jetty bringing up boxes from a boat that had come in from Harris. One that was in my arms had a big tear in it and I could see that inside was a stack of tins of condensed milk. I looked longingly and thought of the sweet yellowy-white liquid, and my mouth watered. At least that night we would have something good with our meal.

Later I was down by the boat with Neil Ferguson. He was perhaps four or five years older than me, with hair as black as basalt. He was whittling away at a piece of driftwood with his penknife, when all of a sudden he looked up. 'So, what do you think of going to the mainland?' he asked. I shrugged my shoulders, uncertain how to answer. I found it impossible to know what I thought; all that was in my head was that I was hungry.

'You wouldn't be hungry if you were on the mainland,' he added, reading my mind. 'Ach, we won't be one bit better off, you mark my words,' he went on. 'All we are is a nuisance to the government in London and an amusement to all the tourists.' I heard the anger behind his words and found myself thinking of my father's last words to me, and of how he had vowed never to leave the island.

'You know how Hirta began?' Neil asked me suddenly, laying down the piece of wood. A low sun broke through at last from the great wall of cloud in the west and lit every wet stone around us; even the dense heaps of seaweed were almost too radiant to look at.

I had never thought of it. I had simply taken it for granted that there had always been people on this island. Again I shrugged my shoulders.

'Well, I heard a story once,' he went on, 'from my grandfather.' Neil was exceptionally proud of his grandfather; he was forever quoting him on this or that. 'Ages ago there were people living in some remote community on the west coast of Scotland. The men were away nearly always at the fishing, while the women gathered shellfish from the shores. Anyway, there was one time the women were busy working and one of them had left her baby up among the rocks, all wrapped up in blankets. Suddenly this eagle that had been circling miles up in the sky saw the baby moving and came down like a bolt of lightning, lifted the whole bundle with its talons and made off. The mother heard the baby crying and looked up, but already the eagle was away out over the water, still carrying the child. It took the baby back to its nest far out to sea among the steepest rocks and cliffs. It fed it like its own chick so that it grew used to raw food and, once it was older, the child learned to climb those cliffs and to fear nothing. And that's how folk first came here.'

'But there was only one of them,' I was quick to object. 'How could they have carried on?'

He rolled his eyes in frustration. 'Always the difficult one, aren't you? It's only a story.' He scrabbled up from the rock on which he was sitting. 'Well, I'm off to get something to eat, something from these boxes.' His eyes were shining. I remembered the food boxes as well and got up too. Soon it would be getting dark.

At that moment, out of the corner of my eye, I saw a flicker of black. A raven. In one moment I had picked up a stone and hurled it at the bird as hard as I could. The huge bird lumbered away, croaking darkly. The raven on the tombstone. An eagle big enough to carry a child to Hirta. We depended so deeply on birds. When did they grow to hate us? We would never be able to come back.

The spring came, and we knew now that this would be the last spring, the last summer on the island. A great part of me felt restless to be away. I was still very aware of my father's grave so close. It was too near the house. The living and the dead were separated by just one stone dyke – and once darkness had fallen that wall disappeared.

We didn't talk about it at home. There was just the one time I remember Morag coming back to the house late on a Saturday evening, when the light was just beginning to go. She had been wandering over in Glenn Mor and her clothes were spattered with mud. 'Och, what would your father say if he saw you in that state?' my mother burst out. Morag was so shocked that she rushed away in shame from the room. But it was my mother who broke into tears. Before my eyes, it was as if she cracked audibly. Leaning there beside the clothes she had been folding, she wept dry, angry tears. Iain and I were frozen where we sat. I do not believe that in all our lives we had seen our mother cry. I recall clearly how his face had burned like a sunset. Neither of us knew where to turn. Often since then I have wished that I had got up and gone over to comfort her. But neither of us moved or said a word. At last she straightened, wiped her face and whispered that she was sorry; then she took up the pile of folded clothes and quietly went into the other room.

I think it was at that moment that I realised for the first time how much she must have loved my father. It must seem ridiculous, I know, but I really believe that it had never even crossed my mind before. My father never showed her any affection whatsoever in our presence. There were times when his tone of voice was different, softer perhaps, when he spoke to her, but there was nothing more. What I do remember most was her kindness to him; it comes back to me in many ways. Once he was down at the shore helping to carry up heavy boxes from one of the Harris boats, and the sleet was fairly driving down from the hills on a raw knife of wind. It was a Saturday and I was at home, arranging a collection of shells in the window and arguing with Iain over which of them were mine. I looked up and saw her outside. He had reached the village and you could see that he was half raw with cold; she had one hand on his shoulder and was feeding him a hot drink. I remember, too, when he came back with a hurt hand after climbing on the Stacs across at Boreray. She had been up half the night before because Morag had been sick and her face was pale with weariness, but at once she got warm water and took the red soreness of his hand gently in her own, washed it carefully and tore strips from an old sheet to bind it. And what stays in my mind is the look on her face as she tended him.

But on that night when she cried I sat mute. Helpless in the face of such depth of emotion. Afterwards I tried to be more gentle towards her, to do a bit more to help her than before. But to be honest, perhaps that is only what I want to believe, so long afterwards and too late.

It was about that time too, I believe, that it came on me suddenly how much I missed my father, and for a special reason. Like all the boys on the island, I had dreamed all my life of the day when I would be old enough to be one of the men, and be allowed to take part in the Parliament, the 'Mod.' It didn't meet in any building, but outside one of the houses in the street. There, all the grown men would sit around, maybe on the ground, or on a dyke, to make decisions about a whole range of things. They would plan what work should be done that day, when the potatoes should be planted, when it would be safe to go out in a boat, how the puffins' eggs should be shared out. And if one of the men had been on a visit to the mainland, you may be sure that every detail had to be told.

And now, at last, the time was coming near for me to be admitted to all of this, but the joy had gone out of it because my father would not be there.

The spring came. We were blown into it. But at last the winds grew gentler and there was a warmth on their edge. Rifts began to appear in the grey skies, showing watery patches of blue. It gave us some slight relief. The days began to stretch and it would not be long before the first ships – the first of the last ships – came with their visitors.

I recall one incident from that time. I had gone running over the island one morning, very early. I had been wakened by the sun on my face. I knew it as no good trying to get back to sleep. I didn't take my shoes; I just ran like a hare up the steep slope at the back of the street and up on to the ridge. I don't think I stopped for a single moment either, just thudded down into the glen on the other side, eager to reach the bay.

When I was still several hundred yards from the beach I caught sight of a huge grey hump at the edge of the incoming tide. I stopped, lost in confusion, wondering for a second if the tide was particularly low and if this was some promontory I had never properly noticed before. But all the time I really knew there had been nothing there. I went forward more slowly, pondering all the time, and was assaulted by the smell of decaying flesh. Then I knew that this was a whale. I stood there retching as wave after wave of that fetid stench invaded my nostrils. I looked at the open carcass and saw that every inch was crawling with life; piece by piece it was being dismantled. Soon, I thought, all that would remain of the great sea monster would be huge hoops of whitened bone. And then everything washed together – Hirta, my father, death – and I bent over, sick and empty and fearful.

During the night, snow fell, starting without warning and growing faster and thicker all the time. I got up because I could not sleep. The nurses in the corridor were talking quietly amongst themselves. I pulled back the curtain and watched the snowflakes fall. I feel shut in my own world. It is as if this room has become a giant snowball, muffled with that deeper quietness which only the snow can bring.

Am I the very last of the people of St Kilda left alive? How do you prove that something actually existed when nothing remains, when the folk are dead and the walls of their homes have reverted to boulders lying on a barren hillside?

The boy in me is all I have left. I have not wanted him to change or fade in all these years. The old shell around me now is meaningless; it is my mind that matters. So long as it remains, Hirta will live, and the place that it was will be like a last small flame fighting against the darkness.

Tonight the snow is falling all across New York; it is drifting over Harlem and Manhattan, over the great spiked thistles of skyscrapers that crowd the horizon. It is stopping the traffic on one street after another, filling them bit by bit until the cars and taxis are brought to a standstill and the quiet returns. The television sets will close their big black eyes and there will be no sound left at all. Only in the morning the birds will sing in the trees of Central Park, and the people will listen, at last.

The day we left the island in August 1930 seems to me now, as I peer back through the years, surprisingly uneventful. I remember that I had slept badly and my eyes were bleary. I recall, too, that I cut my finger on a piece of board and that I nearly lost my footing on the stones outside because my arms were filled with belongings. Unimportant details like these are so very sharp. I remember my mother coming down with difficulty from the graveyard, for her ankles were painful by then. And I remember how empty and cold the house seemed, with not a sound to be heard in it. For the last time I looked at it long and hard – the place where I had been born, where I had learned to walk and talk, where the Books had been brought out round the fire, summer and winter, without fail. It was even harder to believe that long before we were here, children had laughed here, had gone out to the Stacs, had lived their lives under the same vast sky.

And now the last of us formed a slow procession, descending one final time to the shore. The Navy had come for us; and as I boarded their vessel one intense flicker of anger speared me. Like taking prisoners, they made sure that none of us stayed behind. I felt that they were eager to be gone, to get the job over. Their voices were clipped, impatient, without emotion. But of course we came from very different worlds; we were oceans and seas apart.

Only last night we had gathered round the Books one last time. I had felt the deepest sense of kinship, of closeness, with my family. Suddenly I felt very afraid of losing them. It was as if a great storm was blowing us out into the world and would disperse us, so that no holding point would exist again. I had the strongest feeling at that moment of us being as one, but only while we were still on the island. After the ship had taken us to the mainland, we might be splintered forever. My tears said farewell to my kin, as well as to Hirta.

Once we were out beneath the great black base of Oiseval I caught sight of Stac Lee and Boreray, their thorny backs jagging the low clouds. And suddenly all the islands were spread out before me, sinking and leaping among the waves; and as the sun slid from deep among the ramparts of clouds, it lit strange and magnificent fires here and there on the land. I was leaning out over the rail, far away in my thoughts, when Neil appeared beside me.

'Well, what about going back?' he said very fast, and his voice sounded strange, not his own. I looked at him startled as he stared out at the changing and shifting light. His eyes were shining.

Then the light vanished altogether and it became hard to distinguish cloud from land. Our vessel was by now battling in earnest against the mighty power of the waves until at last there was nothing of them left, just the scowling blackness of the sea sweeping in its wide circle.

A sickness took hold of me and I left the rail to sit down. Neil had gone and the rain darted out of the sky, hard and merciless. I remembered that I had not had a bite of food since the previous night. I went to find the rest of the family. I spied my mother, sitting alone surrounded by our few possessions. She was not looking at me, she had not heard my approach, and I stopped, thinking suddenly how small she seemed and how out of place. Her face was white and drawn and she looked deathly tired. I went up to her and bent down to lay my hand on her shoulder. Her blue eyes found mine and her smile was warm.

'Go and lie down for a bit,' I told her gently. 'I can easily look after everything.' But she shook her head, still smiling kindly at me. 'I'm fine, Roddy. Just go and see if Morag is feeling better. She was feeling *fann*, and now with this big sea . . . '

But I couldn't find Morag anywhere. I went down deep into the ship and the smell from the engines made me feel sick and dizzy, and tiredness broke over me in waves. In the end I was forced to sit, my head in my hands, wishing that it was over. I was afraid, afraid of going away from all that was dear and familiar. As the eldest, I realised that I was the one who must now be responsible and wise, with my father dead; I must be strong in the face of adversity. And yet all the time I felt utterly weak. I felt as though inside myself I was still nothing more than a child. And all the time the waves lifted and hissed under the vessel, on and on without end.

There was little time for farewells. All of us were weary, conscious, too, of the curious eyes around us, eager to discover the secrets of this huddle of evacuees. I was swinging a huge pack on to my back when the spotless uniform of a naval officer appeared before me. I looked at him dumbly, blearily. 'Good luck,' he said, his voice brisk but not unfriendly. I saw in his face also, behind the military confidence, a kind of diffidence, a confusion as to how to deal with me. I was from his country, I suppose, but not from his world. 'I hope you'll settle quickly,' he added.

I had no idea how to answer; I had no idea how he expected me to respond. I just stood looking at him stupidly, and then my eyes fell away. By the time I had settled the mule's load on my back, he had gone.

Yet I remember his words now. *I hope you settle quickly.* He meant them quite sincerely; I have no doubt of that, but he unconsciously expressed the hopes of his military commanders, as well as of his government, far away in London. For in the end we had become a burden to Britain. We were a curious and costly outpost on the very edge of the map – indeed, more often than not, off the map – and we had outlived our time.

We must have looked, that day, like people who had come back from the middle of the last century. Perhaps then it was little wonder that they stared at us and our humble belongings. We wanted to be away as quickly as possible from there; we were refugees, without dignity, and we longed for nothing more than to hide away.

The place that had been arranged for us, outside Lochaline in Morven on the Sound of Mull, was not ready for us, so for a day or so we stayed with Neil and his family, sharing cramped attics and stale food. I remember little of that time, but one thing stands out vividly. A shining red car breathed past the cottage in the hot stillness of an early morning. It was the first car I had ever seen, and it both thrilled and frightened me at the same time.

Our own cottage seemed strange. We viewed it with apprehension, suspicious and critical. But certainly we had to admit that there was far more space for living; for the very first time Iain and I did not have to share a room. But I remember how he would prowl around it like an anxious sheepdog; how he would knock walls and pat his hands round each dark corner.

My mother was different, though. That night, she asked me to give thanks when she brought out the Books – thanks for our safe journey, for the provisions made for us, for shelter and the blessing of good friends.

I really believe that from the very beginning of our new life I saw a difference in Iain. He was already taller and stronger than myself, and it almost seemed to add extra years to him. He clearly resented the authority bestowed on me by my mother, and would often sneer at my suggestions. 'That was never the way to set that! When did you think of putting such a thing there? Surely you can see that land is no good for such a thing?' So it would go on; but he was clever enough to keep his remarks out of earshot of my mother. She was ageing, but she held sway over us nonetheless and was not afraid to rule us. I can never forget a night in winter when Iain was invited to a party in Lochaline – the first he had ever attended in his life – and he came back the worse for wear with drink. She met him at the door; it was almost midnight. Without a word she let him into the hallway where I was standing myself. In complete silence, she stood and looked at him. I could see his hands shaking because of the authority she had, indeed, he seemed almost to shrink before our very eyes. During it all I don't believe she spoke a single word, yet her look was enough to reduce him to nothing.

The truth is, though, that I was afraid of Iain myself. It has to be said that I knew much less about the land than he did; I had always been more interested in books than in anything else. Also I had all my life had a fascination for boats and had loved plashing about the shores of Hirta in anything that floated. But when it came to the care of sheep or the yield of the land, I had little interest; so I was uncertain about the handful of acres that lay around our new cottage. Iain took advantage of that uncertainty mercilessly. He took charge more and more with every day that passed; his very confidence made me less sure, and I grew listless and dispirited, and simply shrugged my shoulders in defeat.

But the war between us was not new. It had been there since long before the days of my father's illness. Iain had known that my father had not loved him; these were truths that beat every day in the chambers of his heart. Somehow we all knew it. By the time of my father's illness I believe Iain had come to hate him. I had the feeling that in a horrible way he was taking delight in my father's downfall. Yet I was also aware that when he died that winter night, Iain was shaken to his roots.

Now, although my father was dead and gone, I sensed that Iain could not forget that he had always loved me more. Despite the years that had passed since the beginning of the rift between us, the poison was still in his blood. There were times, I know, that I almost felt afraid to be alone with him. I couldn't imagine what he might do to me, yet I was afraid, aware of his strength.

There was one day I remember in particular. We were putting up a fence to divide two bits of land. Iain had sharpened the ends of the posts and set them in their holes, but I had to hug them as he brought down the sledgehammer to force them into the ground. I blinked every time the wood was struck. I looked up at my young brother's face and caught his eye once. I remember his expression so clearly, as the hammer curved behind his head. There was power rippling in it, mixed with amusement at my suffering.

Morag had meantime found work in Lochaline; though it was winter and the little hotel was quiet, they found sufficient for her to do in the kitchen and the laundry. Perhaps, I used to think, it was partly because she was a St Kildan and they were curious to know what she was like. But at least she had found some kind of place in the community. It was only a matter of weeks before we learned of the first deaths among our people. To me they were the most unexpected, the ones I would have thought least likely to fail. News now came by way of letters, and that was another strange thing. Deaths had always been suffered together, just as we had been together during the joy of birth. But now we were scattered; the thin seed of those who survived had been carried to every corner. Nothing, not even the power of death, could unite us again.

Each death felt unnatural; something else had claimed them, for they had seemed strong and well while on the island. A cancer of the spirit. It was very much later, here in America, that I learned how native American children taken from their tribes in the reservations and sent to school in the cities, died within months of being moved. We were all frightened by the news, each of us in our own way. Vulnerable, powerless now to return, did we choose wisely when we decided to leave our island home?

And then, in the middle of that time of doubt and anxiety, the greatest blow fell – our mother took ill.

The snow had been coming and going for days. Great white flurries came sweeping in from the Atlantic, leaving a light covering which lay for a time before melting as quickly as it had come. That day, she had gone out to gather snowdrops; the first of them were bravely pushing their heads through the snow – the first snowdrops we had ever seen. She had run outside, in between the heavy sleety showers, but then a fierce wind caught her; the whole air was buried in white. I saw her myself from the window. I almost opened it, wanting to tell her to come in quickly, not to be foolish. She hadn't even waited to put on a coat. But I hesitated; she was so eager to have the flowers. And as she bent to pick them, she half-turned towards me and I could see her face. At that moment, she looked as a girl on Hirta. The blowing wisps of hair were dark and shining in the wet, her face momentarily smooth and filled with youthful health. And she was smiling, the smile not changed at all; but it was so seldom now that she smiled.

Iain was round at the back of the house cutting wood. I could hear the dull thud of the axe from where I stood at the window. I did not call to her to come in: I was already aware that both Iain and I ordered her about too much. I left the window and returned to what I had been doing, still hearing the sound of axe blows from behind the house, and I did not think of her again until I went downstairs much later, my task finished.

She was on her own, sitting crouched very near the fire, and there was no light at all in the room. For a second I thought she might be asleep, but as I went over to her she stretched out her hands to the fire and I realised that she was shivering. I dropped the wood I had been carrying.

'Are you all right? What's wrong? What happened?'

I took her hands in mine but they were not cold; they were raging with heat. I saw the snowdrops she had gathered strewn in disarray across the table by the door. I got up, my legs suddenly weak with fear.

'Iain!' I shouted. 'Come here!'

'Let's get her into bed,' he said at once when he saw her, and together we lifted her. I could hardly believe how light she was, how frail. I held her head and as her hair splayed out I was reminded of how I had seen her in my mind only a few hours ago. But the girl was gone. It had been the final glimpse of what had been.

As we laid her down gently on the bed, her eyes searched to find mine. 'Don't trouble to get the doctor,' she said, and I was reminded then of my father. She had not said a single word in contradiction then; what were we to say now to her?

When Morag came home from Lochaline that evening she said nothing at all but got warm water and cloths, and knelt down and bathed my mother's face and neck, arms and hands. She was on fire; her forehead raged with fever and the sweat stood shining on her skin in the lamplight. The white pillows were piled up behind her head for her breathing was now laboured, sounding as though she had climbed a steep hill.

'It's pneumonia,' said Morag quietly. 'We have to get the doctor at once.'

My mother said nothing. If she had properly heard Morag, she made no sign. She was too busy fighting for breath. Iain just stood there dumbly at the end of the bed, his hands clutching the iron, his eyes constantly searching our mother's face. For a moment I looked at him and it seemed as if all his strength and confidence were stripped away. With a sudden stab I remembered the day I had snatched him up to throw him over the cliff, so consumed with jealousy I had been. For all his confidence, his air of power, I realised how close he still was to her, how dependent; he loved her more deeply than words. His knuckles clutching the end of the bedstead were white as chalk.

'I'll go,' I said at once. 'I'll go and find the doctor. Have you the torch, Iain?'

It was as though I had shot him. He swung round clumsily, blundered out of the room and downstairs. Morag was wringing out the cloth again, gently bathing the pale sheen of those fevered arms. Her hands did not shake at all; she seemed utterly calm, as if she was pouring her own calmness into that frail frame.

Iain silently thrust the torch into my hands as I went out muffled against the cold. For a second our eyes met, and he could not but betray the fear and confusion of his inner heart. He said not a single word; I don't think he could have spoken even if he had wanted to. Perhaps, to be honest, I felt a moment of victory, but if I did it was quickly swallowed up in the extremity of our need.

It was snowing heavily as I went out. The wind seemed to be coming from every direction, so that gusts would swirl behind me like wolves, rushing out towards the Sound of Mull and then moments later thick snow would drive right into my face from the Atlantic. It was exhausting to walk against such a storm. The darkness held no terrors for me; I had been used to such nights ever since I was able to walk. Nor did the sea, raging as it was, frighten me at all, for where is any ocean more violent than on the jagged edges of Hirta?

Yet I was terrified nonetheless. I battled on through the blizzard, yard after yard, thinking of my father, of his grave on the island, and it seemed as if all this darkness round about me was somehow composed of his death, of the horror of the grave. I began to imagine that there was something behind me, that I could feel a hand on my shoulder, and I kept glancing fearfully round, more and more at the mercy of my imagination.

At last I saw a light up the hill, at the top of a steep side road. That must surely be the doctor's house at last. I picked up speed and ran up that hillside for all I was worth. I slipped on the icy track and went down hard on my side; pain jabbed through my elbow and knee, but I scrambled up again, desperate now to reach that light. Despite it, the blackness of spirit still pursued me; I was back with the black-clad procession on the day of the funeral, and I imagined I could hear them in the noise of the blizzard. More than one of them was dead, had already slipped away since the evacuation, but I could hear their voices, the murmur of their prayers.

'Is this the doctor's house?' I half-fell at the porch door, my feet slipping on the smooth stones. An anxious woman looked out at me, taking in the sight of my snow-covered coat and raw hands.

'Roddy Gillies?' she said after a moment. I nodded. 'No, I'm afraid it's a bit further yet,' she said with real regret in her voice. Her Gaelic was strange to me; I had to concentrate to catch the words. 'Keep on down the road, and don't turn off before you've passed the lochan.' I nodded again, knowing where she meant, and took a step back out.

'Here, will you not come in and have a cup of tea?' she asked anxiously. 'It's a wicked night to be out.'

I thanked her but shook my head. I tried to tell her about my mother but my voice choked and I felt hot tears in my eyes. I had to hurry before it was too late! I turned away into the blank face of the snow and the torch beam darted about on the banks. It seemed so weak against the strength of the wind, the hugeness of the dark. If only a car would come! If only someone would be going down to Lochaline! I hardly walked now in my panic, but half-ran along the edge of the road. There was now not a light to be seen anywhere. Then all at once the torch beam fluttered. I stopped and shook the thing and once more it grew bright, but I knew that the battery was failing.

I was very cold by now. The snow was wet, falling in great thick lashes and melting as it landed. Rivers trickled down my neck, and my face burnt with the cold. How much further could it be? I tried to work out how long it had been since I left the house; it felt like an eternity. Every moment was precious; I knew, and yet was powerless.

Then the torch failed altogether. When the light went, the darkness flooded in round me like tar. I could not so much as see the outline of the road. I knew night as a brother, but always, on Hirta, there had been something to guide my steps. I knew the island as a blind man knows his own world, dark or light. But here it was different; this place was still new to me, and I felt like a stranger, unsure and slow.

I laid my hands against my knees, sank down on the road in utter despair and wept. With all my heart I knew I had to find the doctor before it was too late, yet here I was, unable even so much as to see the road ahead. I had not known such darkness in all my life; it was like being cast into some deep horrible pit. And then the strangest thing happened. As I crouched there I seemed to hear a sound. At first I did not realise what it was, but then it came to me clearly as the sound of a psalm being sung in Gaelic and I recognised it as the tune Stracathro, sung by the congregation on the island. I could hear their voices, in that slightly discordant sound which comes from the free addition of grace-notes by the singers. And I could see their faces, too, see them quite clearly in my mind's eye, and the familiar music came in on the very wind, sweeping under my feet, lifting me with the power of its sound.

I got up and began to walk, right into the very face of the blizzard, my feet slow but steady, sure now of each step. Whenever I suspected the road curved into a bend, I would crouch down and search with my hand for the surface. And still the singing was in my ears, and I began to say the words of Psalm 121 inside my head as the singing lifted and fell like a strong current within me.

After some time I became aware of a new sound. Twin lights pierced the blackness. I looked round into the dazzling light as a car swept closer through the snow. I stumbled and then awoke from my own world, and began waving the car down madly. It stopped and I peered in at the window.

It was Dr Maxwell himself.

The car was warm. I remember being overwhelmed with sleepiness, despite the strangeness of my surroundings. As we travelled the road to the house, I was lulled by the high-pitched scraping of the windscreen wipers as they pushed away white walls of sleet. The doctor explained to me that he had been out on a call; an elderly man who worked on the Rahoy Estate had been injured while cutting wood. It had been almost impossible to drive up the road from the shore, it was so slippery with wet snow. I listened, content with the warmth and the feeling of security, the dry cocoon that at last shut out the continuous driving of the blizzard. I watched the slow wings of a tawny owl as it ghosted low over the road and on to the moor beyond; in the beam of the lights the bird seemed almost made of snow itself.

The car moved slowly on towards home; we hardly seemed to move at all, so afraid the doctor must have been of losing control and plunging off the road. With a shudder I saw how I might easily have walked off the road completely and become hopelessly lost. The only sound was the low humming of the engine as it slid onwards through the snow. The flakes were beginning to lie now. By morning, I thought, the roads might well be blocked, the wires down. I fought hard to stay awake, although sleep was what I wanted more than anything. Only the fear held me, would we reach her in time?

When the car swung in at last, the upper windows shone out into the night the colour of a fire that has sunk to an orange glow. I did not think at that moment that I possessed the strength to open the car door and step out once more into the teeth of the storm. I felt far away; it was as though I had a fever and saw everything before my eyes as in a distant dream. The doctor spoke to me but my head was so heavy that I did not understand. I got out, swung the car door shut, and stumbled towards the door.

As I looked up, I saw the pale oval of my sister's face; she was waiting there in the doorway of the house.

'It's too late, Roddy. She's gone now. She's gone!'

I think of my mother now, this early morning as I write by the window, so far away. The snow has stopped; it has covered everything and there is not the slightest breath of wind. Only up on the little hill at the side of this Home, a child is playing with a bright orange sledge. It must be seven o'clock.

I can remember it all so well. It is like a film inside my head, so clear that I can actually pick out colours, the titles of books, the lines on faces. Sometimes the film seems to fade, so that it becomes blurred and useless; there are parts, I know, which are lost and will not be recovered. But most of it is intact and I do not want it thrown away when I am dead. This is my inheritance; it is the most precious thing I possess, although it has no value in terms of pounds or dollars. It is precious to those like me who understand the world it comes from, but to the modern age it is incomprehensible and irrelevant, and most would not even care to understand it.

But perhaps one day when there are no more places like Hirta, when the last people have been evacuated to the mainland of society and are none the happier for it, then they will wonder whether there was another way, whether we were right after all . . .

Iain was not in the house when I came home, I realised after a time. Morag was crying somewhere but there was no sign of him. I had gone in to see my mother and her eyes were open. My mind seethed. Had she been happy since she came to the mainland? The question struck me like a blow. I had to admit the truth – I had been so taken up with my own affairs that I simply did not know. Indeed, I had been so preoccupied by the conflict with Iain that I had paid scant attention to her at all. And the swiftness of her going . . . that too beat in my brain. Had she fought to live? Oh, I had seen her fight for breath all right, but how could she just have slipped away like this? Was it because there was nothing much to live for? Had she perhaps lost heart not simply since the evacuation, but long before, when my father was lost to her?

Most of all, though, I knew that if I had found the doctor earlier, she might well have lived.

'When was it, Morag? Look at me; tell me!'

'I can't remember. I wasn't . . . '

'You must remember! You must know! Tell me, please!'

Her eyes met mine in the end. 'Maybe half an hour.'

If I hadn't gone wrong, if I hadn't gone to the wrong house . . . I buried my head in my hands, racked with guilt. And then I recalled the strange singing, the singing that had calmed my worst fears on the road and had set me on my way again; what had been the meaning of it? Perhaps it had been meant and her time had come; perhaps after all there was nothing I could have done. That thought alone brought a measure of comfort.

But where on earth was Iain? I went to the door and saw that the snowfall had grown heavier. And then I saw the snowdrops where they lay scattered on the table, where they had lain since she picked them. At dawn, when it was just beginning to grow light again and the last of the wood dissolved in the hearth, I took some of them and put them in water, and left them beside her bed.

From the back door, just at the side of the birches, I caught sight of two fallow deer before they raced away in fear at my movement. I listened for a long time, hardly breathing. Where could Iain have gone?

I seemed hardly to rest at all during the next few days, with so much to attend to. Just as our custom had always been on Hirta to watch by the body until the day of burial, so it was followed now. I sent word of her death as quickly as I could, but it seemed strange to have to write her name on cold paper. Here, although there were other St Kildans in the new settlement, many were far away. And now, more than at any other time, I missed the strong wall of their presence. Once, I had often found fault with the strictness and unyielding conformity of the bleak religion of the island; now I saw another side which I had been too blind to acknowledge. Imposing it may have seemed, yet it had been composed of an immeasurable love. I felt its loss like a terrible pain in the depths of my heart.

The minister from Lochaline came to see us. He was a quiet man, a little shy of us perhaps, and curious. Morag made him tea and he stayed for a while, rocking where he sat on the edge of his chair, looking mostly into the heart of the fire and drinking his tea very fast. From time to time he would think of a new question to ask, and would speak quickly and nervously.

I do not believe Morag said a single word to him the whole time he was there. By then I was worried, seriously worried, about Iain. He had now been gone two and a half days and, since I had barely slept at all in that time, I knew he had not slipped inside during the night.

After the minister had left, I asked Morag if she would mind being alone in the house while I went to look for him. She nodded, sharing my anxiety. There was not much daylight left and I would not go far.

Outside it felt as though it would snow again. The wind had died down completely; it was perfectly still and the skies were uniformly grey, their clouds high and unmoving. I went up behind the house, on to the brackeny slopes that led away over the first hills into nowhere. Where on earth would Iain have gone? Where could he go? He knew few apart from those in the St Kilda settlement, and as far as I was aware had no close friendships even among them. He seemed to have taken nothing with him from the house. It was as if he had simply vanished and left not a trace behind. I thought again of that special bond there had been between our mother and him; I realised that none of us knew just how strong that had really been, nor how vital it might have become as the battle with his father had grown more bitter. If I myself felt the weight of sadness, of emptiness, at the loss of my mother, what must he have been feeling? And the awful suddenness of it all – to think that she had slipped away within a few short hours. A horrible fear was lurking at the back of my mind, a fear I had hardly allowed my conscious mind to consider. Surely, surely he would not have been foolish enough to do away with himself! Surely he would not have dared. We had been taught, and the teaching was deeply ingrained in us, that this was a sin for which there was no forgiveness. He knew that as well as any, but there was a chill circling my soul.

I reached the top of the first rise and began to find it hard to keep my footing. My breath streamed away in great silver clouds as I looked about me from among the rocks, my eyes circling every hollow and crag, searching for any sign of life. But in my heart of hearts I knew that there would be nothing. I looked out across the Sound of Mull and marvelled at the beauty all around; behind me there was nothing, only the wild lion that was Morven, lying with its head on its paws, changeless, caged by winter.

I longed to shout aloud, to shout my brother's name across those hills with all my strength. But I knew that it was useless; he had to choose to return of his own free will – if he still lived. Even if I found him, there was nothing in the world I could do to persuade him.

I saw the heathery tuft of smoke billowing from the chimney of the house and followed it down the slippery path. My feet were heavy. Tomorrow would be the funeral. All of this had happened so quickly, in the twinkling of an eye, exactly a year since my father's death. Who would have imagined that our lives would change like this? Perhaps Iain would have returned while I was gone. Only Morag's eyes met mine.

The storm came as I had imagined. It came from the west and Mull disappeared as if a great white eye had closed over it. It sent great flurries of white hard flakes against the window like the tapping of hundreds of fingers. I sat in the upper room, watching by the body of my mother, a single candle there on the table, beside a book, beside the snowdrops.

There was a draught from the window. Every time a new gust came I felt the cold breath of it where I was sitting. I remembered how a year before I had kept watch by the body of my father. Then, I had known nothing but the world of an island far out in the Atlantic. How I was changed, older, becoming used to cars and money. And yet, I had not grown accustomed to death and dying. In this I was still the same, vulnerable and afraid, lonely as a child in the dread of a room at midnight.

Darkness came and there was no moon. I felt no tiredness; I had been awake so long that my mind was unnaturally alert. The snow kept driving in against the window-panes. I seemed to be aware of every particle on the glass. The candle had nearly burned down to nothing; the room was utterly still when I glanced round and saw, framed in the doorway, my own brother.

'I wanted to tell you I'm sorry, Roddy.' I was so startled by the sight of him that I rose from my chair without thinking, my heart thudding. The book fell to the floor. 'I know I haven't been fair leaving everything to you . . . but you were always the favourite with him and I turned to her. She was all . . . ' he looked away, unable to finish. He paused. 'I'll be there in the morning.'

I wanted to say something, to ask at least where he had been, but my mouth was dry and useless. I heard his feet slow and steady on the steps up to the attic but I did not know what to say anyway; I was sure I would only annoy him with my words. Then, as I picked up my book again, I saw him there in front of me. He had taken off his coat and his heavy boots. There was not a fleck of snow on him now.

'I'll stay,' he said gently. 'You've done enough. I'll watch for the rest of the night.'

I did not argue with him. He wanted his vigil here. I only nodded and went silently from the room and out on to the landing. I could hear Morag's soft breathing through her half-open door.

I went into my own room but did not go straight to bed. I had been awake so long that it seemed to make no difference now. I closed the door and went over to the window. Leaning on the sill, I looked out across the low rises of hills stretching away behind the fields. About an inch of snow had fallen. Now the clouds were breaking up. A shimmer of silver was struggling to break through. As I watched, it flowed up and up behind the great wall of cloud and swam through into open sky. A ball of moon, a silver balloon rising all the time in the blue-black of that eternity. The hills beneath flashed their snowy backs like hundreds and hundreds of whales in an immense ocean. I could see the waves and I could see the whales; they seemed to move and swim as the light changed and the moon danced between wisps of cloud.

Then all at once my eyes caught another movement. Down below, almost at the very back of the house, a whole herd of deer stood. There must have been thirty or forty of them, ever alert, their ears sifting the wind, searching every sound for danger. They were so thin that they could have been carved out of bone, covered only in a tight-fitting hide.

They had come to find food; they had come down out of the hills to find sanctuary and warmth. This was not their world and they had no love for it, but in the end they had to come rather than starve. And so it had been with us. I thought of that last winter on Hirta, the one that had broken the back of our resolve, and saw we were the same.

The morning of the funeral was beautiful. I had slept like a child and neither Morag nor Iain had wanted to waken me. Iain never told us where he had been, and we did not once ask him. But he was different; it was as if a hard knot that had lain between his shoulders had been snapped, and a new kind of gentleness had flowed into the place where the knot had been.

It was while we were having our porridge later that he dropped his bombshell.

'I'm asking if we can take our mother's body back to Hirta,' he said quietly. 'A stone can stand here in the churchyard, but I think she should go home.'

He spoke so naturally, and with such conviction, that it seemed at once impossible to gainsay him. I looked at once to Morag. She bent her head. 'I have known of Iain's wish from the beginning, Roddy. I would never try to prevent it.' I remember I made some feeble protest, pointing out the cost, the fact that a grave would already have been dug at Lochaline. And then I added: 'I'll not go against you either, Iain, but just one thing – you will have to tell the folk who come.' He nodded in assent. 'Neil and myself are going.' That was all.

In those days the church was not opened for funeral services; the people came to the house, crowding round to hear the minister in the hallway and round the door, even outside if there was not enough room. We had expected that all the St Kildan colony would be with us, as indeed they were, but we were touched that so many had come from Lochaline as well. After the minister's soft words of comfort, we sang my mother's favourite psalm in Gaelic – Psalm 46, 'God is our refuge and our strength.' Then, when all was quiet, Iain stood forward and made his announcement.

I looked at the faces around me, but Iain had already consulted with the oldest of the St Kildans, and they had agreed; their faces bore a look of grave assent. It was not an easy journey; it cost more than we could well afford. But in the end my mother's body was laid to rest in the graveyard of Hirta, beside that of her husband, John Gillies.

Nurse Johnson came this evening and found me writing by the desk. She was already furious because the other patients had been slow in making their way from the dining room and she shouted at me to go back to bed at once. 'You're too old to be writing anyway!' she flung at me. Perhaps I am. It had taken me all of ten minutes to get to the desk, crossing the room by holding on to the table, the chair, the wall hanging and the desk in turn. The more I write, the greater is my urgency to finish. I never had any children, I have lost touch with everyone from the world I once knew, and there is nobody waiting to inherit anything I possess.

Yet this means everything to me. It is the thread of a story that has been wound up in me for many long years. I want it to be written before I die; I am determined that it shall not be left half-finished and lost. No craftsman would leave a piece of work half-done and feel satisfied, so, no matter what Nurse Johnson says, I will go on with this story. All the same, I am afraid that when the last word is written (and I will be very certain of that moment) I will have nothing else left to live for. And so I am caught. I want to be done – for how can I be happy when something remains – and yet I fear I am writing my own death sentence.

I realise I have been thinking a lot about death tonight. It seems to press ever closer. Unlike Iain, I have escaped its touch. He was serving in North Africa. He had only been there a short time, about the same time that I had been in the U.S.

I was sitting in my room on a brilliantly sunny day in June. The whole house smelled of oranges, and outside a cloud of butterflies fluttered among the fresh blooms. Suddenly, quite clearly, I saw the figure of Iain standing by the foot of the bed. He was looking right at me and I could see in detail the whole of his uniform, although he was there for only a few seconds.

'Iain? *De a the e?* Whatever is it?' I said in astonishment. He seemed to smile gently but he had already begun to fade. The strange thing was that while he was there it seemed as if the very furniture and the smell of the oranges, paled and faded. It was he himself who was real and vivid.

It was the 23rd of June, fourteen days before the news came that he had been killed. It seemed they knew almost exactly the time of his death. He had been in the forefront of battle. I stared for a long time at the unfolded letter in my hands, remembering that strange afternoon when he found me. The more I thought about it, the more I came to believe that in the end he did not want to continue living.

All that remained to him was a pocket of land on the mainland, a place for which he had no deep love, among people who, though kindly, would probably always regard him as something of a stranger. He had no place that was truly home to him; all he could do was remember the home he had once had.

So my own feeling is that he threw himself into the very furnace of battle because he had nothing left to lose, nothing for which to go home. I know that my own passing will not be like that. I am too much of a coward. Perhaps I have done a few brave things in my life, but now I have grown old and my world is sheltered and safe. I suppose I just want the pen to fall gently from my hands when all of this is finished.

I think it was while Iain was still away on the island that I heard Morag's news. I was touched that she chose to break her secret to me. It was one evening when we had been outside together. The sky was beautifully clear, for there was a hard frost, and I remember that the going was really tough, for the snow had a thick layer of ice on it now. We reached the edge of the wood in the end, catching each other's hands now and again, and laughing because we were making such heavy weather of it. All of a sudden she grabbed my arm, and gasped, pointing up at the sky.

'Look, Roddy, a shooting star!' Did you see it?'

I hadn't seen anything at all, but a few moments later she squealed with delight because there, in another part of the blue-black expanse, another streamed across the darkness. I was jealous, and I dragged her up one of the low knolls so that we could have a clear view. I craned my neck for a while, searching in vain. We stamped our feet with the cold when all at once the sky seemed full of great silvery trails wherever we looked.

'I remember how old Murdo used to talk about a night when he was a boy, and the sky was just filled with shooting stars.' Morag was speaking softly, with a kind of reverence in her voice. 'I remember him saying that all the boys went up to the summit of Conachair. It was after midnight and it was as if the skies were on fire. They thought that something must have happened, or else that something terrible would happen soon.'

In a few minutes, though, these strange tails began to diminish above us, and all that remained was the cold and the sharp knife of the wind. I turned to go.

'I had something to tell you,' Morag said quickly, not looking at me. 'Donald Angus, you know he lives in the village, well, he asked me to marry him and I said yes.'

I spun round, a flame of happiness rising in me. I took her right off her feet. I was laughing and crying at one and the same time, and I only wished that we might have been going home to share the news with my mother. Morag had hidden her secret well. Donald Angus was a Lewisman. He was as blond as any Viking, tall, and with such a strong accent that I used to think he sounded more at times as if he was singing rather than talking. We had been out in his boat – away in wide, white curls over to Fishnish on Mull, and out further towards the open sea, to glimpse the ledges of Coll and Tiree and the Treshnish Isles. But Donald Angus and Morag getting married! I laughed aloud and ruffled her hair for sheer delight.

'So you're pleased, Roddy?' she asked shyly.

'Aye, I'm pleased. Of course I'm pleased!'

So that was what the starfall brought, the engagement of Morag and Donald Angus. It brought much more than that, of course, if you happen to believe in such things, for those were hungry years, and hard ones for those in the cities who had no work. But that night it brought nothing but joy. And we walked home together in the white shining of the night. After the bitterness of the two deaths, there was happiness, the hope of a spring and a new beginning.

It was decided that Donald Angus and Morag would live in our house at Kinlochallan once they were married. He had come to Lochaline two years before us for the fishing, and the rooms he rented were small enough for himself, let alone for a wife as well.

Iain had now been back from St Kilda for several weeks but Morag was afraid of telling him about her engagement, afraid of his disapproval and the accompanying black and thundery rage. But fortunately he had a liking for Donald Angus, and perhaps the fisherman had been cunning enough to help his cause by offering Iain an occasional bucket of fish that was left over from his catch.

Nothing had yet been said aloud, but I came to decide that there would not be enough room for me at Kinlochallan after the wedding. As for Iain, he had plans for the place; he was going to rent an adjoining piece of land and rebuild the ruin that was on it. Already he was breaking in the ground, land that had long ago returned to heather and weed. He was master of the croft. He was excited by the potential it afforded; it was something into which he could pour his bitterness and frustration after all that he had suffered.

I simply did not know where to go or what I could do. Iain was involved in the work alone. Often he would be out of the house before it had grown light and would not appear again until noon. In the first weeks after our arrival he had called on me to help with certain tasks, but now he did everything himself.

When Donald Angus came to the house of an evening, the two of them would talk away with enthusiasm about what could be done to modify the land or what might be the best solution for this or that problem. Donald Angus was forever quoting examples from his native Lewis, saying: 'I have a cousin in Keose . . . ' or 'I remember when they did something like that in Barvas.' And Morag would sit absorbed in their talk, her face rosy and shining, silently willing them to become firm friends. I, in my turn, would feel a stranger in my own home. Morag had always been the closest to me, closer perhaps than anyone, and it dawned on me that I had lost her. Now I had no one at all. Her adoration of Donald Angus made me desperately jealous; he had taken my place.

So it was that I felt it hard even to talk to her about where I might go or what I could do. Rightly or wrongly, it seemed to me that I was being pushed out without so much as a word. At last I resolved that wherever I did go, I would go to quickly at the time of the wedding. It would be a sudden, shock announcement that would surely make her regret the way she had treated me. With bitterness I would think of the joy I had felt such a short time before, on the night when she had told me the news of her engagement. I had never considered then that it might signal the end of my own life at Kinlochallan. How short a time it had been since I had left Hirta. Now I was having to contemplate leaving my family too. Filled with self-pity, I nursed these thoughts like a black fire in my heart.

In the meantime, talk of the wedding ran like a burn in spate between the houses of the St Kildans and even down into Lochaline itself. At the back of Neil's place there was a courtyard whose slabs were half worn away with time. At the far end, thistles had conquered and speared the air through adder-broad cracks. That was the place where the wedding ceilidh was to be, for it would be high summer by then and there would be light enough to carry on the dancing till two or three in the morning.

It seemed as though half of Lewis would be coming down for Donald Angus's wedding. New cousins were being discovered every week. I think there may have been some envy in Morag for that; so many of her people were now scattered in the wake of exile from Hirta. Not that she said anything of this aloud. Yet she had made friends in Lochaline too, and plenty of them wanted to wish her well. Many of the cottages in Morven would be empty on that June night.

Spring rushed into the sea with frothing burns and glowering dark hues from the moors. The light grew longer and longer, and Iain was hardly to be seen about Kinlochallan the whole day long, so busy were his hands with the rebuilding of the cottage. I think I had never seen him so absorbed or so happy before. When he came in he would be bubbling over with plans of what he would do next, or things Donald Angus had promised to help him finish. And Morag – she was far away in her own happiness; there was a light in her face that had never been there before; as she talked and laughed so easily by the evening fire, I would hardly have known her for my quiet sister. The more they rejoiced, the more I found myself shrinking into a dark world of my own making. I had made my decision, but it was not what I truly wanted. It was simply what I had chosen in my own bitterness and self-pity, knowing all the time that it would hurt my sister most of all.

At last the time came and the courtyard was made ready. Lanterns were borrowed and placed in corners where they would give most light; kitchen tables were laid out also with food and drink. The marriage was to take place at the Manse, where I would give the bride away. It was a bitter irony to me, since in reality, hurt and confused as I was, I was to be leaving her.

The day was cut out of blue crystal. There was not a breath of wind, and the Sound lay like the surface of a mirror as we looked down on it from the Manse. The elderly minister said some kindly words to the bride and groom as we left for the reception, and I remember looking at Morag and seeing with a pang of pure envy the shining in her eyes. A cold wave seemed to wash over me at that moment. The cord with my sister had been severed, I thought then. Iain had become master at Kinlochallan; even my old friend Neil seemed to have his own circle nowadays and had become indifferent since he had begun work in the forestry. I felt as if nobody really cared for me any more; in one way or another I had lost all. Never had I felt more alone.

A motley collection of vehicles made its way along the road later, to begin the reception – one old car carrying the bride and groom, some carts and a few bicycles. I travelled in a cart with some Lewis cousins of Donald Angus. Somebody produced a flask, and I drank deeply, although I was unused to its strength. It stung my throat and made my eyes water. But it would numb the pain. And later, as the celebration got under way, I allowed my glass to be filled again and again. More than once, I know, I was keenly aware of Morag trying to catch my eye, but I steadfastly avoided her gaze. I heard little of the speeches, was unable to join in the laughter. All I knew was that I was thirsty, always thirsty. And I remember that the story of the woman at the well flashed through my mind, the woman who asked Christ for living water to quench her thirst. I thought bitterly of it, and quickly thrust the thought away. Then I started to think of my own story of how St Kilda had got its name, from the Vikings who had found fresh water there . . .

All of a sudden, in a single moment, I was home. Not just vaguely, not in some nostalgic and transient memory, but really there. I was standing above the village, with the graveyard to my left, and I could see the headlands perfectly clearly, the shore below, the water, the men bringing up boxes from a boat that had newly come in from Harris. And it was not just any day; it was that very day. I knew it without any doubt. I could smell the sweet, honey-filled scent of the clover and heard a bee humming away through the grass by my ankles. I had bare feet.

It was so sudden and breathtaking that I reeled. I dived past all the wedding guests, the whisky dizzying my senses; and then at last I was outside behind the houses and I was sick, over and over again. The sun felt like a hot hand on my neck. After a while I looked up and saw Morag standing in front of me. I felt covered in shame, but there was still anger and self-pity like bile inside me.

'I'm going away,' I burst out. 'When you get back from Lewis, I'll not be here.' It was a statement, but it came out as more of a threat. 'I've decided to go to Glasgow,' I added in a calmer voice. 'There just isn't a place for me here anymore.' And then, as she said nothing: 'Go back inside. You're the one person who will be missed today.'

I knew I was, in a way, daring her to leave me; deep down I was hoping she would stay – maybe even put her arms round me and say she was sorry. I longed for her to implore me to stay and say I would always be welcome with the two of them. But she did none of these things. She simply turned on her heel without a word and went back to the reception. She had come of age. She had grown strong without me and I saw it clearly now for the first time. Always until this time she had been my little sister, but now she was herself; she had grown tall in the strength of Donald Angus.

Now I wept. I wept bitter tears of humiliation and anguish, because I felt beaten. For the first time, perhaps, I allowed myself to acknowledge that I was not, in fact, being driven away; I was driving myself away. And I had nowhere to go. For all the men from St Kilda there was the opportunity to work in the forestry; I could have joined Neil in that. But I rejected it. And where would I stay?

All this time I could hear the reception going on happily without me; I heard the laughter and the applause, the clinking of glasses, the music for the dancing. I thought then of one girl I knew from Lochaline, Mairi Ross. She had a single twist of dark-red hair and water-blue eyes. Once she had waved to me when I was passing through the village in the early evening, and since then I had often had her in my thoughts; now my feeling of anguish mounted as I imagined her hand being taken for dance after dance.

I went then. I left the place without a soul seeing me, walking down the road with my head still heavy with whisky and my steps unsteady. Slowly, I made my way towards the house, dreading its emptiness and heavy with guilt at what I had done. I went up to my room and sat on the bed and thought of Hirta and childhood. I thought of Moses and the Israelites, and had a strange picture of a dry path being opened up for us across the sea, back home. And there I imagined my father being still alive, fitting the very last stones of the wall, and my mother working away in the home she had known since childhood, secure and well. But there would be no miracle and though I ached to ask God to hear the cry of my heart, I kept myself hard. I was here, and I was alone.

Upstairs in my room I opened the window as wide as it would go. I leaned out and listened, and heard the sound of a fiddle and clapping. When the dance ended, a new sound drifted to my ears. Away towards the Sound I heard the crying of curlews, crying which seemed to rise and fall all the time as they trailed back and forth through the luminous June light. It was like the saddest music I had ever heard, set against the joyful notes coming from my sister's wedding. And even when the music began for another dance, I could still hear them; the two sounds merging, beautiful and haunting.

I went back and sat on the bed, lost in thought. I simply had no idea what to do. I understood very well that my going, my betrayal, would wound Morag to the very depths of her being. Never in my life had I hurt her, until now, and on the happiest day of her life. Was I right? Had I just been blinded by my own selfishness? Instead of rejoicing with her in the love she had discovered, I had become jealous and harsh. And the thought came to me, too, that perhaps Iain did not deserve my anger either, for had he not been wounded by my mother's death far more deeply than I had myself? Perhaps even now I should go back in, tell them I had been wrong and humble myself. Surely it was foolish not to stay? Was I mad to think about leaving before I had even learned to call this place home?

I had no idea in which direction I should turn. I had to make a decision, right away, that very night. The sun had become a dagger of white-gold in the west; it speared through the windows in a flame which flickered orange and red. The skies became paler and paler, their deep hue lightening to a yellowy white. And still I heard the plaintive calling of the curlews, echoing in the dead-still air. And still I heard the sawing of fiddles and the tramping of feet in the dance.

Far from sober, I realised all the same that nothing was likely to change. Iain had proclaimed himself master at Kinlochallan, and Morag and Donald would certainly remain there until they found a place of their own. It seemed to me that there was always a kind of restlessness in Morag's husband, even if he were to travel to the end of the world he would always be fretting for Lewis. I imagined that they might well settle there some day. Until that time, then, I would continue to be an awkward refugee in a place which was not home.

I pushed my feeling of guilt back down; I was not all to blame. It did come back to me, with some unease, of how Iain had stood in the doorway of my mother's room and apologised. But he had not changed, I told myself. Perhaps it was that his heart had been blackened and twisted by a father who had not shown him enough love? He needed to be given love before he could understand how to return it. And Morag – she did not even see that she had grown away from me; she was too deep in the sweetness of her own happiness.

Nothing would change, I told myself. I had no choice. Denying the jealousy and self-pity festering in the caves of my own heart, my mind was made up. I stared at the road in front of me. The road I would follow. And I would go believing that this was the only course open to me.

I must leave before anyone returned from the wedding. Quickly, I gathered my belongings together, helped myself to a few oatcakes and some cheese, and closed the window to shut off the sound of the fiddles. The road to Corran Ferry wound up the hill past the houses of my old St Kildan neighbours. Instead, I would make my way down to Lochaline, sleep outside somewhere, and ask a man I knew there for a lift in the morning. I took with me every penny I had, which indeed was not much.

I started out just as the light was beginning to fail. There was still a blue-gold glow to the sky that stretched in an arc across Mull, but behind and overhead there was only darkness.

I had never felt so lonely in my life.

As I walked, now and again I would see a flower growing by the roadside. Hardly knowing what I was doing I began to pick a small bunch of assorted blooms, their scent giving a small glow of comfort. It helped a little to pass the time, for the suitcase I carried was not light, and the heaviness of my heart made the way seem longer. I met nobody and saw nothing, except when an otter, crossing the road ahead of me, startled me out of my daze. Then at last I caught sight of a house, high on the hill above the village. Soon I would find a place to sleep.

It was without any sense of having made a decision that I found myself taking the road west towards the old graveyard. Silently, I made my way past all the stones to where one small one bore my mother's name. The light was growing. The night was passing and would soon be over. Already in the east was a bright, hot glow that would become the new day's sun. Not a sound was to be heard as I knelt there.

And then for the second time in two days I was transported. Through the grey, cobwebby semi-darkness of the June night I could make out the strange ring of stones that circled the graves of Hirta, and I was looking out at the open Atlantic, back over towards Harris. I was quite clearly aware of exactly where Iain and Neil had laid my mother's body. I saw the place precisely. I bent over and placed the little bunch of wayside flowers on the simple slab that remembered her, and in that moment I knew beyond doubt, though I could never have explained it, that in some sense I had placed them, too, on the ground where she lay.

Slowly I rose and went over to a grassy corner by the wall and lay down to sleep. I woke to find the sun already warm on my neck. In its comforting rays, I continued my journey. It took all my courage to go and knock on John Cameron's door, but he was a quiet man who would not, I knew, spread gossip. As it turned out, he was intending to take his van to Ardgour the next day.

'No matter,' he said kindly, 'I can just as well go there today instead.'

We spoke very little on the journey.

Three days ago I had my notebook and pen taken away by two nurses I haven't seen here before. I know, of course, that they had been sent by Nurse Johnson. It was early in the morning, and I had left the book over by the window. I had been warned often enough. One of them had a key and opened the cupboard against the wall; she threw the book inside, taking no notice of my protests, and locked the door again. The other one said nothing, and wouldn't look at me. I felt that she didn't want to do it.

I actually cried. I cried like a child when I saw her lock the cupboard. They do not see a person when they look at me; they see an old man with a few strands of white hair, whose hand shakes when he lifts the food to his mouth. They cannot see the person inside me who has lived a proud life, who has loved and raged and learned and struggled. They see a nuisance, but one which will in any case die soon and who has nothing left to say.

For some reason Nurse Johnson could not bear the thought of me writing. It angered her from the start. I never spoke to her at all, but she felt my resentment. She knew that because I wrote, I was capable of stringing a sentence together. So she knew that I was deliberately not talking and it enraged her. Who did I think I was to deny her?

For three whole days, then, my notebook has lain inside that cupboard. There is a small glass panel in the door and through it I can see my book. All day long my fingers have been itching to hold my pen, to get on with the story, because now the words are flowing; now it seems almost easy. I have been lying in bed seeing whole scenes in my head, remembering things one after another, driven mad by the fact I can put nothing to paper and might lose it all again.

The situation has brought back a memory long since forgotten, of when I was a child on the island. Some of the folk had been over to the mainland for stores, before the winter set in. Neil knew how much I loved reading, how I was always longing to get hold of a book; any book at all. He had been with the party and had bought me some cheap paperback – a western I believe it was. Knowing how my father detested fiction, the devil's work, Neil smuggled it to me a day or so after his return. I kept the treasure hidden in my room. If Iain found it he might have betrayed me – in all honesty he had cause enough. One day, when I thought my father was well out of the way, I brought the book out from its hiding place. Lost in the story, a thousand miles away in a land of prairies, fast horses, with the heroine in great danger, I looked up to see my father in front of me.

'What is that in your hands, boy? Where did you get trash like that? How dare you, when you know what we think of such wickedness in this house? Tear it up this minute! Go on, tear it up and put it on the fire where it belongs.'

I had to watch the pages curl orange and burn away through my tears. The same tears as I had shed three days ago, tears through which I had dared to go back to when I really was a child, to touch the raw wounds that have never since been healed.

Nurse Johnson knew exactly how to punish me. To lose that book, of all things. She might have burned it, of course, as my father burned the book long ago, but she did not.

'Well, now, and how are you this evening?'

It is late, Nurse O'Neill has slipped in to see if I was still awake. She had just come on night duty. At once I tell her what has happened and in a moment she has found the key. The precious book is in my hands.

'Thank you, thank you, thank you,' I whisper.

It will take longer, but I can write now whenever she is here.

When I arrived in Glasgow it was in the middle of a heat-wave. I will never forget it. It was the smell that hit me first – that awful smell which seemed made up of smoke and rotting vegetation and urine – and on some days, it merged with a different and even stronger smell which I learned later came from the breweries.

I was completely at sea. John Cameron had said to me that the small post-offices were often friendly places and might be able to tell me of rooms to let. Sure enough, the man behind the counter was kindly and must have sensed my fear and loneliness. He gave me the address of a Mr Semple who rented out rooms. He told me in detail too how to get there, but I soon got lost. I asked directions so often that I almost despaired. The trouble was that I just could not make out what people said; no matter how hard I concentrated or how close I leaned to listen, the words still seemed to roll themselves into a horrible, mangled mess of sounds. I was a foreigner here; the fact hammered home over and over again.

At some point, too, on that very first day I turned a corner and came upon two old women talking away in Gaelic. I was so completely surprised that I stopped dead in my tracks, bemused and happy, not interested at all in what they were saying but simply glad to hear my language. But in a moment or two one of them noticed me and her face seemed to freeze. She jogged her companion's elbow and in a second they had gone, leaving me feeling lonelier and more depressed than before.

Eventually I stopped a youngish man with sandy hair and glasses.

'Follow me, pal,' he said cheerfully, 'I'll show you.'

Off he set at a brisk pace so that I was hard put to keep up carrying my heavy case. Finally he stopped in a narrow lane.

'This is it. You can easily find your way now.'

In a moment I was knocking at Mr Semple's door. I waited a long time for an answer. Three crows rose up from a wall across the road, their hollow laughter mocking me as I stood there. Then an old thin man was opening the door, his cheeks sunken and shiny, the skin drawn taut over his temples. The smoke from his cigarette drifted away slow and grey.

'Mr Semple?' I said, holding out my hand. The one he offered me was thin, so thin it looked like a skeleton's. There was no grip in it at all.

'My name is Roddy Gillies and I'm from the Highlands,' I said. 'Please, have you a room to let?'

I held my breath. I think I would have wept if he had said no. But he nodded and beckoned me inside. He walked very slowly. There was no light on and the place felt cool, even cold, after the heat outside. A smell of cabbage lingered in the hallway. I followed him into a small room at the back. I noticed it had bars on the window. My eyes quickly took in a bed, a chair, a small wardrobe. There were hooks on the wall, and a dreary picture of denuded trees above the bed. I put my suitcase down and we went into a tiny room with a sink, an ancient-looking stove and some shelves. 'The kitchen,' he said shortly. 'You can share it with me but it must be kept tidy, mind.' Then he added: 'It's a gas cooker, so be careful with it.' Shyly I confessed that I had never used gas and he showed me how to light it. Then he led me to the lavatory and wash-basin, and announced that he would take a week's rent in advance. I almost gasped when I heard the amount; it would take so much of my small store of money that I would simply have to find a job within days.

As I was handing over the money, he broke into such a fit of coughing that his whole delicate frame seemed to rattle and threaten to break apart. Then he disappeared into a room marked 'Private,' and there was silence, but for the sound of a huge clock ticking in the hallway.

I went into my room and sat on the bed. I turned back the coverlet and saw that there were clean sheets. Suddenly, despite the loneliness and the strangeness, a wave of sheer thankfulness came over me – I was safe here. It could never be a home, but it was refuge. I muttered a prayer of thanks, brief but sincere. What would I have done, I wondered over and over again, if there had been no room?

Through the wall I could hear my landlord coughing again. It reminded me of my father. I thought of him lying on his bed after his fall, as he struggled to grasp hold of each breath.

Quickly, I packed my belongings away in the cupboard. Grateful though I was for this place, with each thing I put away I told myself that this was not for ever. It could not be for ever. I would wait in this city, with its bewildering crowds of people – never had I seen so many people – and its loud traffic, its heat and its smells, like a goose with injured wings, knowing that when they healed I would rise up into the skies and be away. All the time I was in the city, each day I lived there, I knew it was only a pause in my journey, nothing more.

Outside, the high walls of the tenement opposite blocked the sunset and the road home.

The first Sabbath in Glasgow I was up early. I had no idea where to go, but all the same I found myself walking the streets. The whole place was eerily silent; the dawn's mist was breaking and fading to let through a furnace of June heat.

Singing. I stopped in my tracks. Gaelic singing. How could I ever mistake it? Wave after wave reached me, psalms I had known before anything else, and I rushed without thought towards the door and opened it. I found myself at the back of deep rows of people, in the midst of the loud swell of their singing. I opened my mouth to join in and I could not, overwhelmed by memory. But then I closed my eyes and held my head back. I stood again in our island church, the missionary swaying slightly as he sang. And I sang too, with power, knowing the words without needing any book, and my heart hammered with a joy I had not known for a long time. In this confused sea I had found an island, a strong rock, on which for the moment at least I could stand tall.

After the service was over, I was at once surrounded. I must have been invited to half a dozen homes on the spot, but instead I slipped quietly away, disappeared into a side street. My mind was in turmoil. On the one hand I was warmed and deeply moved to have found that community of Gaelic-speaking people in the heart of the city. In one way, lonely as I was, there was nothing I would have liked more than to be welcomed into a kindly Highland home. But a part of me was afraid – afraid that, as a St Kildan I would not truly be accepted. Despite the bond that linked us, my world had not been theirs for a hundred years or more. A few miles of water had separated us, but an almighty chasm in terms of identity. And I knew I was shabby; I was afraid of being looked down on, afraid of seeing again that look of pitying fascination. This was not simply imagination; I had met it in the past. Like they had encountered someone of a race they had only heard of before.

Perhaps I was afraid of accepting an invitation that day because I had heard plenty of tales about the way other Hebrideans had treated St Kildans in the past. The tourists who had swarmed over Hirta during the summer months, seeking trinkets and postcards, had looked down on us, sure enough; but if the tales were true, other islanders had been far more cruel. My father had told me of Hirta men who had gone in search of nothing more than salt in time of need, being treated like common beggars and turned away. For the St Kilda had always been different, an island set apart, beyond the normal routes and world of the Hebrides. Perhaps they had been a little ashamed of us.

I was afraid and I was proud. So, half angry at myself for turning away, half glad to escape, I retreated to my room. I could not help thinking of the good dinner I might have had, instead of the meal of potatoes and milk which was all I could afford.

I had to find a job, and find it quickly! It was very apparent from the way Mr Semple had wasted no time in taking my first week's rent – and even from the way he counted out the coins – that money was very important to him. I could manage one week, that would be all. I had bought some oatmeal and a bag of potatoes from a small shop just round the corner and I lived on porridge, boiled potatoes and milk. And when sometimes I passed a baker's shop and looked longingly inside, I would say to myself that I was living on the food that had sustained my people for hundreds of years.

Day after day I got up early, dressed as carefully as I could, polishing my shoes until they shone, scanning my image in the mirror a dozen times and tidying every stray stand of hair. I visited offices and warehouses, shops and restaurants, even law firms, anywhere – even in the most run-down areas – I thought there might be the possibility of a job. I knew I had no qualifications but I was desperate and willing. But everywhere I got the same message. This was the Depression, they said with a shrug, and there was no work to be found. Exhausted, I would return to my room, not having eaten since early morning. The air seemed to stink of hops and metal; the hot weather did not help at all and made me think of the life I had left at Kinlochallan, of its security and safety. Why had I left? The quarrels with Iain and Morag seemed a million miles away from here. What had I been thinking of, to come to this city? Why had I chosen Glasgow, for one thing, instead of a smaller place like Oban or Inverness, where I might have fared so much better? Should I just go back? For an answer, I brought out the precious few coins from my pocket to count them, over and over.

It was on one of those days that I suddenly found myself face to face with Sparky. I am not sure which of us was the more surprised. He was a Ferguson, the younger son of Alan and Mairead Ferguson, and he had lived four doors along from ourselves on the island. I could remember him vividly from days in the schoolroom, one hand always supporting his head of fire-red curls. He hated school and wanted nothing more than to go to sea.

He was the last person I would ever have expected to meet in the city. If I had thought of Sparky at all during my days in Lochaline, I would have imagined him perhaps on the deck of some merchant vessel, or far away across the sea in Nova Scotia or British Columbia. But here he was in Glasgow, his hair wild and tangled and dressed in terrible rags, but still Sparky.

I crushed his hand in my own and broke into torrents of Gaelic. The rush hour was beginning and the pavements were full of people. He seemed ill at ease standing there, although he smiled at me, and I noticed that his hand trembled as I let go of it.

'Come with me,' he said in a low voice. 'I'm not going far.'

'D'you live near here then?' I asked eagerly.

He jerked a hand over his shoulder and gestured vaguely, almost irritably. 'Not far from here. Let's get going. I can't stand it when it's thick with folk.'

He thrust his hands into what remained of his jacket pockets, and began walking fast, manoeuvring round people as if they didn't exist. Suddenly he turned left and without a word disappeared through a door. I found myself in thick smoky darkness among old men slouched at tables. There was an unpleasant smell of burnt meat in the air and somewhere under a table a dog whined. Through the cloying air I made out the face of a fat man with a moustache leaning over the bar.

'Your usual, Sparky?' he asked.

'Aye, and the same for him.'

We sat down at a table in the shadows at the back. I was thankful to find it was cool in there, after the long hours spent trailing through the metallic July heat. Sparky brought out cigarettes; he did not talk to me until he had one lit. I wondered whether he realised I had never been in such a place before.

'How are your mother and father?' I asked then.

'My mother died last year,' he said, speaking very low and never once looking at me. 'Father's with me; he never goes out anywhere and he forgets things all the time.' And then, after a pause: 'He's old, you know.'

I said nothing, but it seemed unbelievable to me. Sparky's father had been anything but old. I could see Alan Ferguson so easily in my mind's eye, coming up from the shore with a heavy creel on his back, never once faltering on that steep path. He had been one of the last, and finest, climbers on the Stacs, an iron strength in his feet and hands, and in his mind. I thought of him now, sitting alone somewhere, with nowhere to go.

We sat in silence. Sparky did not ask about my family, even about Iain, with whom he had been good friends. Instead I began to tell him; I spoke of my own mother's death, of the house and the land around Kinlochallan, and Morag's marriage to Donald Angus. I wondered whether he took in what I was saying, for he made no comment at all; he had already finished his first drink and was fidgeting to return to the bar.

'Will you have another?'

I shook my head, bemused and silent, as he walked quickly past the table to get another drink. The place was becoming busier; working men with the long day over were coming in to drink, sitting beside men like myself who had spent the day searching for work. They did not seem any happier than ourselves, yet I envied them. I found myself wondering where Sparky got the money for drink.

'I was lucky,' he muttered. 'I found a job at the first place I tried. I'm an odd-job man at a locomotive engineering works.'

The silence again closed round us. Then Sparky folded his arms in front of me.

'You have to forgive me, Roddy,' he began suddenly. 'I drink a lot; I drink like this every day. I drink to forget, and I drink to remember. I drink far more than I can afford, like plenty others in this place.' He banged the heavy round ashtray with his glass and then cupped it with his hands. 'You see, that's the island, our own island. That's where I want to be and the only way I have of getting there is this.' He swirled the amber pool of whisky in the bottom of his glass. 'Hirta doesn't exist any more, Roddy, not for us anyway, not for any of us. All we can hope to get back to is what it once was.' He looked at me severely. 'What else binds you and me? Nothing. We're not really friends; there's nothing special we have in common. Just that one thing – the island.'

I looked hard at him and saw the shining of his eyes, the intensity of emotion that burned there.

'Every day now I go back there,' he went on, the edge of a smile on his lips, his voice very quiet and calm. 'I know it's costing my life, Roddy. I know the price fine, but it's worth it. It's all I have left now.'

There was no more to say. I drank my whisky, but every last drop of it seemed to smoulder in my mouth. I felt sick as I sat there in that bar while it grew louder and louder and the air seemed to become harder and harder to breathe. I watched Sparky in dismay as he went back for yet more whisky, until his eyes changed and his shoulders drooped. And as I watched, his head dropped on to his elbow and he was again the boy I remembered all that time ago on Hirta. The dreamer.

Neither of us talked any more. At last I became conscious of the time. The whisky lay heavy as lead in my stomach. I had eaten nothing since breakfast. I wanted to get away. I scraped back my chair and softly said goodbye to him. And that was the last time I saw Sparky Ferguson.

I did not write to Morag. More than once I tried to put words on to paper, but they seemed to linger there, strange and remote, and would not flow into sentences at all. I told myself that when the time was right they would come, but I think that even then a worm of bitterness lingered in my heart, and in a way I did not want it resolved. Returning every day to my lonely room in the city, from where I could see no living thing, I had every occasion to think of all the beauty surrounding Kinlochallan, and to feel – however wrongly – that it had been stolen from me.

I found work in the end, fetching and carrying for a fellow called O'Hagan who ran a small furniture removal business. He was a hard man who swore at us and cared for nothing and nobody but money. In the beginning, I seemed to hurt all over, as if someone had taken a big stone and thumped all over my shoulders and thighs and knees. I remember one day we were carrying things up to a third floor room in a tenement in Partick. O'Hagan stood below, watching another man and myself as we dragged a heavy cupboard between us. Every time I passed him I caught the sweet blue smell of his cigarette.

'Come on then, Gillies, get a move on! Ten bloody times I've had to tell you and still you won't shift! We've just half an hour till we're due in Hyndland.'

I thought my knees would never hold out; they felt as if they had melted beneath me. Yet somehow I forced myself on – up and up to the top of the stairs, down again for the next load. Then all at once I saw my father, clear as though it had been the day before, walking steadily up from the boat with a great heavy box on his shoulder. There was a whole line of men; Alan Ferguson was one of them, and Neil's father, too. But it was my father I was watching. His eyes were steady, never wavering at all as he climbed higher and higher on that steep path to the village. And at the top he did not even pause, but began the descent for more goods without so much as a word, the rain and mist beginning to drive in from the sea . . .

The image was so real at that moment that it gave me strength to go on without faltering, to ignore the agonising weight of the load on my shoulder. I would have lost the job if I had failed – that was certain. Sparky's answer had been to bury himself in what had been; my memories had come to me to give me strength to conquer. The voice of O'Hagan grew more and more insignificant; it seemed to me at that moment nothing more than the piping of a young child, the words important no longer. The steep, uneven steps of the tenement stairs no longer mattered; I was carrying provisions for the winter, and I was walking in my father's footsteps.

After that the days and weeks just seemed to merge into one another. I was glad when the heat of summer passed and autumn came – not that there was anything much to mark its coming except that some leaves from the few blackened trees in the small park nearby blew forlornly along the streets. Then the fog descended to cloak Glasgow like a sunken wreck; vague white and yellow lamps shone mistily in the gloom, smudged by the thick scarf of this airless prison. I felt all the time that I had gone below sea-level, that I was clawing upward all the time to the open sky to get my breath.

The traffic was at a near standstill. People were trying to shout directions and I kept seeing a man with a stack of newspapers wandering aimlessly among vehicles, shouting the name of his paper like a plea for help. Even the names of the streets were half-rubbed away by the yellow stain of the fog. I would stand and stare at them, straining to catch one letter and then another until the whole word at last appeared.

It was around that time that the fire happened. I remember because the children were all gathering things for their own bonfires, so it would have been the end of October. I had come home about six o'clock, so exhausted that I could hardly move. I could hear my landlord moving about in his own rooms, slow and heavy; every so often the silence broken by the harsh sound of his coughing. Ravenous, I had no energy to prepare food and it was all I could do to strip off my boots before sinking into the blissful softness of the bed, to fall asleep at once.

I was wakened by the sound of voices outside. I leapt up, dragging on my boots, and rushed out into the close, following the voices out to the back court. It was pitch dark, but as I looked up I was horrified to see flames pouring from a window in the tenement opposite, two floors up. In the middle of a knot of people a woman screamed, 'My bairns! My bairns!'

I still do not know why I did what I did, for there is nothing of the hero in me. I simply did not stop to think. Perhaps hunger sharpened my senses. All I know is that I noticed a pipe running down the side of the building, passing close to the window where the fire blazed. The age of the building meant that there were plenty of holes and fissures by which I could climb up. Breathing a prayer for help, I tore off my boots and socks and launched myself at the wall, holding on to that pipe.

'Are you daft? You'll never do it!'

'For God's sake get down! You'll kill yourself!'

It was as if I was swirled away, out of that time and place altogether, out of the range of their warnings. I bit the end of my tongue, and tasted blood and salt. And there was salt all over my face, and the wind was tugging at my hair, and the voices of seabirds screamed and wheeled below. And it was Stac Lee I was climbing, barefoot as generations of my ancestors had been. I was a hundred feet above the boiling waters of the Atlantic, yet the strange thing is that all fear had gone. Instead, I felt a surge of strength go through my whole frame, a wave of sheer power that I can only call faith. But there was something else too. There was the pride in being a St Kildan. It was as if I was remembering by instinct, as if in my bare feet and my hands were generations of climbers' nerves and sinews of learning.

I climbed until suddenly the searing heat from that window woke me from the other world; I ducked, traversed till I was beneath it. On the other side the flames were less intense. I rushed inside and was almost overwhelmed by the thick wall of acrid smoke. I covered my mouth with my sleeve, heard then the crying and rushed through a door into another small room to find two tiny children huddled on the floor, too terrified to move. They were little blond things, hardly more than two or three. I scooped them up like chickens in my arms, hardly knowing what to do next. Then I turned and saw a fireman standing in the doorway, and heard the jets of water already scouring the walls, and I knew we had been saved.

In an hour or two it will be dawn and Nurse Johnson will begin her shift. I've been writing the whole night and the pen is heavy in my hand. I am dead tired. Through the open curtains I can see the skies beginning to lighten; they have in them the most beautiful white-blue clarity that only comes after a truly severe frost. Nothing seems to breathe in the icy stillness.

Mr Semple was dying. I took to giving him his meals in his bedroom and in return he deducted a little each week from the rent. I still remember how he would stand with his back to me, hunched over at the dressing-table, carefully counting the coins I had just handed to him.

There was nothing left of his body. The skin was taut over his face and the bones beneath his eyes were pronounced; his eyes were bloodshot, his breath so bad that I feared to go near him. I took him food but he hardly ate; he had the appetite of a swallow.

'Give me my cigarettes,' he would whisper. I would wait there until he signalled for me to go. I think now he may have wanted to talk but he did not know what to say to me. He had been in business once, with his own company. His sons had it now, but I never saw them visit him; nobody came to see him. I often tried to imagine him, alone in the house while I was at work all day, waiting in the shadows of that bleak place, hearing only the steady ticking of the hall clock.

The New Year came and went in absolute loneliness, and I thought ceaselessly of Kinlochallan. I pondered for hours on all I had lost. And for what? What was I doing in this place where no one cared whether I lived or died? I thought of the Prodigal Son, but I was not sure where my real home was, or how I could reach it. I felt at times that I had been swept away by a far bigger and more dangerous sea than the one which swelled around Hirta. I knew that I had no direction, that I was pouring away my life fetching and carrying for a man I despised, and who despised me. There was no pleasing O'Hagan, with his sadistic and twisted heart, who taunted me ceaselessly because I often failed to understand a command, and because my voice was soft, not hammered from steel like his own. Each day I struggled home tired and sick at heart, fighting against the sharp wind that drove around each blackened tenement and I vowed I would return to Lochaline. Surely I could find something to do that was better than this? But something held me back. What exactly would I do once I arrived there? Did I think I could survive on the charity of my brother?

Sometimes I went into a pub. I sat alone in the darkest corner I could find and when I looked down at the shining pools of spilled beer on the table, I saw not my own face but the reflection of Sparky. More than once I was tempted to follow his path. But I knew well enough that what he saw was only a broken image, a poor shadow, and that his was no kind of answer at all. I was aware too that it was a waste of money, and I felt guilty and ashamed. Somehow I had to begin again. Break new ground. Stop ceaselessly looking over my shoulder at what had been. Yet I did not know how to do it.

One night I stood on a bridge that spanned the Clyde. The water that flowed beneath was made of oil; its surface was fired by the last glow of the sunset. Pieces of metal and broken wood rose from the banks like the bones of strange creatures. The water reeked of disease. As I looked, I remembered the water of Hirta, the fresh, clear joy of it as it burst from the ground and bounced away like crystals from the hill. I thought of myself, of how I too had journeyed from source to sea, and felt that this was a kind of picture of what I had become; my life felt as useless and corrupted as that oozing river below, silting out brokenly to the sea.

I wandered home quite late that night, hardly caring in what streets I walked. There was a strange mist lying over everything, very low and fine. It streamed across the darkness like fine silk and smudged the lamps and made the silence eerie and deep. I returned at last and descended into a sound sleep. From the depths of it I jerked awake for no reason that I knew, I sat bolt upright. I was breathing wildly, my face and hands shining with sweat. I hadn't had a nightmare, nothing that I could recall at all, but I was acutely aware that something had happened to Morag –

she was ill and in pain. My hands were trembling. They shook so much that I could do nothing with them. I staggered about the room like a madman, trying desperately to make sense of the sensation.

It was still dark. I went back to bed but could not settle so I got up and dressed. What else could I do? Over a cup of strong tea, anxious thoughts chased each other through my mind. First and foremost, I knew that I must get to Morag. But Mr Semple? How would he manage without me? Yet there was sufficient in the house, I knew, and the neighbours along the close would look after him if necessary. Then there was my job – I'd lose it if I didn't turn up. No, surely one of them would come to find me? I sat down, forced myself to be calm, and scribbled a note. Then, taking almost nothing with me, I left.

As I think back on it now, all these many years later, it seems to me the maddest and bravest thing I ever did. Yet it cost little; I truly felt I was leaving nothing but the dust from my boots behind. It was still very early. The wind was raw and I wished I had a warmer coat. The people I met were all going in the opposite direction. That is my strongest memory. Men especially, striving on towards the heart of the city, their faces empty of all but direction and time. It came to me how they would do that year in, year out, unable to find release or to question why. And suddenly, despite my gnawing fear over the thing that had happened to Morag, a wave of sheer elation swept through me at the thought of leaving Glasgow. It was as if I had been longing to remove some kind of horrible skin from my body and could not tear it, but now, in one motion, it was coming away in my hands and the clear smooth skin beneath was visible at last.

I walked on briskly then until I was out on the north-west edge of the city. Soon a man with a cart drew up beside me and offered me a lift. He said not a single word for perhaps five miles; seemingly in no hurry whatsoever. Then abruptly he told me he was going to Campsie Farm and I would have to get off.

For a few moments I stood again on the road, listening to the sounds of spring all around me: the rustling of birds in branches, their calls and chatter. I drank in the sight of grass and hedges, of the red sunbeams which daggered in from the east. Then I saw a rushing burn and threw myself down on my knees beside it, throwing cool water over my face and arms and drinking as if I had never drunk before in my life.

I went on then at a good pace, hardly thinking about the miles under my feet because I was simply thankful to the depths of my heart to be free. It began to grow cloudy after a time, and the sun was shut out like a red eye. A stiff breeze came and on its swirling skirts was a flurry of snow. I stopped, thinking it would soon pass, but it did not. Soon it was snowing in earnest.

I realised then what a fool I had been to come away so fast that I had hardly given a thought to what I might need for the journey; I had no thick coat and already I was cold.

For a while I took shelter beneath some trees, but I knew I would stay warmer if I remained on my feet. Then a car closed in on me, a huge, beautiful, shining red beetle.

'Where are you heading for? We're going to Crianlarich.'

I climbed in, thankful beyond words to the three youngish people who stared back at me. Even I could tell that their accents were cultured and upper-class; the car and the belongings too spoke of wealth. Any room in the car was piled with baskets and jackets and food; my feet rested awkwardly on boxes of fishing tackle. It was clearly not at all convenient for them to take me in, and their kindness warmed me. They chattered endlessly, wanting to know where I came from and where I was going. They saw that I was cold, and insisted that I take a rug for my knees. They plied me with cups of sweet coffee from a thermos flask, and I stared out at the bleakness that surrounded us.

Great thick, feather-like flakes were falling, one after another after another, and the ground was rapidly becoming white. The driver kept leaning forward in exasperation, scraping at the windscreen to clear his view. I did not like to think how I would have fared without this lift. For a long time we crawled along; the world rapidly turning into one huge snowball. The car was beautifully warm and I began to feel sleepy, my head aware only of the murmur of voices, the low humming of the car, and the squeaking of the windscreen wipers as they laboured to push away the snow.

'This is where we go our separate ways, I'm afraid.'

The voice woke me with a start. I must have been asleep for some time. They pressed a bag of food into my hand and then the girl said as I was getting out, 'Here, do please take this coat – it's an old one of Bill's. He won't miss it. You can't possibly go on without a coat.'

Mercifully, it was now much clearer than before. It had snowed hard and the clouds seemed empty; above me they were beginning to split and there was a single patch of yellow with blue behind it. I realised that I was somehow going to have to find shelter of some kind for the night, but there was no point in staying there in the village, for I had no money. So I walked on steadily for perhaps an hour, watching the clouds anxiously for signs of the snow beginning again.

I had, for the time being, forgotten my anxiety about Morag, but now it hit me again. I must get on! Come what may, I must get back to Lochaline as quickly as possible. But walking was so slow. And I had to rest for the night; it would soon be dark. Then the cloud seemed all at once to roll down from the north and in no time at all the road grew blurred. Lights shone out here and there, like lighthouses in a grey sea. By then I was feeling overwhelmed with tiredness, my strength utterly drained.

I looked round me in despair at the night, the cold darkness of the night, and I remembered with great clarity that night when I had gone to find the doctor. I remembered the premonition of her death that had possessed me; I recalled vividly too standing at the side of my father's grave on Hirta. Death, death. I seemed to have been pursued by death, or the fear of death, all through my life. And now Morag – was I about to lose my sister too?

I reached a farm and stood for a while at its gates, wondering what to do. A pale lantern hung outside the house, seeming to make the night bleaker and grimmer than ever. Snow was whirled and drifted against the low windows. Somewhere a door was banging in the breeze, but there was no sign of anyone, no sign of life at all. I resolved to find a corner for myself in one of the outhouses until morning. I wanted shelter but not company. My head was too full of fear and confusion.

I found a dry corner without trouble. The place smelled of beasts, but I jumped with fright when something brushed against my leg. It was nothing more than a cat and for the first time that day I smiled to myself. I sat down on a pile of warm hay and thankfully opened the bag of food my kind benefactors had given me. The chicken sandwiches, rolls and hard-boiled eggs were so delicious and I was so ravenous that I had hard work to restrain myself from devouring the lot. Mindful that this food had to last a long time, I ate only a little and then lay down to sleep.

I did not sleep for some time. I prayed that I might not be too late.

It is a strange thing, but although I recall that first part of the journey and that first night on the road, I find it impossible to remember the rest except as a blur. Looking back after all these years, it seems that I simply kept plodding on through the snow for mile after mile after mile, thinking about nothing but the urgent necessity of reaching Morag. Certain incidents do remain, like when an old shepherd's wife saw me tramping past her house and had me in for a meal of bacon and egg – surely the best meal I had ever tasted. Or when I could find no shelter and had to take refuge behind some haystacks, where I spent a cold, uncomfortable and sleepless night. I cannot now be sure just how many days I was on the road. I remember the long bleak road through Glencoe, the seemingly endless trek round Loch Leven; and I remember too how I was so entranced by the beauty of the loch and the hills as I made my way through Onich that I forgot my misery.

What I remember best is the sheer joy and relief when at long last Corran Ferry came into view; although there were still many miles to go once I reached the other side. I looked across at the thick tan stretches of seaweed, the black inlets whose water seemed like beautiful dark glass, the hillsides that stretched away, slumbering lions lost in a wilderness.

'Is this you back then?'

I whirled round at the sound of a familiar voice, and saw John Cameron waiting for the ferry to arrive; his warm smile cheered my heart.

'Jump in, Roddy! You're in luck again, boy. I'll drop you off right at the door.'

I can't express the relief I felt. I was so tired; I hadn't eaten or slept properly for what seemed like ages. Thankfully, I climbed into the cab.

'Well, you certainly went away in a hurry but it's good to see you back,' John said mildly. I offered no explanation and he asked no questions, but instead started to tell me about the things that had happened since I left.

'Oh, it was a bad winter,' he said. 'Nothing but trouble. Your brother has had a hard time of it right enough.' I looked at him. 'Och, the land he's trying to make a living from is bad – soaking wet. Then he went and had a bad fall in the autumn, broke something up on his right shoulder. It was pretty serious, took a long time to heal right.'

John told me how he was coming back from Fort William, where he had been visiting his brother. He had been there for quite a few days, so he would have no idea what had happened to Morag, I thought. After a while, I felt myself beginning to drift off.

'Just have a sleep, boy – you look fearfully tired.' I was aware of nothing more until the van stopped for some sheep on the road. We were near Kinlochallan. I strained forward in my seat, heart thudding, only to find that there was nothing round the corner but bare hillside.

Then, when I least expected it, we were there. The house covered in snow, and someone appeared from round from the back. I thanked John warmly, leapt from the van and was away, running across the road. The figure stopped, looking up at me. It was Donald Angus carrying two big buckets of coal in his hands.

'What's wrong?' I shouted.

He looked at me blankly for a moment as I sped towards him. Then a huge smile spread over his face as I tore past him, straight into the house.

'Upstairs,' he said. 'She's fine now; they're both fine.'

I took the stairs two at a time and tripped in the middle, almost pitching myself on to the floor. My chest was bursting as I reached the top and went right into her room. There she was on the pillows, her face pale but very calm, and there was in her arms the strangest bundle.

'Look,' she said to it gently. 'Here's your uncle.'

'M-Morag!' I stammered in disbelief, 'I never thought . . . I mean, I came because I felt you were ill, you were in pain.'

'It was bad, right enough, Roddy,' she said. 'A hard time for me, but I'm fine now.' I went forward to the side of her bed, remembering something else. I found myself on my knees, taking her hand in my own, and my eyes filled with tears.

'Forgive me, Morag – forgive me for what I did. I'm sorry, so sorry. I should never have done such a thing.'

She put her hand on my brow so gently, with such compassion, that I knew I had not needed to ask for forgiveness, because she had granted it a long time before. I had the strangest sense of her being older than me, far older now in her new maturity. I felt that I was still searching for myself desperately while she was utterly serene, complete in her contentment. Then I saw that she had tears in her eyes, too.

'You came to me, Roddy,' she whispered. 'You were worried about me . . . we're still close.' She smiled at me, then motioned me to sit beside her. I dried my eyes as she handed me her tightly-wrapped bundle. All the woollen garments that wrapped it round were white, but the face was bright pink, the eyes shut fast as if in prayer. I looked at Morag and then down at this strange pink face and the minute hands that were fastened together.

'This is Calum,' she said quietly, answering the question in my eyes, and in her voice was pride and contentment and relief, all one and the same.

I said his name several times and then I was laughing, laughing despite the tears that still streaked my cheeks. I was thinking of every long mile I had covered from Glasgow and of the fear there had been in my heart. There had been moments when I had wondered whether I would even find her alive at all, when my spirit had been so low that there seemed no faith left in me.

I held the precious bundle in my arms and looked down at him, heard the quick, thick sound of his breathing.

'When was he born?' I asked. But I knew the answer.

With my return to Kinlochallan I felt that a lead weight had rolled from my shoulders. More than the relief at finding Morag well and happy, I knew her forgiveness. It was a feeling more precious to me than gold. Donald Angus came in then and there was laughter in the house; the evening drew in, the fire was lit, and we sat in comfort and talked. I had come home. Donald Angus brought out a dram for us and afterwards I wolfed the meal they gave me; I could hardly remember when I had last eaten. Then I looked out of the window and saw the snow lit like great shields under the moonlight, and a wave of sheer warmth surged through me. I had come home. I was no longer a refugee from Kinlochallan. And all at once my tongue was freed and I reclaimed my Gaelic. It was like a horse which, forced to carry a plough and plod unerring lines for many hours, suddenly scents the moor again, kicks over the traces and breaks away. Those hours seemed to me then as the happiest of my whole life. Probably they felt more precious because of the darkness of the months that had gone before. Perhaps Eden is always at its most beautiful when around it lie desert sands or wilderness.

I was thinking of nothing except my reconciliation with my sister and the joy of being at home with her, when all of a sudden the outer door opened. Donald Angus stopped in mid-sentence. Footsteps sounded in the hallway, the door opened and Iain came in, looking straight at me. I was on my feet by then, trying desperately to find words, but both my mind and my mouth were dry. His eyes held mine for a long moment but he did not say a word. Instead, he turned and went heavily upstairs.

I went on standing there, awkward and shaken, the dream in tatters. Donald Angus didn't say a word at first, but just kept looking into the fire. The house was silent as my brother reached the top of the stairs; then Calum cried softly and I heard Morag comforting him.

'It will be all right, Roddy,' Donald Angus muttered. I saw that Iain's entry had shaken him badly too. 'It will be better after a few days.' But he did not sound as if he believed it himself.

It cast a deep shadow over us, and when I went up to bed my mind was racing with thoughts and questions and fears. I knew now without any doubt that although Morag had forgiven me, Iain most certainly had not. His anger, the black well of his bitterness against me, went very deep, I knew, and was crusted with age. I paused for the barest moment outside his room and thought back to that day in childhood when I had carried him off to do away with him. So, in the very beginning, it had been my own jealousy of the child who lit my mother's eyes which had given rise to the shadow which hung over us now. And although the tables had been turned, nothing at all had really changed.

By early in the morning I had not slept a wink. Tired yet overwrought, each moment was filled with torment from my teeming thoughts. I went downstairs without making a sound, afraid of wakening that fresh, shining shell of a child. It was cold in the kitchen and I stood over in the window, looking out over the grey ramparts that lay massed on the edge of the sky. It was March, and the snow had not lain long; much of it had disappeared.

Feeling him behind me, I turned round and saw him standing in the shadows.

'I don't want you back here,' he said, and there was a kind of black emptiness to his voice. His eyes held nothing but enmity. 'You left. You ran off on your own sister's wedding day. I don't know what you've done since then and I don't want to know; I don't care. But I do know one thing —you can't break into this place as easily as you broke out of it. Maybe Morag forgives you, but I don't. I don't want you here. Go back to wherever it was you were. Leave us in peace.' I made to say something, but he put up his hand. 'You know you can't live here any more. You're a stranger here. This is my place – I've worked every day you were away to build it up. I've slaved to the last drop of my strength, and I'll tell you this – I'm not sharing it with you. You'll not have a corner of what you haven't worked for. I want you out of here.'

He had already turned away, his speech finished. I could take it or leave it. Perhaps it was that arrogance that made me see red, so that I could not just let him walk away in victory. My hands were trembling at my sides.

'This house is as much mine as yours,' I said. 'I am my mother's son, too, and when she was alive I had a place in it as much as ever you did. I left it last year – that's true, but it was because of one thing. You were determined to make Kinlochallan your own and shut me out. I left it because I imagined I was losing my sister – yes, I was fool enough to think that, I know it now. You can't bear me coming back here because you're scared – scared I might be better liked than you, or that I'll get a foothold and maybe even be more successful than you. What on earth is wrong with you, Iain? Why can't you learn to share? Why can't you stop seeing me as an enemy, fighting me at every turn? Why don't you face your own darkness and deal with it?'

The vase flew past my face to smash against the wall. The echoes of it seemed to reverberate in the silence.

'You leave my life alone!' he shouted. I could not miss the threat that lay behind the words. 'The only darkness I have has come from you. Don't ever forget that.'

He turned again and this time I did not stop him. I did not dare. There was no strength left in me at all, and even if I had known what to say, I could not have spoken. A moment later he was out, slamming the door behind him. Donald Angus was coming quickly down the stairs. He entered the kitchen, his eyes taking in the fragments of the vase.

'I'm sorry, Roddy,' he said gently. 'Come and sit down. Never mind the vase.' He put his hand on my shoulder and led me to a chair. 'Iain has changed,' he said soberly. 'You remember, before you left, he and I had got quite close. We were able to talk. All that's changed; it's been different for a long while now. After the wedding, after we came back from Lewis, he said he was going out to St Kilda. Neil was going with him; they were to be staying a few days. When they got back, there was something really strange about Iain. He had a kind of restlessness about him; his eyes were wild. I suppose we felt it was because he had been back, because everything of the past had returned to haunt him. We just thought he would get over it, gradually return to normal. But that never happened. He would fly into the most terrible rages. If there was anything that went against him in his work, it would nearly drive him to madness. And then back in the autumn he had a bad fall and hurt his shoulder; that drove him mad too because he couldn't get on with a thing. That was a hard time. I tried to talk to him often enough, trying to put things back the way they had been, but it never worked. Sometimes there'd be odd flashes, and you'd hope it would be better, but it never lasted.

'When we knew for certain that a child was on the way, we were really quite afraid. We didn't want any child of ours to begin his days here. But there seemed no alternative. My father's croft on Lewis is too small for us, and Iain won't leave here, not for us. He sees it as his and his alone. For the moment we are stuck – there's nothing that can be done. But we'll hope and pray that things may yet change, and somehow you can come back.' His eyes seemed to sparkle for a second. 'It would be good if you were to come back, Roddy. I feel guilty that I pushed you out.'

I smiled. Comforting as his words were, I could only wish that I had heard them before I stormed away from Kinlochallan. But I didn't stay to hear them. Now it was too late. There was no way back. I could not see how Iain and I could live together.

Later that morning I walked up the hill to the high ridges behind the houses. It was difficult going, for deep snow was still lying in many places, with only the boulders exposed like stranded whales where the wind had blown the rocks clean. I stood there for a long time looking down on Kinlochallan, and suddenly it seemed to me that I was looking at it through a window, desperately wanting to come in and knowing that I could not, no matter how I tried.

'He'll kill you,' Morag had whispered to me earlier, her eyes shining with emotion. 'I'm so frightened he'll kill you, Roddy. Don't think he hasn't got it in him – he's full of hatred, and the only way he can pour it from himself is by tearing at that old ruin. He doesn't really know what he wants, but Kinlochallan is all he has. He believes it's only a matter of time before we move out. I feel he only tolerates us because he's sure we're just waiting to find somewhere else. But if you came back now, if you moved into the house, I don't know what he would do. I don't trust him, Roddy, and he's my own brother . . . '

A light shone in the house, the only point of warmth, it seemed, in all that white and grey world. And then, in contrast, I thought of all the poverty and misery and deprivation of the city where I had spent the last months. And it seemed incomprehensible that such a beautiful and serene place as Kinlochallan looked now should be so twisted and spoiled by the bitterness in one man.

My eyes rested on the little washing-green at the back of the house, and I visualized a little boy tottering and staggering there, the grass stems tickling his knees, huge blue eyes full of wonder at the sight of a butterfly. This was a place where Calum could grow, blessed by a thousand natural wonders. There was a rich sea for his father to fish, and a house that was big enough for us all to share, at least for a few years. But it was an impossible dream.

Already the light was beginning to fade and pieces of land to disappear one by one, smudged by the incoming dark. I knew in my heart that I was saying farewell, that I had made my peace, that I might well never see Kinlochallan again.

No one knew where Iain had gone, but I decided in any case to leave quickly. There was not only myself to think of, but a child, a new and beautiful child, of whose birth I had in some strange way been aware. Morag did not want to let me go, and when it came to parting, her face was broken with anguish. I held little Calum for a long time.

'Don't stay in Glasgow, Roddy,' she implored me.

I thought of Sparky and I thought of Mr Semple, and I knew she was right. I nodded, unable to utter a word, and held her close. As I broke away from her she pressed something into my hands. It was a Bible, a little Bible that I knew well, for it had belonged to my mother. Many had been left on Hirta, open at a certain place, in the rooms of houses where they had been read faithfully night after night. Some of the pages of that little book were so worn with use that their pages could hardly be read. But it was a gift precious to me beyond words. It would be a sort of home, a shelter – something I needed most in all the world.

Donald Angus took me as far as he could and left me at a place where I could spend the night. It is a curious thing, but I cannot remember where it was, or indeed one single thing about the journey back to Glasgow. What I do recall clearly, though, was that when I let go of his hand after a long moment of goodbye he took something from his jacket.

'It isn't much,' he muttered, as if he was embarrassed and wanted no thanks at all. 'I only wish it could be more, Roddy, for I feel in a way I'm to blame for all this trouble that's happened. Take it and use it, and promise to tell us at once if ever you are in need. God bless you.'

He went very quickly, and I was left there in the dark, knowing that for the moment at least I had no choice but to return to Glasgow.

When eventually I put my key into the lock of the familiar door and pushed it open, I knew at once that something was wrong. There was a scent in the air that I had never known there before; it was like velvet, the smell of cushions, old and dusty. At once I heard the sound of footsteps and I turned and saw a young man coming towards me. He had very intense blue eyes, his thin blond hair was slicked back and he wore a suit. He didn't smile at all.

'You must be Roderick Gillies. I'm afraid Mr Semple, my father, died a couple of days ago. In due course the house will be sold so I'll have to ask you to make other arrangements for accommodation.'

With that he disappeared into the old man's bedroom and began talking in a very flat tone to someone I couldn't see. I had been so afraid, so certain that I would be blamed for having gone away leaving the old man alone when he was ill; yet he did not seem to care in the least. Later, in the bleak silence of my room I heard sounds of drinking. As the voices grew louder, laughter echoed strangely in rooms where there had been so little noise before. They did not bother about me at all. Mr Semple's sons, Sam and George, had visited at last.

For two days I've been too ill to write anything. Those late nights of writing while Nurse O'Neill was on duty must have caught up with me as the cold had got into my chest. I kept the notebook hidden under my bed, and thankfully Nurse Johnson did not think to check that it was still locked away when she came in yesterday morning. I feel like a child watched over by an angry mother. I don't believe she would ever understand what I'm trying to say. My words would be like a foreign language to her. The world has changed so fast. I have the feeling that it is out of control, that no one knows where it is going, and no one really cares. And that is exactly why my island is so precious, why I have this desperate urge to hold on to its anchor.

Perhaps I am delirious. I hardly slept at all last night, listening to the wind around the house. It was as if a great sea had lifted everything around us and the waves rose and fell beneath the floors. That is what I imagined, that the sea had come in to find me, and was going to take me home. I must have been delirious.

A day or two after my return, I moved out from Mr Semple's house. I had asked nearby for lodgings but had found nothing; then I had been directed to two places that proved too expensive. Eventually, I had found a room in a very run-down boarding-house, where the other lodgers were mostly men who had lost their jobs. Men from Ireland or the Highlands; outcasts like myself. The landlady, Mrs Rinaldi, smokes incessantly and speaks very fast and with great intensity. She tells us exactly what we ought to do to find work; no point in wallowing in self-pity. 'You should go to university,' she told me, 'be a doctor or an engineer.' But there was no advice on how I was to pay for this. 'See those two moles?' she said in the next minute, looking intently at my face; these, she maintained, meant that I would one day become very wealthy indeed.

I could not bear to think of going back to work for O'Hagan again. If I had crawled back and begged him to take me on, he might have done so, but I would have become more chained than ever. Half the city seemed to be in search of work and I even saw men fighting for it. Hardship had bitten deeply over the past winter; it was pitiful to see the old and the poor wrapped in the barest of rags. It was spring, but the wind was bitter; at times it howled like a pack of wolves.

Then, one Saturday, something happened that was to change everything for me. I had noticed a youngish man in the house; I knew that he was called James Bell, but that was all. He seemed different from all the others, with an alert and cheerful air about him. That day I fell into conversation with him and learned his secret. He had a definite aim in life; he had determined to go to America and make a new life for himself.

'I'm booked on a ship which sails in only three months' time, and I'm saving every penny towards the fare.' He urged me to do the same. 'Go all out to find a job and you'll succeed,' he said again and again. 'Once you're in America you'll get a real chance if you work hard.'

I could not sleep that night. The next day I walked in a dream; the thought of a new beginning had gripped me. Until that time I had somehow believed that only two courses were open to me – to stay on in Kinlochallan or to return to Glasgow. The thought of America filled me with a strange fire. It was unknown, fresh, and it would ask no questions of me. I would be accepted for what I was, rather than be mocked for being a kind of savage. The fare I would have to find was enormous, and as yet I didn't even have a job. Yet the fight to find that money had already begun to burn within me.

For three days I went out in a determined effort to find work, no matter what it might be, and on the last afternoon I found a job, as a labourer in one of the few shipyards still in business. I could hardly believe my good fortune; the evidence of unemployment and sheer misery stared me in the face wherever I turned. I determined to work and to save. And I went straight to the shipping office and booked a passage, my only regret that it could not be the same ship as James, as I would need at least six months before I could possibly be ready.

Afterwards, I sat down and with trembling hands wrote a letter to Donald Angus and Morag. Before my eyes I kept seeing the face of Calum and I thought of how I would never see him grow, or run about the fields behind Kinlochallan. It took me a long time to write that letter and my heart as I posted it was heavy as lead. Despite the decision I had made, the thought struck me that if they begged me to remain, I would, because I loved them and their little son fiercely.

I started work at the shipyard. It was hard, very hard, and from the beginning I hated it, but I knew that I had to set my face to it and endure it, no matter what. All day long my ears were filled with the hammering of steel and the shouting of men; it often struck me as a strange irony that I should be toiling and sweating over a ship, for the sake of another ship, one that would take me away forever to America.

One evening I returned home to find Mrs Rinaldi waving a letter. 'For you, Roddy,' she said, her eyes sparkling. 'From a girl, perhaps?'

For once I did not feel like encouraging banter with her.

'No, my sister,' I replied and disappeared into the sanctuary of my small room, tearing the envelope as I went. My hands were shaking so much that I could hardly read.

They had moved; they were on Lewis. It had become unbearable at Kinlochallan. Iain, they said, was growing steadily worse. All his plans seemed to come to nothing and the more he failed, the more his anguish and his anger increased. One day Donald Angus had dared to offer him some advice on a job he was doing, and Iain had become so enraged that he almost attacked him.

That had finished them. There was a tiny house they could have on Lewis, really little more than an outhouse. It was a shell of a place, but they were already working hard to improve it, and at least they felt at peace there. Calum would grow up with Gaelic all around him and in a good community; the sea was not far from the door and there were miles of moorland at the back. Altogether it was a fine, wholesome place to bring up a child, and they were not sad to have left Kinlochallan, not as things were.

At last Morag wrote of America. She said that she fully understood, that she wished with all her heart there was another way, and that if only Iain were to give up his stranglehold on Kinlochallan, I would surely be happy there. But she knew that was a dream. Both of them wished me God's blessing for my new life and begged me to let them know at once if I were ever in need; and ended with their hopes of seeing me again.

I knew, however, as I folded up the letter, that a door had closed for good. But nothing now stood in my way. The hugeness of the step I was about to take suddenly overwhelmed me.

The next six months were very bleak. I worked as I had never worked before, indeed harder than I would have thought possible. James Bell was a good friend, the first person for a long time to whom I felt I could talk freely. When the time came for his departure, I envied him the confidence with which he faced the unknown future, and afterwards I missed him sorely. Before he left, however, he introduced me to a free library. I cannot ever forget the thrill I felt as I looked at all the rows of books. Scarce treasures now abundant, I set myself to read two or three volumes a week. Lost in a book, my tiredness vanished. I read everything – biographies, travel tales, history, religious works, novels. And as I devoured them, my English improved and a new confidence grew in me. I made up my mind then that I would do no more labouring jobs when I reached the New World. I would study and work hard, and one day perhaps become a librarian or a teacher.

For all my new-found ease with English, there was one book I always read in Gaelic, and to me it was by far the most important of all; my mother's old Bible. It seemed to bring her back, to give her memory life, more strongly than even a photograph might have done. Her searching and her tears, I felt, were embedded in those pages. So I read it, not under compulsion as in my boyhood days, but willingly. To tell the truth, I used to shy away from the Gospels; there was too much in them about forgiveness. And I was nowhere near being able to forgive Iain for the life he had stolen from us.

I worked on. Slowly, bit by bit, my savings began to mount up. Other than my rent, I had few expenses. I worked overtime, labouring such long hours at the yard that I hardly knew the difference between day and night. The weeks went by with only my constant reading to lighten them. Sometimes I would go back to the Gaelic church I had found on my first week in Glasgow, but still I shied away from close acquaintance. I went mainly for the psalm-singing, not just because I had always loved the psalms, but because standing there singing, I would find myself back on the island with my own people.

At last the day came to leave. I had succeeded; I had enough for the fare and a little besides. I gathered my things together, such as they were; gently placing the precious Bible on top, feeling that in a way she was coming with me. Standing on the docks that bright morning, the gulls fluttering like tattered pieces of paper over my head in the blue October sky, the people struggling with belongings, running along with little flotillas of children, pushing towards the massive black bulk of the ship. My hand gripped my heavy case tightly as I pressed through the confused ranks towards the gangway.

I heard my name clearly, even above the shouting and commotion.

I stopped dead and turned round. Then I saw them. Making their way towards me were Donald Angus and Morag, with Calum in her arms.

All the words I might have found at that moment were torn from my head. I felt myself as if washed out to sea by a great wave. This was the most wonderful act of love they could have shown me.

'Do you remember the psalm we sang?' Morag asked, her eyes steady and sure, 'that day – the day we left the island?'

I nodded. It was all I could do. So she sang it for me, there in the midst of that huge and surging crowd, amid the emotion and despair of a thousand farewells, and it gave me hope. I felt courage well up in me and gather till it filled my spirit.

I looked about me and already the crowd was diminishing, pressing forward to the gangway. I looked hard at my family for a last time and I held Calum. I caught the bright aliveness of his eyes and I thought that all the hopes of my father and mother, of Morag and myself, indeed of all the exiles from that island, were written into that one small face.

I found them from the deck of the ship. I pressed into a corner of the rail and spied them, miles below. They stayed there until the great craft began to shudder away from the dock, and to boom its last long notes of farewell. I held their faces until they were swallowed into the crowd, and then the crowd itself was just a blur.

One night I got up, very late, because I could not sleep; I went out on to the deck. The air was clear. It was neither dark nor light. Like the summer of my childhood. I closed my eyes and heard the sea-birds crying over Mullach Bi; I felt the soft wind on my face as I walked by the edge of Glen Bay. I looked out from the rail to the north, and imagined that my eyes could somehow pick out those tiny black landfalls – Hirta, Stac an Armin, Stac Lee and Boreray. They would never truly leave me.

That was a long time ago. I am old, but it seems to me that the past is not so old. Inside me the barefoot boy lives on. I never did return home, not even when Iain died and Kinlochallan lay empty. I had no heart left. My torn roots had at last begun to take up water and I had a new life in America. Besides, I had only to close my eyes to see Calum on the hillside behind the house where he belonged.

My mother's Bible has been a strength to me always. In the end, I came to the Gospels and learned to trust, to admit my own need of forgiveness, and to forgive. I was set free at last. And now my story is written, and I am very tired. It is growing dark and I have been writing too long. I am not afraid of leaving once more. I know that I am going home. At last. The boat is dipping into shore, and I know so well where it will take me.